URBAN MERMAID

HOWARD PARSONS

Moonlight Garden

Renton, Washington

Cover Art by Ilsie Om.

Edited by C. E. Moore and S. C. Moore.

Published 2015, Moonlight Garden Publications, an imprint of Gazebo Gardens Publishing, LLC.
www.GazeboGardensPublishing.com

978-1-938281-72-3   (paperback)
978-1-938281-73-0   (e-book)

Library of Congress Control Number: 2015941090

Printed in the United States of America.

For Judi, my wife of forty years.
Happy anniversary, Sweetheart.

ACKNOWLEDGEMENTS

My sincere thanks go to the editorial team at Gazebo Gardens Publishing, LLC for all their hard work, as well as taking a risk on a neophyte author.

I also want to thank my wife for all her encouragement of me to put pen to paper, even though fantasy novels are, beyond the shadow of a doubt, "just not her thing."

Next, I want to thank the very talented Ilsie Om for the wonderful cover art. She has been so easy to work with and made the cover one less headache for me. I hope that we can continue to collaborate on future books in the *Colony Island Series*.

Visit Ilsie's website at: http://thewoodsyfawn.format.com

Thanks also to my friend in fins, Pete Tarsi, for his eagle-eyed typo spotting.

Finally, my deepest appreciation and gratitude goes to my three muses for all their comments, criticisms, and cheerleading:

— S.K. Munt, author of *The Fairytail Saga*
  and other novels

— Emm Cole, author of the *Merminia* series and
  The Short Life of Sparrows

— Marie McKean, author of *Born of Oak and Silver*
  and other novels

Your kind words, support, and encouragement have touched me more than you will ever know.

REVIEWS

"I knew that Howard Parsons was sort of a mermaid expert going into this. Okay, so there's no doctorate one can obtain to officially qualify for such a title, but if there was, this author would have the certificate, the trophy, the PHD, the Monopoly board game mermaid edition, and some sort of Nobel Prize.

Urban Mermaid is unlike any other mermaid book I've ever read. His book isn't even a half-cousin to any of them. There are no off-the wall names, there's no royalty, there are no sparkles, there's no slack-jawed human.

What there is—is warmth. *Urban Mermaid* crosses more genres than any Mer book I've ever read, and what is so cool about it is that paranormal romance and fantasy don't even get a look-in! It's a satire, a romantic comedy, a coming of age, a blue-collar romance, and in the end—just a beautiful story about ordinary people meeting, falling in love, and trying to overcome obstacles together, when one of those people just happens to have a tail sometimes. The characters are not too perfect to be true—they're the average Mr. and Miss, and I am so grateful for that.

Howard doesn't need tsunamis and royal weddings and octopus-people or seahorses named Glimmer to make you fall in love with his characters. They are realistic, flawed, lovely, and practically peel themselves off the page and wiggle into the sea with their believability.

Pulling off a hero in this day and age who isn't loaded or fabulously wealthy, or more kinked than a home perm, is a hard task—but Mr. Parsons does exactly this, and with a lovely, graceful writing style that only the most refined writers can cultivate."

—S.K. Munt, author of *The Fairytail Saga*

"This story illustrates Howard Parsons' extensive research and all of the years he's spent reading and reviewing other Mer tales. The author has sketched out Colony Island in such a way, that I can see the little shops, the beachfronts, and also the Mer who secretly make up this quaint beach town. The mermaid mythology in Urban Mermaid is completely unique and unexpected. Pen and Peter have a love story all their own. Congratulations, Howard Parsons. You've created a very distinct little world with a seemingly normal and average couple who turn out to be anything but by the story's end."

—Emm Cole, award-winning author of the
  Merminia series and *The Short Life of Sparrows*

"*Urban Mermaid* was a treat to read. From the very beginning page to the last lingering sentence, I loved every moment of it. If this is just the start of something greater—for it is, being the first installment in the "Tails from Colony Island" series—I personally can't wait to read the rest.

Packed full of merfolk lore, *Urban Mermaid* is a must read for mermaid fans out there. I won't spoil much, but let me just say, when I finished reading it, I wanted to go swimming and find a mermate of my own."

—K. Lynn Adams, author of *The Father of the Wolf*

"*Urban Mermaid* surpassed all my expectations. It is a wonderfully warm and tender love story encompassing both family love and romantic beginnings. I loved it. I would recommend this book to any reader that enjoys romance with a little excitement thrown in."

—Ali May, reviewer

"*Urban Mermaid* is an old-fashioned novel with an omniscient, head-hopping narrator...with modern day twists and adult situations. Author Howard Parsons lays out his mermaid world with loving detail, explaining the world of merfolk that coexist with American coastal communities, from their mythical origins story to the real-world challenges facing them today...making it a totally absorbing and fun read.

This is not your average paranormal or fantasy novel, reading more like a contemporary romance with a side of mermaid tails. The problems facing our "urban mermaid" are more of the everyday and urbane sort, and both Penelope's insecurities and Peter's are the same ones that face us all. The author gives readers a fresh interpretation of mermaid culture as not so different from the rest of America, dealing with the more unique aspects in a totally matter-of-fact way. A fresh, interesting mermaid story that kept me reading and rooting for that happily-ever-after."

—Katie O'Sullivan, author of *Son of a Mermaid*

"The story was presented in a fresh and bold new way, while still managing to incorporate some traditional mythology. *Urban Mermaid* was an enjoyable read, and I found myself delving deeper and deeper into the story and feeling emotionally invested rather quickly. Howard Parsons portrays a colorful picture of figures and places you can tangibly feel. It is a love story between Penelope and Peter first and foremost, but that doesn't mean that love comes easy. They face everyday problems that are timeless—family, work, stations, stigmas, etc. This is definitely not the childhood bedtime story many of us remember when we think of 'mermaids'! It is much sexier, edgier, and faster paced.

Urban Mermaid is smartly written with the added benefit of breaking away from many of the clichés that are common with this theme of story, while still maintaining the core folklore most mer fans are hoping to see. If you are craving an entirely new mermaid experience, by all means, read *this* book."

—Paige Blue, author of *Finding Summerland*

"*Urban Mermaid* was a fun, easy book to read. Howard has successfully blended the new and the old, mythology and reality, together in one story. A couple meeting, living, and loving in modern day society. Although it is a romantic comedy, the story does touch on the serious side of family dynamics, social stigmatisms, and the self-awareness of adulthood. No person is perfect—free of flaws—and that is reflected in all of the characters, which makes it that much more believable.

The entire book was artfully written—I could smell the beach, feel the water, see the shops in Colony Island, and hear the sound of high heels walking across pavement. An entire new little world was created. Howard was able to accomplish this while using simple words and non-cluttered thoughts. I have not read any other Mer stories, nor am I a fan of romance novels, but I was pleasantly surprised and drawn-in."

—Cheryl Washburn, reviewer

"As my very first foray into the world of the merfolk, *Urban Mermaid* was as comfortable as slipping into the ocean. The main character, Penelope Tench, pulls you into the waves with her trials of contention, but she is just like any other young mermaid....hoping to find the merman of her dreams. Through the course of a not so rational decision, she realizes that the merman she'd hoped for is actually a human named Peter MacPherson. All too soon Peter feels a responsibility towards Penelope and provides the proper 'logistics' for her 'tail time.' As feelings develop, it's time to go to Colony Island and meet the parents. What ensues kept my nose in my book, wondering if Poseidon listens to the requests of humans. Plans, conflict, love, and laughter...it's all there in *Urban Mermaid*. *It* is a lighthearted, enjoyable read. It begs for you to be at the beach, having a sandwich while checking for a caudal fin."

—Gerrie Washburn, reviewer

TABLE OF CONTENTS

PROLOGUE

By all accounts, Poseidon was something of a ladies' man in his younger days. He did more than his share of womanizing, both divine and human. There were even rumors of rendezvous with men—though when asked, he steadfastly held that these were simply idle talk and that one should not believe everything one reads in the scrolls.

Nonetheless, Poseidon was most definitely a playboy who fathered a fair number of children. Some were acknowledged, and some weren't. In those days, the standards for deities were far different from what they became in modern times. There was a "Do as I say, not do as I do" sort of philosophy.

Poseidon was an up-and-coming young deity when he took over running the Mediterranean Sea from the Titan, Oceanus. His tenure there was quite a success, and his name appeared in many legends of the day. Poseidon was so good at it, that he subsequently acquired the responsibility for all the world's waters from Oceanus.

Much of the freshwater work was delegated to various naiads, nymphs, and river gods, and there were a number of lesser gods to help run the saltwater end of things as well. So, aside from his administrative duties, Poseidon had plenty of spare time and found plenty of ways to spend it. If there was anyone who embodied the phrase "wine, women, and song," it was Poseidon.

Then came the temples, priests, and sacrifices in his honor, which only served to feed his ego. Along the way, Poseidon also became the god of earthquakes and horses. The former was a performance bonus doled out by his brother, Zeus, and while he was grateful for the accolade, he was not much interested in making the ground shake every now and then, so he outsourced to a couple minor Indian deities.

Being the god of horses was another story, because he loved to play the ponies and made all sorts of extravagant bets on which horse was fastest, could pull the most weight, or could survive the extremes of wind and weather. When he lost a bet—which was unusual—the winners often had a hard time collecting and on more than one occasion found themselves sleeping with the fishes. Fast times. Fast horses. Fast women. That was Poseidon.

All of this began to change when he visited the Aegean Sea on an inspection tour and paid a call on Nerus. The old man of the sea introduced his daughter, Amphitrite, and Poseidon was instantly smitten. Thunder-struck may have been a more apt description, and he found it impossible to take his eyes off her.

Amphitrite herself was quite taken by the dashing young god of the sea, but word got around the Aegean quickly, and Poseidon's reputation had preceded him. She decided to bide her time and see if he did anything to clean up his act.

Poseidon realized it was time for him to settle down, and since Amphitrite was the one he wanted to do it with, some changes were in order. He started with the horses. For decades, rich merchants had been drowning teams of horses by way of sacrifice in hopes of a trouble-free and profitable voyage. Poseidon called the priests into his temple and let it be known it had to stop immediately. Henceforth, if the merchants wanted a safe voyage, they would be required to give money to the poor. This became a sacrifice in the truest sense of the word.

Burnt offerings were thereafter frowned upon as well. Ordinary people were to give a certain amount of food to the priests in exchange for their blessings, and the rest was to be given to the poor and needy. The priests weren't too happy about the change, but the alternative meant they'd spend the rest of their lives as toadfish.

The gambling was next to go by the wayside. There was the occasional friendly wager, but the bookmakers were in dire straits—until the millennia when football was finally invented.

For Poseidon, dalliances were off the menu too. He'd have an occasional one-night-stand, but on the whole, the god of the seas was living a life of abstinence.

Amphitrite took notice of these changes, and once she was convinced they were not temporary, she was his.

Married life seemed to agree with Poseidon. Their son, Triton, was soon born, followed by their three daughters, Rhode, Kymopoleia, and Benthesikyme. There were several other daughters, but Poseidon managed to keep their names out of the scrolls for the sake of privacy.

He groomed Triton to be his right-hand man and to eventually take over the family business, and his daughters were very accomplished young sea nymphs. Family life was good, and all were happy, until one day, when his youngest daughter brought home a sailor who had fallen off his ship during a storm.

She was quite taken with him, and like any doting father, Poseidon wanted his daughter to be happy. All it took was a wave of his trident, and the young mariner could don a tail with scales like the rest of the family. His youngest was ecstatic. Yes, Poseidon had become a real softy, but he was left with a quandary. He couldn't grant quasi-divine status to every sailor, fisherman, or castaway his daughters—or granddaughters—brought home.

One lazy Sunday afternoon, Poseidon watched his children playing a complicated game of tag with a pod of dolphins, and it suddenly struck him that something was missing from the sea. He loved his dolphins and whales, but there had to be more...somehow.

After a few hundred years, he decided that "something" was people. He wished he'd mentioned it to Zeus at the time he took over from Oceanus, but it was too late now.

Of course, being a god, he could create things ex nihilo, but since Zeus was the father of gods and men, creating a new race of people would only get him in trouble with his brother. Asking for a special favor was next to impossible, because Zeus was always changing himself into a swan, a bull, or a man, and canoodling with every milkmaid or shepherdess he took a fancy to.

It occurred to Poseidon, however, that the gods were regularly turning men into stags, doves, or swine without any repercussions, so why couldn't he retrofit some humans to live in the sea?

He and his son sat up late for decades discussing how all this would work and what his new merfolk would look like. In the end, he and Triton decided they would look like ordinary mortals—at least above the hips—and would have a single appendage below for locomotion, somewhat similar to that of Poseidon and his offspring.

The perfect solution looked and acted like a fish tail. Triton wanted to give them gills, but Poseidon was not fond of the aesthetic. Instead, he took a page from the amphibians and decided to give them the ability to breathe through their skin. He also decided to correct a number of things he privately regarded as design flaws—mostly dealing with sex and reproduction.

Why, Poseidon wondered, should a little lovemaking have to result in a big pregnancy? Yes, it caused the mortal population to grow rapidly, but more often than not, it brought additional misery to a species already suffering as it was. Females would use pregnancy to ensnare males, and males often left a trail of fatherless children in their wake.

Poseidon had a better idea. Mermaids would have the ability to control their own fertility. In other words, mermaids would remain infertile until they were ready to breed. When a mermaid wanted to hear the flippy-flapping of little fins, she could will herself to ovulate. This would also have the added effect of eliminating a regularly occurring inconvenience.

In order for mermen to understand exactly what they were getting themselves into, the process of ovulation would produce a redness of the skin, later to be known as the breeding flush. The act of breeding itself would serve to celebrate their piscine heritage and acknowledge they were creatures of his sea.

Finally, Poseidon wanted to increase their lifespan and give his modified humans the ability to communicate telepathically underwater and to change their tails into legs when they wanted to stroll about or live on land for a bit. After all, humans walked on land and could swim in the sea, so why should his race of merfolk be at a disadvantage?

Now, how to accomplish these changes? Of course, Poseidon could have waved his trident, and poof, it would have been done, but that wasn't very practical in the long run.

Triton came up with the solution—what would become known as recombinant DNA. He created a virus that would deliver these changes to each cell in the human body and live in the fruit of a rather large bush, which sometimes grew into a small tree.

The fruit was the size of a grapefruit with skin that

resembled a nectarine. The inside looked rather like a blood orange, and it was very, very juicy. Eating the fruit might make the person a bit ill, but after three or four days, they would have an irresistible urge to run into the sea.

His fruit trees were placed on bits of land where storm and shipwreck survivors were likely to wash up, and they were in constant bloom. All Poseidon had to do was sit back and wait for the results.

It didn't take long for things to happen, but there was a bit of a problem. Most of the people on ships in those days were men, as very few women traveled by sea. This resulted in a lot of libidinous mermen fighting over a handful of mermaids and was no way for the race of merfolk to grow.

It was Amphitrite who had the answer. She recruited her daughters and had them deliver bowls of the fruit to the coastal homes of young widows, jilted brides, and forsaken lovers. This had the unforeseen effect of shifting the population balance toward the opposite extreme, but at least the mermen weren't fighting over a limited supply of mermaids anymore.

Those mermaids who wanted mates all to themselves spent much of their time on or near the surface, hoping to find a good candidate on a passing ship. This was most likely the reason why mermen were so seldom mentioned in sailors' tales and ancient legends. They were otherwise occupied below the waves.

It wasn't instantaneous, but eventually, the population began to redistribute and right itself, and many a young widow who had lost her husband at sea was joyously reunited with him beneath the waves.

Poseidon and Amphitrite were pleased with the progression of their "children," the merfolk, or mer, as they sometimes called them, and they relished in helping them grow and flourish in the following millennia.

CHAPTER ONE

One Sunday afternoon, Penelope was napping under a low-water dock...or at least trying to. Ordinarily, her dreams were either the usual nonsense that plays through almost anyone's subconscious or a newsreel with scenes and reminiscences from her past. On this particular day, it was the latter, and the one playing now seemed to be a favorite of whoever was in the control booth. It certainly wasn't her favorite, as it only served to remind her of the current state of affairs in the miserable existence jokingly called her life.

"Mom, there is absolutely not a single boy in town that interests me. There is no one here at all that I'd want to choose for a mate."

Her mother looked up from her sewing. "Penelope! You're eleven years old. Don't you think it's a little early for you to be worrying about choosing a mate?"

She knew her mother was serious when she used her first name. "But it's true, Mom. Really! None of the boys on the island like me, and I feel the same way about them."

"Well, Anne, I'm sure you will find the right boy sooner or later," she replied in a less stern, more tender tone.

The trouble was that no one came along in the years that followed. Penelope tried to be patient and bide her time, but every year, her despair deepened. Once the merboys reached thirteen or fourteen, she had a pretty good idea about how things stood, and none of them were for her.

Although it was not uncommon for a mate to be a few years older or younger, it would be a decade before their life experiences caught up to hers—especially if she went to college, as her father hoped she would.

Penelope knew she could always choose a feral for a mate, but that came with its own set of problems. Most feral boys wanted as little to do as possible with things on land, and once they had completed as much education as they thought was necessary, they dropped out and went to sea.

The feral girls weren't much better, and they soon followed the boys. It was common for a feral girl to choose a mate at fourteen or fifteen years of age and breed within a year or two afterwards.

On the other hand, island girls were highly encouraged to postpone choosing a mate or becoming sexually active until they were eighteen, because if it did happen before that point in their lives, then their grades went to Hades and they would drop out, become pregnant, or both. The town's camouflage depended upon staying within the statistical norms of people on the mainland, and if they continually placed outside of that range, it might attract unnecessary and unwanted attention.

The other problem Penelope faced was that three days was the most she could spend at sea without wanting to come back to land for a while. Sea trips were like camping trips. She loved sleeping underwater and making friends with whales, but a long weekend was about it for her.

If she chose and bred with a feral, she and their child would spend most of the time on shore. She had already seen what that sort of arrangement did to the children of such a match. Amy's father was a good provider, but being feral, he was at sea for months, or up to a year, at a time. His absence had left Amy shy, withdrawn, and insecure around men, which portended the odds of her choosing a mate to be slim to none. Penelope couldn't do that to her child.

To cope with the ongoing failure of her love life during high school, Penelope did what she'd always done—threw herself into her school work and swam so deep, she was unaware of the human girls and their seemingly unlimited supply of boyfriends, and she wouldn't notice the island mergirls and boys who were already starting to take an interest in one another. Sure, Penelope had boyfriends and crushes along the way, but both parties knew it was only temporary. Better than being alone.

Then came her Senior Prom. Penelope had been looking forward to it for ages, but no one from Colony Island asked her to go. It hurt a little bit—okay, a lot—because the junior and senior classes from the island were unusually large. The moonlit beaches must have been very well visited by mer couples during the two years those merkids got their start in life. Still, one would have thought there'd be someone left for her to go with.

Penelope considered suggesting to Anthony that they go together, but he was taking her cousin, Lindsey, so that was out. Feral boys wanted nothing to do with human customs, so she didn't even bother considering one of them.

A boy from the mainland was the only one who ended up offering to take her to Prom. Penelope suspected he had a crush on her, and while her mother would have ordinarily insisted she go with one of the island boys, the only other choice was to stay home and miss it, so she gave her blessing.

Richard turned out to be a complete gentleman, and their evening was magical. It was one of the few times growing up that Penelope had felt normal on the mainland, or at least as normal as a mermaid could amongst humans.

They had a couple dates following Prom, one to the movies and the other to a restaurant on the other side of Royston. Both evenings were wonderful, but the currents of life pulled them in opposite directions.

Perhaps a reason they hadn't worked out was because Penelope had remained absorbed in her studies during the few weeks following Prom Richard had attempted to woo her. It was quite the shock when the principal called her into his office and handed her a letter saying she had, by far, the highest GPA in her class. She, Penelope Anne Tench, was to be valedictorian at commencement in four weeks' time. The news was a welcome distraction from yet another breakup.

Neither she nor her parents knew what to make of it until the scholarship offers began to pour in. In the end, she chose the school she'd planned on attending all along, Florida State University. Penelope's father was proud, her mother was in awe, and she would get away from Colony Island and the deep, dark despair it caused her—at least for a while.

In Tallahassee, Penelope was adrift in a sea of humans. Her old, familiar anchors were gone, and she found herself fascinated but lonely. Most of all, she missed her time in the high school chorus with Amy, Lindsey, and Cindy. The choirmaster had been around long enough to learn that everyone from Colony Island—male and female—had a beautiful singing voice, and to land four of them in their freshman year was a major coup.

At Florida State, no one had ever heard of Colony Island, and thus no one sought her out. She wasn't brave enough to try out on her own, and as a result, she had more time for her studies.

There were sporting events and parties, but they were only occasional diversions, and she didn't trust herself to keep her secret, given the copious quantities of booze that everyone seemed to consume.

Yelling, "Hey, everyone! Watch this!" and diving into a swimming pool would have been a disaster. If she did to go to a party, she simply had a glass of wine or half a beer and then left to "meet someone."

Her sober lifestyle caught the attention of the highly religious girls in her dorm. Penelope was fully aware of Christianity but not at all interested. On Colony Island—and in the sea—there was a folk religion centered on Poseidon, but there was no dogma or temple with priests. On the cusp of each New Year, her father offered a prayer to the god of the sea, but that was about as religious as anyone on the island got. She could've told the girls that she was a Poseidonion, but that would've required even more explanation.

To avoid all of this, she spent her time in the library in the welcome refuge of her studies. Her weekends were spent either doing homework or swimming in the Gulf of Mexico. Even though she had come to enjoy university life, the darkness of her isolated existence continued to deepen.

When Penelope went home at the end of her sophomore year, Amy mentioned that she was a different girl than the one who had delivered the valedictory address on their graduation day. Lindsey and Cindy agreed.

Soon after, the tides turned. Penelope was both flattered and stunned when Anthony asked her to dinner in nearby Royston. At least she wasn't destined to be lonely on one night this summer, and going out with an old friend would be a breath of fresh water. Of course, she accepted his invitation almost immediately. The dinner was relaxing, and it was so good to catch up on things with an old, old friend.

After they drove back to the island, it was still light out, so Anthony suggested they go for a swim together. By the time he dropped her off at her parents' house, she'd had the best evening since Prom—in fact, even better than her prom. So this was what she'd been missing! Naturally, she accepted his invitation to go out again in a few days' time.

As the summer wore on, spending time with Anthony became an almost everyday occurrence. They went on a lot of swim dates, and Penelope knew the town gossips would be having a field day soon, if they weren't already. The common wisdom on Colony Island was if a couple started swimming together exclusively, then a big announcement would be forthcoming in the not-too-distant future.

Penelope was well aware of this and did her best to be open-minded about Anthony. Her parents tried to be as nonchalant about things as possible, but she could tell they were quietly hopeful. She certainly enjoyed her time with him, and she had known him nearly forever, but was that enough? Was this what things were supposed to feel like?

Anthony seemed to be playing it cool. No hands, no tails, just a quick peck on the cheek when he dropped her off at her house. She didn't mind him taking things slowly. Penelope wasn't looking to choose a mate this summer. She still had to finish university, and the simple act of choosing would change everything.

No, the most she wanted was a letter of understanding— sadly nowadays, an email or even a text message—saying that he would like her advice on choosing a mate at some point in the future. In human terms, it was as close to being pre-engaged as one could be.

Finally, after a series of sleepless nights in early August, she made her decision and went for a walk with Anthony along the beach.

"Tony, this summer with you has been so much fun—the best time I've had in years. I've been giving this a lot of thought though, and to me, you'll always be the boy I used to play tag with along the reef. I'm sorry, but I just can't see us being any more than good friends."

Anthony dropped to his knees on the sand, and Penelope thought she'd broken his heart.

But when he opened his mouth, his first words were,

"Thank Poseidon!"

She wasn't quite sure what to make of his reaction.

"Anne, I've been so worried about this—wondering how to tell you, what to tell you. Lin and I had some fun times together, but we both knew anything more would drive the two of us crazy. It's not like that with you and me, though. And she thought that might be the case. Lindsey asked me to see if there could be something between us, Anne. That's why I asked you to dinner a few weeks after you came home from school. I hope you're not mad... And she almost turned out to be right! I think we'd be good together if we could both get beyond those memories from our childhood. But I can't, and it looks like you're the same way. I'm really sorry, Anne. I hoped this could all work out for us."

"Tony, I was so worried about how to tell you and what your reaction would be. I'm glad you feel the same way. And I'm not upset about Lindsey, either. It was sweet of both of you."

"Oh, good." He paused for a moment. "Ummm, Anne, you know that Lin and I...you know...we could...do the same...if you need it."

Penelope knew what Anthony had done for her cousin, Lindsey. Merfolk had an entirely different attitude toward mating than humans. While it certainly wasn't any kind of hook-up culture, it wasn't straight-laced either.

Mermaids, and merboys to a lesser degree, were terribly sentimental about that first time, and if there were no prospective mates or even boyfriends on the horizon, they would often ask a good, unattached friend—like Anthony—if they would do the honors. Sometimes, these alliances would wind up choosing each other as mates. Other times—as in Lindsey's case—the two would wind up being even better friends with a wonderful shared memory of the first time they mated.

"Tony, thank you, but I'm just not there yet. If I am ready but not seeing anyone, you'd be the first person I would call. Anyway, would you mind if we still hung out together? You're a good friend, and I'll miss spending time with you."

For the rest of the summer, Penelope and Anthony went to the movies, as well as doing other "human things," and still swam together on occasion.

Penelope hoped they could occasionally see each other when she came home for visits during her junior year and that the next summer would turn out to be even better than this one. Unfortunately, that was not to be.

In early October, Anthony emailed her to ask what she could tell him about Gwen Delamar, a casual acquaintance of hers from high school. During Christmas break, Anthony announced he and Gwen had chosen each other as mates. They scheduled their joining ceremony so Penelope could attend while she was on Spring Break, and their vows were the sound of a door closing on Penelope's last chance of finding a mate on Colony Island.

Penelope didn't go home again for nearly five years. She was on a prestigious internship in Chicago the next summer and away on another one in New York following her graduation—Summa Cum Laude.

Between those two summers was her senior year...and Jimmy. He was achingly handsome, witty, and attractive in every possible aspect. And human. Penelope really thought he just might be the one, and she seriously considered mating with him for the sheer joy of the experience. Something told her, though, that once—or even twice—would not be enough.

She remembered all the lectures in school about the dangers of falling in love with a human. It usually wasn't their fault it happened, though in nearly all cases, it would not end well for the mermaid.

Having to put her emotions on hold because Jimmy was human had shaken Penelope to the core, and she began to harden her heart toward humans so it would never happen to her again. It wasn't long before the barrier extended to family, friends, and the world in general.

After graduation, she moved to a tiny apartment far from Colony Island. She was living in self-imposed exile, and her father began to remark regularly that going to see his daughter was like visiting someone in the "big house." You could see them through the glass, have a conversation—sort of—through the phones, but there was no real contact. No touch. No feelings. Nothing came through.

Eventually, her parents stopped visiting. It was too hard on her...and them. There was more warmth and light six hundred feet below the surface of the ocean than where she was.

When Penelope received an email some months ago from her mother with an article from the Royston News about someone she hadn't thought of in years, she sank into a whole new level of depression. Richard had met and married a girl from college, was working his way up the ladder at his father's auto dealership, and there was a baby on the way. Since humans had much less time in which to breed, it was easy to see why they'd gotten an early start.

Her mother had sent the information with the best of intentions—her old Prom date had found and chosen a mate, and so could she. But instead, it served as a reminder that she had yet to find one and probably never would.

Penelope had a bit of consolation, but it didn't help to lift her mood. Her three best friends from high school hadn't found a mate either, at least not yet. Cindy had gone to nursing school. According to her mother, she had her eye on someone from the island. Lindsey had gone off to school in—of all places— Nebraska, and had enjoyed it so much, she'd taken a job out there after graduation. She'd probably choose a human for a mate, and that would be the last they'd ever see of her. A tragedy in the making.

As for her very best friend, Amy, she'd most likely never find the courage to come out of her shell to choose a mate. If she ever did feel the need to breed, she'd have her father fix her up with a feral merman. They'd meet on the beach, mate, and Amy would raise the child on her own. Not at all unheard of, but it did underscore an existence that would be forever solitary.

Though Penelope wasn't what humans would call "marriage-minded," she was much like most females, mer or human. She just wanted to find a mate and have children with him. That seemed almost impossible now, and her world was getting darker by the day.

There had to be another settlement like Colony Island somewhere in the world, a place where she could have a second chance at happiness. Over the years, there had been rumors of other merfolk like those on Colony Island, but no one knew where they lived. She'd considered asking the ferals, but they were notoriously close-mouthed about things unless it was in their interest to divulge the information.

She'd thought about setting off and swimming—around the world if need be—in search of a place where her mate would be waiting for her...or not. But if Penelope went down that path, she would surely get her hopes up over each new lead, each new clue, only to have them dashed repeatedly when the island, the settlement, the place either didn't exist, or lacked potential mates. Over and over again until her dying day—which could be a very long time away—she'd search, find nothing, and search again.

No, she couldn't do that. It had become more than she could bear, more than she could take. It had to end.

The newsreel in Penelope's mind flickered, her eyes opened, and the wooden dock was all she could see. While many mermaids would have been in awe of life on the mainland, Penelope was sick of living among humans, sick of humans themselves—sick of everything. She suddenly realized there would be no fulfillment or happiness in this world, so it was time to leave it, and leave it quickly.

She couldn't call her parents to say goodbye since that would only delay the inevitable. She couldn't send them a letter or email because they would only come looking for her...or her body. Telling them would only bring more anguish to everyone, and she'd had more than her fill of it.

Leaving her parents to wonder for the rest of their lives was bad enough, but the bare hope that she was still alive might sustain them. She had no hope to sustain herself. They would wonder, worry, and grieve, but they would—sooner or later—move on and breed again. A new someone to erase the pain and failure that would be her legacy. Penelope prayed child number two would be a success for everyone's sake.

Forget tomorrow. Forget life. Forget everything. She'd take a one-way trip out west somewhere—they'd never think of that—and find a place where she could make her exit. Mermaids dehydrated much faster than humans, and two hours in the afternoon sun would do the trick nicely.

She had to get going. She'd swim back to her car, go home, do some research online, and get a ticket on the first plane out of the city—the first plane to where it was hot and dry and lonely enough for what she needed to do.

CHAPTER TWO

The parking lot at the boat ramp was an island in a sea of black mangrove, saw palmetto, coin vine, and turtleweed. It was well off the beaten path and though it had been built with the best of intentions, few sportsmen ever came here to launch their boats. The county made occasional visits to keep things trim and clean, but the abundant foliage threatened to phagocytize the site in the not too distant future.

It was remote. It was lonely. It was the perfect place for Penelope to hang out on a sunny spring afternoon.

The crunch of gravel immediately caught Penelope's attention. *Crap! Crap! Crap!* No one ever came to this unused boat ramp. That's why she liked to nap under the dock. It was bad enough that she had to spend most of her time among humans, and now they were interfering with her plan. *Crap!*

She heard the sound of shoes as they stepped onto the dock and stopped near the end. She moved to where an angled knothole gave her a view of the human above her. It was a man, around six feet tall and of average build. His hair was a darker brown than hers, the standard short human length, and he was clean-shaven. Not her particular taste.

Overall, he was not bad looking, but no Adam Levine, either. She couldn't see his eyes, but that really didn't matter at the moment. All she cared about was avoiding contact. He suddenly disappeared from view as she heard the sound of someone lying down on the planking. Depending on which way he was facing, she might be able to make a swim for it.

Cautiously, she poked her head out from under the dock and looked up toward the surface. *Double-crap!* The man was looking over the edge and down into the water. Penelope could easily see his eyes were green. *Why the hell do I care what color eyes he has?*

She was about to pull herself back under the dock and try to escape out the other side when a voice—a voice that she'd never heard before—said, "He has a kind face."

Penelope was trying to figure out where the voice came from when another voice said, "Yeah, whatever. Let's go mess with his head!"

The second voice made her throw caution to the wind. Maybe she could have a bit of fun before she ended her life. It would give her something to smile about on the plane trip to the desert and oblivion.

With a few powerful flicks of her tail, Penelope launched herself out of the water like a submarine executing an emergency blow.

The man had just gotten to his hands and knees when Penelope's sudden appearance nearly scared the life out of him. He fell backward, almost going over the far edge of the dock. If he did, she'd have to clean up the mess.

She wanted to have a bit of fun—not feel guilty—so she rested her left arm on the dock, grabbed his ankle with her other hand, and furiously paddled her tail fin so she wouldn't sink back into the water and pull the guy in on top of her.

"You okay, buddy?"

"Yeah, I think so. I'm okay. Why'd you scare me like that?"

As he pulled himself back up onto his hands and knees, he caught sight of Penelope at the edge of the dock, resting on her forearms and elbows with her tail fin mildly churning the water. His eyes immediately bugged out, and she worried she might have to perform CPR.

"What the *hell* are you?"

"I'm a mermaid, silly. See?" She leaned forward and curled her tail backward so her entire fin rose above the surface. "Go ahead! You can touch. I won't bite!"

With a Cheshire Cat grin on her face, she watched him hesitantly reach out, touch her hip, and run his fingers from her skin down on to her scales. She felt a small tingly kind of shock—static electricity or something—but managed not to twitch.

"Wow...a regulation tail and everything. I always knew you guys existed!"

Well, hooray for you, bright boy, she thought.

"What on earth are you doing here?"

Looks like I got a live one! "Like I said, I'm a mermaid. I live in the water." *Duh!* "I saw you on the dock and thought I'd say hi."

"So...where do you come from?"

Penelope rolled her eyes. *Why did she have to pick this wahoo?* She nodded her head back over her left shoulder toward the salt marsh and the sea in the distance.

"Yeah, right. Of course I know you come from 'out there,' but where out there? Out there is a pretty big place."

Well, score two points for the home team. You're not quite as dumb as you look. "I grew up a few hours down the coast."

"What's your diet like?"

Diet? I'm not on a diet! I'm one of the trimmest mermaids on Colony Island, thank you very much.

"I mean, what do you usually eat?"

Huh? Penelope was caught off guard by this, but she recovered nicely. "Oh, the usual. Kelp and other seaweed, krill, shrimp, fish that aren't fast enough to get away." She wanted to add hamburgers, pizza, and ice cream but caught herself. She was breaking enough rules talking to a human like this. No need to give away all of the secrets.

"Do you run into much pollution out there?"

At this, Penelope scowled and scolded, "Do I? *Do I?* It's like swimming in a toxic toilet with all the crap your species dumps into the ocean! Do you idiots even know what you're doing to the sea?"

The guy frowned. "Hey, don't blame me. I sign petitions, participate in beach and waterway clean-ups, and protest ocean dumping...loudly! So do a lot of my fellow 'idiots.' Don't paint all of us with the same brush."

Penelope had not expected this strong a reaction, and she tried to deflect his criticism. "Well, if I had legs, I'd come up on land and kick some major butt!"

"And I'd be right there beside you," he added.

As the sun began its slow descent to the western horizon, there were other questions in a similar vein that were asked and answered until he finally said, "Aside from all that, what's it like to live in the sea?"

"I wouldn't know. I have a nine to five job just like everyone else." *Oh crap! Now I've done it. I gotta get out of this thing fast!* "What time is it?"

The guy showed her his watch. "Damn! Look, I gotta swim. It's been great talking with you." Penelope pushed off the dock and sank below the surface.

The man leaned over the edge and stared down at the brackish water.

Thirty seconds later, Penelope rose up—more slowly this time—took his face between her hands, and planted a big, wet kiss on his lips. Smirking at his stunned reaction, she sank back below the surface and disappeared.

Thirty minutes and half a mile away, Penelope was back in the front seat of her car, drying her hair and laughing hysterically. "The look on the poor guy's face was priceless! I can't believe it. This is the best fun I've had in ages!"

That same unknown voice spoke in her mind, though more sternly this time. "You should be ashamed of yourself! You were entirely rude to him. He was such a nice young man. Your mother didn't raise you that way at all. What in the ocean would she think of you doing something like this?"

"Yeah, right," she mumbled. "If I can do this sort of thing every now and then to some dumb human like him, I just might stick with this mermaid gig a little longer."

CHAPTER THREE

It had been one hell of a Monday morning, and it wasn't even 10:00 a.m. yet. Peter was trying to avoid running around like a headless chicken, but it appeared to be a losing battle, as he was a one-man band. One member of his staff was out with a new baby; looked like he'd *have to* contribute to the office's baby gift pool this time around. Another was out with the April fifteenth flu—he was desperately wrestling with his tax accountant. And Peter had no idea where the third guy was. Oh yeah! Something called a vacation.

On any other day, he would have taken all of this in stride—but not today. There were a couple new people starting, and their workstations had not shown up until this morning. It had been a mad dash unpacking the machines, setting them up, and at least trying to start configuring them before the newbies made their way up from H.R., or as he liked to call it, the Anti-Personnel Department.

One of the new hires was supposed to sit in the cubicle next to his, and he was now wrestling the test server that usually sat on top of that desk into a space under his cubicle's desk. This old boy was heavy, but once he had it in place, he could start pulling and connecting cable. Under the circumstances, things were looking up. Or at least they *were*, until Vickie from up in Accounting stopped by.

"Is this where the new assistant comptroller will sit?"

"Yep. At least until they finish playing musical offices upstairs, and who knows when that will end."

"I know. Isn't it terrible? All this moving and shifting because they simply want to refurbish a couple offices."

"I hear you, Vicks, but unfortunately, I don't decide things like that. Now, what may I do for you?"

"Nothing, really. I just wanted to know where the new comptroller was going to sit for the duration. By the way, I was thinking we could go out together some time...maybe for a couple drinks after work...maybe for something else..."

There it was. Another one of the ladies who had the hots—or at least thought she did—for the eligible, young systems administrator.

"Uh, I don't know, Vickie. I'm still trying to get over my last relationship, and I'm just not ready to try again."

It was true. He was indeed still trying to get over his last relationship—which ended eighteen months ago. And the one before that, and the one before that, in a steady succession that reached all the way back to his freshman year of high school.

It started when Peter first discovered girls. You know, *really* discovered girls. They were these wonderful, soft, fascinating creatures of mystery who also smelled nice...and were totally disinterested in him. Given the different rates at which the sexes matured, that was probably to be expected.

Fast forward to his junior year in high school, and little had changed. Most of the girls were still disinterested in him, but there were a few he went out with a time or two.

When his father passed away after a long illness, none of the girls at school came to comfort him or even to simply say they were sorry for his loss. With girls, nothing ever seemed to last very long, even when he was a senior. His relationships lasted a month, at the very most, while other guys had been dating their girls for an entire semester.

Peter finally did find a girl to take to Prom, but he got the feeling it was a mercy date when she abandoned him after the first dance and spent the rest of the evening whispering with her friends and asking other guys to dance with her.

He went off to college hoping things would be different, and they were...a bit. He slept with a few girls and went out with a lot more, but only one relationship lasted beyond four weeks, and that was only because of a technicality.

It was time to call in some professional help—his best friend and roomie, Billy King. Billy was a music major and most definitely a ladies man. At a party, all he had to do was sit down at a piano and play "Bridge Over Troubled Water," and every girl within a thirty yard radius would dump their dates to flock around him. If anyone would know how to help, it would be Billy.

Peter walked his roommate through a typical date and a typical relationship. The latter didn't take very long, but Billy couldn't find any fault with what Peter did. They even double-dated a few times so he could observe Peter in the field, but again, he saw nothing wrong with either his actions or behavior. If anything, Peter was better at relationships than Billy. He had a certain wit about him. Peter was charming, entertaining, and attentive.

Finally, in desperation, Billy set him up with some girls he'd handpicked. Maybe Peter was just making bad choices. It didn't work. In only a few weeks' time, each girl had ended it with Peter, who was starting to feel like he was cursed.

This curse didn't stop with the girls. It extended to their parents as well. One example was the long weekend where the girl's mother had barely set foot on campus before she was in his face telling him she despised his kind and threatened legal action if he didn't stay away from her daughter. Later on that same weekend, he saw his most recent ex-girlfriend with one of the campus lowlifes, and her mother was fawning all over him. Peter learned afterward that the mother had even footed the bill for a motel room so the two of them could have some private time together—not just for the weekend, but for nearly every one thereafter.

Then, there was Katie. She went to a different school, an hour away. They had met toward the end of summer break and stayed in touch after classes started. There was definitely a mutual attraction, and Peter felt like things might finally be going right for him.

When he visited her campus one weekend, they spent a good part of his time there in bed together. He was her first. It was warm, tender, and everything he'd hoped love would be. Before he headed back to his own campus, they made plans for him to return the following weekend and texted nonstop for the next four days. On Friday, Peter learned his 11:00 a.m. class had been cancelled, as well as the one scheduled for mid-afternoon. Since he was already packed, he decided to hit the cafeteria early and leave for Katie's school to surprise her.

Katie's dorm room was on the second floor of a former motel, and Peter climbed the outside stairs and followed the walkway to her room. The door was open slightly, so he peeked in and heard a noise coming from behind the partition for the sleeping area. There, Peter found Katie...and another guy...completely naked and on top of the covers. She seemed oblivious to everything except what they were doing.

Between the sounds of passion and his heart breaking, someone tapped him on the shoulder. He turned around to find a second guy standing there.

"Are you next?"

Peter shook his head and left the room. He passed a third guy on the outside walkway that was hurrying in the opposite direction, unbuttoning his shirt as he went.

Peter never bothered to ask Katie for an explanation, and she never bothered to give one, or even apologize. It was as if their six weeks together had never even happened, and it was months before Peter tried to re-enter the dating scene. Even then, it was only a half-hearted attempt.

Peter's mother was there to see him graduate that spring, and two weeks later, she passed away. While the doctors attributed it to natural causes, his mother had never stopped grieving for his father. Peter was convinced she had died of a broken heart.

His older brother came east from Seattle to take care of the estate, pack up, and sell the house. Their parents had moved in only a couple of years before their father's death, so there were no real emotional ties to the place. Some things were sold and some things were put in storage. His brother told him to go ahead and get started on his life, and Peter did just that. He fled to Florida, lured by an open position at a publishing company. A new start in a new state.

Peter had hoped all of it was behind him now, but things were still the same no matter where he went. After three or four relationships had gone south—each well within the four-week time frame—Peter simply gave up.

Maybe he'd try one more time in five or ten years, but he'd resigned himself to the idea that he was not meant to find love or happiness. Ever. Still, that didn't stop the unattached women at the company from lining up to tear his heart out...

"Okay, Peter."

The sound of Vickie's voice brought him back to the present.

"I hear you. Just keep me in mind once you're over her. Maybe I can help things along."

"Yeah. Sure. I'll let you know." *But who will help me get over you?*

Peter pulled the chair away from the desk and crawled underneath. There was a wretched tangle of wires there and it was going to take a while. He had just daisy-chained a power strip when he heard Mr. Williamson walk in.

"And this is where you'll be sitting until your new office is ready. Now, let me introduce you to some of your neighbors." His voice faded in and out as he walked between the cubicles, introducing the new hire to some co-workers.

Peter was about to plug some Ethernet cables into a switch when Mr. Williamson stopped in front of his cubicle.

"And sitting right next to you is our IT lead, Peter MacPherson."

Peter stuck his hand up from under the desk and waved.

Mr. Williamson chuckled. "He'll come up to the surface sooner or later, and when he does, he'll be able to help you with logging in, setting up your email, and so forth. Now if you'll excuse me, I'll let you get settled while I see about our other new hire."

Peter heard the sounds of a notebook and pens being placed on the desk, as well as the squeak of an office chair and drawers being opened and closed. He pushed the On/Off button and heard the reassuring beep from the server.

He backed out from underneath the desk, stood, and brushed the dust from his trousers. Once he felt he was reasonably presentable, he turned and held out his hand.

"Hi. I'm Peter MacPherson."

The new hire was female, about his age, with brown eyes, light brown hair, and a look of absolute shock and horror on her face.

Peter followed with, "Have we met somewhere before? You look awfully familiar."

Penelope sat, frozen to her seat, with her mouth flapping open and shut in perfect imitation of a fish as her worst nightmare stood before her, smiling. *This can't be happening. This can't be real. It must be a dream. Wake up, Anne. Wake up!*

She began to tremble and move her hands in random motions across her desk as if she had suddenly gone blind.

Her nightmare withdrew his hand, sat down, and scribbled something on a sheet of paper. When he finished, he pushed the paper across to her.

Shakily, she picked it up and read, "Yes, I remember you from yesterday. Don't worry. I won't say a word. "

As warm and comforting as those words sounded, she was even more terrified now. He knew what she was. She stood up and sat down again, twice, then on the third try, rushed off down the hall.

Al, who sat in a cubicle across the aisle, rose and walked over to Peter. "What's going on with her?"

Peter calmly replied, "I think it's just a case of first-day jitters. A lot of things hitting her all at once."

Peter glanced at his watch and sent a quick email:

Mr. Williamson,

If you have no objections, I'd like to take the assistant comptroller to a long lunch today. That will give me some time to explain procedures and software to her without disturbing anyone else in the office.

Peter

Five minutes later, a reply appeared in Peter's inbox:

Peter,

That would be wonderful. I usually take newbies at her level to lunch at the club on their first day, but we've got a small crisis developing up here, and I'm trying to arrange a conference call with the board and the rest of the company officers. I appreciate you offering to do this. You're a real team player!

H.W.

Penelope dashed into the ladies room, shut herself in the stall furthest from the door, and began to cry. Her little bit of fun had resulted in a huge disaster. She had spilled the beans about merfolk to a random human, and it had come back to bite her—hard! Of course, her new job *had* to be in the same office as the guy who could, at any moment, claim he'd chatted up a mermaid on a Sunday afternoon.

Now, he knew where she worked on land, and he was an IT guy to boot! He could pull the information from her personnel file and use it to track her down and sell her to Sea World or something like that. No one was safe. Not on Colony Island. Not in the sea. Not anywhere. What had she done?

Penelope decided the best thing to do was run. Run fast. Run far. She'd send a letter of apology to the company, thanking everyone for their time, but it was a bad fit and wouldn't work out. The only thing stopping her from running at this point was her purse. She'd left it in her cubicle, and she had to get it back before anyone started looking through its contents.

Once she got control of herself and dried her eyes, she'd calmly—very calmly—walk to her desk, grab her purse, and since it was almost lunchtime, calmly walk out. When she was well beyond the building's front door, she'd run like hell. After she determined she looked as presentable as she was going to, Penelope left the restroom and headed for her cubicle. She turned the corner, and there was Peter, waiting for her.

"Are you okay?"

Damn him to Hades!

Peter didn't wait for an answer and showed her the printed copy of Mr. Williamson's email.

"Our boss wants me to take you to lunch so I can start explaining procedures and software to you. So, if you're ready, let's go."

After Penelope grabbed her purse, Peter guided her toward the elevator.

Okay. This can work in my favor. I'll let him escort me out of the building, clobber him with my purse, and make a run for it.

The elevator stopped at the second floor, and Peter escorted her down the short hallway to the company cafeteria.

Poseidon, why have you forsaken me?

Peter steered her into the serving line. He ordered a bowl of tomato soup and a grilled cheese sandwich while Penelope put together a salad.

Remain calm. Don't resist. Wait for your opportunity to escape.

Once he paid for their meals, he directed her to an isolated table in the far corner of the cafeteria. Peter claimed the seat facing outward so he could be on the alert if anyone approached. After they were both seated, Peter bit in to his sandwich. Penelope sat there and stared at her plate.

"Hey, the best way to attract attention to yourself is to sit there with food in front of you and not eat it."

Penelope began to slowly nibble at her salad, watching Peter all the while. The MacPherson motto, "Touch not the cat," was sage advice for this situation, and Peter was not about to make things worse. When they were both close to being finished, he put down his soupspoon and looked her squarely in the eye.

"Please understand that I'm your friend, not your enemy. No matter what you may say or do to me, I'll carry your secret to my grave. I have absolutely no intention of turning you in or selling you out. I don't know if yesterday afternoon was intentional or an accident, but it happened, and we're stuck with the consequences. You must need to earn a living, or you wouldn't be applying for jobs on land. That's fine with me. I'm going to do my best to protect you, even if you fight me every step of the way. Now, I understand you prefer to be called by your middle name, correct?"

Damn it! I've had more than enough of his smug, self-satisfied attitude. This whole thing is his fault, and I'm going to make sure he pays for it. Penelope's eyes flashed, and she was seething at the thought of cooperating with him.

"Look, Peter, I've had other jobs before this, and I'll have other jobs after I'm done here. I can take care of myself very well both in and out of the water, and I don't need your help to do it. And no—call me Penelope."

He shrugged. "All right, Penelope. Do whatever you wish, but I wanted you to know you're not alone in this."

Penelope wanted to reach across the table and smack his fool of a human face, but she stopped short of doing so. It would draw too much attention to them, and that was the last thing she wanted to do. Instead, she stood up and stormed out of the cafeteria and all the way back to her desk.

Trying to make a run for it at this point in the day would raise too many questions, and she wanted to make a clean and unremarkable escape. Besides, this Peter person would probably shadow her steps. *If I hadn't worn these damn human high heels, I might have had a shot at making it.* No, the best thing for her to do was to work the remainder of the day, quietly leave at five, and not come in tomorrow.

When Peter caught up with her a few minutes later, the air temperature seemed to have dropped forty degrees. She deigned to acknowledge his presence with a frosty glare that would have withered even the hardiest variety of arctic moss.

Peter spent the rest of the afternoon showing her how to log in, reach her email account, and locate the appropriate software, all the while wishing he had brought his parka with him to Florida.

When 5:00 p.m. rolled around, Penelope promptly shut her workstation down, took her purse, left without a word, and went straight to her apartment. She hadn't gotten a wink of sleep the previous night, and though she was groggy, she knew exactly what she had to do. Get the hell out of town.

There was one thing complicating this course of action; she had left her binder on her desk at the office, and it contained references, contact information, names, phone numbers, addresses, and plenty more that would give Peter, or anyone else, a way to track her down, as well as follow her trail back to Colony Island. She had to retrieve that binder before it was too late.

It shouldn't be too hard. She'd simply slip into the building as soon as they unlocked the doors on Tuesday, run up to her floor, and grab the binder. She'd send a letter of apology in a day or two. She wanted to mention that asshole, Peter, was the cause of all this but decided to keep it simple and avoid unnecessary questions about her background.

After another restless night, Penelope's plan was off to a promising start. Peter had not come in yet. She picked up her binder, and Poseidon was with her. *Goodbye and good riddance!*

She walked quickly toward the stairwell, and as she passed the elevators, the door opened, and out stepped Mr. Williamson.

"Ahhh, Miss Tench. I see you're here early. Good. Good. We have an emergency situation on our hands, and we need you to join us in a meeting right now."

Penelope was starting to think Poseidon had it out for her. Maybe she'd been meant to mate with Tony, and this was retribution. Before she could open her mouth, the stairwell door opened, and Peter strode out. *Great. Just great.*

Mr. Williamson turned toward him. "Peter, I'm going to have to borrow your colleague for the rest of the day, but don't worry. I'm going to make good on my plans for lunch at the club, and I'll explain procedures—and a whole lot more—to her. Now, come along, Miss Tench. Everyone should be waiting for us in the boardroom."

It had been a long day and Penelope was exhausted. If she hadn't been so out of it that morning, she could have said, "No, thank you," and walked away from the company. But no! She was now the acting comptroller for the Harriman Company. The real comptroller was supposed to return from vacation the next week but had phoned in the day before to announce he'd decided to remain on vacation permanently.

Mr. Harriman and the board had decided she was the best possible choice to take over in the interim. He even intimated that with her degree in finance, academic honors, internships, and references, she was already the front-runner for the permanent job.

This career path had been suggested by her father and was not one she would have chosen, but she had to admit, she was good at it. There was so much to think about and so much to plan and decide.

When she finally made it to her apartment after work, she had a quick bite to eat and then readied for bed. Once her head hit her pillow, she could no longer keep her eyes open and instantly fell asleep.

It was newsreel time again, and this one was a golden oldie. Back when Penelope was old enough to be left with her grandmother for part of the day, her mother had taken a volunteer job at the county library in Royston with the hope she could eventually help set up a library on Colony Island.

On one particular morning, her mother took Penelope for her state-mandated preschool shots at the county health department. She was a good little mermaid and only whined once, so her mother stopped by the library on their way home to introduce her to the other ladies working there.

"Well, hello, young lady. What's your name?"

"My name is Penny, though it really is Penelope, and you know what? My mother and I are mermaids."

Penelope's mother rolled her eyes. "I'm sorry. There's not a single little girl on Colony Island who isn't a mermaid. It must be because we live so close to the ocean."

"But, Mommy, it's true! You said..."

Her mother gave her five-year-old one of those looks that said, "Hush right now, or there'll be big trouble when we get home!"

"Oh, it's quite all right," the librarian said. "Over where we live, every single little girl is a princess."

In the months and years that followed—until Penelope was well into adolescence—the library ladies would send her books about mermaids, mermaid princesses, etc. When she completed her first young adult novel on the subject at the age of twelve, she went to find her mother.

"Mom! The people who write these books must be stupid. The mermaids in the stories are nothing like we are."

"Penny, that's because they don't know anything about us. When your father and I were on our honeymoon, we swam down to the Caribbean and stayed on a remote island. In the evenings, we'd sit around a fire your father made on the beach, and ferals would join us and tell horrible stories about humans. There was a grain of truth in some of them, but otherwise, it was pure conjecture because they'd never known any humans. Now, since we have to live next to humans and have our secret to keep, you must never, ever, reveal your mermaid side to a human."

"But why, Mom?"

"You know perfectly well *why*, young lady."

"But what if I really want to?"

Penelope's mother had had nothing to say to this, so she'd sent her to wash up and set the table for dinner.

"You were absolutely right, Mom," Penelope said out loud as she rolled out of bed after her alarm went off.

I should've listened to you. Now, I have to go into work, find Peter, and see if I can do some damage control.

CHAPTER FOUR

After spending most of the morning in the server room, Peter returned to his desk and found an email from Penelope waiting for him. At least she was finally speaking to him.

He opened the message and found that though brief, it contained no profanity or death-threats.

Peter,

We need to talk. Meet me on the benches outside at 12:45.

Penelope

The building they worked in had a little park on one end where two streets intersected at a forty-five degree angle, and there were a couple benches in that small, green space. Peter hoped that was where Penelope meant.

This girl was smart. Most people would have finished their lunch by then, and the park would most likely be empty.

Peter left for lunch early and stopped by the lunchroom to order a ham and provolone sandwich to go. He bought a bottle of diet soda and a bag of corn chips and was soon on his way outside.

The benches were empty, so he grabbed the furthest one from the door, as it offered the most privacy. He had finished his lunch and was flipping through messages on his smartphone when he heard the clip, clip, clip of high heels approaching on the paving stones. He looked up to see Penelope standing before him, but when he began to stand up, she shook her head.

"Stay where you are. I've been sitting in meetings all morning, and I don't mind standing. Besides, it will keep anyone from getting any ideas."

Including me, Peter thought to himself.

Including you! "First of all, I need to apologize."

Peter wasn't quite sure about her sincerity, as she was speaking through clenched teeth.

"I'm...sorry, but you need to understand my position. Humans think it's so easy being a mermaid. After all, I don't have to do anything but sit on a rock somewhere, sing, and comb my hair all day. Lah dee dah!

"Well, let me tell you what my average weekend is like. First of all, I get up at 2:00 AM on Saturday morning, skip breakfast, drive like hell to whatever beach I'm going to so I can find a safe place to park, and get in the water before anyone sees me.

"I swim around all day eating sushi—which I *hate*—until it gets dark. Then, I have to try and get out of the water before the food places all close so I can have something decent to eat. If I don't, then it's more sushi. Either way, I have to move the car, get back in the water to sleep, and swim around all day Sunday until it's dark again and I can go home.

"One time, I didn't get home until 6:00 AM on Monday because some of *you* were having a beer party next to my car. I couldn't really walk up to them dripping wet and say, 'Excuse me, but I'm a mermaid, and I'd like to go home now,' *could* I?"

Peter tried to mumble an apology for the beer party and say that humans weren't all like that when Penelope cut him off.

"Oh, I saw that look on your face. Just so you know, I wear a bikini to and from the water. I usually leave it, and my car keys, under a rock or tied to a pier, but one time, some kids found it. I saw them dragging it around and playing with it on the beach. I had to wait until the beach was completely deserted before I could sneak back to my car, break into it, and drive home.

"I *finally* found an isolated dock and a safe parking place nearby that'll work very well if I don't use it too often. But now I can't use it at all because *you* know where I hang out.

"It was just another Sunday afternoon, and some guy came to the dock where I was taking a nap. I decided to have a bit of harmless fun with him—only to discover the next day that not only does he work at my new job, but his desk is next to mine as well. I should have let you fall off of the other side of the dock, hit your head, and drown. That was my second mistake. The first was deciding to pop out of the water and wind you up.

"Now, do you understand why I'm more than a little upset over all of this? Do you understand why I don't particularly care one way or the other if you're my 'friend?' *Do* you?"

Peter slowly shook his head. "Look, I'm sorry that..."

Penelope's eyes were glowing at this point, and not in a nice way. "You damn well better be!"

She turned and stormed off to do whatever it was that acting comptrollers do all day.

As Penelope was walking toward the building's entrance, she heard the unknown voice say, "You call that damage control? You might as well have stomped on his foot and kicked him in the shins while you were at it."

Peter wasn't sure why he'd apologized. He'd empathized with Penelope's human problems, but he was not his species' keeper. As for the thing on the dock, she'd admitted it was all her idea from start to finish. He was the innocent party who'd been left wondering if the whole thing was some kind of "candid camera" stunt. Still, it was his nature to try and fix things where fuming females were concerned. He had the beginning of an idea about how to remedy her situation, but it would take the remainder of the afternoon to come together.

When he got home that evening, Peter began doing some research. He ended up staying awake half the night finding and printing out all the information he needed, but in the end, he felt like it was worth the effort.

When he arrived at his office in the morning, as soon as his PC finished booting, he sent Penelope the same message she had sent him the day before.

Penelope,

We need to talk. Meet me on the benches outside at 12:45.

Peter

Sure enough, at the designated time, he heard the clip, clip, clip of high heels on the paving stones.

"You wanted to see me?"

"Yeah, I did, but before you bite my head off again, let me finish, all right?"

Penelope slowly nodded her head. She'd have to hold her tongue, but that was all right. It would give her more self-righteous venom to unleash when it was her turn to speak.

"First, I'm sorry about your troubles with humans. As I said on Sunday, we're not all like that. Second, I'm sorry I happened to be the object of your prank on Sunday, but that could not be helped. Third, rather than apologizing for moving to Florida or even being born, I'd like to explain how we can fix things, or at least make your life easier. But, before I do, please remember that no matter how much you think you may hate me, I'm still your ally—not your enemy."

Penelope was starting to get irritated again, but nonetheless, she said, "Go ahead."

"Okay. I want you to know that what I'm about to propose is not new for me. During my summers in college, I was on the nature staff at a summer institute in the Blue Ridge Mountains, and I did something like this. Though instead of juggling canoes, I'm going to be managing a mermaid.

"On Fridays after work, we'll drive to the coast, check into a motel—separate rooms, of course—and have a nice meal out somewhere. The next morning, we'll head to the beach at sunrise and get you into the water. At lunchtime, we'll rendezvous at a spot further up or down the coast, and I'll provide you with the lunch of your choice. In the evening, we'll get you out of the water at a third spot, go back to the motel, change, and then go out for another nice dinner. On Sunday, we'll do it all over again, only using different locations. I'll check us out of the motel, and when we get you out of the water on Sunday evening, I'll have something ready for you to eat on the way home.

"The beauty of all this is, you'll get a good night's sleep, decent meals, a short drive to and from the water, and you'll only be at each spot once, so no one will notice any kind of pattern. Now, here are maps showing each of the locations I'm considering, along with street views. I realize it's short notice, but I'd like to know your thoughts so I can get going on the reservations."

Penelope looked at the papers in front of her. "Well, this spot won't work because they've put up a fence here since the place was photographed. However, there's a spot two blocks north that should be fine."

Am I actually thinking of doing this? What's wrong with me? I should be telling this guy to go pound sand. But, the stupid voice in her head insisted this would make her weekends considerably more enjoyable and kept begging her to say yes.

"Hmmm…this might actually work. Not bad for a human. Who's going to drive?"

"I will. I'll take care of all the expenses as well."

"Okay, if you can find a decent motel that's not too far from the beach, I'm in." Penelope walked—not stormed—back into the building, wondering why she was so enthused about his idea.

Penelope began fuming again on Friday evening as they drove toward the beach. *If this clown thinks he's going to get some tail just because I'm a mermaid, he's in for a rude awakening.*

Once more, that unknown voice spoke to her. "He seems like a nice young man and a gentleman as well. He's doing all of this just for you. Why won't you give him the benefit of the doubt?"

Penelope refused to even dignify that question with an answer.

Peter looked at Penelope from the corner of his eye. She was sitting as far away from him as possible with her arms and legs tightly crossed in front of her. Not even a blind man could fail to recognize the "keep away from me" body language.

Message received and understood! Peter had no intention of going anywhere near her, but he couldn't see the harm in casual conversation. He only had to glance at her, though, to realize that pleasantries were not going to fly.

When they reached the motel, Peter handled the check-in and returned with the keys, as well as an apologetic look on his face.

"I'm sorry about this. I asked for two rooms next to each other, and they interpreted that as a request for adjoining rooms. But don't worry. There's a lock on each connecting door, and I can't get into your room unless you unlock yours."

"I understand how adjoining rooms work, human. Let's get

something to eat. I'm starving."

Peter ate his dinner under Penelope's baleful glare. It was a nice restaurant with a good mixture of entrées. She hadn't ordered seafood, but what did he know about mermaids? His meal tasted good and would have tasted even better without Penelope's dirty looks.

Finally, he had enough of her glowering at him. "Look," he hissed. "I know you'd rather not be here with me, and honestly, I feel the same way. However, we are both here because of you, and you alone. I wasn't the one who decided to pop out of the water and scare the crap out of someone.

"If you'd stayed under that dock for another two or three minutes, I would've been in my car and on my way home. But that doesn't mean we wouldn't have met. I knew you were coming to work at Harriman a month ago. I even knew your name and set up your email account. All of the decisions have been made by you, not me. So, if I'm going to waste my time on you, will you at least give me the courtesy of civil conversation?"

Penelope closed her eyes. He was right. This whole thing was her fault, and her mother would be furious over the way she'd been acting. She wasn't about to apologize—but she did turn off the hot and cold running hate for the rest of the meal.

She said nothing on the way back to the motel, and when they finally stood outside her room, Peter asked, "So, how do like your morning coffee?"

"I'm sorry, but I only drink tea."

"Ahhh. A mermaid after my own heart. So, how do you take your tea?"

Penelope was furious with herself for saying, "I'm sorry." Where had that come from? As she turned to open the door to her room, she snapped, "You seem to be pretty smart for a human. You figure it out."

"Earl Grey with lemon. No sugar."

Penelope was even more furious now. How did he know that? How? She wanted to slam the door in his face, but for some inexplicable reason, she gently closed it behind her. After laying out her bathrobe and bikini, she brushed her hair, turned out the light, and went to sleep.

It was time for another blast from the past, and this time,

she was four years old. There was a shop on the main street of Colony Island called The Mermaid's Purse that sold new and gently used children's clothing, as well as maternity clothes and other such things.

The yellow frame building sat on a corner, and there was a room facing the side street that held toys for mer girls and boys. There were mermaid dolls, stuffed sea creatures, little wooden tridents, plastic gold crowns, and little treasure chests with plastic strands of pearls and gems inside. There were also toy boats, fire engines, and police cars.

One day, her mother found Penelope in that room, gazing at the wonderful things that lined the shelves, and asked if she would like something to take home with her. Penelope rushed for a stuffed dolphin, which she immediately named Mr. Splashy and subsequently took wherever she went.

To her, Mr. Splashy was as real as a dolphin could be. She talked to him constantly, told him all her secrets, slept with him, and simply loved him to death. Every time she and her mother would walk by the window to the shop's toy room, she'd stop, wave to all of Mr. Splashy's friends, and beg to be taken inside so she could tell them how much her stuffed dolphin missed them.

On one of these occasions, Penelope decided a mermaid doll looked lonely and asked to take it home so that Mr. Splashy would have someone to talk to. She became increasingly concerned that Mr. Splashy's friends stayed on the shelves, week after week and month after month with no one to love them.

Her mother was about to tell Penelope to stop being silly until she saw how serious her daughter was. So, instead, she told her—as any good mother would—that stuffed animals were chosen for their patience and didn't mind waiting until the right person came along for them. That mollified Penelope for the time being, but long after Mr. Splashy had been relegated to a place of honor on her bookshelf, she still felt bad about the stuffed animals at the shop.

Penelope awoke to the sound of someone knocking on her door. Who the hell would be waking her at this ungodly hour of the morning? She determined the knocking was coming from the door to the adjoining room, and after opening it, she squinted at Peter with bleary eyes.

"Whadaya want?"

"Rise and shine, sunshine! Sunrise is less than thirty minutes away. I have hot tea and donuts for you. I'll be waiting in the SUV out front."

Penelope took the tea, closed the door, and fumbled for the light switch. Five minutes later, she stumbled from the room wearing her bathrobe. *To hell with the bikini. No one in their right mind gets up this damn early, anyway.*

Peter wanted to remind her that her old routine had her getting out of bed hours earlier but decided to keep quiet, as she'd yet to bite his head off.

On their drive toward the beach, Penelope sipped her tea, munched her donut, and began to feel less on edge. Once she was a little more awake, she decided to ask about something that had been nagging her since the previous night.

"Peter, how did you know I like my tea this way?"

"Well, that's the way I drink it. I took a stab in the dark about yours."

Penelope wasn't totally convinced. He'd sure sounded positive about it last night.

About ten minutes later, Peter pulled up to the spot where they would make their way between the hotels and restaurants en route to the beach. The oceanfront hotels were older along this stretch and didn't consume every square inch of their lots. Traffic was almost nonexistent at this time of day, and Peter had no qualms about slipping into a space marked "Loading Zone – 10 minutes" and leaving the motor running.

Penelope was fully awake now and seemed eager to get in the water. Peter stood behind her at the ocean's edge, scanning up and down the beach several times before saying, "It's clear. You're good."

Peter held her bathrobe as she stepped out of it, and in an instant, she disappeared into the water. He stood there for a minute or two, but she was apparently gone. After one more scan of his surroundings, he turned and headed back to the SUV. With any luck, he'd be able to get in a nice nap before it was time to worry about lunch.

Three hours later, Peter was on his way to a gas station. Once the tank was full, he inflated an inner tube he'd kept handy for tubing trips back home. He spread a piece of netting over the center of the tube and looped the attached cords around the rim and back through the center. This would serve as a table in case

Penelope didn't want to come all the way out of the water for lunch.

It was still early, but the rendezvous was well south of where he was at the moment, and Peter wanted to be there with plenty of time to spare before she surfaced. After picking up a pastrami sandwich, a cold soda, and a large chocolate chip cookie for her at a deli, he was on his way. His lunch could wait until Penelope was done with hers and safely under the surface again.

The parking lot at the meeting point was empty when he got there, but that didn't last for long. As Peter was gathering his bits and pieces to take down to the water's edge, a fifteen-passenger van pulled up. Its occupants disembarked and began preparing what appeared to be a cookout on the beach.

With Penelope about fifteen minutes or less out, Peter pulled on his life jacket, grabbed the inner tube and her lunch, and headed for the water. Once lunch was safely stowed aboard the inner tube, he pushed it out into the water and began dog paddling after it. He was over three hundred yards from shore when Penelope surfaced next to him.

"What are you doing way out here? I thought I was supposed to meet you at the shoreline."

"Change of plans. We have a hot LZ!"

"A what?"

"LZ. Landing Zone! There's a bunch of people setting up a picnic where we were supposed to meet, and I can't risk them seeing you," he said while treading water.

As Penelope ate her lunch, she couldn't help but notice the frantic look in Peter's eyes and the fact that he was holding on to the inner tube for dear life.

"Are you all right?"

"Scared...to...death! Even though we're actually in the sound here...I'm afraid of being in the ocean. Got caught in a rip current when I was twelve or thirteen and pulled out to sea. Almost drowned. I'm okay in fresh water or in a boat, but put me in the ocean...and I start to freak out."

Penelope rolled her eyes—she was good at that—and shook her head. Maybe she should simply drown him now and be done with the aggravation.

"Shame, shame, shame on you! You were raised better than that," the unknown voice scolded. "What would your parents think? We both know he has nothing to fear, but as far as he's concerned, Peter is putting his life on the line so you can safely have your lunch. Cut him some slack!"

Penelope sighed inwardly. This voice—wherever it was coming from—was starting to get really annoying, but it was right. She was a much better person than that and felt guilty for even thinking that way.

"As soon as I'm done, I'll give you a tow back to shore. Where is your lunch, by the way?"

"Haven't bought it yet. Waiting for you to be on your way before I eat."

Shaking her head, Penelope put the last bit of her sandwich down and ignored the cookie. "Okay. I'm done. Let's get you back on dry land."

"No. You haven't finished your lunch. I can wait."

Penelope went ahead and finished the rest of her lunch—a bit faster than she ordinarily would. "That's all of it. Now hang on!"

Peter and the inner tube returned to shore more quickly than when they were on the outbound leg. Once his feet touched bottom, he turned around to thank her, but she was nowhere to be seen. He got some rather strange looks from the picnickers as he came on shore but paid them no mind. He stowed his gear in the back of the SUV and threw a couple towels on the driver's seat. He needed to pick up some lunch, get changed, and then go shopping.

The isolated strip of beach serving as the pickup point, was virtually deserted when Penelope emerged from the water. She wrapped herself in the large towel Peter provided, pulled on her bathrobe, and they walked to the SUV.

"Ridiculous. Simply ridiculous," she muttered to herself.

When they reached the parking area, Penelope stopped and gaped at the SUV. Or rather, what was on top of it.

"What in the world is that?"

"It's a sea kayak," Peter answered with a touch of pride in his voice. "I've always wanted one. This afternoon, I went to a place to see about renting one for tomorrow, and they had this one on sale for half price. It's an older model they used for demos and the occasional rental, so I decided it should go home with me."

"You mean we're really going to do all this again tomorrow?"

"That's the plan. Like I said earlier, I'm okay if I'm in a boat, though we should probably meet for lunch in the sound again. Once I get used to handling it, I should be okay in open water, provided the waves cooperate."

Penelope shook her head and climbed into the front seat of the SUV. After returning to the motel for a shower and dry clothes, they drove off in search of dinner. Penelope remained fairly quiet during the meal, but the overall atmosphere was more pleasant than it had been the previous evening.

Though she didn't want to admit it, the day had been more relaxing than her usual Saturday swim, and her sleep that night was much better. There were no dreams—or at least none she remembered—and this, in and of itself, was a welcome change.

She was more rested and refreshed when Peter knocked on the connecting door about thirty minutes before sunrise the following morning. As they drove to the drop off point, Penelope was the cheeriest he'd seen her the past week. She wasn't bubbly by any means, but anything was an improvement over "grump-o-matic," as he secretly called her.

"Do you have everything packed and ready to go?" Peter asked.

"Well, for the most part, yes. There are a couple things left that should be obvious when you get back to the room."

"Okay, I'll wear latex gloves so you won't get *cooties*."

"You do that," Penelope said with a barely perceptible chuckle in her voice.

The drop off went as well as it had the day before. The two of them reviewed the lunch and pickup points, and Peter asked what she'd like for dinner.

"You know, I've used that pickup spot in the past, and there's some bushes I could use to dry off and change in. Let me do that, and we can pick a restaurant on the way home."

As before, Peter scanned the surroundings prior to giving her the "go" signal, and then he headed back to the motel for an hour or two of sleep before he collected their things and checked out.

The lunch rendezvous was a success. Peter was comfortable in his new watercraft, and Penelope enjoyed being able to lay her lunch out on the forward deck of the kayak. While the previous day had been overcast, there were only a few cumulus clouds in Sunday's sky. With nothing left to do until it was time to go to the pickup point, Peter enjoyed a glorious afternoon maneuvering the kayak up and down the sound.

Beneath the surface, things were a bit different as Penelope glided through the water on her way out to sea. There was a thick patch of sea grass just south, and it was where she intended to take her nap. As she worked her tail in a slow rhythmic motion, her mind ran through the events of the past two days.

Her main concern was the return visits of the strange voice that had bothered her so much. Why was it there, and where was it coming from? It was starting to go from annoying to worrisome. Was she losing her mind?

Maybe she should go visit a sea shrink, if such a thing existed. This was the problem living as an isolated mermaid. There was no one to talk to, no one who could help. She could always swim home to her parents', but that would just make things worse.

Then there was the matter of swimming itself. Merfolk didn't have to swim every day or even every month as long as they stayed hydrated one way or another. Lindsey, residing in Lincoln, Nebraska, was living proof of that. Penelope just didn't like the idea of cowering in her room every weekend when there was an entire ocean in which to escape from humanity. The trouble was, she had a human helping her do exactly that. She really had lost her mind.

Penelope located the sea meadow and slowly swam back and forth over it, looking for the right spot. She found a corner where the leaves seemed to be extra tall and thick. No predators in sight, just small, colorful fish weaving their way through the grass. She settled in to the middle of the patch and played finger tag with the fish before drifting off to sleep.

It was early evening when she woke and made her way to wait offshore at the pickup spot for Peter to give her the "all clear." While there was a bit of momentary concern when three joggers went by on the beach, Penelope was able to exit the water without being observed.

Once she'd changed into dry clothes, Peter pointed the SUV in the general direction of the city. Though the return trip was relatively quiet, the tension of the past forty-eight hours was somewhat diminished. Her body language was more relaxed but still not very friendly.

Peter insisted on escorting Penelope into her apartment building and up to her door when they arrived there. As he set her bags down and prepared to return to the SUV, he asked, "Well, did you have a good time?"

This was the hardest thing Penelope had asked herself to do

in a long time. As she searched for an evasive answer, that annoying voice spoke up. "Go ahead. Tell him. You know you enjoyed yourself for once, so why won't you tell him?"

It was almost like opening her mouth to have a tooth pulled, but she finally responded, "Yeah, I had a pretty good time."

"That's great. Can we do this whole thing again next weekend?"

CHAPTER FIVE

Looking back on the weekend, it was the easiest in and out of the water she'd ever had in the vicinity of humans. Peter had made things safer and easier for her. *Damn his human ass!* Why did he have to be right? Why did he have to be so good at this?

Penelope had to admit she liked getting some decent sleep, being chauffeured to and from the water, having lunch delivered, and dining at restaurants rather than subsisting on fast food. And she'd actually enjoyed her time in the water!

She was still uneasy that Peter knew her secret, but if he was going to spend his time and money on her again this weekend, why should she refuse? Penelope made one stipulation, though: no more adjoining rooms. She'd make sure she was completely packed on Sunday morning before leaving for the sea.

The retiring comptroller cleaned out his office on Wednesday so Penelope could move into it. It felt good to get away from Peter, but at the same time, she missed sitting next to him. Whatever was causing this, she hoped she'd get over it soon.

This time, Penelope let Peter handle all of the planning and only gave the maps a cursory glance. They'd be a bit further south than where they were last weekend, and she was not familiar with the locale, so she simply rubber-stamped his suggestions. If he made a muck of things, it would be all the easier to tell him to get lost.

Two hundred yards offshore, Penelope was relaxing in the gentle current thirty feet below the surface when she realized she hadn't heard the annoying voice all week, which was a relief, as she had been starting to question her own sanity. Still, she was curious as to why she'd even heard it at all, as well as why she only heard it in connection with Peter. Perhaps she had been around humans for too long, and it was starting to take its toll on her. Who knew what she might do next? Go on a mad shopping spree for clothes? Get a complete makeover?

As a few clown fish swam lazily by, she couldn't help chuckling over the makeover thought. While mermaids did wear clothes—at least those who lived on the shore—they were hardly slaves to fashion. A dress or skirt would be worn until it was no longer wearable. Wardrobes were small, but then, folks who spent much of their time in the water really didn't need a whole lot. There were some mermaids on the island who worked in Royston and kept up with more recent styles for appearance's sake. She imagined the same thing applied to those who lived in the Royston enclave.

As a rule, mermaids were not much concerned with makeup, either. After all, what was the sense of putting it on, when it would only wash off if you went for a swim? The trouble with humans—or at least human females—was if you spent much time amongst them, you were expected to wear at least some makeup. Thankfully, human males seldom seemed to notice one way or another.

Although mermaids tended to rely on their natural beauty, the after school program at the Colony Academy gave lessons on how to apply the stuff so the mermaids would fit in with the human girls at the mainland high school. Otherwise, one of the operators at Bab's Kut and Kurl on the island could do it if there was some special need to be made up…like a joining ceremony.

Suddenly, Penelope's mind went blank, and she found herself in the dark, icy grip of despair being dragged down below the point where sunlight glittering on the surface was only a rumor. She was being crushed by the unrelenting pressure and was powerless to save herself.

She had felt so much better for the past week; why was this happening to her? Why now? She had no answer, but in that moment, the voice spoke again.

"Don't give up, child—not now when you're so close! Love is on its way to you, I promise. You'll find what you've been hoping for, sooner rather than later."

Okay. She was definitely losing it now! She was so immersed in trying to determine just how far around the bend she'd gone, that she didn't notice the light returning to her soul. The only way she could reconcile all of this was to believe that Peter had been sent to make it easier to swim and easier to enjoy being what she was. At some point in her swimming, she just might meet the one she wanted most, the one thing she needed.

It may only be a fantasy, and a silly one at that, which would sooner or later abandon her, but for the moment, she had something to cling to. If Peter was indeed part of all this, then she needed to treat him better. She was still somewhat mad at him, but she was starting to find it hard to explain why. Maybe—just maybe—if she saw this through, all would be revealed in the end. Penelope had planned to ask the strange voice just who or what it was, but now, she was glad she hadn't. She was too afraid of the answer.

She was not ready to drop her defenses—at least where Peter was concerned. She'd still keep him at arm's length, but she'd try to be as civil as possible and refrain from yelling at him—unless he truly deserved it. In retrospect, she hadn't really enjoyed doing it anyway. One thing was certain, though. She was not about to allow him to call her Anne, the name she preferred, and probably never would. Hearing him call her Penelope gave her just one more reason to dislike him. If she stuck to her plan, all of this just might work out.

When Penelope's head broke the sunlit surface, her worries, her doubts, and the darkness remained below. Her world seemed a bit brighter somehow, and for once, she felt no need to wonder why.

The rest of their weekend went as well as the first. Both drop offs and pickups were flawless, and lunch became something to look forward to. Peter seemed to have a knack for security and finding the safest locations for her to start the day's swim, as well as wrap it up. By the time they returned to the city on Sunday evening, Penelope found herself hoping Peter would want to go again next weekend.

The following Wednesday, Peter sent an email asking Penelope to join him in the lunchroom at their usual meeting time. She supposed it was about the upcoming weekend, though she'd requested he email her the maps and necessary information. It was bad enough she spent Friday through

Sunday evening with him. Anything that kept the contact to a minimum was all for the better.

Once they were both seated in their corner on the far side of the lunchroom, Peter pushed the information for the upcoming weekend toward her. "I've decided I can't be emailing this stuff to you. There's too much risk in it."

Penelope was disgruntled they would have to meet, even for a half hour, during the week and asked sourly, "Why's that?"

"Well, there's too much chance someone might stumble across our messages. Even if we emptied our 'sent' and 'trash' folders on a regular basis, our email transactions are logged by the mail system, and the actual contents of the messages are logged as well. If someone suspected you were what you are, it would be easy from a hacker's standpoint to recover my messages to you and arrange a nasty surprise at the beach. I could write some code to purge this stuff from the logs, but there are also the back-up copies to worry about. It's just more secure to print you copies of the information.

"I'll have to change how I do things on my end. Just so your eyes won't glaze over, all I'll say is there are ways to do the searches I need without giving away too much of who I am. It'll take some effort, but I'm willing to do this for the sake of your security."

Penelope thought for a moment and then asked, "Peter, why are you doing this...*all* of this?"

Peter smiled. He wasn't sure why, but he felt the need to keep her safe. Need was a strong word, though, and it had the potential to scare her off. "Penelope, I want to protect you."

Those six words set her heart fluttering. To merfolk, there were connotations and implications to this phrase a human wouldn't understand. Rather than explain—the less he knew about her world, the better—she'd interpret it using the human meaning and enjoy the fact that she wasn't dead.

Peter continued, "Now, I know you're accustomed to taking precautions and have done this longer than I have, so if you want me to get lost, I will. However, I'm not going to let anything happen to you...not on my watch."

Rather than her usual sneer, Penelope earnestly asked, "Do you really think there's an issue with my security?"

"To be honest, probably not. However, humans can become terribly obsessed over things, and I don't want to take any risks if I can help it."

Well, this human is certainly doing his best. More than I would have expected. If we go past this weekend, I'm going to start paying for at least part of these outings.

The next few weekends passed without incident. Peter had suggested they work a couple extra hours during the week so they could leave about 3:00 p.m. on Fridays and be a bit ahead of the traffic as they drove to their destination. Penelope readily agreed and marveled at how many sensible suggestions the human was capable of.

Before he could make plans for their sixth outing, Penelope asked if they could meet over lunch. That was definitely not like her, and Peter was on high alert as he headed toward their usual table in the lunchroom. Maybe she was going to put a halt to all of this. After all, she'd insisted on paying for everything the past weekend.

Peter had salvaged some of his honor by taking care of tips and lunches. Overall, he wouldn't mind having his weekends back, though he would miss these trips to the beach. Penelope's attitude had improved over time, and the outings were actually becoming enjoyable.

He was not, however, prepared for what he saw sitting down at the table waiting for him. "Well, aren't you something! A dress, of all things. It's nice to see you in something different...and flattering, I might add."

Penelope blushed slightly and smiled. "Thank you. Honestly, I've been wearing the same business suits since my first internship. There was even a joke about me at my last job. 'If it's Tuesday, the suit must be brown'. I just decided that I could use a few new things and went shopping yesterday after work."

"I'd say your expedition was a success, then. Now what did you need to see me about?"

"I'd like to make a change for this weekend, if that's possible. I know I said otherwise a number of weeks ago, but I'd like to go back to having adjoining rooms."

This was a switch. Penelope had been all about limiting contact, and now she was in favor of a little bit more. "Any particular reason why?"

"A number of reasons, actually. As you know from the last couple weeks, having completely separate rooms meant we were in two different parts of the motel. Not a good idea for security or efficiency. I think adjoining rooms would also be more convenient. What do you think?"

Peter had been brewing tea and dispensing toast, donuts, and oatmeal from his room for most of their weekends, so all three reasons were good for him. "I'm fine with it if you are. I'll see what I can do for our upcoming trip. Meanwhile, I have a request of my own. As you've probably noticed, the sun has been setting later and later since we started our expeditions. Factor in that more and more people are hitting the beach now, and it's really difficult to bring you in before dark. That pushes dinner further and further back for us both, and I figure you need at least some time to relax after a day in the water.

"I'd like to suggest we do pickups on the sound when it's feasible. I'll paddle out to you with your bikini, and you can follow my kayak in. If the surf's not too bad, I can wade out a ways in the ocean, but...you know me."

Peter's phobia was irritating at times, but Penelope's weekly swims were so much more enjoyable now, that she was very willing to cut him some slack. "How about this? If we know the surf is going to be heavy, I'll swim over to our alternate spot. Otherwise, I'll surface and check the beach. If I see you waving me off, I'll go to the alternate spot. If I see you waving me in, we'll meet in the middle."

"Deal!" Peter was pleased. This was the first time they'd really worked together to solve a problem.

Penelope had to admit she felt much safer and more secure with this new arrangement. There had been an incident the previous Saturday afternoon when a very forward and somewhat intoxicated guy accosted her just after she had left the water and was adjusting her bikini top and bottom. Peter had run up and stormed his way in between them, told the guy off, and sent him scrambling for safety. It was almost as if...as if...no. It was simply a coincidence.

Still, Peter was looking out for her wellbeing, and she was really beginning to feel he was for real, and she could trust him. Someone to trust—she hadn't had that luxury since leaving Colony Island.

From Peter's standpoint, overall, things had become more friendly between them over the past couple weeks, and the tension had evaporated. At least she didn't call him "human" anymore, and when she entered the water in the morning, he would see a flash of her tail fin before she disappeared for good. That was a hopeful sign, wasn't it?

Peter would readily admit she was attractive, especially now that she smiled rather than scowled. She'd be a good catch for some lucky merman. He walked back to his workstation, wondering why the thought of Penelope dating one of her own kind was more than a little troubling to him.

It was the following Monday night that the dreams began—the ones that included Peter. If it had happened weeks earlier, she would have been alarmed and stopped their expeditions immediately. But at this point, Penelope was relatively unfazed by it.

After all, she spent time with him every weekend and he was...well...a friend now, and she guessed he had been all along. She was happier than she had been in years and had started to hold out hope that she would finally find the merman of her dreams. Perhaps it would be due to what Peter had done for her. She owed him something and chuckled at a couple of the ideas that sailed across her mind.

At first, she thought of giving him some of those floaties she had seen human children using. *Better yet, how about one of those inflatable life-ring things with a horse's head?* That would make a great gag gift, but she needed something for a friend.

She could always fix him up with Amy. *They'd be perfect for each other.* Penelope quickly scuttled that idea—somehow, the thought of Peter seeing another mermaid did not appeal to her. She thought of one other thing, but she couldn't do that to him. It would be cruel, and she was not a cruel person.

As for the dreams, they were mostly about Peter delivering lunch or meeting her at the pickup point, though there was one brief flash that seemed to occur at the end of every dream. She saw him slipping away from her underwater.

Penelope wasn't sure what it was all about, but given the crazy stuff that most dreams were made of, it probably meant nothing at all—if dreams meant anything to begin with. At least there hadn't been any newsreels of her younger self. Things were looking up all around, and she hadn't thought of suicide in ages. One thing was certain: their weekends had become more cordial, and she was glad for that.

On Saturday evening, Penelope and Peter were chatting over dinner at a Mexican restaurant. To Peter, it seemed totally incongruous for a mermaid to like Mexican food, but she was the one who'd suggested it, and this was a good choice. Apparently, mermaids were more than adept at selecting good places to eat.

"Tell me, what do you see when you're down there?"

"Well, marine life mostly. Lots of fish, of course, kelp forests, an occasional wreck—no gold and jewels, I'm afraid."

Peter smiled at that. "Darn! I wish I could see some of those things. You know, before I moved down here, I traded a canoe for an underwater digital camera. I'm not sure how good it is, but if I clean it up, would you be willing to take it with you some time?"

"Not a problem, Peter. I've wanted to try my hand at photography from time to time but never had the equipment. I'd love to see what I can do. It sounds like a win-win kinda thing to me."

"Great! I'll have it ready for next weekend."

Peter was relieved that Penelope seemed to have dropped her defenses. It made things much less awkward for them, which made for a better weekend in every aspect.

One thing he'd noticed was a change in the morning drop off. Once she dashed into the ocean, Penelope would vanish under the surface and presumably put her tail on. He wasn't quite sure how it all worked. She would then surface off shore, wave, and flash her fin before diving beneath the waves. In the evenings, she appeared to be relaxed and pleased to see him at the pickup point.

Peter attended to getting the underwater camera in shape over the following week. It needed a new battery, and he tested the case to make sure it was still waterproof.

At dinner on Friday evening, he showed it to Penelope. "It's rated at forty-five feet, which is good, because you lose fifty percent of the light thirty feet down, more or less."

"Our eyes work better underwater than yours do, so we can see well below that point, but I get the idea."

"It also has a timer, so you can set it and then back away. I suppose it's so you can still get pictures of shy fish. I also added a larger memory card. Unless you get snap-happy down there, you should have plenty of space for your photos. I'll off-load the pictures when we get back to the motel, and we can look at them over dinner."

"How about you give me the camera at lunch tomorrow? We'll be able to make the most of the light, and I think after three hours or so of taking pictures, I'm going to want to come in a bit early."

Once they were back at the motel after Saturday's swim, Penelope warned him she'd probably taken a number of selfies testing the camera and its timer. Peter assured her he'd take care of deleting them first thing.

He put two copies of that day's pictures on a thumb drive and then wiped the contents of the camera's memory card. That done, he decided to take a shower so his hair could dry while he looked through Penelope's pictures.

He was just starting to undress in the bathroom when he heard the most angelic voice singing "If I Loved You" from *Carousel*. He looked around to see where the voice was coming from, and when the singing began once more, the song had changed to "I Loved You Once in Silence" from *Camelot*. The vocal came from a vent high up on the bathroom wall—the wall separating his room from Penelope's.

Peter ran from the bathroom and began to pound on the connecting door. After a few moments, Penelope opened it and stood before him in her robe with her hair wrapped in a towel and a puzzled look on her face.

"Was that you...singing? I recognized the songs from albums of show tunes that my grandparents used to play all the time. That was the most beautiful rendition of them I've ever heard. Please, please say it was you."

Penelope blushed. "Yes, that was me. My senior year in high school, the chorus did a program of Broadway show tunes for our spring concert, and those two were my solos."

"I don't know what to say. You have such a beautiful singing voice..."

Penelope blushed even more this time. "No, I'm not *that* good. My best friend, Amy, has the best voice on the island." She suddenly realized she had accidentally blown part of her hometown's cover, but at this moment, she really didn't care.

"I guess all this comes from luring ships to the rocks."

"Ugh! Inaccurate reports from unreliable sources. Most shipwrecks were due to storms, navigation errors, or inept seamanship. If any mermaids were on the scene, it was to rescue as many sailors as possible, though I will admit that some of them may have been husband hunting. You know, mermen's voices are just as good as ours. Unfortunately, no one seems to care much about singing anymore." Her scowl had dissolved into a face full of sadness.

When Peter finally closed the door, he had the look of a deer in headlights, and all he could say was, "Unbelievable."

All through his shower, he puzzled over something else. Why did his heart start racing each time she blushed? He didn't want to think about the possibilities, but it was curious how the two events coincided.

All of this was forgotten when he sat down to look at the pictures from that afternoon. Some of the shots were okay, and some were quite good, but he was totally unprepared for Penelope's selfies.

A couple were looking up at her face, with the sunlight filtering down through the water, giving both her head and hair a sort of halo. Others were simply test shots of her tail fin.

Then came the last one, which must have been taken to test the timer. It was a full frontal shot with her tail curled out behind her. She looked…beautiful…as beautiful as her voice sounded.

The rich, brown hues of her hair and eyes really didn't come through underwater, but the soft, sweet lines of her face framed lips that would easily entice a sailor into the sea. Her smile was honest and open, and she seemed to be smiling *at* him as well as smiling *for* him. She was not big-breasted, but that made her all the more real, all the more adorable. Her curvy, trim frame merged seamlessly with her wonderful mermaid's tail he had seen too little of until now. Reluctantly, Peter looked away, collected the selfies, and moved them to a separate folder on the thumb drive before copying the rest of the photos to the laptop.

The restaurant was very casual, and they found a booth toward the back where they could look at the photos without disturbing anyone. Penelope narrated the slide show and told Peter where she had taken each photo as well as the species of each fish. Peter would have thought that knowledge just came naturally, until she mentioned she'd had to learn all of them in elementary school.

Peter observed a very relaxed and secure Penelope Tench sitting across the table from him. Most of their one-on-one contact for a little over two months now had occurred at meals. It had started out as trench warfare, but it appeared that recently, some sort of peace agreement had been signed. She gave no indication that she wanted contact outside of lunch and dinner, but the slight smile that played across her face showed that mealtime had become a more pleasant experience for her. If that was the case, Peter would be more than happy for things to continue as they were.

"By the way, thank you for getting rid of all the selfies. I really do appreciate all you do to protect my secret."

Peter felt like a traitor, but after seeing her like that, there were a few photos he was just not able to part with. At least not yet.

As he was pondering ways to securely store them, Penelope intruded on his thoughts. "I'd really like to relax and take a nap tomorrow, but we can try this again next weekend."

Peter was fine with that, and the following day, he arrived at the lunchtime rendezvous around 11:30 a.m. Since he wouldn't have to worry about putting the kayak in the water for half an hour, he whiled away the time looking at Penelope's photos...including the selfies.

He puzzled over why he was so drawn to them. It was most likely because he'd never seen a mermaid underwater before, but still...he wished for a fleeting moment he could be a merman. That was impossible, of course, but there was another wish behind that one. It was best he dispose of all such notions right away, before things got out of hand.

CHAPTER SIX

As the week progressed, it looked less and less likely they would be able to do any photography on the upcoming weekend. Although they'd been blessed with remarkably good weather the past two months, a tropical system moving up from the gulf promised to ruin things for them.

Where and when it would cross the Florida peninsula were the big questions, but Peter decided they should at least have some time for Penelope to swim on Saturday. As it turned out, the storm was not the only source of problems.

When Peter checked them in to the motel, he discovered that even though they had adjoining rooms, Penelope had hers for both nights, while his was only for one night.

"Looks like some kind of glitch in the reservations system," the desk clerk said apologetically.

Peter realized that getting himself worked up over this would accomplish nothing. "Well, could you give me another room in the motel?"

"Sorry. We're booked solid on Saturday night. In fact, I'm wondering how you got your reservations booked at all."

Peter resigned himself to Sunday's breakfast being more of a bother than he would have liked. "I guess I'll just have to take a room somewhere else."

"Don't think you're going to be able to do that either. Between the usual weekend traffic and the Seaside Scottish Games, everything in the area will be full."

Peter gave the desk clerk a wry look. "Seriously? Highland Games this time of the year? All that wool?"

"Afraid so. They usually hold the event in late February,

but this year's edition was washed out. This weekend was the first date they could schedule that suited everyone. Big pipe band competition, you know."

"You seem to know a lot about these events."

"Clan Grant. From the look of your name on the reservation, you're Clan MacPherson," the clerk said with a wink. "You and the pretty lady in your car could double up for Saturday night."

Peter glanced out at the car where Penelope sat waiting patiently—or as patiently as anyone could who hadn't had dinner yet. "Ahhh, sorry. We're friends, but without the benefits. I'll figure something out."

After they'd placed their bags in their respective rooms, Peter and Penelope drove off in search of dinner. Peter decided that he'd keep the accommodations issue to himself. After all, these weekends were for Penelope, and she shouldn't have to worry about where he was going to sleep.

After seeing Penelope off the next morning for her swim, Peter returned to the motel to collect his things and find out the latest on the weather. The experts didn't appear to know any more about where and when the storm would hit than they had the previous night. They seemed to be talking in circles about this front and that high-pressure system, and the upper level steering currents. No one would probably know anything until early the following morning.

Before it was time to vacate the room and get Penelope's lunch, Peter fired up his laptop to check a weather site he knew about. The links he needed were on his thumb drive, and so were Penelope's selfies.

"Yep, you make all this effort worthwhile," he said to himself before closing the image viewer and powering off. *Time to get lunch and head toward the noontime rendezvous.*

Usually, Penelope would finish her meal, exchange a pleasantry or two, and then submerge to get underway. Today, however, she seemed positively chatty and reluctant to leave.

"Peter, remember the afternoon we first met? What did you think after I swam off?"

"The first or second time? There was that kiss, you know."

Penelope blushed, and she wanted to know why she kept

doing that. She hadn't done it since she was in high school. "After the second time, I guess. After it was all over."

Peter was glad she was opening up, but at the same time, he wanted to know why her blushing kept affecting him this way. He would seek medical help, but explaining that a blushing mermaid did this to him would land him in the psych ward. Better to take a cold shower after she was gone.

"Well, I wondered if I was on one of those 'candid camera' shows where they pull a stunt and then watch your reaction. But then, I had always known—or hoped—that mermaids were real, so it really didn't faze me much."

Penelope gave him a shy smile and said, "I'm sorry...not sorry I met you, but sorry for doing that to you."

"It's okay. You gave me an afternoon to remember!"

After dinner that evening, Penelope was brushing her hair when she had an idea about what they should do the next day. She opened her side of the connecting door and knocked on Peter's, or what used to be Peter's door—because the man who opened it was definitely not Peter, and there were two young girls bouncing on the bed.

Penelope apologized profusely and closed the door. Where had Peter gone? What was wrong? He wouldn't abandon her...at least not intentionally.

She looked out the window for the SUV. The motel's parking lot had been nearly full when they got back from dinner, so he'd dropped her off in front of her room and then—supposedly—driven off in search of a parking spot. She scanned the lot and was about to give up when a bit of motion on the far side caught her attention.

There it was, the SUV with the sea kayak on top, and Peter doing something or other inside. Penelope waited for Peter to come back across the lot and explain what had happened to his room, but he didn't get out of the car.

She left her room and hurried across the lot to find Peter stretched out in the SUV. She rapped on the glass, and when he woke with a start, she asked, "What are you doing?"

Peter sheepishly explained about the mix-up and how there were no other vacancies in the area. Although he insisted he was fine and it was just for one night, Penelope was having none of it.

"Why didn't you tell me about this?"

"I didn't want you to worry or offer to go sleep in the water. This is my problem, and I'll deal with it."

Penelope glared at him—something she hadn't done for at least six weeks. "Oh, no, you're not. There are two beds in my room, and you can have one of them."

Peter could tell she was serious, so he gathered up his things and followed her back across the lot to her room. He was too tired to argue, and anything seemed better than the back seat of the SUV at that moment.

Peter settled on the end of his bed and turned on the TV to see what the weatherman had to say. Penelope decided she'd better go ahead and take her shower, so she casually stepped out of her clothes and headed for the bathroom. Bathing in a place that's not your home usually involved a bit of seemingly aimless wandering around, and though she was a mermaid, Penelope was not immune. Each time she walked past, Peter averted his eyes. This did not go unnoticed.

When she emerged from the bathroom, she purposely stood in front of him. "For Poseidon's sake, Peter. You see me naked every single weekend! You don't have to look away."

"I know that. It's just…you're off duty now, and I thought you might want a bit of privacy."

Penelope had always found the human aversion to nudity to be utterly silly, but things were suddenly different. Here was this human who was more than willing to sleep in the car so she could have a room to herself, and he was trying to give her privacy when she needed none. Peter was not an ordinary human. He respected her and was concerned for her wellbeing. Something somewhere inside her melted.

"Thank you, Peter, for your thoughtfulness. The bathroom is all yours now."

Peter grabbed the few things he needed and went into the bathroom. Following his shower, Peter brushed his teeth, pulled on his pajama bottoms, and walked into the main room. Penelope was disappointed by his attire but didn't mention it. He went to his bed, crawled in, and turned off his light. Shortly thereafter, she did the same.

It was a glorious day to be out on the water, and in it as well. There was not a cloud in the sky, and the bountiful sunshine felt pleasantly warm rather than scorching hot. A very light breeze and a gentle swell had caused Peter to set their lunchtime meeting to take place off shore, rather than in the protected sound.

Peter delivered Penelope a hot pastrami sandwich with Swiss cheese, and she dug into it immediately so they could chat a bit before it was time to get underway again.

She had just rinsed her hands in the water and taken the last gulp of her soda when she turned to find the yellow sea kayak upside down, floating on the surface. Peter must be practicing his Eskimo rolls, she thought at first, but the kayak didn't right itself. Twenty seconds later, his paddle floated to the surface, followed by his life jacket.

Peter's in trouble! Penelope ducked under the surface, and sure enough, the cockpit was empty. She swam back and forth and suddenly saw him below her, drifting downward. She had to get him back to the surface, quickly. She dove, but it was like swimming in Jell-O. No matter how hard she beat her fin, she couldn't get anywhere very fast. It seemed to take forever, but she started to gain on him. As she reached out to grab him, she saw what she didn't want to see.

He was dead.

"Peter!"

Penelope awoke to find herself sitting up in bed, bathed in a cold sweat and breathing heavily. She turned to see Peter sound asleep in his bed, blissfully unaware that anything had happened. Her pulse began to slow and her breathing settled. *Do I have feelings for him?*

"Of course you have feelings for him. You've had them since the very beginning. Remember that kiss? I had to give you a bit of a nudge, but you went willingly. So, here is your assignment. Determine what those feelings are, and then decide what you're going to do about them. Now, if you don't mind, I'd like to get back to reading this romance novel, because I'm getting to the really juicy part. Class dismissed!"

Penelope didn't know what to make of all this, but she rolled on her side and watched Peter sleep for a long time.

When she awoke in the morning, Peter was sitting on the edge of his bed watching the weather forecast. The electric kettle began to boil, and he got up and poured her a cup of tea. After dutifully squeezing a lemon into the cup, he put two chocolate frosted donuts on a plate and brought her breakfast to where she was sitting up in bed.

"I've checked online, as well as what's on TV, and I think we're good until at least noon, and maybe a little after. If we get going soon, I can have you in the water with enough time for a good swim before we have to pull the plug."

Penelope nodded mutely, and after a few sips of her tea and a bite of her donut, she got up, pulled on her robe, and stuffed a bikini into a side pocket. She was not as much eager to hit the water as she was to have some time and space to think about the previous night's revelation.

They were at the drop off spot early enough that she was able to go straight into the water. The sky was becoming overcast as the breeze picked up, and there was a small chop to the water.

Penelope didn't turn and wave as she usually did, but Peter chalked it up to wanting to get as much swimming in as she could before they had to leave. He quickly turned to head back to the motel so he could have a look at the weather update at least two dozen times before he had to check out.

It was with some apprehension that Penelope surfaced for lunch. The morning's swim had resolved nothing, and what time she had left in the water today would probably do little—if anything—to help.

She watched Peter's kayak approach, and she pondered what she should say or do. She need not have worried, for once he handed over her half of the Italian sub, he divided his time between eating and checking radar maps on his smartphone.

"Okay, here's where we stand. If you do the complete afternoon swim, we're gonna get stuck here through tonight. However, I have a plan that should give you at least two more hours in the water and have us on our way in time to beat the storm. We're just going to have to play it by ear after that."

"I'll let you make the final decision, Peter." *Dear Poseidon. Now I'm deferring to him!*

"Do you remember where we first met? That's the closest safe pickup spot I can think of. It'll take me at least ninety minutes to get back to the car and load up the kayak. Depending on traffic, I think I can make it in about thirty minutes, maybe a bit more. Then I can get you out of the water and straight into dry clothes for the trip home. Okay?"

Penelope nodded and immediately swam off.

As Peter paddled back to where he'd left the SUV, Penelope vacillated about what she should do. Part of her wanted to head toward the dock, part of her wanted to swim toward home, and part of her wanted to put to sea and ride things out. She was literally swimming in circles at that point.

Finally, she had an idea. She would swim back toward the city. Yeah, that was what she should do. Of all people, Peter would understand. She'd explain everything tomorrow or the next day. Better yet, next month.

As she turned to swim up the coast, a series of images flashed through her mind. Peter waiting and waiting for her to arrive, standing there and calling her name. The wind picking up, and Peter paddling out into the gathering storm. Peter being buffeted by wind and waves, him being struck by lightning or the kayak capsizing. Peter drowning.

"NO!" *Sweet Poseidon. I do have feelings for him.*

She couldn't let anything happen to him! She'd never be able to live with herself. Penelope turned and swam in the direction of the dock where they'd met two and a half months ago. She arrived at the pickup point after about forty-five minutes. The parking lot was empty, and she swam under the dock for a nap, which she hoped would settle her soul.

Traffic had picked up considerably while he was out on the water, and Peter pushed his way toward the pickup point. He pulled into the empty gravel lot well over an hour behind schedule.

Since there was no sign of Penelope, he pulled on his swim goggles and waded in to see if she was sleeping under the dock. She was lying between the pilings, looking as stunning as a sleeping mermaid could. He hated to wake her.

Peter surfaced beneath the dock to take a deep breath and then swam down to where she lay—an aquatic version of Sleeping Beauty, resting on the white, sandy bottom amongst gently waving blades of Manatee Grass. As much as he wanted to kiss her, or even just give her a peck on her perfect, freckled nose, he didn't want to ruin things between them. Instead, he gently tugged on her flukes and was rewarded with a fin-slap that sent him backward into a piling.

Penelope was terrified, and ready to slap whomever it was again, when she realized her mistake. Peter rose to the surface holding the back of his head, and she swam up to him.

"Peter! Are you all right? I'm so sorry. Please forgive me. Let me look at your head."

Fortunately, it appeared he'd have a bump there at worst. Once she completed her examination, Peter turned to face her.

"The gravel lot is empty. Let me get back to the car, get the towels ready, and you can come straight out and dry off."

Penelope nodded her agreement and Peter swam from under the dock with a still-throbbing head. Once out of the water, he strode to the car and opened the front and rear doors on her side so she'd have a little bit of cover. Peter opened her bag and put it on the front seat so she could easily reach her clothes.

Grabbing the large towels, he held them out and shouted, "Ready when you are."

She walked out of the water on the ramp. Peter enveloped her in a towel and handed her a second one to help her dry off. He felt as if he was her guardian, her protector, ready to do anything for her comfort and safety. Penelope moved between the two open car doors to finish drying off and pull on her clothes. Peter stood in front of the opening with his back turned, trying to shield her from prying eyes.

"Peter, you don't need to do that. No one's here."

"I don't want anyone to get the idea that a naked girl...woman swims here and then comes snooping around the next time we use this spot."

Penelope was touched. He was wounded—thanks to her fin—and yet he was still trying to protect her. It was so sweet of him, but it made things all the more difficult for her.

Once she was dry and dressed, Peter hurried around to the driver's side to get in and get going, but she stopped him.

"Peter, don't you dare get in until you've dried off and changed. A couple more minutes won't affect things one way or the other."

The wind had picked up considerably by the time they turned on to the main road and headed north. There were still plenty of weekend visitors on the road, and traffic soon slowed to a crawl.

"I should have risked taking you back to the car with me," he muttered to himself.

"Peter, I trust your judgment. We'll be okay."

That was small consolation as far as he was concerned.

After forty-five minutes, they approached the entrance to the bridge and causeway that would take them to the most direct route home, and Peter saw what the problem was. The entrance was awash in blue and red lights as emergency workers tried to deal with the results of too many vehicles trying to occupy the same space at the same time. He couldn't count the number of the vehicles involved, and once he spotted the HAZMAT team, he was sure things weren't going to be cleared up for hours. A glance across the water showed something similar going on over there as well. They might as well keep heading north. Once they were past the bridge, traffic thinned out considerably.

A few miles further on, there was a restaurant on the right almost devoid of cars. It promised to be a long evening, and it was better to drive on a full stomach than to run on one that was empty. Peter and Penelope were quiet during their meal; he was preoccupied with the route home, and she was preoccupied with other things.

Five minutes after they pulled back onto the road, it began to rain...and rain...and rain. Not content to come down in buckets, the rain came down in bathtubs. Visibility faded fast, and Peter was forced to drop his speed.

"I'm going to turn the navigation over to you so I can deal with the driving. If the water gets too deep, you'll have to swim the rest of the way, and I'll follow in the kayak."

Penelope offered a small smile in response to his joke. "Don't worry, I'll give you a tow."

Penelope looked up from the roadmap laid across her lap and glanced at Peter. He was the perfect picture of determination as he gripped the wheel with both hands and peered into the rain sodden darkness ahead.

He's going to get me home safely no matter what. She hadn't seen that kind of look on a male since leaving home. *I guess I was wrong. Some humans are capable of kindness and nobility.*

Her opinion of people on the mainland might have changed, but that alone wasn't going to get them home in one piece. They would have to work as a team.

It was a long, slow trek home. They had to pull over a number of times and wait until they could see more than a few feet ahead. In some spots, they had to creep through flooded sections of the road, while in others, they had to wait until they could get around a wreck.

Finally, they were able to turn inland and head toward the city. The going wasn't any easier. Indeed it was worse in some places, but after two hours that seemed to last forever, Peter pulled the SUV into the garage underneath Penelope's apartment building. They carried her bags up the stairs to the fourth floor and arrived at her door, exhausted. As Peter turned to leave, Penelope stopped him. Ordinarily, she would have told him to drive carefully and go straight to bed, but that was last weekend.

"Peter, the weather is awful and you're worn out. My couch opens up into a bed. I'll get some sheets and a pillow, and you can stay here tonight."

Peter was too tired to argue with her. He mumbled something about going to get his things and securing the kayak as he turned toward the stairs. By the time he returned, the door to her apartment was closed, and he half expected she had reconsidered and locked the door. If that was the case, he'd simply sleep here in the hall. But, to his mild surprise, the doorknob turned, and he walked into Penelope's tiny apartment. Actually, tiny was an overstatement. Miniscule was more like it; the open sofa bed took up half of the space called the living room.

Peter was ready to collapse when Penelope pushed him toward her bedroom and the bathroom on the far side of it. The hot water revived him, and once he dried off, Peter felt like he was good for another thirty minutes or so. He waited in the living room until she was done with her shower, and soon she was standing in the doorway toweling her hair.

"Peter, if you don't mind, I'm going to leave my door open. The air doesn't circulate very well when it's shut."

"Sure, no problem. Feel free to come and shake me if I snore."

Penelope smiled and stood there, unable to move as she fought the urge to go kiss him good-night. Finally, she simply said, "Good-night," and turned back to the safety of her room.

She sat on her bed in the dark and rested her head on her knees, wondering what she should do. There were two factions within her that were at war with each other, in what was turning out to be an emotionally bruising conflict. There was the voice of reason, which pitched each and every argument from every lecture Penelope had sat through as to why mermaids should avoid relationships with humans. On the opposing force was that strange voice that returned fire with all the reasons why she should act on her feelings for Peter. Penelope's loyalty wavered back and forth.

When the voice of reason ran out of arguments, it resorted to a snark attack in the hope of landing a direct hit on her feelings of guilt. "If you had quit your job like you should have, you wouldn't be in this mess right now. You'd be back in the sea where you belong."

The other voice tossed that bomb right back at reason. "If you had quit your job, you wouldn't have discovered your feelings for Peter. You wouldn't have the loyal and supportive friend you have now. You wouldn't be on the cusp of having what you've been longing for."

And so it went, for what seemed like hours. Each side would take a major hit and retaliate with a blow of its own. In the end, the defeated voice left the field of battle and limped off into some dark corner to lick its wounds. The winner was bloodied but unbowed.

She knew she'd been doomed from the start. If it was going to mean the end of her, at least she would go out in a blaze of glory. Now that the battle was over and her fate was sealed, she had one question for which she needed an answer.

"Just who or what are you?" she asked the strange voice.

"Haven't you guessed by now? I am your heart, and I want the very best for you. Now, go to him. This is your time."

CHAPTER SEVEN

Peter was dreaming. He knew this for a fact, because he was underwater, watching Penelope swim back and forth, something he'd never seen in real life. This same image had been appearing in his dreams for the past three weeks, but something was different tonight.

The look on her face was frantic, and when she met eyes with him, the expression became one of alarm. Penelope started swimming toward him, and her progress, though slow, was steady. She came close enough to touch, and that's when it happened. She kissed him.

Peter woke up with a start to a peal of thunder. Lightning flashed, and there was more thunder as the storm cell moved through. He turned to find he was not alone in the bed. Penelope was there, next to him, holding on to his arm. He leaned over and gently kissed her on the forehead. It was too dark for him to see the sweet smile that slowly spread across her face.

It was still raining when Peter opened his eyes the following morning. Penelope was still there, snuggled up next to him. There was only one thing for him to do at this point—leave before any more damage was done. He slid his arm out of her grasp and inched out from under the covers to go put his clothes on. Unfortunately, he only got as far as the edge of the bed.

"What's wrong?"

Caught. He wasn't going to get out of this as easily as he'd hoped. At this point, he wanted to jump up, grab his clothes, and run for the car. Instead, he turned and whispered to her, "It's all right. Go back to sleep."

Penelope sat up in bed with a hurt look on her face. She

didn't bother to cover herself. This was not the time for her to conform to human modesty. "It's not all right. You wouldn't be trying to leave if it were. Please tell me what's wrong."

It wasn't an order. It was a request—one he could not ignore. Why was she making this so hard? Why couldn't she just let him leave and salvage what was left of his ego? Instead, he was going to have to go through one more round of rejection, and it was one he didn't want to endure. But, he was too much of a man to run—no matter how much he wanted to. No, it was time for him to fall on his sword, and his shoulders slumped at the thought.

Peter couldn't bring himself to face her and instead looked down at the sheets. "Penelope, I think...I've fallen in love with you." Let the bleeding begin.

"Peter...I don't think I've fallen in love with you."

There it was. What he'd been expecting all along. Why did she have to make him suffer more than he already was? He looked heavenward in the hope of some divine mercy.

"I *know* I've fallen in love with you."

What? That wasn't in the script! She was supposed to laugh and tell him to get lost—just like every other girl he'd ever fallen for did. He couldn't come up with a response and couldn't help but look at her.

"Peter, are you sure about your feelings for me? Last night when I came to your bed...you didn't do anything."

Peter was in new territory here. He was going to have to wing it, which meant he was going to have to expose his battered heart to her.

He winced as he began to speak. "Penelope, I haven't had the best luck with relationships over the years. Last night, I wanted to hold you...to love you. But I didn't, because I had hope. I hoped this would turn out to be something good— something lasting—and I stopped because I love you very much and I didn't want to rush things and ruin our chances of something real. If we're patient, maybe the right moment will present itself in the future."

There it is, Penelope thought. He was trying to protect her, protect her love, and protect her heart. This was the man that had looked after her since the day after they'd met and had persevered in spite of how mean she was to him. She had fallen in love with Peter MacPherson—a human—and she was not the least bit sorry about it.

She reached her hand out and took his. "I understand, Peter, and if it means we can have each other forever, then I'm willing to wait...as long as I have your love. You know you have mine."

Penelope leaned forward and kissed him. It wasn't perfectly choreographed, but it was so achingly good, so wonderfully sweet, that she could have done it for the rest of the day and into the night.

Unfortunately, reality cut in. "Peter, what time is it?" They glanced at the clock in unison. "Shit! We're supposed to be at work. I'll give the office a call and let them know I'm on my way in. You should call from your cell after I'm done."

Penelope left Peter and walked into her bedroom, not so much for privacy while she made the call, but to hold herself and wonder how he felt when she was in his arms.

Meanwhile, Peter dug through his things and pulled out his smartphone. He was scrolling through his collection of music when Penelope walked back into the living room.

"Sweetheart." That was the first time she'd used that term of endearment, and it sounded wonderful. "We don't have to go to work today. There are power outages downtown and flooding out in the suburbs. Mr. Williamson feels it will be better if we just take today off with the hope things will be back to normal tomorrow, more or less."

Peter was ecstatic. He was going to have a whole day alone with this wonderful person who had said she loved him, and so far, shown no sign of rejecting him. He found the song he'd been searching for—"Can't Help Falling in Love With You"—took Penelope in his arms, and pressed play.

They slowly danced to the love song, not once, but three times before she took his face in her hands and kissed him like she'd wanted to for so long.

Peter held her close—close like she'd always hoped someone would but never expected to happen. It felt so good, so warm, so loving. He had held girls in his arms before, but the episodes had always been brief and the affairs short lived. He'd experienced enough rejection to be wary, but this felt so wonderful. *Please don't let this end . . . ever.*

Penelope and Peter spent the rest of the morning in each other's arms, neither one wanting to let the other go for fear they'd vanish. In the afternoon, there was cuddling, napping, and more kissing. Penelope had never spent a day like this, and she hoped it wouldn't be long before she did so again.

She was watching Peter nap when her heart spoke to her. "Are you happy?"

"Happy, content, in love."

"Then take today as a gift from Poseidon. No one deserves it more than you."

Penelope was suddenly concerned. Was this a way station? A temporary fix? Something to tide her over? And what would happen to Peter if it was?

"I'll let you be the judge of that, dear," it replied.

Evening approached, and a peek out of the apartment's only window revealed the Chinese place down the street was open. After calling in their order, Peter threw on his clothes and braved the wet streets and pools of standing water to go retrieve their dinner.

As he climbed the last flight of stairs, takeout in hand, he was suddenly seized by the fear that Penelope may have had a change of heart.

He approached her door anxiously, it opened, and there she stood in a T-shirt with a smile that would have instantly melted the polar ice caps.

"Welcome home, sweetheart."

Peter followed her inside and closed the door behind him. "It's good to be home. It's good to be home with you."

Peter fervently hoped it would remain that way for a long time to come. Though he didn't know it, Penelope hoped with all her heart it would be that way as well.

After dinner was over and the dishes were washed, dried, and put away, they sat on the couch together. She folded her legs and rested her head on his shoulder.

"Peter, what were you afraid of?"

"Afraid of? When?"

"This morning when you woke up. It almost seemed like there was something holding you back. Preventing you from saying what you wanted to?"

"Oh."

It wasn't one of those accusatory questions, nor was it anything like an inquisition. It was simply a question from someone who cared for him—someone who wanted to understand more about him. Peter sighed and began to explain the history of his life, thus far.

He didn't give a blow-by-blow, rejection-by-rejection account of what had transpired since he turned thirteen. That would be too depressing. He did mention Katie and a few other notables, however. Peter wasn't looking for sympathy, especially from Penelope. He just wanted to let her know there was baggage she might have to deal with.

Penelope was stunned. She couldn't believe that human females could be that cruel…especially to someone like Peter. She'd had a number of female human friends—both in high school and afterwards—and none of them had seemed capable of behaving like that. Then again, maybe she'd been tied up too much in her own woes to notice what went on around her.

This led to a larger question. What should she tell Peter about her life? Okay, he knew she was a mermaid, and he'd been unfazed about learning that, but should she tell him about her home, or anything else for that matter? What about their customs? What about her fourteen-year quest for a mate?

She wasn't really looking for one back when she was eleven years old, but she was old enough to see the writing on the wall. And how would Peter take the news that she was looking for a mate in the first place? Would he think she was desperate? Would he think he was a candidate? It hadn't even occurred to her to think that far ahead, and if he was truly intended to simply be a way station, she didn't want to. She just wanted to enjoy the moment and enjoy being with him.

Penelope took a deep breath and began, "Well, it's a bit different for us…"

When the evening was drawing to a close, Penelope didn't want Peter to leave. Peter didn't seem inclined to go, either. She decided to break the ice herself.

"Peter, do you have to go home tonight? I don't want to kiss you goodbye. I only want to kiss you good-night."

Peter mulled his options. His work clothes from last Friday were still in the SUV. Since he was a guy, no one would pay attention to the fact that he was wearing the same outfit again on Tuesday, so there wasn't much of a barrier to him spending the night.

"I don't see why not, if you really want me to stay."

"I really do want you to spend the night here, Peter. Could you do one thing for me, though? Could you leave your beach shirt or something here with me when you go home tomorrow? It's probably just a silly mermaid thing, but it would be nice to have something of yours for me to keep here. Something I could touch or smell when you're not around."

Peter chuckled to himself. "Well, if you want to have some of my stinky old stuff, I suppose I can leave a couple of things with you."

Penelope was over the moon, and Peter was happy she was pleased by the little things like that.

It was getting late, and Peter eyed the sofa thinking it was time to open out the bed and get ready to go to sleep.

"Sweetheart, you let me share your bed last night. Please come and share mine tonight."

It was difficult to turn down such an offer, so he joined Penelope in her bed and turned out the light.

Her dream was the most pleasant and comforting one she'd ever had. Penelope was in her element, being gently rocked in the arms of the sea. So warm, so enfolding, so safe. She wished Peter could be there, sharing the feeling with her.

Penelope awoke to find that Peter had been holding her while she slept. She turned her head to kiss him and soon drifted off again.

Paula Revelle was the office gossip. She knew who was on their way up, who was on their way out, and who was seeing someone on the side. She didn't consider it to be a bad thing, but rather, a badge of honor. Paula went to great lengths to ensure that everything reported as fact was indeed factual, and everything that was mere speculation or rumor was presented accordingly. From her command post in the building's lobby, she was privy to who was meeting whom for dinner after work before going home to their respective spouses or partners.

She knew, for example, that Mr. Smithson regularly received packages from a maker of plus-sized fashions for ladies that were addressed to Miss Smith. It was not Paula's job to rat him out to his wife, though she did wonder what Mrs. Smithson would think of her husband's new wardrobe.

Then there were Lisa Morris and Priscilla Buford, for whom the phrase "going out with the girls" meant they were going out with each other and almost always visited a lesbian wine bar before going home to one's house or the other's, depending on which spouse was out of town that evening.

Paula was queen of all she surveyed. She had a network of reporters spread throughout the company, and she kept her subscribers regularly informed with lunchtime whispers and discrete texts. Paula was the acknowledged mistress of group messaging.

There was always the chance of being found out, but Mr. Williamson was an easygoing sort of person and was always excluded from her network to be safe. Still, the higher-ups probably would take a dim view of her activities, no matter how vital they were. Paula relished the danger.

On this particular Tuesday morning, she was reviewing the contents of her upcoming broadcast when Penelope and Peter walked through the lobby, hand in hand. "At least they're finally being open about it," she muttered. This wasn't headline news—at least not yet—but it did deserve a highlighted mention.

Once the couple had stepped into the elevator, Paula watched as the car ascended to Penelope's floor and then come back down to Peter's. Yep, those two had it bad.

They didn't call her "Paula Revere" for nothing. In less than five minutes, her subscribers would know about this turn of events too. The news traveled quickly throughout the Harriman Company, but if people were expecting a bit of kissing in the copier room or assignations in the supply cupboard, they would be disappointed.

There were a couple of texts sent back and forth during the day and some handholding at lunch, but that was the extent of Penelope and Peter's fraternization. Both of them were trying to make up for Monday, as well as work extra hours so they could leave mid-afternoon on Friday. After most of the employees had left for the day, Peter and Penelope were still hard at work. Once 7:30 arrived, they called it quits.

They stopped for soup and salad on their way back to Penelope's apartment and awaited the inevitable moment when Peter would have to go home. Neither one of them wanted to part, but they only had two more evenings before leaving for the beach. As promised, Peter handed her one of his weekend T-shirts.

"You know, sweetheart, you could leave a couple sets of shirts and pants here for when you stay over."

Peter grinned. "You know, sweetheart, I'm giving you all of my stuff, but I'm getting nothing in exchange."

Penelope thought for a moment and then removed her ponytail holder. "Here, take this. You know, you'd look cute with long hair and a ponytail."

Peter rolled his eyes and kissed her goodbye.

When it was time for bed, Penelope took his T-shirt in her arms and held it close all night long.

CHAPTER EIGHT

"You okay?" Peter asked as he watched the highway ahead of them. The Friday night rush-hour traffic was a drag, and the beach they were headed for was two hours down the coast, but he sensed that was not what was bothering her.

Penelope was startled out of her deep concentration. "Oh. What? Yeah, I'm okay."

Peter decided to leave well enough alone. If she was anything like he was, every attempt to pry out more details would only be met by ever increasing resistance. Penelope was entitled to her thoughts and her privacy, and if it was important, he would learn it soon enough.

On the subject of privacy, Peter had been prepared to book separate rooms so she could get a good night's sleep, but she would have none of it. Penelope had insisted on a single room with a king-sized bed, if possible, saying the two of them had slept apart long enough.

Penelope seemed to come up to the surface during dinner but quickly submerged again on their way to the motel. Thank goodness for late check-ins.

Peter asked if she wanted to take her shower first, but Penelope declined, deciding she was good until morning.

He was just about to turn the shower on when she called out, "Peter, I need to talk to you."

Peter's heart sank. There it was—no "sweetheart," "honey," or other term of endearment. He'd heard this same sentence a number of times before, and he knew by rote what would come next. Penelope'd had a change of heart, and their relationship was over. Peter hated being so insecure, but experience had taught him well. He wrapped a towel around his waist and walked out of the bathroom like a condemned man on his way to the gallows.

"I need to tell you something." Penelope motioned for him to sit on the bed with her.

Yeah, I know. Let's get this over with so I can get outta here.

"Peter, where I come from, mermaids are not forbidden to, but are strongly advised against having relations with human males. We sit through lectures twice a year as to why we should avoid your kind like the plague, and that advice sticks with us long after high school is over, and for good reason. Mermaids tend to make bad choices when it comes to humans.

And I'm a prime example, right?

"I'm ashamed to admit it, but we have an inferiority complex."

Huh? Peter was stunned. How could a wonderful creature like Penelope feel she was inferior? Maybe he was missing something.

"Ever since we moved on shore, we've felt like we're not good enough—like we're half-human. I mean, we're glad to be what we are, but next to you guys, we just don't compare, and it comes out when a human pays attention to a mermaid. We feel like Cinderella—lifted out of the ashes by a handsome prince. The trouble is, we don't pay attention to what kind of prince has chosen us, and we wind up falling head over fins—even when that person is the worst possible choice we could make.

"If there *are* loving relationships, they are very few and far between. We're so willing to give up the sea to be with our mate, we fail to consider the consequences. We become trophy wives, more like possessions than life partners. Sometimes, we don't even tell our mate what we are, and then it gets dangerous. Too often, we want to take a break, even if it's in our own bathtub, and enjoy the feel of having a fin again, and we get discovered and rejected. We are beat, thrown out of the house, or worse. If a mermaid has given her human a child, he often keeps it and sends her away. And she can't risk revealing her secret during a custody battle, so she looses her child as well as the love of her life.

"Some mermaids commit suicide because they can't stand living without their human, no matter how badly he's treated them. Others are too ashamed of what has been done to them and disappear into the sea forever. Either way, when a mermaid chooses a human mate, her parents are unlikely to ever see her again. Only a few—a very few—return to their home, and if they do, it's because the man threw the child out with her."

Penelope had watched the growing look of horror on Peter's face as she described the catastrophic consequences of falling in love with a human. She wanted to say more but Peter stopped her.

"If I ever do something like that to you, please kill me. Shoot me, drown me, I don't care. I'd be a monster and would not deserve to live one moment longer. If you're afraid I might do something like those bastards have, then maybe you should end this before we get any more involved."

Peter had given voice to his greatest fear, that she would decide at some point to leave *him*. He refused to give it any more thought, as his prime concern at this moment was Penelope.

"Ever since I met you," he said, taking her hand, "I've had this overwhelming urge to protect you. I fell in love with Penelope Anne Tench, the person. I didn't fall in love with you because you're a mermaid—I fell in love with you because you're you, and I will do all I can to keep you safe and happy. Now, is there anything else you need to tell me?" Peter asked, hoping against hope she wouldn't want call it quits in spite of what he'd said.

Thankfully, she shook her head. "No."

"And you still love me?"

"Yes," she said softly.

"Good, because I will always love you, and I will never be like those men. I promise you that." He kissed her on her forehead and stood up to go take his shower. As he walked toward the bathroom, Penelope announced she was going to get sodas for both of them.

Washed and scrubbed, Peter stepped out of the bathroom to find the door wide open and Penelope gone.

A quick peek outside showed the SUV was still where he'd left it. *She must be on foot.* Peter surmised she was either headed back home or on her way to the ocean. Even if she was leaving him, he would have driven her to either one; walking on roads after dark was dangerous.

Throwing on a pair of cargo shorts, he decided to scour the motel first before hopping in the SUV. There was nothing to be found up front, so he headed toward the back end where he'd noticed a lone soda machine earlier in the evening. There was no one there either, but over the loud hum of the machine's refrigeration system, he heard a noise that sounded like a sob.

Peter walked around to the other side of the building to find Penelope with two cold sodas at her feet, sitting in the stairwell, crying her eyes out.

"Sweetheart, are you all right? Did I say something wrong?" he asked as he touched her shoulder. He was totally unprepared for Penelope's arms wrapping around him like a starving squid.

"P-P-Peter. You came for me. You can't be human. You just can't!" she said between sobs and sniffles.

"Well, I hate to disappoint you, but last time I checked, I was human, and I'm pretty sure my parents were too."

"I...I...love you, Peter. I told you about mermaids and humans because that was my biggest fear...what might happen," she explained with a snivel. "You don't act like a human, but you still *are* one and I'm not sure how to make this work after living my entire life in a town that is wary of relationships like ours."

"Honey, please don't give up on us. We'll find a way."

Peter helped her up, stuffed the soda cans into his pockets, and with his arm around her, walked Penelope back to the room. She cleaned her face with a damp washcloth, and when she felt presentable, Peter helped her into bed and climbed in after her. She held on to him tightly for the rest of the night.

Peter's affirmation had somehow given Penelope the permission she thought she needed—the permission to be in love with a human and relish every minute of it for as long as it lasted.

The following week—and the subsequent ones as well—were very different from the previous one. It all started when Penelope announced a review of the company's material assets was underway, and she wanted to see the server room. Peter was hoping he might get a hug and a kiss out of it, but once the door closed, she touched his face for a moment and then pushed him up against the door and proceeded to kiss the life out of him. A few minutes later, they exited the server room somewhat rumpled but more or less presentable.

There were weekly or even semi-weekly one-on-one

meetings to discuss the company's IT assets, their depreciation, future needs, and the ideal length of Ethernet cables. Peter would arrive with catalogues, spreadsheets, and printouts in hand, and once the door to her office was closed, the materials went on her desk, and she wound up in his lap.

Penelope's PA, Julie Simmons, and the other women in the department, thought their rendezvous were cute and conspired to keep Paula Revelle in the dark as much as possible. Besides, considering how cold Penelope had been during the first months of her tenure, it was a blessing to see her happy and in love.

The right moment for them to consummate their love had not presented itself yet, but with their increasingly steamy meetings, they knew it was just around the corner. In a way, Penelope was glad Peter had asked to wait. It had made things less complicated, and she believed their relationship was the better for it, as long as they didn't wait *too* long.

During their weekend outings, she would often hold his hand as she floated below the surface next to his kayak and wonder what it would take to get Peter into the water. He was human, but they could still swim together, if only for a little while.

After one particularly enjoyable lunch break, Penelope left to take an afternoon nap in a sea grass meadow nearby. She found a choice spot and curled up.

"Every mermaid should have a human," she sighed.

"Every mermaid should have a merman," a voice added.

Was that her heart or her head talking? She wasn't sure.

Penelope felt a drowsy, floaty feeling, and suddenly, she and Peter were swimming together through the water with her wrapped up in those warm, protective arms of his.

She wasn't sure just how he was able to swim with her, but it didn't really matter. The water caressed both skin and scales in the same way Peter did, and bright sunlight filtering down from the surface turned the corals and kelp into a salty wonderland. Penelope's ears rejoiced at the familiar sound of her home beneath the waves, and she was sure Peter could sense everything she felt.

She awoke with a jolt. *You know better than that. Just enjoy this moment in your life while it lasts, and memorize everything so you'll have something to hold on to after...* Penelope refused to consider what was probably inevitable.

As swam toward the surface to meet Peter, part of that

dream was still with her. *There's always a chance.*

It was two weeks before Labor Day, and Penelope figured they had been a couple for two months. Not a major milestone by any stretch, but it was two months longer than she would have expected back in April.

So much had happened in that time, and Peter had given so much of himself to make her happy and change her outlook on life. She loved what she was once more and found herself being comfortable on land and in the sea. Peter deserved something special.

They'd chosen Titusville as their base for the weekend, and Saturday was their usual drill—the daytime in the water and a quiet dinner with Peter.

On Sunday, Penelope was unusually slow in getting ready for the beach. There wasn't much for her to do, really—throw on a robe, stuff a bikini in the pocket, and go. But she seemed to be on her own schedule and even asked for a second cup of tea and another donut, as it was too warm for oatmeal.

Peter stood by the SUV, fuming as the sun rose. He'd already scratched their intended drop off point and was looking at alternates. It was well past time for her to go straight from her robe into the water without being seen, and now he was considering spots where she could enter the water like any other tourist and not attract too much attention when she ducked under the surface and didn't reappear. If they hurried, they could still get to the water's edge before the lifeguards came on duty.

Peter heard the door to their room open, and he turned to see Penelope stroll out in a pretty sundress, floppy straw hat, and sunglasses. She looked just like any other human at the beach. This was really going to throw a wrench into the works.

"I'm sorry I took so long. I couldn't find a bra that would work with the way this dress is cut, so I decided to use a bikini top instead."

Peter was astounded, and since he could think of nothing else to say, he asked about the bikini bottom.

"Oh, I wore it instead of underwear. Hey, I'm a mermaid. I have to be ready for anything."

He was still trying to figure out how all this was going to work when Penelope said, "I thought I'd spend the day with you instead of going for a swim. I don't have to put my tail on both days. You've done so much for me over the past two months. We can do whatever you want today."

"How about a leisurely breakfast for once?"

"Sounds like a plan to me," she responded with a warm smile.

After a very relaxing breakfast, they did a bit of window shopping and then bought food for a mid-afternoon picnic. They toured the Merritt Island Wildlife Refuge and ended up on Playalinda Beach at the Canaveral National Seashore. They parked the SUV at the end of the road and walked up the beach a way until people became distant objects.

The sand dunes separated the beach from the saltwater marshes and were held in place by myrtle oak, golden creeper, and sea lavender, along with other plants and grasses. White-tailed deer had made their way along the leeward side of the dunes in order to nibble on the fruit of the seagrape trees and cautiously watched the couple as they walked along the shore. Penelope and Peter were truly alone, and they enjoyed the isolation.

Peter set up a pop-up beach cabana he'd found on clearance at one of those stores that specialized in sunscreen, souvenirs, and T-shirts. They'd eaten their picnic lunch and settled in for an afternoon on the beach when Peter noticed Penelope was getting antsy.

"You know, it's okay if you want to go for a swim."

"Peter, that wouldn't be fair. This is your day, and I planned to spend it with you."

"Honestly, sweetheart, nothing would make me happier than watching you enjoying yourself in the water and flashing your fin at me."

Penelope was up on her knees now. "Are you sure it's okay? I promise I won't be long."

"Take as much time as you want, sweetheart. Just remember we have a bit of a drive tonight."

She peeled off her sundress and held her hand out to him. "Come on. You can grab my bikini once I have my tail on."

Somewhat reluctantly, Peter followed her across the sand and into the water. It was particularly calm that day, but it didn't matter; Peter got nervous whenever seawater went much above his ankles.

Penelope ran ahead and dove in. She surfaced two minutes later with her bikini in one hand and yelled, "Come and get it!"

Peter was more than nervous at this point, but he couldn't let her know. Gritting his teeth, he waded in further, and suddenly, there was nothing under his feet. Being brave for his girlfriend carried almost no weight now, and he felt panic begin to set in as he furiously dog paddled to stay afloat.

Penelope was there in a flash. "Here. Put your legs around my hips and your arms around my neck."

Peter did as he was told, and suddenly his chin was at water level as Penelope churned her tail to keep their heads above the surface.

"See, you're safe. We're together, and now we can do this." She kissed him hard and didn't stop.

Peter did his best to lose himself in the moment—but even her bare breasts against his chest were not enough to completely distract him.

He held out as long as he could before he said, "If you're not careful, you'll wear your tail out trying to keep me afloat. Swim me in closer, and I'll take your bikini so you can go enjoy yourself."

Penelope wanted to protest. She was enjoying herself like this, and it would take hours before her tail got tired, but she felt she shouldn't push it and did as he asked.

She watched him wade out of the water with her bikini in hand. *We can't go on like this. I'll always be grateful to him for giving me my life back, but I can't leave the sea for him. This is where I belong. I don't know what he'll say or do when I tell him or how I'll tell him, but I know I have to, and I can't wait much longer.*

Penelope dove and resurfaced a few times. She had to think things out and wouldn't be able to do so with Peter watching. She plunged into the water, flashing her caudal fin as she slipped below the waves. Penelope headed for deeper water, where she could have a bit of privacy as she decided how to handle all this.

When Penelope didn't come up after five minutes, he was pretty sure she'd be down there for a while. This was perfect, because he couldn't do what he needed to with her watching him. He'd been a real wimp when he was out there, and she was probably deciding right now that he was no longer worth her effort. She was probably right, and that was why he had to do it. He pulled out his smartphone, did a search, and scrolled through the results.

"Seaforth, Seafield, Sea World…here it is." Peter dialed the number and waited for someone to pick up.

"Hello. Would Mr. Paul happen to be in today? That's okay. I don't blame him at all. Would you take a message for me? Tell him Peter MacPherson called, and I'm ready to proceed. Yes. He has all the information including the measurements. He'll know what to do."

Peter ended the conversation. "What's done is done. No turning back now."

Both Peter and Penelope were quiet during the drive back to the city—both lost in their own thoughts. Penelope had returned to the surface about an hour after Peter made his call. She wasn't hungry and neither was he, so they decided to skip dinner and head home.

They didn't sit close to each other as they had come to do over the past seven weekends. In fact they barely realized the other was in the car.

There was not much traffic to speak of at that hour, and Peter pulled into the garage beneath her apartment building well before their usual arrival time. After helping to carry her things into her apartment, they stood there awkwardly, not knowing what to say or do.

"Well, I suppose I should take advantage of the early hour and head on to my place...give myself a chance to catch up on things," he said glumly.

Penelope replied, almost as glumly as Peter, "Yeah. I could use a bit of time to work on stuff myself."

"If you don't mind, I'm going to take my clothes in your closet home. I need do some laundry. I'll bring fresh stuff the next time I'm here." *If there is a next time.*

Penelope nodded. "Sure, do whatever you want." *He's taking his clothes back. It's probably for the best.*

They shared a chaste kiss, and Peter wished her good-night.

After his footsteps receded down the stairwell, Penelope sat on the sofa, put her head in her hands, and cried.

CHAPTER NINE

It was 8:00 a.m. on Monday morning, and Paula was seated at her command post in the building's lobby. There were only a smattering of incoming calls at this hour, but that would change when 9:00 a.m. rolled around. The calm before the storm was the perfect opportunity to review her newsfeed.

At 8:15 a.m., a grim faced Penelope Tench hurried in and took the stairs up to her floor...alone. For the past two months, she'd arrived every Monday around 8:30 a.m., hand in hand with Peter MacPherson. This could prove interesting.

At 8:35 a.m., Peter came through the door, looking dour himself. He nodded at Paula as he hurried past, and she made a mental note to see what happened on this coming Friday afternoon. Usually, Peter and Penelope left together, and if that was not the case this Friday, they would become an item in the following Monday's noontime gossip.

Penelope closed the door to her office, sat down, turned on her PC, and spun her desk chair around to stare out the window. She hadn't seen Peter yet—which was good and bad—and she had no idea what to do or say when she did. This was going to be a tough week, and she pledged to try and not take it out on others...especially Peter.

She was woken from her reverie by her phone alerting her to a meeting in ten minutes. *Almost nine already?* When they came in separately, Peter would've stopped by her office or emailed by now. Was he avoiding her because he was planning to dump her? At least then she wouldn't have to deal with the aftermath of telling him what she wanted to say...

All Peter could do was fidget, look at the clock, and then fidget some more. It was 9:00 a.m., so technically, someone should be there to open up. He knew the department head never came in before 10:00 a.m., so he decided to wait another hour before he made the call.

He glanced at the clock; it had advanced a whole three minutes. He would go crazy before the end of the week. He had to do something to keep his mind off things.

Sure, he could always do what he was paid to do—his job. The trouble was, he had absolutely no interest in that at the moment, and his only meeting of the day was not until 3:30 p.m. Maybe he should update his resume. There were going to be too many damn questions afterward, and he wouldn't be able to deal with everyone second-guessing his motives. Time to start the job search.

Where was Peter? Penelope had left the meeting expecting to find an email or voice message from him when she got back to the office. According to her PA, he had not stopped by while she was out.

A quick check around the floor revealed he hadn't even been up today. In fact, no one had seen Peter yet. Was he even here at all? She was going to check with the receptionist but thought better of it. If Paula Revere got the slightest hint that something was not right between them, it would be all over the company at warp speed.

It was 10:45 a.m., and she had to do something soon. Penelope decided to have her PA block off the rest of the day for her. No calls. No visitors. Nothing, unless it was the president of the company. She'd work on the quarterly financial statement, even though it wasn't due until the fifteenth of October. There were other reports she could look at too. With any luck, she could hide out in her office until well past 5:00 p.m., bladder breaks notwithstanding. She'd do anything to keep her mind off the next item on the agenda— figuring out when and where to tell Peter.

It was 11:10 a.m. before Peter had finally been able to get the head guy on the phone. Everything was going swimmingly according to him. *Swimmingly. Just great!* The guy had to use that particular adverb.

Peter opened Penelope's online calendar to see what her schedule was for the rest of the day. She usually had more meetings and visitors than he did, and Peter didn't want to catch her at the wrong time. His plan was to keep things on an even keel until the day arrived.

Penelope's calendar said she was booked solid for the rest of the day, something about the quarterly financial statement. The message behind the words "DO NOT DISTURB" came through loud and clear.

Over the past few months, Peter had learned he could pop in while she was busy and still be warmly received—or at least without too much grumping. This situation, though, was out of the ordinary. His chances of executing his plan would be nil if she became angry and showed him the door too soon.

Peter might be able to catch her at lunch, but he doubted that would happen. There was some actual work he needed to do now, and if he kept his head down, the time between now and that meeting would pass quickly. He could break things up if he worked on his job search in the background.

Penelope had given up asking people if they'd seen Peter. If she asked too much, they would get the idea something was wrong. Then Paula would get wind of it, and Penelope wanted a little time before the storm broke and everybody knew. It was going to be bad enough when it did. *Poseidon, please, just a few more days.*

She allowed herself a bit of respite from hiding out by wandering down to the lunchroom. It was exactly noon, and Peter was pretty regular about his meal times. She had planned to innocently walk in, get a cup of tea and maybe a bagel, and then stop by his table on her way out.

Peter wasn't there. She decided to find an empty table and keep her eyes on the door, which she did until 1:00 p.m., when the lunchroom crowd slowly filed out. The place was nearly empty, and she would stick out like a sore fin if she stayed. A whole hour and no Peter. Time to get back to work.

It was getting close to Peter's 3:30 p.m. meeting. His job search had turned up one good possibility—a position as a systems administrator in Fort Collins, Colorado. The odds were he'd never run into anyone from this company out there, and he'd be pretty far away from the sea. There couldn't be any mermaids in Fort Collins, could there?

Peter opened a new tab on his browser and pulled up a map. North of Fort Collins was Interstate 80, which he traced west through Wyoming and across Utah. There couldn't be any mermaids in the Great Salt Lake—too shallow and too salty—but going further west across Nevada and into California, there was always the distinct possibility of mermaids living near the ever-blue waters of Lake Tahoe. Still further west was San Francisco, San Jose, and Santa Cruz. His virtual road trip ended on Monterey Bay at the small town of Aptos. There were bound to be plenty of mermaids in those waters, and he'd need to steer clear of places like that.

Penelope couldn't take it any longer. She took the stairs to his floor and arrived at his empty cubicle. Peter had left his PC on, and there was a reminder for a meeting in the president's office that had begun twelve minutes ago. Her breath caught as she saw the job posting for Fort Collins in his browser window. He really *was* planning to leave.

Defeated, Penelope decided to finish things up at her desk and go home early. Their relationship had begun with a string of sleepless nights, and it looked like it was going to end that way as well.

Peter's meeting was finished by 4:40 p.m., so he headed in the direction of Penelope's office. She should be wrapping things up soon, and it would be easier to interrupt now. He arrived to find the office empty and the lights out. She was gone...probably in more ways than one.

Neither one of them benefited from what little sleep they got Monday night, and they both decided to go in to the office early rather than toss and turn for another hour or two. That was how Penelope ran into Peter as he was unlocking the front door at 6:30 a.m.

There was no place to run, no place to hide, so they sat and made cordial small talk over a cup of tea in Penelope's office before the rest of the staff showed up. They both apologized for Monday. She recounted a litany of things she'd had to take care of, and he intimated he'd been busy in the server room most of the day. Neither one really believed the other, which only served to fuel their fear and uncertainty.

The conversation was about to turn toward the matter of the coming weekend when people began arriving for the workday. They parted with the promise to talk again later in the day, and each wondered what the best time and location would be to get this over with—but they never got together.

On Wednesday, Mother Nature intervened. A tropical system was going to be moving up the coast on Saturday. While it did not promise to match the deluge from two months earlier, it was going to make being outside uncomfortable. Penelope decided they could get together for dinner or something on Friday or Saturday instead.

When she passed Peter in the hall outside the lunchroom Penelope said, "I've been thinking. We really do need to talk this weekend."

Penelope had just used two of the most feared phrases in the female lexicon. The countdown had begun.

By late Friday morning, Peter was a nervous wreck. If Penelope dropped the hammer before everything was ready, he'd lose all access to her, and his plan would fail. At 12:15 p.m., his phone finally rang.

It was the head of the department saying everything was ready to go. All Peter needed to do was to stop by and sign some papers.

He took a deep breath and texted Penelope: " How does dinner together tonight sound? Chinese okay?"

Time crawled by over the next ten minutes before she responded: "Sounds good. Let's do it at my place."

For the fifteenth time in two days, Penelope stood and looked out her office window. She could almost see the river. It would be so easy to take the bus and get off on the bridge. From there, she could dive in and swim to the sea—and freedom.

As much as it was out of character for her, the thought of living at sea with a feral mate almost sounded too tempting to resist. No, she needed to speak her mind first. She could swim down to the sea after tonight was over and done with. Meanwhile, she needed to draft her letter of resignation.

It was 3:05 p.m., and Penelope was on her fourth revision of the letter when she sensed Peter was on his way to see her. She didn't understand why or how she knew, but she was not surprised when Peter rapped softly on her office door. She asked him to come in as she covered her draft with another document and pretended to read it while taking notes.

Penelope could tell that Peter was nervous about something. He had this fidgety little thing he'd do with his fingers when he was anxious, and his dancing digits were in plain view. When he opened his mouth, Peter's voice confirmed her guess.

"Uhhh...hi, sweetheart. I have to run an errand. Anything I can get for you?"

"No, I don't think so. If you're going to pick up dinner, I'll have my usual order."

"Sounds good. See you between six thirty and seven."

Penelope stood and walked around her desk to hug Peter, to hold him one last time. To both of them, it almost felt like things were normal between them.

On his way back to his cubicle, Peter stopped by the server room. Locking the door behind him, he sat down at the work desk...and sobbed for the next fifteen minutes.

It was 7:15 p.m. when Peter finally arrived at Penelope's tiny apartment with their Chinese takeout: Szechuan beef,

Hunan Tofu, and an order of fried dumplings. Peter sat in the parking lot behind the restaurant for over half an hour before going in to place the order. The moment he did that, the evening would start to progress to its inevitable conclusion.

Dinner was awkward to say the least. Both of them were jumpy, wondering if the other suspected what they had planned. Except for some very minor small talk, very little was said during the entire meal.

When they'd eaten all they were going to, Penelope removed the dishes and began to wash them. There wasn't enough room for two people to be comfortable in the kitchen area, so Peter went into the bathroom, where he closed and locked the door. He stood with his head resting on the door, trying to think of some happy memory as a distraction. The only one that came to mind was of sitting in the den with his dad, listening, for the umpteenth time, to his grandfather tell stories of his exploits with the 101st Airborne back in World War II. Both Dad and Gramps were gone now, and all Peter had were memories of memories.

The closer the moment came, the more his fear began to grow. His thoughts drifted to the Band of Brothers on D-Day. Those guys were probably scared and reluctant to some degree, but they had a job to do, and they got it done. Now it was time for Peter to hook up to the central anchor line, and when the green light went on, step out into the prop-wash from the C-47's engines…just like gramps had.

Penelope silently begged him to stay in the bathroom longer. Anything to forestall telling him what she had to. Much to her disappointment, the lock clicked, and Peter hesitantly stepped out. Penelope excused herself, and while she was indisposed, Peter positioned what he was going to need for what he had to do and sat down on the couch.

His plan was to maneuver the conversation in the desired direction and strike while the iron was hot.

Penelope's plan was to go with the flow and act when the right moment presented itself. She brushed her hair and then left the bathroom. Peter was sitting on the couch, a map and note pad in hand. She slowly walked over and sat down beside him.

"Well, I guess we should take this opportunity to figure out where we're going to go this weekend," he said.

"You know, you don't have to come every time. I'm a big mermaid, and I can look after myself." She tucked her legs under her and wrapped her arms around them. "Besides, I'm sure you have things you need to catch up with at home."

Peter began to feel panic setting in. Things were already going south, and he needed to keep the conversation away from where it seemed she wanted to take it.

"Sweetheart, I do not resent one second of our weekly trips to the beach. I love handling the logistics and bringing lunch to you. The only thing I regret is that...well, that I can't go with you when you swim."

Penelope took a deep breath, and Peter knew he had to think fast. The boat was pulling away from the dock and he wasn't on it. He was going to have to wing this and he prayed that Penelope wouldn't call him on any of it.

"Pen, before you say anything...I've been giving this a bit of thought and I may have a solution to our situation."

"Such as?" Penelope asked skeptically. Whatever idea he had, it wouldn't match what she wanted, what she needed to say to him.

"Just hear me out. All I need is a snorkel, mask, and fins. I'll have to stay near the surface, but it's better than nothing."

Penelope shook her head. "Peter, that's only a temporary fix."

"Okay," Peter said, hoping his next idea would keep her from breaking up with him, since the first one clearly failed. "I can get an open water certification and rent some scuba gear. I'd be able to spend more time with you and go deeper as well."

"No, Peter...in the long run, that won't work either," she said with a sad smile which belied the anxiety she was feeling just below the surface. Penelope planted one foot on the floor as if she wanted to suddenly jump up and flee. She couldn't take much more of this.

"Well then, I could always use a re-breather. It would take longer to be certified, but I'm willing to do it."

"Peter, I appreciate you thinking of solutions, but I just can't see you overcoming your fear of open water so easily. No snorkel, no scuba gear, no mermaid's kiss is going to resolve our situation."

Peter was frustrated with the course of the conversation and worried that the next stop would be a miniature submarine. "Okay, I give up. What, then?"

Now was the time. Penelope had agonized over which part to say first, but either way, it was probably going to be a lose-lose situation. *Poseidon, give me strength!* "Well, there is a way, the only way, really…you could become one of us. You could even become my mate."

Penelope almost wanted to look away. She had just torpedoed her relationship with the love of her life and it was more than she could bear to watch.

"You guys can do that?" he asked with an incredulous look on his face.

"Uh huh," Penelope replied, slowly nodding her head. She was suddenly holding her breath. Peter had focused on the first part and totally missed the fact that she had essentially proposed to him. No going back now. The catfish was out of the net.

Peter stared off into space with a distant look in his eyes. After about fifteen seconds, he said, "Wow! Become a merman? Be able to live under water and really swim with you? Penelope, that would be amazing. Okay. You've got me. I'm in!"

Whatever response she may have anticipated, this was the very last thing Penelope had expected him to say, and now it was her turn to be incredulous.

"*What?* Is that all the consideration you're going to give this? You don't even know what this entails."

Peter looked at her and said, "Fair point. So, does this change involve radical surgery?"

"No."

"Do I have to wrestle a shark?"

"No."

"Do I have to drink fish blood?"

"Umm, no."

"Well, what then?"

"I don't know. It's not like they do this in the middle of Main Street. The only human I've ever known who became one of us was Ed Waterman's mate, Gail. She was such a wonderful, sweet person. It's a shame she's gone now and I can't ask her."

"Well, Pen, if Gail could handle this, don't you think I'm

capable of doing whatever it takes?"

"Sweetheart, I'm really touched...touched and flattered you would so willingly do this, but you need to understand it would be permanent. There's no going back."

"Oh, crap! I dropped my pen. I don't want it to bleed onto the carpet." Crouching, Peter began to fish around under the couch. "Please go on, honey. Believe me, I'm listening to every single word you say."

Penelope sighed. "Peter, this is not like a club you can drop out of if you lose interest. It's not like a magazine subscription you can cancel when you're tired of it. You really need to give this some serious thought."

"Ahhh. Found it!"

Peter started to climb back onto the couch but stopped with one knee on the floor and looked Penelope in the eye. "My love, believe me. I've given this a lot of thought, and this is what I've come up with."

Penelope was suddenly mesmerized by the small velvet box in the palm of his hand. When he opened it, she gasped.

It was a one-carat, round cut diamond set in white gold, with the tiny dots of a milgrain detail running along both edges of the narrow band. Simple and elegant.

"It's...it's a ring." She glanced at him for a fraction of a second before continuing. "It's...an engagement ring! I'm going to be a bride!"

Suddenly, Penelope began bouncing on the couch, and in a childish singsong voice, chanted, "I get to be a bride! I'm going to be a bride!"

Peter threw back his head and laughed. "Miss Penelope Anne Tench, may I take that as a yes, you will marry me?"

Penelope launched herself from the couch and bowled him over saying, "Yes! Yes! Yes! You silly human!"

As her mouth found his, there was an explosive ripping sound, and the air filled with a fine cotton dust.

"Dammit! I don't care about the panties, but those were my best blue jeans!"

As her agitated tail fin flapped against the couch, Peter said with a dazed look, "Ummm, what just happened?"

"Sweet Poseidon! I'm so embarrassed. Whenever I'm really, really happy, I lose control and my tail happens. It's not uncommon for merkids to do this, but most of them grow out of it by the time they reach third grade. This hasn't happened to me since high school. I couldn't have sleepovers with human girls, and only Amy, Cindy, or Lindsey could share a room with me on class trips. This is so humiliating!"

Peter eased himself out from under the teary-eyed mermaid, rolled her on to her back, and said, "You can't be comfortable like that. What can I do to help?"

"Well, you can help me get my top and my bra off. Clothes feel so damn weird when I have my tail on."

After removing them, and the remnants of her blue jeans, he asked, "Now what?"

"Could you put me on the bed so I can stretch out? It's going to take a little while before I get my legs back. We can't flip back and forth like turning a light switch on and off—the process uses up a lot of energy. "

Peter nodded. Tenderly, he lifted her, tail and all, into his arms, and her embarrassment vanished. Penelope snuggled her head against his neck. She felt like she was one of the poor stuffed animals that had sat on the toy department shelf for years. Someone had finally come along and was taking her home to be loved.

Peter smiled at her. He could tell she had relaxed in his arms, and he was happy to know he had that effect on her. Her body was so beautiful, her skin so warm and soft, and her scales were smooth, almost like pearls—definitely not slimy.

Penelope startled him by saying, "Our bodies secrete mucous only when we're in the water. It's a very thin film, and it evaporates once we're on the shore."

"Hmmm," he responded, focused more on how to get her safely into bed and less on the fact that he hadn't thought he'd been contemplating her scales aloud.

Penelope's tail added extra weight to her frame, as it was mostly solid muscle. She was also around two feet longer, and it was tricky maneuvering her through the bedroom door. The last thing Peter wanted to do was hurt her fin or bump her head on the frame.

As he held her above the bed, ready to lay her on it, she giggled. "You're going to have to get some tips from Avery Johnson. He's the only human on Colony Island. He insists on carrying his mate to and from the water every time she decides to go for a solo swim."

Peter cocked an eyebrow and laid Penelope down. As he

ran his hand down her scales, he marveled at the fact that he was going to have some of these himself before long. Turning to face her before she could say, "My eyes are up here," he asked, "Now what?"

Penelope grinned. "Well, you can take your clothes off. I'm tired of being the only one naked around here."

After ditching his boxer shorts, it suddenly occurred to him that he'd left a very important item back in the living room. Peter stepped out and quickly returned with the little velvet box. He placed the engagement ring on her finger and kissed her hand.

"You've made me the happiest human in the world," he said with an adoring smile.

The look of joy on Penelope's face was priceless. "I never...never...thought I'd ever actually find a mate. Never even dreamed I would have a wedding."

Peter sat beside her and took her hand in his, resolving never to let it go. However, her last statement puzzled him. "Don't you have weddings where you come from?"

Penelope shook her head. "No. In the sea, my people don't do weddings. When we came ashore on Colony Island, they came up with the idea of the Joining Ceremony. The whole thing takes about ninety seconds, and that includes signing the registry. Back home, having an actual wedding is an almost impossible dream." She looked away, her lower lip quivering. She had suddenly been granted so much happiness and was almost ready to cry over her good fortune.

"The one brief shining moment of being a bride, eh? Well, I'm going to make sure you have a wedding, even if I have to pay for it all myself."

"You'd do that for me?"

"Of course! Why wouldn't I? If it's within my power, and legal, I'll do anything for you."

Penelope's face looked as if the sun had miraculously risen for the very first time. It clouded over a bit, however, when she said, "Well then, could you answer one question for me? I've been agonizing over it all week, and I need to know. What was the job in Fort Collins, Colorado all about?"

Peter looked downcast. He immediately knew how she had found out and wished he'd remembered to close his web browser. He took a deep breath. "I finally decided to ask you to marry me last Sunday while you were swimming and called Sewell's Jewelry Store directly from the beach. I'd put your ring on lay-away until I was absolutely sure I was ready to ask if you'd marry me. I was afraid you'd be insulted, though, or there was some arcane law about mermaids and humans. I figured you'd say no and wouldn't want anything to do with me, so I was looking to go as far away as I could. You've been so distant all week, I'd assumed the worst."

"Honey, I've been worried about how I was going to tell you—about how you'd react when I asked you to become my mate. I was scared you'd be offended and leave *me*."

"Pen, I could never do that. I love you too much. You have given me the two greatest honors I could ever hope for—your desire for me to be your mate, and the possibility of becoming a merman."

"Peter, you will probably think this is a silly mermaid thing, but a thought struck me just a second ago. Somehow, I believe we were always intended to be each other's mates."

"Ahhh, kismet," he said, and kissed her. "That would help explain the past ten or eleven years of my life. It's a lovely thought, sweetheart, but whether or not there is such a thing, I can't say. All I know is, the most wonderful girl in the world wants me, and I'm more than content with that."

Peter stretched out on the bed next to Penelope, and she rested her head on his outstretched arm before he continued. "I'll be your mate if you will be my wife."

Penelope brought her face close to his and whispered, "I'd like that. I'd like that very, very much."

She kissed Peter on the lips…and then she kissed him again. Soon the kisses turned in to some serious making out. Penelope lay her tail across his legs and then curled the end of it up so her fin rested on and beside his thigh.

She smiled sweetly. "Do you remember a couple of months ago when you said that if we were patient, the right moment would present itself?"

"Guilty as charged. I don't want to wait any longer."

"Me neither."

And so, things progressed. Her body seemed to realize what was required of it, and her tail straightened itself out, morphing into a pair of legs. Peter's body realized what was required of it as well, and Penelope was quite aware.

Over two months of pent-up passion drove them, and after pulling Peter on top of her, she paused and took his face between her hands.

"Is something wrong?" Peter asked.

"Nothing's wrong, sweetheart. I'm just looking at my mate…and I'm so glad it's you."

Any fleeting pain was swept away in the joy of receiving her mate for the first time, and when they were finally joined, Penelope rode wave after wave of pleasure.

This feels so good, so right. Sweet Poseidon, I love this man! I've waited so long for this, wanted him for so long…I'm going to be his bride!

Suddenly, she felt as though she was floating, rocking in the arms of the sea, the sun warming her tail, her face, her breasts. Her legs were still intertwined with Peter's, but this felt so real. Penelope let go and gave in to the feeling. She stretched her arms out above her head, arched her back, and dove beneath the surface. It was as if she was becoming one with the sea, and her world faded to white.

CHAPTER TEN

The rain continued all day Saturday and into the night. Penelope and Peter really didn't care or even notice. They were snugly wrapped in a cocoon of love and happiness and wanted nothing else. Or at least they didn't until Penelope's small cupboards ran perilously close to being completely empty.

Buying groceries had been the last thing on her mind during the week. Now, with two hungry lovers in the house, the supplies, which would have lasted for Penelope until Tuesday or Wednesday, had all been devoured by sometime Saturday afternoon.

At that point, the only thing to do was to relocate to Peter's apartment. Fortunately, Peter had sought to calm his anxiety about proposing to Penelope by giving his place a good cleaning, which included dusting and restacking the collection of old PCs, laptops, and servers that occupied a significant part of his living room. While Peter's apartment was somewhat larger than Penelope's, the advantage afforded by the extra space was negated by all the computer hardware lying around.

The mission to move to Peter's place was two-fold. First there was the food aspect, and second was his need for a change of clothes and underwear—not that he or Penelope had worn much over the past twenty-four hours.

Penelope took along several changes of clothes, including one of her nicer dresses. Peter's apartment was now her place as well, and she wanted to leave some of her things there to stake her claim.

Where they were going to live was another question entirely. Their respective leases did not expire for at least another five or six months, and finding someone to sublet would take three months or more, so there was little incentive to search for new digs and set up housekeeping together until their leases were almost up.

In the short term, the solution was obvious. They would spend their weekends together by the sea and spend one or two nights at each other's apartments. The rest of the time would be spent solo in their own places taking care of the chores associated with everyday living.

Once they were settled in Peter's place for the evening, Penelope thought it would be nice to mate with Peter in *his* bed, and she initiated a session that was blissfully romantic. Afterwards, they snuggled in each other's arms and drifted off to sleep on a sea of happiness and contentment. Life had suddenly become good, very good indeed.

The following morning, over a breakfast of tea, toast, and jam, Peter asked the inevitable question. "Penelope, shouldn't we be using protection?"

He hated killing the mood, and it wasn't that he didn't want to have children with Penelope—he most certainly did—but that was a topic for later when things had settled down a bit. The time to talk about kids would be once he'd learned the facts of life—mermaid style. It could well be that former humans and mermaids couldn't have children, or something like that, and he didn't want to get himself worked up about being the father of a merbaby until he had all the facts.

Penelope giggled and replied, "I can't get pregnant, darling…"

Peter felt his hopes for a family going down in flames.

"…unless I decide I *want* to. If and when a mermaid wants to breed, she wills herself to ovulate. It's not something we can spring on you unaware, because a mermaid's skin becomes kind of reddish when she's fertile. We call it the breeding flush, and it alerts males to the fact we're ready to reproduce. You have so much to learn about us, you silly human."

Peter's mind was flooded with a sense of relief knowing he wouldn't get an unexpected text message telling him she was swimming upstream to spawn. Yes, he did have a lot to learn about things in the mer world, and he was comfortable with setting the baby discussion aside for the time being.

That question taken care of, he changed the topic of conversation to groceries. He thought it would be safe and mundane, but Penelope became just as excited as she had with the previous subject.

Ordinarily, Penelope wouldn't have been so enthused, but this was the first time she'd be going shopping with her mate. *My mate!* The prospect of a joint jaunt to the market was further proof that a whole new world had opened up before her, and it was one where her hopes and long-deferred dreams were starting to come true.

They soon arrived at an agenda for the rest of the day. They would have lunch at a nice restaurant in town, go grocery shopping, and then wind up back at her place for dinner where they'd spend their third night as a mated couple. This would put them back on their regular weekend schedule, and they'd go to work together the following morning.

That afternoon, they found themselves at Paul's Chophouse, sitting in a window seat, holding hands, and discussing plans for their immediate future together.

"I suppose I should go home and tell my parents next weekend. Colony Island—that's where I grew up—is a little over two hours down the coast, depending on traffic."

"Do you want me to stay here? You haven't seen them in a long time, and they'll probably want you all to themselves." Peter wasn't sure how this whole thing was going to work, and he was concerned he might be turned into chum by an enraged merman or two.

"Don't be silly! They'll definitely want to meet you. You're my chosen mate. You'll probably be seeing a lot of my parents from now on. I know my mom is gonna want me to come down every weekend for a while."

Peter was still a bit skeptical, but he was willing to tag along if Penelope wanted him to. Besides, he'd feel better if she were not on the road by herself for over two hours.

Penelope had her own reasons for wanting Peter to accompany her the following weekend. Of course she wanted to introduce her parents to her mate—something they probably thought would never happen. But there was another reason, a reason she had dreamt about the past two nights but not mentioned to Peter. She wanted to get started turning him into a merman as soon as possible, and with the three day Labor Day weekend, there should be plenty of time for announcements, introductions, and the other things that went along with being newly chosen, as well as that one very important item.

Friday night, she dreamt of kissing Peter in the waves, and suddenly he was able to follow her underwater. Last night, she'd dreamt of mating with Peter as the waves washed up on the shore. Her tail had suddenly appeared, and then Peter had one too.

Yes, those were her dreams, and that kind of thing seldom happened in real life, but she imagined it wouldn't be too hard or take very long to take care of Peter. After all, she could go from legs to tail in a few seconds—so how long could it take to go from human to mer? A long weekend? A week? It should be rather easy.

Peter noticed the faraway look in her eyes and asked if she was okay. Reluctantly, Penelope returned to reality, smiled, and squeezed his hand.

"Sorry, just daydreaming about everything...about us."

While Penelope and Peter were caught up in their own private world and oblivious to everything around them, they were under observation. Paula Revelle and her husband frequented Paul's Chophouse, and she had been quick to notice them sitting by the window, holding hands.

Apparently, whatever problem there had been between them last week was now resolved, and the couple had returned to the realm of ordinary, at best, gossip.

High above the restaurant, the clouds had been getting thinner, and at that moment, the sun broke out, sending its welcome rays through the restaurant's windows. One of those sunbeams found Penelope's engagement ring, and the diamond refracted the sunlight into a halo, which surrounded her hand and dazzled Paula's eyes.

Is that an engagement ring? Paula excused herself and contrived to walk past their table on her way to the ladies room. The happy couple was too wrapped up in each other to notice her, and Paula subsequently ducked into a stall and pulled out her smartphone. She composed a text advising her loyal followers to stand by for a very important gossip blast before 9:00 a.m. the following morning.

Paula was at her desk bright and early Monday and immediately set to work composing her text. She wanted one more sighting for confirmation before pressing the send button and did not have to wait very long.

At 8:20 a.m., Penelope and Peter walked in, hand in hand. The ring was obviously there, and the public display of affection before they separated left no room for doubt.

Both Peter and Penelope had separate morning meetings to attend on different floors. His was with the Software and Acquisition Committee, while hers was a review of earnings for the past fiscal year.

Penelope was head down, reviewing the details of the report she should have looked at over the weekend—instead, she'd been too busy cuddling up next to her new mate and enjoying the wonderful bliss that was suddenly hers—when her turn to speak quickly arrived. She stood, started her presentation, and launched into her analysis of earnings and profits areas—a subject she usually relished but today seemed exceedingly trivial and dull.

She had just completed the second slide when someone's phone announced an incoming text. That was quickly followed by a chirp from another device, and then another. Penelope wished people would learn to silence their phones while they were in a meeting.

Ignoring the pings and the soft murmurings that accompanied them, Penelope continued on with the rest of her presentation. When she was done, she turned around to face a host of Cheshire cat smiles. *Humans!*

In the meantime, Peter was less than enthused with his meeting and had been trying not to doze off while participants argued the pros and cons of switching to a new Linux distribution on the company's server farm. This was exceedingly ironic since well over half of them could not tell you which operating system ran their desktop computers.

While one participant was holding forth on the virtues of a Linux distribution that even Peter had never heard of, chirps and pings of the assorted smartphones in the room began. Apparently, some football player with the Dolphins or Buccaneers was being traded or let go at the end of pre-season, or a NASCAR driver had a new ride for next year. It really didn't matter to Peter, and he occupied himself with scribbling the specs for a new Perl script that would solve a ton of issues—provided it worked as expected.

When Peter finally escaped his meeting, he headed for his desk and encountered guys giving him "Way to go!" head nods or punches in his bicep accompanied by, "Nice, man!"

He was somewhat mystified by all of it until he reached his desk and saw a waiting email from Penelope's PA, Julie, that read, "Congratulations! I'm so happy for both of you!" There had been no discussion of keeping everything secret, but he had hoped to be able to inform Mr. Williamson about their news—office relationships could be a tricky subject and he wanted to start his engagement off on the right foot with his boss.

On the whole, the company was pretty easy-going about dating as well as married couples and there had been two other office weddings during his tenure. Peter was rather pleased that his co-workers appeared supportive, but he was concerned about how Penelope would take it all. He had already gathered things were done quite differently where she came from, and Penelope might not be prepared for the way human females reacted toward an engagement.

Once Penelope's meeting was finally over, she headed toward the break room on her floor. She still couldn't understand what all the smiles and grins were about. Was there something stuck on the back of her skirt? A huge run in her tights? Maybe she could sort it out over a cup of tea.

She had just poured the water over her tea bag when Julie walked—no, ran—in, locked her in a bear hug, and squealed, "I'm so happy for you!"

That was apparently the signal everyone had been waiting for, and before Penelope could answer or even extricate herself from the hug, there was a stampede of women from her floor, and several other floors as well, accompanied by general giggling and questions like, "Where did he ask you?" "How did he ask you?" "Were you expecting it?" "Have you set a date, yet?" "Where are you going on your honeymoon?" "Have you chosen a designer? My cousin's roommate knows Vera Wang's secretary."

Penelope was hugged at least once by everyone in the room and repeatedly asked if she was going to keep her job, her maiden name, and her apartment. Her engagement ring was examined by one and all and subsequently declared beautiful, perfect, and elegant—though there were a few snide remarks from several ladies who were disgruntled that Peter was off the market before they'd had a chance with him.

Slowly, the crowd began to filter out, and Penelope was finally able to have one or two intelligent conversations about her engagement. When the last well-wisher had returned to their desk, it occurred to her this was the first time in her life she'd ever felt like a human.

Peter bought a couple sandwiches and a bag of chips in the lunchroom and headed out to the little park on the north side of the building. Penelope was waiting for him on their usual bench with a dazed look on her face.

"You look shell-shocked. Everything okay?"

"I'd probably say I'm more pixilated than anything else." Penelope went on to describe the events of earlier that morning and was almost at a loss trying to explain the scene with all the office ladies in the break room. "I just don't understand. Why'd they do that?"

Oddly, Penelope knew the question Peter was going to ask and beat him to the punch with an answer. "On Colony Island, most mermaids—or at least the ones you care about—already know who you've been swimming with, and when you announce you've made your choice, there's not much of a fuss made about it. Sure, they're happy for you, but still, it's not like this. I don't get why everyone here thinks it's a big deal."

"Welcome to the human world, my dear. Most folks at the company seem to have known we were dating—but that was probably about it. Even if everyone knew how serious we were getting, they still would've congratulated you like that when the official news broke. Remember, sweetheart, they think you are just like them. They think of you as human."

Penelope needed time for all this to sink in. At the age when most mer on the island were preparing to attend high school on the mainland, they were enrolled in an after-school program known as Mer School. Its purpose was to educate them on the facts of human life.

Apart from their general studies, the boys took special classes on how to protect the girls from detection—which always included the usual smirking and sniggering typical for their age and gender—and the girls took special classes on things like makeup and fashion, among other things. Penelope didn't remember a lesson on females flocking around engagement rings, but she did learn a lot about how to act like a typical young human, which was essential to keeping their secret. For instance, telling an adolescent human you would like to mate with them when they came of age was not a good idea.

Learning to pass for a human in high school was one thing. Being accepted as a human in the everyday work world was something else entirely. What's more, Penelope *had* felt like she was human back in the break room. She didn't know whether to think of herself as a traitor to her species, or an honor graduate from Mer School. The fact that she'd chosen a human as a mate only served to make things seem even more complicated.

"Pen, they really like you. They care about you and are happy for you. You can't just swim away from things anymore. You're one of us, too."

How did Peter know she was thinking about that? It must have been a lucky guess. Regardless, she was a mermaid living and working in the human world, and her mate was a human who wanted to join her world. In the meantime, she needed to concern herself with how she was going to introduce her world to Peter.

"Sweetheart, I hate to ask you this, but would you mind if we slept apart tonight? We have a big weekend coming up, and I need some time to think about how to handle a few things."

"As long as you let me text you every forty-five minutes to say I love you."

Penelope grinned. "If you'll compromise and make it every sixty minutes, then we have a deal! I'll even throw in a call before I go to sleep." *It's so wonderful having a mate.*

How was Penelope going to announce—out of the blue—that she was coming home? To say her correspondence with her mother over the past year had been sparse would be overly generous, and up until three months ago, almost nonexistent would have been a more accurate description. She pulled up her email and chose a letter at random.

Mom,

I'm doing okay. Thinking of changing jobs.

Penny

That was the extent of her communications for the month of January. By mid to late May, the frequency had changed to every two weeks, and toward the end of June, they had become a weekly affair with an increasingly sunny outlook. In late July, they were a twice-weekly kind of thing and had become downright chatty compared to a year ago.

Now she was going home and taking her newly chosen mate with her. There was no way her mother could fail to suspect something was up, and she didn't want to give away the news in her email. On the other hand, to say too little might create more problems than it solved. In the end, she compromised.

Hi Mom!

Busy, busy, busy! I'm planning to come down for a visit late Friday afternoon and stay until Monday afternoon. I'm really looking forward to seeing you and Dad.

I may have some exciting news for you. Otherwise, everything is fine here. Looking forward to this weekend.

Love, Penny

She hit "send" and then promptly logged off. If her mother asked too many questions, she'd feign being too busy to respond properly and say she'd explain everything over the weekend. There certainly would be a lot to tell everyone on Friday, but now it was time to shower and go to bed. She'd call Peter once she was snuggled in between the sheets and the lights were out.

Penelope kept busy on Wednesday, trying to get ahead on work so she and Peter could leave without any guilt on Friday and be ahead of most of the traffic. She expected they'd arrive around 6:30 p.m. and maybe pick up dinner for everyone on their way in.

When her mother's email came in, Penelope thought of replying to her by saying, "Guess who's coming to dinner? My mate!" but set that temptation aside. The message conveyed she was relieved, excited, happy, and thrilled that her daughter was *finally* coming home, and Penelope decided to leave things as they were. Her mother had not tried to pry about the "exciting news," which immediately told Penelope she knew something was up. Friday evening would be interesting to say the least.

An "all hands" meeting was scheduled for the lunchroom at 4:00 p.m. Mr. Williamson called the meetings every few months to announce new acquisitions, staffing changes, etc. Maybe this time it was to announce everyone could leave at 2:30 on Friday.

Peter planned to swing by Penelope's office around 3:40 so they could go to the meeting together and find a place to sit or stand. Just as he walked in the door, Mr. Williamson called to ask if he could stop by her office and double check some numbers concerning last year's profits. Penelope sighed. It looked like this meeting was one of the usual kind.

Mr. Williamson was a genial sort of man and an old-fashioned corporate executive who firmly believed his employees were the key to the company's success. While he tended to be more formal with women—a legacy of his southern upbringing—he nonetheless tried to be as casual as decorum allowed.

"Ah, Peter. It's good to see you here," he said with a genuine smile. After a glance and a smile in Penelope's direction, he continued. "I understand that congratulations are in order. I'm always glad to see young folks like you find that special person and settle down. Peter, if you'll pardon me, I need to double check some figures with your bride-to-be."

Actually, the figures he asked for were already in the report she'd emailed him, but he often misfiled things—so it was said—and his stopping by was simply a regular part of everyday business.

Noting it was now past time for the meeting to start, he

borrowed Penelope's phone to call his PA and let her know he was on his way. Penelope and Peter followed in his wake down to the lunchroom.

Ever the gentlemen, he held the door open as they went through to the lunchroom where Penelope and Peter were greeted with cheers and thunderous applause. The room had been decorated with streamers, balloons, and a banner that proclaimed, "Congratulations Penelope & Peter." It was a surprise engagement party, and Mr. Williamson was quite pleased with himself.

"Miss Tench, our PAs and a few others were able to put all this together for you two."

Penelope was flabbergasted, speechless, and debated whether to stay or flee.

Peter leaned in and whispered, "It's okay, sweetheart. Relax. They did this because they really like you."

As Penelope was accepting hugs and handshakes, Mr. Williamson pulled Peter aside. "Tell your fiancée all of us are very happy for the both of you, but I've got to slip away. I have an offsite meeting with the Board tomorrow that I'm not looking forward to." And with that, he waved to the crowd and left the lunchroom.

At 11:00 a.m. on Friday, Mr. Williamson called Peter and Penelope into his office.

"I'm not going to beat around the bush, so here it is. The Board wishes you two the best of luck and happiness, but they're not comfortable with the thought of a married couple occupying two sensitive positions in the company. They have no problems with two people who are dating, which, to my way of thinking, is rather stupid, since you two could do just as much damage to the Harriman Company single as you could married. They're really afraid of the Internet, and half of those old farts have never even been online. One of them steadfastly believes the Internet is just a series of tubes," he said with a roll of his eyes.

Peter and Penelope chuckled at this notion then exchanged a look of concern—all joking aside, this could seriously affect their careers.

"Suffice it to say, one of you will have to leave the company, and I believe that person should be you, Peter."

Penelope took Peter's hand. While this blow was not fatal, it certainly put a kink in their marriage plans. Mr.

Williamson noted their obvious concern.

"So, here is how we'll make this work. Peter, your last day with the company will occur right before your wedding, and you'll be given a month's leave as well as severance equal to one year's pay. When the two of you return from your honeymoon and everything has settled down, Peter will work here as a contractor. While your pay won't be as much, Peter, you'll receive a monthly retention bonus that'll bring your compensation to about the same level as your current pay.

"At the end of next April, Miss Tench, you will be given a substantial pay increase as recognition for your invaluable service over the past year. The end result is, you two will make more money married than you did single, and that will send those old buzzards a rocket. I expect two or three of them are going to stop breathing within a couple of years, and if I'm still around, I'm going to make sure their replacements are well below the age of ancient. If you're interested, Peter, you can come back on board with the company at that time. There are a few details to be worked out, like your pension and medical, but we'll take care of that later. Any questions?"

"I…I don't know what to say, sir." Peter replied.

"There's nothing you need to say. I want my two favorite lovebirds to go ahead with their wedding plans without a care. Now, as I understand it, you two are off to break the happy news to Miss Tench's parents. I want both of you to finish up and hit the road as soon as possible—while I look up some recipes for buzzard stew."

Peter and Penelope were on their way to Colony Island by 1:30 p.m. and spent the first hour of the trip reviewing Mr. Williamson's plans—and wondering if it would make any difference to things in the long run. They eventually decided it would require a bit of adjustment but not have much overall impact, and the conversation subsequently drifted toward their weekend on Colony Island. There was more to life on Colony Island than Penelope could explain in a whole day, so she decided to stick to the bare minimum facts.

"Peter, everyone there is pretty friendly, though because you're a human, some folks might be a bit standoffish. Those will mostly be the ones who work on the island and don't usually see anything from the mainland. There's a community of merfolk in Royston—the county seat—that is fairly cosmopolitan, and the rest of us are pretty easy going. If anything goes wrong, I doubt it will result in angry mermen with torches and tridents," she said with a sly grin.

"One thing you'll notice is that many of the males wear their hair in a ponytail. It's an old custom, but no one thinks less of anyone cutting their hair short. Though my mom says most Colony Island mermaids would think of an unchosen male with a beard and ponytail as the hottest thing since George Clooney."

Penelope decided to switch topics at that point. She couldn't care less if Peter had a beard, but she was definitely interested in seeing him with a ponytail. She didn't want to ruin her chances by talking about it too much and too soon.

"If any mermaid was ever created for the sole purpose of being a mother, it's my mom. I should warn you, though, she can be very emotional at times—in a good way. She's not one of those gushy types except when it comes to her family. You'll probably see her tear up two or three times this weekend, but it's nothing to be alarmed about. She just loves Dad and me, and now she's going to have someone else to love as well.

"As for Dad, he makes his living as a private investor, and nothing comes between him and the Wall Street Journal. He comes across as gruff and a bit old-fashioned, but in reality, he's a real softy. He calls my mom 'Mother,' and the last I heard, he bought a Hummer because he liked the way they look. Mom is always fussing with him about his hair. He'd prefer to wear it human style, and Mom prefers him with a ponytail. He has a very small one just to keep the peace. I think the two of you will get along fine." *I hope!*

"If you say so, dear. I just hope he doesn't come after me with his trident."

"He doesn't have a trident, silly. He has a speargun."

CHAPTER ELEVEN

Centuries before Columbus made his voyage, merfolk migrated to the New World. The waters were hospitable, and food was plentiful, so their numbers grew, and there they stayed. Life was good, but they had overlooked one minor fact—over time, even iron rusts in saltwater.

No matter how well they cared for them, one by one, their trident spears became useless. They were able to sharpen shells and affix them to wood shafts, but these were, at best, makeshift. At worst, they were less than effective tools in deadly situations, as there was nothing better than an iron trident when it came to dealing with great white sharks.

Possible solutions to the problem were debated, but no single answer was completely satisfactory. One idea was to swim back across the Atlantic and obtain new tridents from forges along the coast of the Mediterranean. The flaw in this was finding those mer-friendly forges, and carrying hundreds and hundreds of tridents across the Atlantic was daunting to say the least. Even if they towed small boats or rafts, one good storm at sea would leave them back where they started.

One well-traveled merman had observed their counterparts along the East Asian coast using bamboo for shafts and sharpened shells or stones as spearheads. However, they had no tools to cut and shape the wood, much less fashion good, dependable spearheads. There were other suggestions like using whalebone, but it all came down to one thing: they didn't have the proper tools to do any of this. It was then suggested they steal the tools from the humans, but that option was considered too risky and dangerous.

Merfolk had occasionally bartered with humans over the centuries, so finally, it was agreed they would trade their most plentiful commodity—fish—for metals or things that could be used to buy tools. They passed themselves off as fishermen, supplying seafood in exchange for the commodities they needed, as well as fruits and vegetables. Their business with humans necessitated rafts, dugout canoes, and nets, all of which the merfolk learned to make.

When the Spanish began to colonize the New World in the 1500s, the merfolk learned to build boats and became expert sailors. They set up what appeared to be seasonal fishing villages and traded fish for land commodities. Every two to four months, they decamped and moved up or down the coast to a new location. By the early 1700s, they had chosen an isolated island off Florida's east coast as a permanent location to do the work necessary to maintain their fleet.

Colony Island was approximately a mile wide and nearly four miles long. It was protected from the mainland by a large swamp to the west that ran the length of the island, what would later be known as the Royston River to the south, and a series of marshes and narrow inlets on the north end. The backbone of the island was ten to fifteen feet above sea level, with the land sloping gently down to the sea, and was separated from the mainland by a small stream at the northwest end. Other than crossing the narrow bridge at that point, the only practical way to reach the wooded island was by water.

While most of the merfolk swam south for the winter months, a contingent stayed behind to effect repairs and fashion replacements where necessary. Some of them traveled to human settlements, where they worked as apprentices, journeymen carpenters, metalworkers, etc. They brought their new or enhanced skills back to the island and proceeded to build basic huts and shacks to live in. By the time the main body of merfolk returned, the colony had established itself, and both new and repaired boats and equipment awaited the start of their fishing season. At the end of the season, more merfolk chose to stay for the duration.

After five years, all but a handful of mer were staying on the island year round. They'd learned other crafts from the humans, and the colony was thriving. The quality of life improved, and as more and more houses were built, the merfolk found that living on the shore had its benefits.

They still thought of themselves as mermaids and mermen, but they also thought of themselves as having one fluke in the ocean and one foot on land. In effect, the seducers and seductresses of the sea had themselves been seduced by comfy chairs, warm beds, and hot meals. By the turn of the 19th century, the town of Colony Island had prospered, and they were quite satisfied with the way things had turned out.

As the decades passed, the main road became lined with storefronts, and though the primary industry was still fishing, businesses sprung up to service the needs of the fleet and residents. Many of the island's houses had large garden plots, and the owners made money by selling produce. Colony Island had an economy of its own.

Not everyone, though, was happy with the turn of events. The merfolk who remained in the sea considered the residents of Colony Island to be sellouts. They had always thought humans to be a nuisance they could do nothing about. They looked down their noses at the merfolk living on shore, considering them to be pretenders, mer who were trying to be like humans. The island residents referred to those in the sea as "feral"—an expression that was returned in kind by them labeling the islanders as "domesticated."

Some ferals decided to try living on land, but the results were less than promising. Out of every fifty who tried, all but five returned to the sea within a generation or less.

Things didn't always go well for the islanders, as they considered themselves to be not quite as good as humans. Over the years, the residents developed something of an inferiority complex, and anyone who tried too much to emulate humans was considered to be putting on airs. For their part, the people on the mainland thought the merfolk were ordinary fishermen and shopkeepers—a bit odd perhaps, but human, nonetheless.

It was tricky adjusting to human customs, none more so than that of marriage. Traditionally, a couple would appear before their friends and family to announce they had chosen each other as mates—whether for a single breeding cycle or for life. But, after years on land, mermaids began to want weddings like their human neighbors.

Memories of life in the sea were still fairly fresh in the

minds of the town fathers, so they compromised, and in the 1830s, the joining ceremony was born. It was close enough to ancient tradition to be easily recognizable yet close enough to mainland customs to placate the mermaids. Couples also had the choice of either living in what humans referred to as a common-law marriage or taking out a marriage license for the legal benefits it conferred. Most couples, especially those who considered themselves to be life mates, opted for the latter.

In the late 1800s, one of their fishing boats snagged a net on something in deep water. Two of the fishermen, William H. Tench and Thomas Waterman, shifted to tails and swam down to free the net. They found the wreck of a Spanish ship from the Queen's Dowry treasure fleet that sank with all hands in a hurricane off the Florida coast in 1715. The cargo was Columbian jewels—and gold. Lots of it.

There was so much gold that humans would certainly ask questions as to where it was found and how it was recovered. The answers to those questions would raise even more questions and ultimately endanger the Islanders' secret. The town fathers decided the money should be used for the benefit of the island residents.

Most of the gold was melted into ingots, and one by one, quietly sold on the Havana exchange, as well as in other countries in the region. The full value of the gold was not realized, but nonetheless, Colony Island was fabulously wealthy by the standards of the day. While the largest share of the treasure was claimed by the town, a modest, but still quite valuable amount was given to the crew of the fishing vessel that found the wreck. The lion's share of that amount was divided between Tench and Waterman.

In the early 1900s, the town began to put its share to use buying kit homes from Sears & Roebuck. Many mermen found work demolishing old houses and assembling new ones to replace them. By the end of the century, there was a cadre of tradesmen, builders and construction workers descended from these men who did most of the building and repair on Colony Island and worked construction jobs on the mainland when there was nothing for them at home.

When America entered World War II, the residents realized their life on Colony Island would be over if the Allies lost. Many of the mermen chose to stand shoulder to shoulder with the humans and enlisted in the armed forces, but not all of them returned.

The postwar prosperity that blessed the rest of the nation seemed to bypass Colony Island, and nothing was more affected than its fishing business. The whole industry was starting to change. Factory ships and centralized processing facilities began to make their appearance, and there was no way the Colony Island fleet could compete.

In the late 1950s, the island's processing plant shut down. The fleet began taking its catch to a facility up the coast or selling it for local consumption. This sent the island's economy into a tailspin, as the residents were ill-equipped to deal with such a radical shift in such a short time. Some returned to the sea, while others sought work on the mainland.

An enclave of Colony Island merfolk sprang up in Royston as a way to avoid the daily commute and in time was made up mostly of young professionals with a more cosmopolitan outlook than the islanders. While they would go back on weekends to swim and catch up on things, the island was no longer their home.

The inferiority complex that had all but vanished during the war years quickly reasserted itself, and the islanders turned inward. As a result, members of the Royston enclave stopped going to the island on weekends—as they deemed the whole town too depressing—and found other places to swim.

Participation in activities that were perceived as human fell off, and music was seldom heard in town. The phrase, "Awww, that's just something humans do," became common, and anyone who did things such as attending their child's school play was perceived as trying to pass as human. The merfolk were more or less happy, but Colony Island was not what it once was.

The post-war population boom also affected Colony Island, as mainland housing developments crept closer. While the swamp to the west of the island was an unbuildable barrier, the town decided to buy land buffers to the north and south. The marsh and narrow inlets to the north were designated a wildlife refuge, and the land south of the Royston River was developed as a small, wooded buffer community, where some members of the enclave were persuaded to move.

For decades, children were educated on the island through high school. As education standards improved, the town could no longer maintain a K-12 system for the relatively small number of children, and it was decided they would attend the county high school, and also the middle school, if the parents wanted.

The elementary school became The Colony Academy, more commonly known as The Academy, a private school that taught most of the island children in that age range, as well as a significant number of children from the Royston enclave.

The Academy gave the island children a chance to learn the ins and outs of interacting with humans—flashing your fin was not a good idea for show and tell. The merkids also studied the usual elementary school subjects, as well as those associated with life in the sea, and there were after school programs for those being home-schooled and those attending the county's public schools through twelfth grade.

For the majority of the children, attending high school was their big adventure in life, and they made the most of it. Upon graduation, some attended the local community college, and a few went on to university. Over the years, Colony Island produced tradesmen, professionals, artists, musicians, a few all-Americans, and one high school valedictorian: Penelope Anne Tench. But, in the end, most mer returned to the island or lived within the Royston enclave.

CHAPTER TWELVE

Peter turned off the interstate, as Penelope directed, and headed east. There was nothing particularly out of the ordinary along this stretch of road. Strip malls, fast food restaurants, gas stations, a donut shop.

They passed the intersection of the main road to Royston, and once they were beyond the supermarket, things began to thin out quickly. The terrain became even flatter, if that was possible in that part of Florida, and the fields were interspersed with small marshes and low-lying land.

There was an intersection with another road to Royston, with a handful of houses on the left, and on the right, was the beginnings of a true swamp. The sign indicated that Colony Island—the first time Peter had seen it mentioned anywhere—was straight ahead but gave no mileage.

The cypress trees in the swamp were quite tall at this point, and the land on the left was giving way to marsh. They passed a road leading toward some trees half a mile away and finally drove across a small concrete bridge—the kind that usually spanned a very minor creek. As they drove around a curve, the town and a small harbor came into view.

It was a typical small town that could've been anywhere on the east coast of the United States, Peter thought, with the ubiquitous old-fashioned water tower and a mix of older brick and frame buildings. The sky was overcast, and at first impression, the town seemed to blend in with the general grayness. A gas station and a garage were on the right followed by a few small buildings. The car clattered over the steel deck of a bridge that spanned the very eastern end of the harbor as they slowly drove down the main street.

There was a pizza joint and a nondescript City Hall on the right. The shops on the left—nothing out of the ordinary—were mostly in old buildings with a fair number showing "FOR RENT" signs. A Greek Revival building of some kind stood on the right across from the fire station. They passed a restaurant, a bar, a few more blocks of shops, and suddenly left the business district. It had taken only two minutes to drive through town, and it looked so normal, Peter felt the merfolk must surely live further down the island.

As they headed on south, houses and buildings on the right gave way to woods and old fields. The left hand side of the street was still residential, though the number of houses decreased, and there were more trees. As in the downtown section, the ocean could be seen six or seven blocks to the east. Eventually, a very small commercial area appeared on the right consisting of another pizza joint, a mom and pop grocery store, and a boarded up white cinderblock building.

Penelope directed Peter to turn around there and head back toward town. Her rationale for coming this way was twofold—it gave Peter a small tour of the island and forestalled arriving at her parents' house. "It's pretty much the same from this point going south to the private beach at the end of the road," she explained.

As they reentered the business district, Peter began to notice some subtle signs that this was not your average town populated by average people. A sign across the side of one old brick building read, "SUPPORT YOUR LOCAL MERCHANTS," and Peter was fairly certain the small caps used for the last six letters were not because the sign painter had run out of space.

The bar they'd passed earlier had a Tudor façade and was named The Mermaid Tavern, and there was a mustard yellow storefront just ahead with a sign on the window that read, "The Mermaid's Purse." It was here that Penelope asked him to turn right, and almost immediately the area turned residential. The homes seemed to be out of the first quarter of the last century when craftsman-style houses were popular.

A few houses here and there were obviously pre-1900s, and a number of homes had large, grassy side yards where vegetables had probably grown once upon a time. One of these houses had a large extension on the back that spilled over into the side yard. No telling what that was.

Penelope asked Peter to turn left at a cross street and left again at the end of the block. It was easy to spot Penelope's house; there was a black Hummer parked in the driveway. Peter pulled over and cut the engine.

As they got out of the car, Penelope said, "Leave our bags in the trunk. We can bring them in later." Her resolve was weakening by the second.

Her mother would most likely be good with the choice Penelope had made, as she had seemed to be favorably disposed toward humans in the past—a bit baffled by them, but inclined to like them, nonetheless. Her father was the big unknown. He could be gruff and grumpy at times, but she loved him dearly. Penelope was going to need the cooperation of both parents if Peter was to have scales of his own.

They entered through the front door, and Penelope guided Peter into the living room. She would rather have left him in the den across the hall, but at least here, he had an additional route of escape through the dining room if things came to that.

"Sweetheart, wait here, and I'll go find Daddy."

Penelope knew exactly where he'd be—in his office at the back of the house. At least this would buy her a little more time with Peter before he got too nervous and ran off. At that moment, she would have been happy to join him.

The office door was partially open, and she stuck her head in. It was a small space with one window. The room was a little more than a third of its original size, as her parents had reconfigured this part of the house to give them an en-suite bathroom with a small shower stall and an extra-long bathtub, known locally as a lounging tub—the perfect place to put your tail on and unwind at the end of the day. There was enough space in the office for a desk, a couple chairs and bookcases, and a PC with a twenty-four inch monitor.

"Daddy? I'm home!"

"Princess. How's my beautiful Fishyface?" He rose from his chair and gave her a warm hug. Then he held her at arm's length and studied her face with a smile. "You look so much better than the last time I saw you. It's wonderful to have you back with us. Everything okay with the new job?"

"I'm quite happy there, and I'm starting to really love it. I'm the full-time comptroller."

"I can't believe it. I'm so proud of you, Princess. With your mind and that degree, you're really going to go places—as long as you remember where your home is."

Penelope had held off as long as she could, and it was now or never. She straightened up, looked him in the eye, and said with the biggest smile she could muster, "Father, I have chosen a mate."

Absolute joy crossed his face as if the sun had finally made its appearance after a long, dreary week. A fatherly tear trickled down his cheek. "That is the most wonderful news in the world! Your mother will be thrilled. I knew you'd find the right merman. Now don't tell me. Let me guess. Your friend Anthony separated from his mate…"

"Dad, it's not Tony."

"Eh? Well, he's a good kid, but not the right match for you, anyway. Now, Tom Sturgeon's boy, Tim, would be a good catch."

"It's not Tim Sturgeon either. My mate's not from around here."

"So he's a feral? Some of them can be quite odd and off-putting, but I do know a few good feral families. Let's see…"

"He's not a feral, either. Daddy…he's human."

Suddenly, the joy in her father's face vanished and was replaced by the most stricken look imaginable. He had lost his daughter. His princess. She had merely come home to say goodbye, and he most likely would never see her again. What had they done wrong? Was she really so desperate that she had to choose a human? Did she think so little of herself that she fell for the first human that paid any attention to her?

Before his anguish overtook him completely, Penelope said, "Dad, he has asked to become a merman."

He wasn't losing his daughter after all. But a human convert as her mate? His son-in-law? How was he supposed to deal with that? He knew humans sometimes asked to become mermaids or mermen, but the only one he'd ever met was Gail Waterman—Poseidon bless her soul—and he was not sure how a male would work out as a merman, much less as a son-in-law. He sat down and attempted to pour a stiff drink, but Penelope stopped him.

"Daddy, his name is Peter MacPherson, and he came with me to see you and Mom. He's in the living room, and I really want you to meet him."

Penelope's father was still dazed, but he managed to follow his daughter down the hall and around the foot of the stairs into the living room, where Peter was waiting nervously.

"Peter, I would like you to meet my father, George. Daddy, this is my mate, Peter MacPherson."

Peter stood up straight, squared his shoulders, and shook her father's hand. "Mr. Tench, I'm very pleased to meet you. Your daughter is the most wonderful, beautiful, and intelligent woman I've ever met. You must be very proud of her."

Penelope had quietly backed herself out into the hall where she held up her left hand to show her engagement ring to her father. She pointed to it while mouthing, "We're getting married!"

Peter noticed his future father-in-law had leaned to one side in order to see around him. "Sir, is something wrong?"

Peter was about to turn around to see what was going on when George returned his attention to him saying, "No. I'm sorry. My daughter was making faces at me."

Penelope figured this was as good a time as any to make a run for it and let the boys get to know each another. Hopefully, she wouldn't find bloodstains on the carpet when she returned.

"Dad? Where's Mom?"

George was grateful for another opportunity to break away from this awkward situation for a moment and glanced at his watch. "She wanted to go for a swim before you got home. If you don't meet her coming back from the beach, you'll certainly be there when she comes out of the water."

Penelope made a hasty departure and called over her shoulder, "Thanks, Dad! We'll be back in a few."

Penelope had bailed on him. Frankly, Peter couldn't blame her too much, and maybe she was simply going for reinforcements. After all, he'd gotten the impression her mother would be easier to win over.

George and Peter engaged in small talk about the weather, the economy, Peter's job, and computers. There were only a few pieces of software they both used, so that topic was quickly exhausted.

Peter was starting to panic in the extended silence when George said, "Son, I know why you're here, and I should tell you that Penelope's mother and I have absolutely no say in the matter. The choice is hers and hers alone."

Peter could not let things rest there. It was show time. "I understand, sir, but I want to do this the right way. Mr. Tench, I have become extremely fond of your daughter and feel that much of the credit for her wit, intelligence, and caring nature should go to you and her mother, and the way she was raised. I want to assure you, I will do everything within my power to protect, provide for, and care for her. Your amazing daughter is the love of my life, and I want to be with her for the rest of my days."

George Tench had straightened at the sound of "protect." That was the first vow that every merman made to his mate, and this young man sounded very serious about it. The other items were also important, but the desire to protect his mate was hardwired into every son of Poseidon. Maybe this wasn't going to be so bad, after all.

Peter had no idea where his words were coming from. He would readily admit he was not great thinking on his feet, and he hadn't had a drink in over a week. Even so, another proposition immediately formed in his mind, and his mouth eagerly opened in order to give it voice.

"Mr. Tench, you no doubt take pride in the protection of your family, correct?"

George nodded, not sure of where this was going.

"Well, think of this as my request to take responsibility for your daughter's safety and security. I have been doing it for the past four months or so, and I would like your permission to do it permanently. So, with that in mind…"

Penelope slipped out the back door, opened the gate, and crossed the Watermans' side yard. Out of habit, she turned to look toward the kitchen window to see if Gail was watching. It hurt not to be able to wave at her neighbor anymore or stop by after school and ask if she wanted to come along on a swim in the ocean. She hoped Mrs. Waterman was somehow watching from the waters of Elysium and approved of her choice in a mate.

It was doubly sad she was gone, because she would have been the first and probably the only mer Penelope could ask about how weddings were done. She knew of no other mermaids on Colony Island who'd had a wedding on the mainland and then stayed close to home.

Penelope turned down the street and began walking toward the beach. She fought the temptation to run like a little girl with a bunch of flowers for her mother. Nonetheless, there was a spring in every step she took.

Ilene Tench tied the bow in the strings of her bikini top and then shifted to legs so she could tie on the bottom. She thought she didn't look bad at all for a fifty-year-old mermaid, and on occasion, she might even be mistaken for her daughter. Certainly, to human eyes, she looked like a slightly older sister, and human eyes were what was important at this moment.

Poking her head above the surface, she scanned the beach and found it as deserted as when she had first entered the water. One could never be too careful, especially when the police would occasionally stop by to make sure the residents followed the rules. All this was a bit of a bother, but it was the price one paid for the convenience of being able to walk down to the end of the street, rather than drive all the way down to the private beach in order to swim. She kicked her feet to catch a wave she could ride in toward the shore. Swimming was so much easier with a tail.

Ilene left the water and retrieved her towel and the bathrobe she used going to and from the beach. The robe had seen better days, and most anyone would have thought it fit only for rags. She had no sentimental attachment to it, and she would replace it with something newer either when she got around to it or the robe itself disintegrated to mere threads. She slid into her flip-flops and began to weave her way between the dunes. She wanted to get back to the house, change, and start on dinner before Penny arrived.

She left the shore behind and crossed Beach Street. Needless to say, she was a bit anxious about her daughter's first trip home in years. She wasn't sure what had precipitated the visit, but she was more than grateful for it.

Penny's self-imposed absence and isolation had been rough on Ilene and George. Ilene had noted the shift in mood and content of her emails over the past few months. She appeared to be coming out of her despair, and that was encouraging—very encouraging—but Ilene had kept her own counsel and not told George anything other than she seemed to be doing a bit better of late. Her husband had taken all of this so hard, and she didn't want to offer him false hope. She hadn't told him about the promise of exciting news, either. With any luck, she'd be able to sound out Penny first.

Ilene looked up the street and saw Penny coming toward her. By the way she walked, it almost seemed that the Penny of ten or twelve years ago had magically returned. Did this have something to do with whatever exciting news she was bringing? It appeared she was going to find out very quickly. Penny had picked up her pace and literally skipped the last thirty yards toward her. This was too good to be true.

"Hi, Mom. It's so good to be home. I missed you and Dad so much!"

Ilene embraced her daughter and tried to stifle the tears that were sure to come any second. "Dear, it's so good to have you home. Your father and I have been so worried about you all this time. We've missed you so much too!"

Penelope was so excited she was bouncing on the balls of her feet. "I'm glad you're still here to come home to. I know I haven't been the best daughter to you for a long time, but I'm doing so much better now."

Her mom was really trying to hold back the tears, and Penelope saw an opening. She stepped back, cleared her throat and said, "Mother…"

Penny using the formal title of "Mother" put Ilene on high alert. She could only think of one situation where her daughter would use that word. *Could it really be true?*

"I have chosen a mate."

There it was! The five words every mermaid hoped to hear from her child had finally been spoken. Ilene studied her daughter for a moment. "He's human, isn't he?"

Penelope was undeterred by this, and indeed, was half expecting it. Her mother was pretty sharp about reading her. "Yes, Mother. He is human, and you know what? He wants to become one of us."

Penelope saw her mother's eyes instantly soften. It was time for the rest of the news. "You know what else?" She held up her left hand to show off her engagement ring. "We're getting married!"

This was unbelievable. Ilene had never even dreamt such a thing could happen for her daughter. They hugged and then began to dance around each other in circles, squealing and laughing like ten-year-olds. There was such joy in both their faces.

Mother and daughter finally slowed enough to catch their breath.

"Did he come home with you?"

"Yes, Mom. I left him back at the house with Dad."

"Well then, we'd better go and rescue him."

Life was suddenly so good. Ilene felt the weight from the past years lift from her shoulders. Her daughter had chosen a mate, and they weren't just being joined, they were getting married. And Colony Island was about to get a new merman! Ilene silently thanked Poseidon for his three-fold blessing and proceeded to walk the rest of the way home with her daughter as fast as her flip-flops would carry her.

Peter was shaking hands with Mr. Tench when he heard the back door burst open.

A voice nearly identical to Penelope's excitedly asked, "Where is he? Where is he?"

Peter began to wonder if he'd misjudged things, and Penelope's mother was the real force to be reckoned with. Suddenly, there in the living room doorway, *two* Penelopes appeared. Well, sort of. The one in front looked a bit shorter and a bit older than the other one, and only one was wearing an engagement ring.

George turned to them and announced, "Mother, this young man is Peter MacPherson, and he has asked for Penelope's hand in marriage. I believe their choice of each other as mates is quite promising, and accordingly, I have given him my...is it blessing or consent?"

"Blessing is more common, sir."

"Very well. I have given them my blessing—*and* my consent."

Ilene could no longer contain herself. She crossed the space between them in two steps and nearly knocked Peter over as she threw her arms around his neck and squealed, "Welcome to our family. It's so wonderful to have you as Penny's mate, dear."

Over her shoulder, he could see Penelope smiling at him. Ilene finally let Peter grab some air, turned to her daughter, and said, "Penny, come over here. I want to look at the two of you together."

Penelope did as requested and took hold of Peter's arm with her left hand to ensure her engagement ring was plainly visible.

"Don't they look nice together, George? They look so much like we did at that age."

George nodded. "I believe you're right, Mother."

"Of course, I wanted us to have a wedding, but my parents were traditionalists and told me that a joining ceremony was good enough for them and should be good enough for me. We asked George's parents, and they said the same thing," Ilene explained.

George nodded his head once more.

"We're not going to stand in your way, though. We're going to give you the best possible wedding a mermaid can have. Aren't we George?"

Penelope's father rolled his eyes heavenward and replied, "I'm sure we will, Mother."

"Right. Penny, you look after your mate while I go and change. When I'm dressed, we'll talk about dinner. George, you go and do...whatever."

George replied, "Yes, Mother," and disappeared down the hall to his office and a well-deserved glass of Scotch.

Ilene kissed both Penelope and Peter on the cheek and also disappeared down the hall, humming to herself.

Peter wasn't sure, but it seemed like her feet were an inch and a half above the floor.

Penelope turned to him. "It looks like we did it. I'm so proud of you. Later tonight you can give me all the details of what happened with Dad while I was gone." She took this opportunity to give him a big kiss.

When they finally came up for air, Penelope whispered, "We should probably go see if there's anything we can do to start on dinner."

Peter was ready to go see if Penelope's father had any good single-malt Scotch on hand but instead followed her down the hall. As they passed what appeared to be her parents' room, Ilene could be heard over the noise from the shower humming and singing snatches of tunes that vaguely sounded like wedding music.

They had been standing and whispering in the kitchen for about ten minutes when Ilene bustled in, buttoning up her blouse. Peter didn't see just a little, he saw a lot, and Ilene didn't seem to notice or really care. He was sure Ilene hadn't flashed him—at least, he was pretty sure—and surmised that since Penelope always swam topless, it stood to reason Ilene would do likewise and really not be concerned at who saw what. Peter had a lot of adjusting to do here.

"I thought since we're running a bit late today, the best idea would be to order a couple pizzas and keep everything totally informal. Does that sound okay to you kids?"

"Sounds great to me, Mom. What about you, sweetheart?"

Peter gave two thumbs up.

The list of toppings Ilene rattled off was completely conventional, and Peter sighed with relief. No seafood toppings like squid, tuna, or shrimp, thank goodness. Pepperoni, Italian sausage, and things like that were the order of the day.

"You two go and hold hands or something. I'll check with George and then phone the pizza place."

Penelope led Peter down the hall as Ilene headed toward George's office.

"Honey, I'm surprised. I would have thought all of you would want seafood toppings, or something like that."

"Just because we're part fish and can live in the sea, it doesn't mean we want seafood most, or even part of the time. In all the times we've eaten together, how many times have you seen me order fish?"

"Ummm…once or twice."

"Exactly. We probably eat a bit more seafood than humans do, but we like beef, pork, vegetables, and fruits, just like anyone else."

Peter was secretly relieved. He wasn't going to have to switch to a diet solely consisting of seafood after all. He hadn't paid attention to what Ilene was doing in the kitchen and was slightly startled when she walked into the living room.

"We're in luck. Carl had three large pies waiting for toppings and they just went in the oven. Peter, would you mind picking them up for us?"

"Not at all," he replied.

"Thank you. If you leave now, they should be ready by the time you get there. North End Pizza is the building on your left just before you get to the harbor bridge."

"Saw it when we drove into town this afternoon. I'm on my way. Be back in a bit."

Peter kissed his mate before hurrying out to his car. Having a pretty good memory for directions, he reached North End Pizza without any trouble. The pizzeria looked like any other restaurant of its kind near the beach. It was mindboggling to think this place was probably owned, operated, and patronized by merfolk.

After taking a deep breath, he walked through the door and found the inside was no different than what he would have expected, and the place looked fairly busy. There was a guy with a dirty blond ponytail and a small beard behind the counter who looked to be a few years older than he and carried himself like a surfer. Peter walked up and asked for the Tench order.

"Dude! You must be Penelope's mate. Congratulations, and welcome to the species."

Peter felt like the cowboy from the movies who walked into a saloon. Everyone stopped to look at him. The noise level dropped as the patrons turned in their seats for a better view. If there had been an old-time piano playing in the background, it would have been perfect.

The guy behind the counter said in a stage whisper, "Don't let it bug you. We don't get many of your kind in here—I mean humans. When we do, they're usually lost. Don't worry. The novelty will wear off, and you'll soon be just an ordinary customer."

The patrons slowly turned back to their meals and conversations. A man with a stack of pizza cozies walked in and immediately went behind the counter.

"This dude is Tony. He's working deliveries tonight."

Tony nodded in Peter's direction.

The counter guy then added, "My name's Carl Fisher,

but everyone calls me 'Carl, the Pizza Guy.' Look, if you've got any questions about all this, man—and I know you're going to have a bunch—give me a call, and I'll do my best to answer them."

Peter smiled and thanked Carl for his offer. After he paid for the pizzas and walked out the door, he heard Tony ask, "Who was that?" just before it closed. The feeling everybody's eyes were on him did not go away.

Once inside the house, he walked toward the kitchen, pizza boxes in hand.

Ilene was on the phone. After saying, "Hold on a second," she covered the mouthpiece with her hand and told Peter, "Dear, until we can get a fourth chair for the breakfast nook, we'll all eat in the dining room. Penny's in there setting the table right now. She'll show you what to do."

Peter walked through the swinging door to the dining room where Penelope had already set things out, including mats for the pizza boxes to rest on.

"Hi, honey! We have iced tea and cola to drink. Which would you like?"

Peter chose iced tea, grateful the list of beverages did not include seawater, dolphin milk, or something like that.

Before Penelope turned to go into the kitchen for beverages, she whispered, "Mom's been on the phone ever since you left. I'm not sure who she's talking to. Your chair is right there next to mine."

Figuring he would be told what he needed to know when he needed to know it, Peter took his seat. Penelope returned shortly with four glasses of ice tea—obviously the drink of choice in the house—followed by her mother, and eventually, her father.

After everyone was seated and the selection of pizza slices had begun, Ilene said, "I was speaking with the mayor. Since things will be closed on Monday, he'll be happy to meet with us at 9:30 a.m. to discuss the wedding, and…other things. He performs the joining ceremonies here on the island, and now weddings, I guess. He also handles the…other things, too. I'm sorry, Peter, but I'm not sure what the proper term for this is, or how it's accomplished."

Peter indicated he was okay with that for now and launched into a slice with Italian sausage. Everyone dug in as well, though Penelope did find a few minutes to play footsies with him under the table. Did merfolk call it "finsies"?

There was a natural break in the action as everyone finished their initial slices and prepared to get a second helping, and Ilene used this opportunity to speak up. "So, when do you two plan to breed?"

"Mother!"

"I was just asking. Your father and I are planning to breed again before long, and I thought it would be fun for your first child to be able to play with their aunt or uncle."

"Mom, we only chose each other a week ago. We've been busy with…other things. When we find the time, we'll sit down and discuss it alone."

Peter was staying out of this one. While he was open to having children—breeding—with Penelope, he wanted to have a few years to get used to being a merman before he became a merdad. George, the other candidate for becoming a merdad, sat there shaking his head as he worked on his second helping of pizza.

"Well, you can't blame a mermaid for trying…"

Ilene was captivated by the thought of being pregnant at the same time as her daughter and considered the fun they would have going through it together. Thanks to Poseidon's gift to mermaids, they could even arrange to breed beneath the same full moon. The possibilities were endless!

The rest of the family continued eating while Ilene indulged in these flights of fancy. Before long, everyone was full, and Ilene cleared the dishes. Penelope consolidated the remaining slices in to one box before carrying everything into the kitchen. Peter took this opportunity to slip out to his SUV and retrieve a box from the back seat.

Ordinarily, George would have gone to his office at that point, but he was curious about the box Peter had brought inside and decided to remain at the table to see what it was. When mother and daughter returned to the dining room, Peter cleared his throat.

"Honey, I have a little present for you. Two, actually." He pulled a large book called *Planning Your Wedding* from the box. "This has a lot of good factual information in it as well as suggestions and examples. Plenty of drawings and photos too. There's even a section on wedding etiquette."

Ilene's ears perked up immediately. "Ohhh! I want to see that. I need to do everything by the book."

George Tench was quick to speak up. "Mother, do we really need to do all that? I mean, joining ceremonies are pretty simple and straightforward."

"Dear, this is going to be the first wedding *ever* on Colony Island, and as the mother of the bride, I want to make sure it's done right."

Peter pulled another book from the box and said, "This is a wedding organizer. It has some facts and tips, but it's mainly geared toward checklists and calendars."

"Peter, Poseidon sent you to us for a reason. You are invaluable—isn't he, Penny?"

Penelope quipped, "Well, Mom, I do find Peter to be quite useful myself."

George just sat there shaking his head. It seemed he did that quite a bit.

CHAPTER THIRTEEN

Peter was out of the spotlight—not that he'd relished being there in the first place. Penelope and her mother were in the midst of washing up the dishes, and every once in a while, words like, "the book," "organizer," "wedding," and "gown" wafted from the kitchen. Penelope's father had retired to his office to read the Wall Street Journal online. All in all, it looked like a typical Friday evening, and the casual observer would be hard pressed to discern anything to indicate this house was inhabited by merfolk.

Penelope had asked Peter to bring their things in from the car and carry them upstairs, which he dutifully did, but he was in a bit of a quandary as to where he would lay his head that night.

There were three rooms at the top of the stairs in this craftsman-style house. One had a large bed, and by the looks of things, definitely belonged to Penelope. Another was an ample-sized bathroom, and the third room, was probably going to be his for the duration. A peek inside told him otherwise. There was no bed, and it was partially filled with boxes and other such domestic clutter.

Every so often, the phone would ring, as apparently the news was starting to spread. Ilene would talk for five or ten minutes then put Penelope on the line for another ten or twelve minutes—and so it went.

There was little else to do, so Peter grabbed his e-reader and ensconced himself in the den with the hope he'd be able to talk to Penelope before bedtime. That moment finally arrived when she appeared in the doorway asking him to take his shower and get ready for bed.

Peter gallantly offered to sleep on the couch, but he found himself talking to empty air as the phone had rung yet again. Penelope sounded a bit cross as she talked with somebody named Anthony.

Ilene dashed upstairs for a few minutes, and Peter caught her as she breezed by the den. He made the same offer to sleep on the couch, but she stopped only long enough to say, "You'll do no such thing, dear. Your place is upstairs."

Peter protested that he didn't want to evict Penelope from her room but found he was talking to her mother's back as she retreated down the hall toward the kitchen. Peter turned off the lamp in the den and retired upstairs to take his shower and perform other nightly chores before going to bed. When he was through, he found the covers turned down, and he climbed in between the sheets and turned off the light on the bedside table.

He lay in the dark recounting the day's events and considered things could have been an unmitigated disaster. Instead, everything had gone quite well, and he intended to keep things that way. He'd had enough trouble with girls' parents over the years, and merparents were an unknown factor.

Peter was about to slip off to sleep when the hall light outside the bedroom switched on. From downstairs, he could hear the sounds of lights being switched off and the house shutting down for the night. He heard Penelope walk into the upstairs bathroom and take a shower. After she was done, she brushed her hair, pacing and occasionally looking into the room where Peter pretended to be asleep. If he was lucky, he might get a good-night kiss before she went off to bed.

Finally, the hall light went out, and he could see her figure silhouetted by the faint glow of a lamp downstairs. The door closed, and Peter heard the soft rustling of someone in the room with him. He was going to get that good-night kiss after all.

He felt the sheets being pulled back and was happy at the prospect of having a good-night cuddle as an extra bonus. He reached for Penelope and discovered she was bare as she could be. Peter found this a bit strange, as Penelope usually slept in a T-shirt and panties. He was going to ask what was going on when her mouth clamped down on his and her

URBAN MERMAID

tongue frantically searched for its mate.

Evidently, a good-night kiss was evolving into a good-night quickie. Peter's mind flashed back to a night in college when he'd found himself in big trouble after his girlfriend's father caught them kissing right before bedtime. He'd been summarily dumped the minute he'd returned her to her dorm on campus.

Penelope was intent on pushing the envelope, as she almost purred in delight, her hands exploring beneath the sheets. Peter's body began to respond to the unexpected but very welcome attention it was receiving, and he really didn't want to dissuade her. This might be fun, as long as they kept things quiet.

They had made love—or mated, as she liked to say—three times during the past week, and they were still learning each other's body signals, but this moment left absolutely no doubt that Penelope did not plan to spend much longer on the preliminaries.

This was confirmed when she moved on top of him and guided him inside her. Penelope let out a gasp of pleasure that would easily be heard downstairs, and it was ride 'em cowgirl time.

The bed felt like it was jumping off the floor, and her moans became loud enough to be heard out on the front porch. Peter was terrified at the amount of noise they were making and was sure her father was loading his speargun at that very moment. Penelope seemed not to care one bit about her parents hearing them as her ecstatic vocalizations became louder and more impassioned.

Peter felt conflicted. None of his partners—what few there had been—had ever enjoyed things this much, and he was rather pleased he was part of it. On the other hand, he was sure her father was going to end him in a minute or two.

As her body grasped him tightly, Penelope let out a cry of ecstasy that surely had dogs barking two blocks over. "Oh, Poseidon! I love you, sweetheart! So much." She sighed as she rested on top of him. Penelope soon rolled onto her back, carrying him with her. "Now it's your turn, darling. Give me everything ya got!"

There were times when a man's brain ignores everything going on around him and switches to autopilot. This was one of them. Peter was probably going to feel the spear from her father's gun in his back at any moment, but he just didn't give a damn. If he was able to protect Penelope at the end of it all, his life would be well spent.

The bedsprings began to squeak again, and Penelope soon joined in the chorus. It felt like a giant wave beginning to build, and when it finally broke, she released her own joyous cry at what they'd accomplished together.

Peter's muscles quickly turned to jelly, and he managed to whisper, "I love you and always will," as he gently slid off her and lay at her side gasping for breath.

Penelope kissed his nipple and laid her head on his chest. She was able to whisper, "I love you, too. So much. You were wonderful," before they both drifted off into blissful sleep.

Peter awoke at the first sign of light with Penelope's tail lying across his legs. He was pleased he'd been able to make her so happy, but that sense of satisfaction was short-lived. He was certain there would be hell to pay if he didn't do something, and quickly. He slid out from under her tail and began to devise a plan to escape before her parents woke.

If he could get the window open, he could crawl across the porch roof, lower himself via the downspout, and hit the ground running. He'd call Penelope from the motel out by the interstate and see about arrangements for getting her back to the city. He threw a few essentials into a bag and started to pull his clothes on.

Penelope awoke to find her tail had appeared sometime during the night. Peter had been so wonderful when this happened a week ago that she felt pleased rather than embarrassed. Her mate could do this to her. How wonderful was that? She felt quite sexy and wondered about possibilities in the bedroom when he had a tail as well.

Then, she noticed Peter struggling to pull his pants on from a standing position. "Honey, what are you doing, and where are you going?"

"Shhhhh. I have to get out of here. There's absolutely no way your parents didn't hear us last night, and your dad is going to kill me!"

"You're right about the first part. They were listening to

us from the bottom of the stairs."

"Ohhhhh. I'm dead. I'm really dead!"

"No, you're not, honey. Take your clothes off and come back to bed."

Peter looked at Penelope, weighing the outcomes of doing as she asked or running like a scared rabbit.

She patted the bed. "Please, dearest, come sit with me."

He finally relented, removed the clothes he'd struggled so hard to pull on, and sat next to her. Penelope leaned forward and curled her tail behind her so she could brush his back with her fin. The contact seemed to make at least some of Peter's anxiety melt away. She rested her left hand on his leg, which she hoped would become part of a tail soon.

"Dearest, there are some things I've been meaning to tell you but just have not had the time. I wanted to do it yesterday evening, but people kept calling the house.

"For one thing, sex is important to merfolk...I mean really important. We don't seem to have the hang-ups that you...I mean that humans do. Peter, the sea is a very large and lonely place. Mating is how we connect. We cherish our time with our mates or partners, and we value how mating helps us express the emotional bond we have. There is an unwritten law that no one—not *anyone*—comes between a mermaid and her mate. When you and I chose each other, my decision was final. You were my first, and you will be my last. No one can change that.

"The thing is, it's the custom here on our island for parents to listen the first time or two their children mate under their roof. All parents want nothing more than for their children to find a mate and be happy. The belief is, if there is anything wrong between them it will come out during mating. So, we—their children—make sure they know how happy we are and how happy our mate makes us."

Peter looked at her for a moment. "So then, last night was all an act?"

Penelope gave him a wry smile. "When I was around seventeen or eighteen and choosing a mate became an approaching possibility, my girlfriends and I would sit around and talk about how we'd fake it. You know, put on a good enough show that our mothers and fathers would be satisfied that we built a strong and lasting bond with the mate we'd picked."

Peter frowned at this.

"The funny thing is, when you're suddenly there—your first night with your mate under your parents' roof—you have no desire to fake it. It all comes so naturally, you just let yourself go."

Penelope squeezed his leg. "Honey, I was *not* faking it last night. We've only mated four times, and each of the first three was special in its own way. But last night...*damn*, that was amazing!"

"I agree. Very amazing," Peter whispered. He wrapped his arms around her waist and kissed her. "But I have to be honest, sweetheart. Knowing they were listening is still very strange for me. Making love should be about just you and me...no one else. Coming from a human perspective, I guess don't quite get why they feel the need to eavesdrop."

"Well, it's not meant to be intrusive. My mother would be embarrassed beyond belief if she walked in on us. It's just that merfolk are very open about mating. We communicate about it differently than humans do—if they communicate at all. If I said, 'Mom, Peter and I are going upstairs to mate,' we would not be inviting them to listen. Saying that would simply tell her that we're going to have some intimate time together, and we don't wish to be disturbed. Her reaction would be joy in knowing we love each other and are very happy together," Penelope explained.

Peter gave her a small smile of relief. He still felt as if he'd fallen down the rabbit hole, but at least some things were starting to make sense. "Okay, I think I understand. Hearing us make love is about them knowing we're a good match, not about the actual act of listening."

"Exactly. You know, when I was nine or ten years old, I began to understand what the sounds coming from my parents' room were, and it made me happy because it meant I had two parents who loved each other. I knew I was safe in a home they made together for the three of us. I would go to sleep and dream of the time when I would have a mate of my own and know the joy and love my parents shared. Dearest, that time is now, and that mate is you, and I am so very happy and in love. Mom and Dad certainly know that now, and I wouldn't trade this island tradition for all the fish in the sea. If anything, they are thrilled and relieved because their daughter has found what she had always hoped for.

"Yesterday afternoon, and especially last night, you and I restored the joy and happiness in their lives that they had lost because of my sadness. We reassured them that their love was being carried forward to this new beginning you and I share. But, even if they had disliked you for some reason, there's nothing they could have done about it anyway. A joining ceremony celebrates a preexisting event. The moment we agreed to be each other's mates, we became a 'married couple' as far as everyone here is concerned."

Peter looked thoughtful. "So, we're already married?"

"That's correct—at least here on Colony Island we are. Of course, if that bothers you, we can call it off..."

"No, no!" Peter exclaimed. "I find the thought that we're married already to be comforting." He squeezed her hand and kissed her. "I guess this means that a wedding isn't necessary now," he teased.

Penelope grinned. "Oh, no, you don't! You're not getting out of this one." She held up her left hand. "See this ring? It says I'm your fiancée, and we're going to have a wedding. Besides, my mother would be devastated if we didn't."

Peter held his hands up in mock surrender and cried, "Okay, okay. You win! We'll have our wedding."

As he leaned in for a kiss, there was a knock at the bedroom door, and her father's voice called out, "Hello? Anybody home?"

Peter flipped part of the sheet over his lap as Penelope bade her father come in. The door swung open, and there were Ilene and George in what appeared to be ancient bathrobes, each bearing a breakfast tray.

Her father noted, "Well, I see someone's happy."

Penelope took Peter's hand and blushed. "Yes, Father, I am very, very happy." She smiled at her mate.

Ilene came around to Peter's side of the bed, and as she placed the tray over his lap, told him, "Here you are, dear. Penny mentioned this is what you might like for breakfast." Ilene gave him a motherly peck on the forehead and sat down next to him on the edge of the bed.

George did likewise with Penelope and once he had settled himself, cleared his throat.

"Well, Princess, I've been thinking it has been ages since we all took a family swim together. Do you feel up for one today?"

Penelope's face lit up like the sun as she bounced on the bed and accidentally slapped Peter's back with her tail fin, almost spilling her tea in the process.

"Sorry, Peter! Dad, that would be wonderful. I've really missed those swims, especially over the past few months."

Ilene cleared her throat. "Penny, aren't you forgetting someone?" She nodded in Peter's direction.

Penelope gasped and put her hand over her mouth and slapped Peter with her fin a few times. "Oh, sweetheart. Sorry again! And I didn't mean to overlook you. I really didn't."

Penelope moved to take her tail out of range when Peter stopped her. "Pen, as long as it's your fin doing the slapping, I'm happy with it. As for the swim, all of you go ahead, and I'll handle the logistics."

"Logistics?" her father asked with a bemused look on his face.

"Oh, yes, Daddy. He's wonderful with logistics. Tell him, honey."

As Penelope beamed with pride, Peter explained. "Well, sir, once I met your daughter, I became concerned for her security and safety when she went to the beach to go swimming each weekend. Long story short, we worked out a plan where I would drive her to a drop off point early each morning and make sure she got in the water without anyone noticing. Once Penelope was underway, I would order whatever she wanted for lunch and meet her at a pre-determined rendezvous point with her meal and anything else she might need.

"In the late afternoon or evening, I'd meet her at a third spot, and once I determined the coast was clear, she'd come out of the water, and we'd drive back to wherever she was staying. I'd be happy to do this for all of you today and in the future."

George Tench rubbed his chin and said, "That might just work. We won't need the kind of security you provided your mate, but it would be nice not having to worry about things as much. You two enjoy your breakfast together, and I'll go pull out some maps. Are you coming, Mother?"

After they closed the door, Penelope gave Peter a brief kiss, and lifting her tray, brought her tail back to the front and swapped it for a pair of legs.

"Awww. I like your tail."

Penelope gave him one of those *you've got so much to learn* kind of smiles. "I need to shift back now, or I won't have the energy to put my tail on when we get to the drop off point. We can only do so many legs to tail to legs cycles a day before we're exhausted. Like I said a week ago, shifting takes a lot of energy, and for Mom and Dad's sake, I want to be refreshed and ready to go when it's time to hit the water."

Peter nodded and then dove into his breakfast. Penelope seemed to enjoy her sausage and eggs, and the two of them sat there, sans clothing, making small talk between mouthfuls. Both Penelope and Peter had very quickly become accustomed to being nude in front of the other. Peter had always thought modesty was a bit overrated and more than a little unnecessary on the beach or by the pool. For Penelope, it was her natural state, and she'd always thought humans were silly about the whole clothes thing.

"You think your mother's going to turn into a Momzilla? She was pretty hyper over those books last night."

"What's a Momzilla?"

"It's a play on the word Bridezilla, which is a play on the word Godzilla, which is—"

"Okay. I get the picture. We watch *a lot* of old movies on cable around here. Now what exactly is a Bridezilla?

"Well, a bride usually wants everything to be absolutely perfect on her special day, and—"

"*Their* special day, love," Penelope said before giving Peter a peck on his cheek.

"Okay, *their* special day—and she morphs into a monstrous control freak. Everything has to be just how she wants it, and everything has to be done *her* way. Her poor bridesmaids discover they have no life because they're spending all their time catering to the whims and desires of the bride, and any disagreement usually causes them to get kicked out of the wedding—at least temporarily.

"The Bridezilla makes everyone's lives miserable, and they wish she and her fiancé would elope and leave them alone. In the case of a Momzilla, it's the mother of the bride who does this. The idea of a Bridezilla and a Momzilla conspiring together is too terrible to even think about!"

Penelope shuddered at the thought of turning into a Bridezilla, or in the case of her mother, a Momzilla. "I don't think that's the case here. She's just excited that her daughter is the bride in the first wedding ever to take place on the island ever and wants everything to be done right. I'll tell Dad to keep an eye on her, just in case."

"I hope you're right. This is the only time I plan to get married, and I hope *our* day is a happy one."

Penelope's mother called up the steps for her to come down and have a look at the maps for the day's swim.

"See you downstairs, sweetheart," she said after giving him a quick kiss.

When she scooted off in the direction of the stairs, Peter decided it was probably time for him to get up too.

He had just finished pulling on his pants when Penelope's mother again called up the steps for him to come down and have a look at the tentative route. Peter shoved his feet into his loafers and trotted down to the kitchen.

He walked through the kitchen door and saw them clustered around the table in the breakfast nook. He should have been tipped off by the bathrobes hanging on pegs, but it was too late. Penelope, her father, and her mother were studying a coastal map…stark naked.

Peter swallowed hard and was about to make a hasty retreat when Ilene looked up. "Come over here, dear, and tell us what you think of this route."

Peter tried to appear as casual as possible as he walked over to the table keeping his eyes firmly fixed on the map. George was no problem for him. If you've seen one guy naked, you've seen them all, and years of showering after gym class, had more than taken care of that hurdle.

The problem here was definitely Penelope and her mother. Below the neck, they were almost identical, and he mused that mermaids must keep their figures longer than human females. Peter didn't want to stare at Ilene, and if he looked at Penelope, his body was going to call for a repeat of last night's exertions.

The map was his only sanctuary, and he hoped he could get all of this over with quickly. Otherwise, he was going to develop a very stiff neck. Fortunately, George spoke first, so it was "safe" to look at him.

"Son, years ago, we—I mean the town—bought up all the land between the north end of the island and the humans' beach resort as a buffer. It was mostly marsh and swamp land, though there was enough solid high ground to support a few roads, and we turned it into a wildlife preserve. It's off the beaten path, so humans don't go there much, and if they do, it's because they're lost. On the whole, there's not much of a beach, but there are a few narrow inlets that open directly to the sea. I thought you could drop us off there.

"We'll take a leisurely swim down to the south end of the island where you can meet us for lunch. The sign over the entrance says 'Colony Beach Club,' though most folks refer to it as the private beach. To get in, you'll need a key card."

George absentmindedly put his hands where his pants pockets should have been and realized he wasn't wearing anything.

"Oops! I'll get the card for you in a bit. Anyway, I thought that rather than running the risk of a pickup point further south where we might be seen or you might get lost, we'd swim south for a few miles and then circle around and return to the private beach around five o'clock or there-about. How does that sound to you?"

Peter continued to avoid looking at Penelope and her mother and answered, "That seems fairly simple to me. All I have to do to get to the private beach is to head south here on Main Street. I would, however like to find some more safe pickup points in the near future."

"Excellent!" George said with a smile. "I'm one of the few people here in town with a key to the wildlife sanctuary's gate, so we can drive in to the drop off point. Let me get that and the key card."

While George stepped away, Peter returned to intently studying the map. If he looked at Ilene, he'd be rude. If he didn't look at Ilene, he'd also be rude. It was definitely a no-win situation. Penelope sensed Peter's unease and explained where the house was in relation to everything else until her father returned with the keys and a note pad.

"Here you go, son. If you don't mind, we'll give you our lunch orders now, and you can take them to Hazel at the deli on Main Street. You'll see it on the left as we drive to the wildlife sanctuary."

Peter diligently took the lunch orders and wrote down exactly how they liked their sandwiches. After that, Penelope decided to provide Peter with an easy escape.

"Sweetheart, you should probably go put on your swim shorts and take some towels out of the linen closet. When you're dealing with mermaids, you're bound to get wet sooner or later."

Peter agreed and scurried upstairs.

Ilene whispered to Penelope, "What was wrong with Peter? Why wouldn't he look at us?"

"Mom, he did that to me the first time we shared a motel room. It's because we're...well, naked."

"Humans sure are funny about things."

"Mom, I know, but he'll adjust. Don't worry. He was just trying to be a gentleman, and I really like that."

Peter was upstairs, rolling a T-shirt, shorts, and underwear into a towel just as he used to do as a kid on his way to the lake for a swim. He located his flip-flops and was about to slide them on when Penelope tapped on the doorframe. Peter looked up to see this beautiful creature—his wife, according to Colony Island standards—standing there, wonderfully bare. Skin or scales, he loved her either way. He was about to lose himself in the soft curve of her breasts and the angles of her hips when he realized she was speaking.

"Peter, I'm so sorry. Mom's sorry, and even Dad's a bit embarrassed."

"Pen, what is there to be sorry about? You and your family were doing what is perfectly natural for you. I'm the stranger in a strange land, and I'm really sorry I upset everyone. I was caught off guard. Don't change anything you normally do just for me. I'm a visitor in your home, and I need to adjust to this environment."

"Peter, it's your home now, too. You're my mate."

Peter smiled at that thought. Here he was, someone of a different species, being welcomed into her parents' house and home, simply because their daughter had chosen him as her mate. His mother-in-law—that concept would take a bit of getting used to—was a bit over the top, but he could see a lot of her in Penelope. He still wasn't sure about her father yet and didn't want to get too chummy at this point, but still, he'd been very friendly this morning, and Peter began to feel some guilt over how he'd reacted. They probably took his actions as a sort of rejection, which it wasn't. He had experienced enough rejection from the parents of his various girlfriends. He knew that sting all too well, and he was not about to return the favor here.

"Sweetheart, please tell your parents it's all my fault,

and they did nothing wrong. Nothing at all. When you encounter two beautiful women like that, well, it's hard to keep your cool."

Penelope blushed at the last part and paused for a moment before saying, "I have...I mean, I will. Peter, my Mom likes you, and even my Dad has taken to you, so please don't worry. I'll try and give you some advance notice from here on out, but still, there will be occasions like this morning."

Peter smiled at her. What was it about this girl that had him so enraptured? He didn't know, and frankly, he didn't care. What he did know was that he would do anything to protect her and take care of her. "Well, can I have a hug from my mate?"

"Of course you can. You always can. But I do need to get some clothes on."

"I hope that's not because of me." Peter would have been happy to look at her naked all day long.

"Absolutely not. If we were driving down to the private beach at the end of the island, the bathrobes would be enough. But, because we're going off the island—even if it's for a short amount of time—it's best to act like humans and dress conventionally." She paused. "I don't mean it the way it must sound to you. Anyway, give me five minutes, and I should be ready to go."

CHAPTER FOURTEEN

George had insisted Peter drive so he could get a feel for the Hummer before he had to drive it back to town, solo. This only served to increase Peter's anxiety about messing up, but by the time he turned onto Main Street, he was feeling fairly confident.

"Peter, there's the deli on the left," George pointed out. "Everything here in town is within easy walking distance, so the best thing for you to do is to park here when you drop off the order, walk to wherever you want to, and then come back for the vehicle when it's time to pick up the food."

"And that lowers my chances of hurting your baby," said Peter, patting the dashboard.

"Son, we understand each other completely."

Northbound traffic was moving slowly up Main Street toward the harbor bridge, and Peter speculated this was the closest thing to a traffic jam that Colony Island ever saw. At the head of the backup was—to use a kind word—a vintage Ford apparently being nursed up the street to the garage and filling station. The conga line came to a halt when the Ford got halfway across the bridge and promptly died.

Everyone was watching the efforts to resuscitate the ailing car when Peter was startled by a tapping on the driver's side window. He lowered it to face the friendly grin of Carl, the Pizza Guy.

"Dude! Mr. T., Mrs. T. Congratulations, Anne!"

"Thank you, Carl. That's sweet of you," replied Penelope. She looked at Peter's face in the rearview mirror. "Folks around here refer to Carl as the honorary mayor of Colony Island. He knows almost everyone, and sooner or later, goes to just about everyone's house to make a delivery."

"And the real mayor even pays me money for managing the two locations. It doesn't get any better than that!" Carl related. Tapping Peter on the shoulder, he continued, "Man, I'm off Monday afternoon. Wanna grab a beer at the tavern?"

It was impossible to ignore Carl's good-natured attitude. "It depends if Pen and her parents will let me off the leash."

Ilene spoke up. "Carl, I think that's a lovely idea. Penny and I need a few hours to start planning her wedding, so that would be perfect."

"All right, Mrs. T. Noon or so okay with everyone?"

"That'll be fine, Carl."

"Okay, dude. See you then."

The decrepit car had finally been pushed across the bridge and into a turnout. As the backup began to disperse, George told Peter, "Carl Fisher's a good man. It's a shame about him and his parents."

Peter raised an eyebrow.

"He's the third child of Abe and Rebecca. The South End shop had been very short handed, and Carl was pulling double shifts every day for weeks. He was staying at a friend's for the duration, because it was much closer than his house. When they finally got some new help on board, Carl went home only to find his parents had 'retired,' closed up the house, and gone to sea for a year or two. They left him a short note, but that was it."

"They just disappeared on him?"

Ilene sensed Peter's distress. "Peter, dear, that's the way merfolk used to be up until about a hundred and twenty years ago. People would just pick up and go to sea for six months, a year, or permanently. They'd simply walk out, even leave the house unlocked, and go. There are still some folks around here that are like that, and it's why the town now owns most of the real estate and rents it out to residents. It was easier to deal with things that way than to wait however many years for the owners to come back. You don't have to worry, though. George and I aren't like that at all. We may eventually retire to the Bahamas, but that's fifty or sixty years away, if not more."

Peter was starting to get the picture that merfolk lived a lot longer than humans and wondered if it would apply to him once he became a merman.

They'd crossed both bridges and were westbound in the

direction of the interstate. George directed him to turn right on the same gravel road Peter had noted the previous day, and he eased the Hummer along to avoid potholes. The road seemed to end at a parking area near the trees up ahead, but George motioned Peter onward. They picked their way through the trees, along an increasingly bumpy stretch, until they reached a red livestock gate blocking the road. The sign on it read, "Colony Island Wildlife Refuge. No Trespassing."

George got out and walked forward to unlock the gate. The land on either side of the road became more swamp-like, and when they reached a crossroad—more like cross trail—George bade him to continue straight ahead.

Surprisingly, the roadway improved and appeared to be well maintained. They were soon driving next to one of the narrow inlets that Mr. Tench had mentioned earlier, and Peter was directed to pull into a turnout on the right. Once he'd cut the engine, George handed him the gate key with the admonition not to lose it.

"Here's where we hit the water. Give us a few minutes and we'll be ready to go."

Peter got out of the Hummer and promptly began scanning the surrounding trees, as well as the road.

"Put a bug in his ear, give him some dark glasses, and he'll look like the perfect Secret Service Agent," George chuckled.

"Daddy, that's what he did every time I was about to go in the water. It got so I didn't feel safe until he'd checked things out first."

"Hmmm. I'm starting to like your mate more and more."

After completing his second scan of the surroundings, Peter opened the driver's side door.

"The path down to the water is a bit rough. If you brought shoes, you can wear them down to the water's edge. I'll collect everything once you're underway."

"That's very sweet of you, Peter. Penny, dear, hand me my flip-flops, please."

See, Mom? He means well, Penelope communicated to her mother telepathically.

I never doubted that, dear. It's just going to take a bit of time to adjust to having a human around.

That's fine, Mom, but I really believe we need to start teaching him to be one of us. After all...

I believe you're right, dear. In fact, I know you're right.

Peter did one last scan then gave the signal it was okay for the family to leave the Hummer. He opened both doors and helped a very appreciative and very naked Ilene make her exit. She quickly followed her mate down the path to the water. Penelope took her time getting out and stayed with Peter while he shut and locked the doors. When they finally reached the waterside, George and Ilene were already swimming down the inlet and out toward the open sea.

"I don't want to go for a swim. I'd rather stay with you."

"Sweetheart, I thought you were looking forward to this," Peter countered.

"I was, but things have changed since the last time I went in the water. You're my mate now, and I don't want to go without you."

"Pen, if it's any consolation, I don't want you to go either, but…"

George's voice could suddenly be heard from the mouth of the inlet. "Penelope, are you coming or not?"

As George slipped back beneath the surface, he was faced with a very irritated Ilene. *George, you should be ashamed of yourself!* she scolded with her thoughts. *Isn't it obvious? She doesn't want to leave her mate.*

I know, Mother, but it's been so long since I've had the opportunity to pull her tail, I couldn't resist.

Poor thing. We need to get going on Peter's transformation first thing Monday.

Yes, Mother. I think we should.

"You better get in the water before your dad accuses me of keeping you here."

"Oh, don't worry, sweetheart. He's just winding me up. I should get going, though. Wait here while I put my tail on."

Penelope dove in, and Peter threw off his shirt before wading in after her. He was waist deep when Penelope surfaced in front of him.

"Sorry to get you wet, but somehow, I feel better about kissing you goodbye like this."

Penelope gave Peter an extended, passionate kiss, hugged him, and disappeared beneath the surface.

"Goodbye, my dear," Peter whispered. "See you at lunch."

Her head broke the surface, and with an achingly sweet smile, she called, "Goodbye to you too, sweetheart. Don't be late for lunch!"

The water was too shallow at this point for her to properly dive, but she did flash her caudal fin at him before swimming to catch up with her parents.

After drying off and changing, Peter wrung out his swim shorts and stowed them for use at lunch. Turning the Hummer around, he retraced his route to the gate and secured it. After checking that everything was okay with George's beloved Hummer, Peter relaxed and headed toward the main road.

As he drove, he repeatedly told himself, "This is just another Saturday. This is just another Saturday."

While he was pretty sure George and Ilene had no hidden agenda, too many fantasy novels had the princess, mermaid, whoever, being carried off by an irate father to whatever enchanted place there might be, never to be seen by her human lover again. The fact that one of her father's nicknames for Penelope was "Princess" did not help matters at all.

Peter parked in town and walked toward the deli, and from the sidewalk, he saw a patch of ocean. With a sigh, he said, "They're out there somewhere."

Ilene and George swam beside each other, hand in hand, the way Penelope hoped she and Peter would soon. She was directly behind her parents and a little above, so she could stay out of their fin-wash as they moved through the water.

From this vantage point, she could easily compare their tails and fins. While she and her mother were almost clones of each other above the waist, below it, the color of her own scales more resembled her father's medium green with yellow edges, though there was enough of her mother's silver green to make an interesting and attractive mix. Her fin was more like her mother's in its shape, though again, she did have a mix of her father's lighter green and her mother's reddish silver coloration there. Penelope had always felt her tail was her best asset, though she tried to avoid being vain about it.

Penelope remembered the books of mermaid stories the ladies from the library sent her when she was a young girl. The stories had bits of adventure and fantasy, and on the whole, she'd enjoyed them, except when it came to how the authors had described the mermaids.

For one thing, she had never ever seen a single mermaid

swim around in a dress or a bikini top. But it was the way the authors described the tails that was so ridiculous. In the real world, there were no Technicolor tails or extravagant fins resembling tropical fish. As for their shape, some illustrations showed mermaids with long, curling tails, while others tapered down to the point where the end was little more than a fin on a scaly green stick. Nether idea would get a mermaid anywhere very fast, if indeed those tails were useful at all.

Real mer tails and fins were of ample length, size, and flexibility to efficiently get them from place to place beneath the surface, and that was it. A periwinkle tail! Really?

Finally, there was the matter of where a mer torso ended and the tail began. In some of those silly illustrations, the mermaids looked like a girl cut in half at the waist with a fish's tail stitched on. Other pictures had scales that reached high enough to cover their breasts. Stupid humans! How was a mermaid supposed to nurse her young? The reality was, mer scales began just below the hips and blended with the skin, where there was a narrow band of color just before it actually turned to scale.

Penelope began dreaming of what Peter's tail would look like. Tail color and shape was sort of like hair and eyes, hands and feet. To be sure, there were variations, but only within a limited range, and one could usually see from which parent or ancestor they had inherited certain traits.

What happened in the case of a human who became one of them, since there were no merparents to inherit things from? She tried to remember how Gail's tail had looked, but she had not paid attention to that sort of thing, since she was in the third grade. It was a tail, after all, not a party dress.

Perhaps Peter's would be ginger. There was a population down in the Caribbean that had orange tails with a reddish tint to them. He would look so handsome with a tail like that. On the other hand, those merfolk kept to the old ways—mermen with multiple mates—and though all parties involved seemed quite happy with the arrangement, Penelope wanted Peter all to herself. She wasn't sure if the tendency to have more than one mate came from having a ginger tail, but she was not going to take any chances by hoping for one. She would find out what his tail would look like soon enough.

Ilene disrupted her daughter's reverie. *Penny, we're going to take a break from swimming here while your father has a look around the area,* she communicated.

Sure, Mom. It's been years since I've tried swimming in formation, so I don't mind the rest stop at all.

Ilene had engineered this pause so she could have a mother-daughter chat with Penelope. The two of them settled on the bottom, sitting back to back, with their tails curled around them so their fins lay across each other's lap. It was one of those touching gestures they had done since Penelope was thirteen or fourteen. They were able to use each other's backs for support and keep an eye out for predators. Penelope wondered if she and Peter would sit this way. The thought left her with a warm glow.

Tell me, Penny, how did you and Peter meet?

Penelope groaned inwardly. She knew this would come up sooner or later, and she'd really been hoping it would be later…much later. She had little choice but to grit her teeth and get it over with.

Well, Mom, one Sunday afternoon back in April, I was taking a nap under a dock, when…

After she'd recounted how they'd met and what happened in the following days, Penelope was astounded when her mother didn't seem upset at all.

Penny, I'm a firm believer that you will know your mate when you first see him—even if you aren't looking for a mate at the time. It just happens. That's the way it was with your father, and your risking everything on Peter has been amply rewarded. Well done, dear.

Thanks, Mom. I'm so happy you feel that way! I was worried you'd be mad about how I handled things. But something has been on my mind since yesterday. How come you accepted Peter so easily?

Penny, of course you know, I have no say whatever in whom you choose, but the most important part is that I trust you to make the right decision for all involved. You're not a little mermaid anymore. I could tell he'd made you so very happy, and when you said Peter wanted to become one of us, how could I not accept him? There's been a rough spot or two, but I have to remember that he's human…or will be for a little while longer.

Hazel's Main Street Deli was a typical sandwich shop. Peter walked in and stood in line until it was his turn to order. Hazel was a pleasant, older woman—Peter was totally lost at sea when it came to estimating the age of mermaids—and she took a moment to read the order Peter had given her.

"This looks like what Ilene and her family order for takeout. You're him. You're Penelope's mate!"

Peter mused that news traveled extremely fast in small towns like this, but Colony Island must have an amazing bush telegraph. He'd been here about eighteen hours, and it seemed like the entire population knew that Pen had chosen him as her mate and he'd asked to join them.

"When are you two going to have your wedding?

"Well, ma'am, we haven't set a date yet. I hope we'll have an idea sometime on Monday."

"Oooh, I can't wait! Now, what are *you* going to have, hon?"

Peter ordered an Italian sub along with four iced teas and mentioned he was planning to rendezvous with the Tenches at 1:30 p.m., so he hoped for the order to be ready by 1:00 p.m. at the latest.

"No problem, hon. *Your* sub, by the way, is on the house."

Peter thanked Hazel and headed back out to Main Street. There was nothing to do for over two hours, so he decided to take a look around downtown.

Walking south, Peter looked in the various shops along the way. There was a grocery store, a hardware store, a clothing store that also carried shoes, a storefront with lawn and garden equipment, as well as seeds and such, and a place that sold appliances—everything he would have expected in a town this size. Peter stopped just past the fire station to look at the Greek Revival building he had noticed yesterday afternoon. Just below the pediment were the words, "The Temple of Poseidon." Was this their church?

He continued past the tavern where he was to have a beer with Carl on Monday and the restaurant that appeared to be a breakfast and lunch sort of place. Further on, across the street from Colony Burgers and Dogs, was a large wooden building—vintage, of course—that took up most of the block and seemed to have had a series of storefronts in a previous life. It had been opened up into one large space with a smaller unoccupied space or two on the corner. Painted on the front window was "Edna's Home and Bath," and on the other side of the glass was a display of furnishings.

The next window down displayed a variety of things for

the bathroom, including an extra-long bathtub. There were bath mats and towels, the fittings necessary to turn one's bathroom into an oasis, and two mannequins dressed in terrycloth robes. An idea quickly formed in Peter's mind, and he went into the store to act upon it.

The girl that came forward to greet him looked to be about Penelope's age and had sandy red hair, freckles, and a shy smile. As Peter glanced around the store, he could feel the girl's eyes on him, so he turned his head, and she suddenly blushed. That same shy smile showed through the fluster.

Peter inquired about the bathrobes and the girl told him—with a renewed blush—they had just started carrying them, and the ones in the window were all they had up front at the moment, but she would check with the manager.

"Good morning, sir. May I help you?" were the first words out of Edna's mouth as she came out onto the sales floor with the ginger-haired girl in tow. The next words were, "You're Penelope's mate. Peter…MacPherson, isn't it?"

Peter slowly nodded his head and smiled as Edna continued, "Well, congratulations to the both of you. I hope Penelope will consider registering here. I could use the business, and frankly, I've never done a bridal registry before. Now, I understand you were interested in the bathrobes."

Peter noticed the shop girl had turned bright red and fled the sales floor in obvious distress, but he went ahead and answered, "Yes. I noticed their robes and towels were…threadbare, and I thought I'd surprise them with new ones. By the way, is everything all right with your assistant?"

Edna looked toward the door to her office. "Well, Amy is quite shy, and I have the impression she thought you were not chosen. I'm sure you've heard about no one coming between a mermaid and her mate. Anyway, I think you have a lovely idea. I'll get some sets from the back."

Amy didn't show her face again, and Edna soon returned with a stack of robes and towels.

"Here you are. I picked the extra-large towels and found robe sizes that will fit George and the ladies. There's also a set in there for you, at no extra charge. Think of it as an early wedding gift. Will there be anything else?"

First a free sub and now a free bathrobe and towel? The generosity of the merfolk was beginning to overwhelm him. "Well, this is a long shot—but do you know a place around here where I can get these robes embroidered with their names?"

"I think I just may be able to help you with that," Edna said as she reached for the phone.

"Hello, Mildred, how are you? You'll never guess who I have in my store at this very moment. No, I've got Penelope's mate here. No, I'm not kidding. He's bought some towels and bathrobes for the family, and he'd like to have their names embroidered. I'm guessing by late this afternoon. Wonderful! I'll send him right over. Give my love to Gordon. Bye!"

Hanging up the phone, Edna said, "That was my best friend, Mildred. We were in high school together back in the day. She has her own embroidery business, and while most of her clients are from the mainland, occasionally I'm able to send business her way."

Edna gave Peter directions while she rang up the sale. As he left the store with his purchases, he noticed Amy peeking out from behind the counter. Peter gave her a friendly wave, and her face turned scarlet again.

Mildred's house was up one of the residential streets on the right, and Peter walked up it, counting the requisite number of houses. He needn't have bothered. There was only one house with a glassed-in front porch, and Mildred was standing on the front steps waiting for him.

"You must be Peter. I'm so glad to meet you. Please come in so we can have a look."

Inside the porch were a variety of machines to do all kinds of embroidery work, as well as a laptop, a PC, and a stack of boxes with "Polo Shirts" hand written on the sides. Peter said he was thinking of a dark blue for the letters, and Mildred showed him what she had available.

"I had an idea while you were on your way over here. A few years ago, I bought some stock graphics, and they included a mermaid and merman. I thought they would look nice next to the names." The graphics were simple silhouettes with the merman wearing a crown and holding a trident.

"Those would be great. Edna gave me a complimentary bathrobe and towel, though I'm not sure the merman would be appropriate for me. I'm...just a human."

"Oh, I'm sure that won't last much longer. Let me see if I can find something else for you."

As Mildred flipped through her book of samples, Peter suddenly had an idea. After asking if he could use her laptop, he sat down and typed in a web address. When the page came up, he scrolled to find the graphic he was thinking of.

"Mildred, this is from my webpage—it's a vanity page, really. This is the crest from my dad's coat of arms, and it goes back—I think—to my great-great-grandfather. Could you put this on my robe?"

The centerpiece of the MacPherson coat of arms was a shield with waves topped by a canoe and a Scottish thistle. The actual crest rested upon a helmet atop the shield. It was a wildcat holding a crescent moon. Above the shield was a banner with the motto, "I WILL ENDEAVOUR SO TO DO."

"Well, that's pretty. Only a handful of colors and no tricky spots. I do this kind of thing all the time, and it won't take very long to set up."

Peter saved the graphic to a thumb drive and handed it to Mildred. "Great! Would you be able to put this on Penelope's as well? Either above or below her name? She's my...mate, and therefore entitled to wear it."

"That should not be a problem at all. I can have all of this done for you by four o'clock."

"Mildred, that would be perfect. I'm running logistics for them, and I need to pick up their lunches from the deli in about thirty minutes."

"Young man, what do you mean by logistics?"

Peter explained the whole idea. Mildred thought it was brilliant and wondered why no one had thought of it before. Peter offered to pay for the work right then and there, but Mildred refused to take a dime, saying it was a gift to the family and if enough residents saw the robes, she and Edna might be able to make some money off his idea.

Peter thanked her profusely and hurried back to the deli where his order was waiting for him. He carried the food and drinks to the Hummer and headed south on Main Street.

Penny, according to your father, we're ahead of schedule, so we'll wait here for a bit.

Penelope watched her father swim off to do a sweep of the area for predators.

Mom, there's one other thing you need to know. Peter had absolutely no idea about last night. Humans can be funny about their privacy when mating, and I didn't want to scare him off by telling him about it before we got into town.

Ilene was downcast. She had so wanted everything to go well from the moment she learned her daughter had a human as a mate. *That poor young man. Now I really feel badly about things. Everything seems to be going wrong between us, doesn't it? Penny, you go on up and meet Peter, and I'll talk with your father about this before we come to the surface.*

Peter arrived at the gate with ten minutes to spare. Much to his relief, the key card worked, and he drove down the narrow winding road that led to the private beach. After finding a good place to park, he changed into his bathing suit and carried lunch down to the waterside. He had just finished laying things out on a towel when Penelope surfaced.

"Hi, honey. Where are your parents?"

"I think they're…having some private time or something. They should be up in a few minutes," she called out. "Sweetheart, please do me a favor. Take off your swim shorts for me."

"Uhhh…sure. How come?"

"No time to explain—just do it right now."

Peter had just stripped his swim trunks off when George and Ilene surfaced. The couple swam ashore and hauled out, tails and all, onto the sand along with Penelope, who sat apart from her parents.

What had he gotten himself in to? The thought of being totally bare in front of Penelope's parents, especially her mother, was unnerving. On the other hand, Peter had always thought the idea of mythical creatures wearing clothes underwater was silly at best, and here were Penelope and her parents, people whose race was born in the sea and lived in the sea, dressed—or rather, not dressed—accordingly, doing what was common sense and natural. It was not they who had the problem. It was Peter.

Peter served Ilene, George, and then Penelope. Finally, he retrieved his Italian sub and sat down next to his mate.

"What's going on?" he whispered.

Penelope replied very softly, "Mom's just a bit upset. I told her you were in the dark about last night, and she feels like she's been messing up since she met you."

"Crap. It's not her fault at all," Peter whispered through gritted teeth. "As you can see, I'm trying to get in the spirit of things here. Last night was just a communications mix-up."

"Peter, she doesn't see it that way. But I just felt Mom relax when she saw you, so that's a good thing. Don't worry."

They spent the rest of the meal break whispering and sitting as close as possible to each other without things getting too out of hand. When it appeared that Penelope's parents were done with their meal, Peter went over to collect wrappers and empty cups.

"Peter, this was a great idea. Would you be willing to do this for our family swims in the future?" George asked.

Before Peter could reply, Ilene stepped in. "George, before too long, Peter will be accompanying us on these swims."

"Hmmm, so he will. Maybe we can find someone else to do this for us. It's a thought, anyway. Son, we're going to do an easy swim for the rest of the afternoon. We should be back at four thirty."

Yikes! That's going to cut things close.

"Sounds good," Peter and Penelope replied in unison.

George moved himself into the water, and Ilene followed. It didn't look too difficult, and they were afloat in less than a minute. Ilene turned and flashed Peter a warm smile before following George into deeper water.

Peter jogged over to Penelope and scooped her into his arms before she could protest. As he carried her out into the water, he told her, "It's all part of the service, ma'am. By the way, I'm going to need you out of the water first when you get back. I want you to help me with a little surprise."

Penelope appeared to be a bit mystified, but agreed nonetheless, and kissed him soundly before she slipped into the water. She waved at him as she swam out to where her parents waited, and then all three sounded, showing their caudal fins as they disappeared to dive deep under the surface. Peter watched the water for a moment and then waded back to shore where he quickly cleared up from lunch, changed into his shorts, and drove back into town.

He didn't want to show up too early at Mildred's, so he parked and strolled along the west side of Main Street. There weren't as many businesses along this side, but the buildings had a certain look and feel to them that much of the east side did not.

One of those buildings, in particular, fascinated him. It

almost looked like it might have been a small liquor store at one point or another in its history. There were large windows up front, though the sales area seemed to have been foreshortened. A long hallway ran the length of the building with the south side cut up into a number of offices. It was hard to tell what was on the north side of the hall, but there seemed to be only one or two doors at the most on that side, indicating at least one large, open space.

There was a wide parking area on either side of the building and ample room in the back. The fringe of the swamp that formed the western border of the island was a good distance away from this building, and there seemed to be a considerable amount of useable acreage available. Peter had no idea why this building was calling to him, but as he headed down the sidewalk, he decided to make some inquiries in the future.

Bordering the north end of the parking area was the Main Street Deli. On the south side was a building that looked like it was trying to be the offices of a general contractor, and on the other side, there were a bunch of rusty old bikes resting on their kickstands. They appeared to be still in use because the tires seemed to be properly inflated, and the chain and gears were oiled. Peter then realized he'd seen a lot of bicycles on the streets in the past twenty-four hours, all of them old and rusty, and he didn't know what to make of it. It seemed he had a lot to learn about everything around here, but it was now closer to 4:00 p.m. than it was to 3:00 p.m. He quickly walked up to the deli, ordered four small iced teas, and drove south to Mildred's.

Everything was waiting for him on the glassed-in porch, and after a quick inspection of the work, Peter again offered to pay her for her efforts. Mildred once more refused him, and there was nothing left to do but to thank her one more time and head to the private beach. He might just make it in time.

At the beach, Peter removed his clothes without thinking twice and arranged his gifts on the old towel he had used at lunch. He had no sooner done this than Penelope walked out of the water.

"Hey, Pen, how was the swim?"

"Terrific! I might do another swim tomorrow, if you don't mind."

Peter responded, "You'll owe me extra kisses if you do," and handed Penelope her towel.

She quickly realized it was much larger and softer than the

one she'd brought. It even had her name on it. After she'd dried herself off and protested he shouldn't have done something like this, he presented her with the new robe, and she began to protest all over again. Fortunately, he was able to silence her with a kiss.

"Sweetheart, this was my pleasure, and it's nothing, really. There's a set for your parents, and I'll take care of your mother's if you take care of your dad's."

Penelope was about to say it was much more than nothing when Ilene and George surfaced and started to wade toward shore. Peter greeted Ilene at the water's edge.

"Peter, what's all this? This really wasn't necessary."

"It was my pleasure. I saw what everyone had for towels and robes this morning, and I felt replacements were needed."

"Peter, we really don't deserve this, especially after last night and this morning. I'm so sorry about what happened. You must forgive us."

"Mrs. Tench…"

"Ilene, dear."

"Okay, Ilene, it all came down to a miscommunication, I promise I'm having a wonderful time here."

"Peter, you must find our ways to be very strange. We'll put these robes to good use around the house, dear."

"Ilene, please don't do that. You'd be changing what you and your family ordinarily do, just for me. I didn't come here to disrupt your lives. I happily volunteered for all this, and I'm the one who needs to change—in more ways than one. Just one thing, though. Would you and Pen please give me a bit of a warning concerning clothes in the future?"

"Of course, dear," Ilene assured him.

Everyone began comparing and admiring their new robes and towels as they followed Peter to the Hummer. Once they were seated, he distributed the ice tea and then pulled his own clothes on.

"Peter, this is absolute luxury. What do you think, George?"

"Mother, you're right as always. Princess, don't let this human go."

"I don't plan to, Dad," she said with a smile, though her eyes were fixed on her mate.

Feeling he had finally scored a small victory for team Peter, he started the engine and drove the family back home.

CHAPTER FIFTEEN

Dinner on Saturday evening was a pretty casual affair. The day in the water had left Ilene hungry for seafood, so she cooked a bit of fish and shrimp—and the leftover pizza from the previous evening was available for all.

Peter split his time between the shrimp and the pizza, and everyone enjoyed a relaxing meal. If anything, it helped to convince Peter that merfolk were pretty much like humans—well, up to a point. Peter had missed gathering around his family's dinner table, and it looked like meals would continue to play a significant role in his life with Penelope. As strange as it seemed, Peter felt as if he had finally regained some sort of normalcy.

He helped Penelope clear the table after the meal and volunteered to help wash the dishes, which meant they spent the time giggling and whispering at the sink. It took twice as long as it would have ordinarily, but no one seemed to be particularly concerned. As they were finishing up, Ilene walked into the kitchen wearing her new robe.

"I thought we could go relax in the Watermans' pool, Peter. Ever since that terrible road accident, Ed has spent less and less time here, and more time on the road. George looks after the house while he's away, and by way of thanks, we get to use his indoor pool. Feel free to stay here if you like."

"I'd be happy to join you, Ilene," Peter said, and then quickly scurried upstairs after Penelope.

As Penelope shed her clothes and put on her robe, she told Peter, "You really don't have to come if you don't want to."

"Ummm, are you saying I shouldn't tag along then?"

"Of course not, silly. Mom's just giving you the chance to

opt out. You've been through enough today, so there's no pressure to join us."

Peter removed his own clothes and wrapped himself in his robe. "Pen, I might be the fifth wheel, but I'm going to roll along with you anyway."

"Honey, you are so not a fifth wheel."

It was still light out as the four of them went through the back gate and crossed the Watermans' side yard to reach the door to the indoor pool. Once inside, Peter could see how huge it really was. The concrete deck surrounding the kidney-shaped pool sat about two feet above the lawn outside. There were several café-style tables along the house side of the pool with a couple of wrought-iron benches along the wall. The pool featured steps leading into the water, a circular conversation pit at the same end, and gently curved corners—perfect for merfolk swimming laps. Ilene saw him gaping at the pool and spoke up.

"Ed Waterman built this for Gail just after she moved here. She was still getting used to the idea of being a mermaid and didn't like swimming in the sea by herself when Ed was on the road. So, he made it a saltwater pool that's mostly a ten-foot deep end with a nice conversation pit. It also enabled him to have a swim immediately before going to the airport or after getting home."

Peter collected the robes and towels and hung them on a row of pegs along the outside wall. Ilene flashed him a smile of gratitude as the family dove in, transitioning to tails along the way. Peter could either stay where he was all evening or join them—at least for a little bit. He took off his robe and dove in.

Penelope began swimming toward the conversation pit so she could talk to Peter, but the moment she heard him enter the water, she turned and immediately swam back. He was holding his own underwater, though his breath wouldn't last very long. Penelope cupped his face in her hands, giving him such a look of love and adoration, that he could have drowned a happy man at that very moment. Then she locked her lips on his and emptied her lungs. That gave them another thirty seconds in the water before he had to go to the surface. She followed, and once they'd both filled their lungs, she pulled him under and began some serious underwater kissing. After about three sessions, Penelope took him by the hand and swam toward the conversation pit.

"Mom, could you and Dad give us about fifteen minutes alone?"

"Certainly, dear," Ilene said.

George grumped, *We certainly never asked for anything like that, did we, Mother?* and then escorted his wife down into the deep end of the pool.

The water was waist-deep in the conversation pit, and once Peter had his feet under him, Penelope let go and swam to the bench that encompassed the pit, about one foot below the surface. She turned, scooted up on the seat, and curled her tail around her to the right.

With an admiring glance and a touch of envy in his voice, Peter said, "I still think that is so cool."

"With any luck, you'll be doing this shortly," Penelope replied as she patted the bench directly in front of her fin.

Peter sat next to her on the bench, and as he put his arm around her waist, Penelope felt a shudder of joy run through her. While she was quite sure of his feelings for her, the little things he did—like resting his hand on the line where skin and scales intermingled—conveyed a sense of love, tenderness, and acceptance she could not help but revel in. In return, Penelope caressed him with her fin, and Peter's sense of mellowness and contentment was easily palpable.

"Peter, you're probably going to think this is some sort of silly mermaid thing, but…"

"Pen, why would I think anything you say is silly?"

Happy and relieved her words would receive a fair hearing, Penelope continued. "Some years ago, I read a bunch of romance novels trying to figure you guys…I mean humans…out. A number of things in the novels seemed so strange and almost alien to me—I guess because we're taught to be self-contained and independent—but now I realize they were so right. It came to me in the pool a few minutes ago. Peter…you complete me."

"Of course, you mean above the waist," he said with a wink.

Penelope shook her head. "No, 'me' is everything from the top of my head to the end of my fin. I can't separate one half from the other, and with you, I wouldn't want to. You complete me…all of me…and now I feel like 'I' is 'we,' and we can do anything together."

"Sweetheart, all I can say is, I don't know what I'd do without you, and I don't want to find out."

"Honey, you know I can't wait to become your wife, but this is one time I'm so glad I'm a mermaid, because you're my mate and I'm yours...right here, right now...and I don't have to wait at all for that. I love what you did today for me and for my parents and that you were able to put aside your fears and join me underwater, even just for a little while."

"Pen, I'm fine...okay, only slightly nervous...in a pool or a river. It's when you actually put me in the *ocean* that my fear really overtakes me."

"Well, dear, I have an idea as to how to help you get past this. I'm not going to tell you right now, because I don't want you to get worked up over it in advance, but do you trust me?"

"Absolutely."

"Peter, that's all I needed to hear, and please know, I'll be there for you."

Any hopes that either one had for some more kissing were dashed when her mother and father swam into the conversation pit and settled themselves on the opposite side. Ilene and George arranged their tails so their fins brushed against each other's back.

So that's the way we're going to look, Peter thought, smiling to himself. *I think I'm gonna like that.*

His thoughts were interrupted by Ilene.

"Peter, would you be a dear and go get my cell phone? If yesterday evening was any indication, there's no telling who's going to call me tonight."

Peter carefully stood on the bench—trying to avoid treading on Penelope's fin—and stepped out of the pool. He walked over and fished Ilene's phone from the pocket of her robe, and retrieved Penelope's as well. He placed both phones where they were safe, or as safe as they could be from the water, and still easily reachable.

As Peter returned to the bench, George spoke. "I heard from Ed Waterman the other day, and it looks like he won't be coming back to Colony Island. He met a widow—one of us, of course—on the Pacific coast, who's in a similar situation, and they have chosen each other as mates. It seems there's another colony out there in California—some place named Aptos, I think—and he's going to give up this house and permanently relocate."

Ilene was about to ask a question when her cell phone rang. She rolled her eyes and picked it up on the third ring. "Hazel. How are you? We haven't had a chat in months... Why, thank you... Yes, we're quite happy about it. He's one of the family now… I don't know. Why don't you ask him? …Peter, it's Hazel from the deli. She wants to talk with you."

Peter waded across the conversation pit and took the phone. "Hello?"

"Peter, this is Hazel from the deli. We spoke earlier today."

"Of course. What can I do for you?"

"Peter, I hope you'll keep me in mind as you get things started. I can offer you a good deal on sandwiches and such. We could even come up with an exclusive menu."

"Uhhh…right. Don't worry, I promise I won't forget you."

After Peter hung up, he handed the phone back to Ilene saying with a shrug, "Hazel evidently thinks I'm starting some kind of business." No sooner had he settled on the bench next to Penelope, than Ilene's phone rang again, and she motioned him across to speak with the caller.

"Peter, this is Mildred. How did everyone like their robes?"

"Oh, hi. They loved them, especially the graphics."

"Wonderful. I told Edna all about it, and she's so excited. She's got some ideas of her own, but I've got to run. Gordon's ready for his dessert."

Peter had no sooner hung up the cell phone, than it rang *again*, and he answered it without thinking.

"Peter? This is Edna. Mildred told me all about what you're doing, and I think it's wonderful. We've got some ideas for your business that we want to discuss with you. We'll pick you up at ten a.m. tomorrow."

After hanging up the phone and handing it back to Ilene, he scratched his head and said, "Apparently, I *am* starting some kind of business. Edna and Mildred want to talk about it tomorrow morning at ten."

George looked interested in this turn of events, while Ilene simply raised her eyebrows at the thought. Peter gave the phone back to her and waded over to Penelope, settling on the bench just as her cell phone rang.

"Amy. How are you? I wanted to call you, but I've been just sooo busy, as you can imagine."

Amy's voice came through the phone with an urgent tone into Penelope's ear. "Anne? I'm sorry. I'm sorry. I'm sorry. I didn't mean to—honest. I didn't mean to! I didn't know he was your mate. He's so hot! I couldn't help flirting with him. Please, please, please forgive me."

Penelope was rather amused by this. She was quite pleased

Amy was so taken by Peter and even more interested that Amy was actually crushing on and flirting with a guy. She was so shy, this was probably the only time she'd ever done this. Amazing! Penelope waited for Amy to stop and catch her breath.

"Amy, it's okay. I'm not upset. In fact, I'm happy you think he's so cute."

"Cute? He's smokin' hot, Anne! I'll share him with you…"

Penelope was starting to worry Peter might actually turn out to be a ginger, though if there was any other mermaid in the world she'd want to share a mate with, it would be Amy.

"Amy, we'll have to discuss that later," she said with a laugh.

"Anne, the moment I heard you were coming home, I called Lindsey and Cindy. Lindsey flew in this morning, and Cindy has tomorrow off. Can you come over to the house at ten thirty so you can tell us all about your hot human?"

After she hung up her phone, Penelope turned to Peter and said, "Well, it looks like we're both busy tomorrow morning. I've got to go and catch up on things with my bridesmaids."

The next morning, Penelope awoke, still in Peter's arms. The warmth of his chest felt so good against the skin of her back. The three full cycles of legs to fin changes from the previous day had left her too tired to mate, but she had insisted they sleep together, sans clothing. It felt so warm, so wonderful sleeping with him with intimacy just a touch away. She had adopted the T-shirt and panties combo at university so she'd fit in with the rest of the girls there, but this was the way she'd sleep now…at least when Peter shared her bed.

Penelope gently untangled herself from Peter's arms, trying not to wake him, and sat up in bed so she could watch her mate sleep. She wasn't sure what it was about him that had Amy so excited. Yes, he was good looking, but Peter was no pretty boy— thank Poseidon! He had no rippling muscles, but then, he hadn't worked on the fishing boats since the age of twelve like many of the younger mermen in town. Peter didn't have much in the way of abs, but six or seven months of swimming would take care of that. No, he was strong in a different way. The way she wanted and needed him to be. If Amy had any ideas she could share Peter, she was sadly mistaken.

Penelope carefully got out of bed and pulled the sheet over his body. They both had a busy day ahead of them, and she wanted to help her mother with breakfast.

Peter sat on the front porch next to Penelope as he polished off one last donut. Breakfast had been a quiet family affair, and he felt like maybe—just maybe—he was starting to fit in with his new in-laws. To be sure, more surprises awaited him, but for the moment, he was enjoying being comfortable in his surroundings. He did have a couple questions for Penelope though. "Is there anything I should say or not say? Anything I should watch out for?"

"Peter, you're among friends now. Just be the gentleman I know and love."

Peter was about to explain his propensity for unknowingly putting his foot in his mouth when Edna and Mildred pulled up in a Jeep—apparently a somewhat popular vehicle here on the island. He kissed his mate goodbye as the ladies clapped and whistled. He had no sooner climbed in to the rear seat next to a cooler, than Edna threw the Jeep into gear and stepped on it.

"Sorry about the whiplash, Peter," Edna apologized. "We've got a bit of grocery shopping to do on our way to the private beach."

Mildred turned in her seat to face Peter. "We're throwing a surprise cookout for your mate. Can you do hamburgers on a grill?"

"I've done it a time or two before."

"Good. We came up with this idea after we spoke to you last night. Edna called Amy, and she mentioned Penelope was coming over this morning, and we took it from there. The girls are going for a swim around noon, and Amy's going to lead them to the south end of the island where we'll be waiting."

Peter gamely nodded and pulled up a recipe for Italian hamburgers on his smartphone. The local police must have still been in bed, as the jeep was moving along at well over the speed limit, and for a quiet little town, seemed to be flying south on the main road. Edna pulled into the parking lot for the mom and pop grocery store he'd seen on Friday afternoon—a lifetime ago.

When they walked in to the store, Edna began conversing with the owner, Avery Johnson, Mildred went in search of his wife, Helen, and Peter got down to doing the actual shopping. Meat, cheese, spices, garnishes, and buns all went into his cart. There were other things like charcoal, paper plates, etc. to pick up, and he'd just collected the last items when Mildred introduced him to Helen.

"I'm so glad to meet you, Peter. You're a godsend."

Peter wasn't quite sure what that was about, so he decided to keep his ears open once they were back in the jeep. The answer was not long in coming.

As Edna pulled out on the road and headed south, Mildred turned to Peter. "Avery is just about the only other human on the island. Edna, how long have he and Helen been together?"

"At least thirty years," she replied. "She's begged him to join us, Poseidon knows how many times, and his standard answer is he doesn't have time for any 'fishy foolishness.'"

Mildred harrumphed. "I wish she'd tell him how insulting that phrase is. Has she decided what she's going to do? Avery's going to run out of time soon, and I know she won't want to choose another mate."

"Well, he's devoted to Helen—insists on carrying her in and out of the water when she goes swimming—and I know she adores Avery." Edna explained. "The last time we had a good talk, she said she was contemplating using the 'Nuclear Option'—whatever that is."

"Well, she'd better hurry and drop the bomb before it's too late," Mildred noted.

Penelope grabbed her robe and towel and headed for Amy's house, two streets over. It was one of the older homes on the island and predated the housing boom of the early 1900s. It had obviously belonged to a well-to-do family at some point, but for the past sixty years or more, it had belonged to Amy's—a family that was as close to being feral as could be.

Amy's grandmother had grown up at sea but settled on Colony Island to raise her daughter. Amy's father was feral but was a good provider, even though he was away from home for long periods.

Though she enjoyed being at sea for longer stretches than Penelope, Amy's roots were firmly planted on the island, and she could no more leave it for the ocean than she could move inland.

Just as Penelope climbed the steps on to the front porch, the screen door burst open, and out ran Amy with her arms open. "Oh, Anne! Welcome home. All of us were so worried about you.

We were afraid we'd never see you again."

It felt good to hug her very best friend again after all this time. "Well, that almost happened, but I'm better now. Much better and much happier than I was. I won't say I'm back to my old self, because the way I feel is such an improvement on how I was as a teenager. Where's everyone else?"

"I kinda fibbed on the time. Cindy and Lindsey will be here in fifteen minutes. Call me selfish, but I wanted a little time with you all to myself. Mom wants to see you as well, so I thought the two of you could chat in the kitchen until the girls get here. Then you can make your grand entrance."

For someone as shy as Amy, she did have a flair for things like this—something that must have rubbed off from Edna.

Penelope remained in the kitchen until Cindy and her cousin, Lindsey arrived, and everyone had a brief update on everyone else.

Finally, Lindsey asked, "Where's Anne? Did she bail on us?"

Penelope walked in through the dining room. "No, I'm right here, waiting to see my best friends."

There were hugs, kisses, and squeals of delight as each girl tried to show she had missed Penelope more than the others.

When at last they were all seated in the living room, Cindy piped up, "Okay, Anne. Let's hear about this human of yours."

"Well, first of all, you don't need to call me Anne anymore. I've finally come to accept my first name and even like it— especially the way Peter says it."

Her friends said, "Oooh!" in unison as Penelope proceeded to give the condensed version of how she and Peter met and fell in love.

"And then, a week ago Friday, I told him about it."

Lindsey was the one to ask, "How did he take it?"

"He was very cool about it. So cool, I thought he wasn't taking it seriously. But, he was, because he went down on one knee and gave me this." Penelope held out her left hand to show off her engagement ring, and there was a miniature stampede to ooh and ahh over it and declare it was the most romantic thing, ever.

Once they were back to sitting on the edge of their seats, Cindy asked, "Then what happened?"

"I said, 'Yes,' of course." That was all Penelope was going to tell. Only Amy would hear the full story when they had some private girl time together. "There's one other thing, I want you three to be my bridesmaids!"

There was dead silence, and Penelope wondered if she should have toned down her enthusiasm when she asked them.

The three mermaids exchanged glances at each other, and Lindsey asked hesitantly, "Uhhh, bridesmaids…like at a human wedding?"

"Yep," she said more casually. "Bouquets, gowns, and shoes dyed to match."

For a long moment, the three looked at one another, uncertain what to say, until Amy broke the spell by jumping up and down and squealing, "We're gonna be bridesmaids!"

That was the signal for the other two to do likewise, along with repeatedly hugging each other, and Penelope, too. Amy's mother walked in to see what all the commotion was about and was caught up in the general excitement.

After the little group of mermaids finally settled down, it was unanimously agreed that a swim was necessary to cool things off. Once their clothes had been swapped for bikinis and robes, the four of them trooped down the street to the beach and into the water. After legs had shifted to tails, Lindsey and Cindy paired off to catch up on things, and Amy swam next to Penelope.

"Okay, now tell me *everything* about your mate."

There were a number of picnic tables along the landward side of the private beach, and Edna pulled up next to the furthest one from the entrance. There was a small stand-alone charcoal grill there, and four yards away, a small, low-water dock extended into the estuary formed by the Royston River. They clambered out of the jeep and carried the cooler and groceries to the table. As Peter worked on making the hamburger patties, he listened to Edna and Mildred talk about what a wonderful idea he had for a business.

"Peter, this is going to be terrific for our town. Naturally, we all enjoy swimming, but going to the same places every time is so boring. You'll find that out for yourself, soon. It's probably the only downside to living here on land."

Mildred piped up, "Edna, don't let any ferals hear you say that. You'll never hear the end of it."

Peter tried to hide his exasperation. He had no plans to start a business anywhere, but he wanted to keep things cordial with his new neighbors.

"Edna, that may be so, but will there be enough demand for this service to pay the bills and provide a living?" Mildred queried.

"I don't see why not. Everyone I've spoken to is very enthusiastic about it, and there are other opportunities as well.

"See those houses across the river? That's our buffer for the beach. The town bought the land long ago and built houses for a number of mer families. Most of them work in Royston, but they come here for groceries and socializing. They'll swim over towing a rowboat, or something like that, tie up here at the dock, and then walk up to Avery Johnson's, or all the way into town, to get what they need. It sounds extreme, but it's a long drive through Royston to get around to the north end of the island, no matter which road you take. You could fetch them from the dock and drive them to wherever."

It was Mildred's turn to jump in. "You could provide a water taxi to downtown and save them the swim. There could even be a bus service to Royston. Most of the girls on my street would kill to be able to go shopping in Royston when they want to."

Fighting a losing battle, Peter tried a diversion.

"Ladies, before we do anything, some research is in order. People are going to get tired of the Wildlife Sanctuary trip pretty quickly. We need to be able to offer a significant variety of trips, and that requires recon.

"Since I'm not a local, you two need to find secure places to drop off, have lunch breaks, and later, pickup. We also need a survey to determine if there's interest in those trips and at what price-point. If that all comes out in our favor, we *might* consider the possibility of starting a business and adding other things to it."

That took some wind out of their sails, but only for a moment.

"We'll get on it." Edna agreed, and looked at her watch. "We've got about an hour and fifteen minutes before the girls get here. Let's use the dock to serve on. They can either stay in the water, or haul out, but they'll have a choice. We'd like to go for a swim now, if you think you've got it under control."

Peter pretended to be interested in the condiments as the

two ladies nonchalantly removed their clothes. While these two were obviously significantly older than Ilene, they appeared to be in great shape, and he could think of a couple of the women back at the office who were twenty-nine or thirty who would probably kill to have bodies like theirs.

"Peter, you'd better lose those bathing trunks right now before anybody gets the wrong idea about you."

Ninety minutes later, four heads broke the surface just off the tip of the island and began to swim toward the dock. Luckily, the coals were perfect for cooking and Peter had already set out drinks, plates, and condiments near the dock's edge. He quickly laid half a dozen burgers on the grill and waved in the girl's direction.

In short order, it was time to flip the burgers, and Peter laid on slices of mozzarella. One by one, he placed the freshly cooked burgers on the buns, which were waiting with the garnishes.

Hearing Edna's voice, he started the next round of burgers and carried the completed ones to the hungry mermaids waiting by the dock.

"It was so sweet of you to do this for us, honey." Penelope said as Peter knelt down to kiss her. "And, you look great." She was, of course, referring to his lack of clothes.

"Thanks, but I did have help on this."

"Hey! Look at that ass! I can't wait to see some scales on it!" Cindy catcalled.

Penelope mouthed, "Me too."

Once the meal was over and everything put away, Edna and Mildred swam off in the direction of the reef, leaving Peter alone with the girls. As her bridesmaids hauled out on the small beach to rest, Penelope coaxed Peter into the water.

"Are you ready to try something?"

Peter nodded somewhat reluctantly.

"Okay, take three cleansing breaths and then hold the fourth," she instructed, before putting Peter into a lip-lock and pulling him under. Peter came up spluttering a moment later.

"Are you okay?"

Peter nodded.

The combination of the giggling bridesmaids and the knowledge of what was waiting for him two feet underwater stiffened his resolve, and the next try was much more rewarding. As his confidence began to grow, Peter relished his time underwater and tried to stay there longer.

"I just don't get it. We all had the same lectures in school about humans, and she not only chooses one as a mate, but she's going to marry him, too." Cindy snarked. "And what is she trying to do with him out there?"

Amy turned, saying, "She's trying to build his confidence in the water. He was caught in a rip current when he was twelve and almost drowned. He's been afraid of the ocean ever since."

Cindy rolled her eyes. "You see what I'm talking about?"

Amy's eyes narrowed. "That can be very frightening to humans, and you have no right to talk. We all remember what happened the first time you ran into a shark. If someone would go through all this for me, I'd mate with him in a heartbeat."

Cindy shifted uneasily.

Lindsey giggled. She was interested in a certain human herself but was definitely not going to mention it now. What intrigued her, though, was the seemingly sudden interest Amy had in choosing a mate. Everyone assumed she'd never mate or breed because of her shyness around males.

Lindsey decided to pair up with Penelope on the way home so she could ask her about what it took to transform a human into a merman. She didn't have any need of it at the moment, and probably never would, because Brad from the west coast underwriting group barely knew she existed. Still, there was something about him she liked, and because merfolk had a longer lifespan than humans, she could afford to wait a while longer.

CHAPTER SIXTEEN

It had finally arrived—the day they would meet with the mayor and get things rolling. Penelope awoke at 5:30 a.m. and fidgeted as time crawled by. Peter woke around 7:30 a.m. and quickly surmised that his mate was not going to let him get any more sleep. After kissing her good morning, he struck up a conversation in hopes of keeping her mind occupied.

"I wanted to ask you about what Cindy said yesterday."

"Oh, don't worry about it, sweetheart. Cindy can be a loud mouth and cranky at times, but she's actually really sweet. She's a nurse at the hospital outside of Royston now, and she puts in some long hours. Her boyfriend, Mike, is in med school at Duke University, and they don't see each other very often. Amy said she gets like this when he's been away for a while, so the girls cut her some slack.

"When Mike is finished with everything, he's coming back here, and the town's going to set up a clinic for him. He'll handle patients from both species, but most importantly, he'll be able to run tests for us. Most merfolk are scared to get an x-ray or have blood work done because of what doctors might find, and that's one of the reasons the town paid for him to attend med school."

"Well, that's good to know for future reference. Now, who is it we're supposed to see today?"

"Bill Marlin. He's been the mayor of Colony Island for as long as I can remember. He's the one who knows the details about how to turn you into a merman, so be nice to him."

That did it. Peter was on edge.

Bill Marlin tidied up the meeting room in Colony Island's municipal building. It was originally intended for exclusive use by the Town Council, though nowadays, all meetings for any purpose involving more than two people usually wound up there. This meeting, however, would mark two firsts—and the mayor was looking forward to it.

Residents choosing mates here had three options available. The traditional route was quite simple, really—the couple announced their decision to become mates to their friends and family, and that would be it. This was mostly done by ferals and their offspring. The second option was to get a marriage license, appear before the mayor, and simply repeat the traditional vows to finalize the process legally. The third was the public, and slightly more elaborate, joining ceremony, which took ninety seconds—and that included signing the license and the registry. But a wedding? This was going to be a very special day in the history of Colony Island.

The conversion of a human to a mer ordinarily happened, at most, once every few years, and was usually done quietly, as most of the converts wanted to either seamlessly blend into Colony Island life, or not be identified as a former human. Peter's, though, had become almost common knowledge by late Friday evening and was now the talk of the town. It would be another first, the first publicly known conversion that he or anyone else could remember.

Bill was jolted from his reverie by the sound of voices out in the hall. The appointed hour had arrived, and both couples walked into the meeting room. He warmly greeted Ilene, George, and Penelope, who proudly introduced him to Peter. Then he motioned for everyone to have a seat.

"The first thing I want to say is congratulations to all of you, especially to our newly chosen couple. I assume everyone here wants to go ahead and have a wedding on the Island?"

Ilene and her daughter vigorously nodded their assent.

"Good, good. Let's talk about a venue, first. Island tradition dictates that all residents are automatically invited to our joining ceremonies, and I don't see why it should be any different for a wedding. Naturally, most residents do not attend, but you can count on a large turnout due to the uniqueness of this event. I highly recommend you use the town hall for the ceremony, for which there will be a nominal fee for setup and cleanup. Do you have a date in mind?"

Penelope spoke up. "I was thinking of the third Saturday in May. I heard it might take a while to have my dress made, so that should give us time to prepare, plus three weeks for a honeymoon. I have to be back at work by the second week in June so I can get ready for the end of my company's fiscal year."

"That will be perfect. The entire month of May is open. I assume you want me to officiate?" There was a general murmur of agreement, so he continued. "As for the service itself, there are the vows, of course, but the whole thing is pretty much open. We can begin working on those details in a month or two. Now, is there anything else you had in mind?"

Peter looked uncomfortable. He didn't know what he should say, and while this was the moment Penelope had been waiting for, she was tongue-tied as well.

It fell to Ilene to speak up. "Mayor, Peter has asked to become one of us." Penelope looked at her in gratitude.

"Ilene, please call me Bill. I've known you for ages, and we'll be working pretty closely over the coming months."

"All right, Mayor Bill, how exactly do we make Peter a merman?"

The mayor chuckled at her rewording and turned to Peter. "Is this what you truly want? To become one of us?"

Penelope was vigorously nodding her head before Peter could even put his in motion.

"Okay, then. This is what it will take to do that." The mayor reached into a box beside his chair and placed something that looked like a grapefruit with the skin of a nectarine on the table.

They are much fewer in number now, and the fruit is not as potent as it used to be. Our own plants came from an island in the eastern Caribbean. Now, before I really get going here, please feel free to ask questions at any time."

Penelope and Peter nodded in agreement while the mayor took a deep breath.

"Right. The transformation from human to mer is accomplished by consuming a certain amount of this fruit for a specified period of time. Because merfruit is rather juicy, you'll consume it in the form of a drink we'll make for you so you won't have to spend all day slurping it from the pulp. The only side effect you'll feel is being under the weather—much like the reaction from a flu shot—when you first start taking the juice, and even that goes away after a couple days.

"There are two ways to get you from here to there. The first is, you drink the juice for an indefinite period of time, and at some point, the change simply happens. I call that the spontaneous method. One minute you've got legs, and the next minute, you have a tail. It's unpredictable and can be very embarrassing—not to mention a secrecy risk—if it occurs in the wrong place at the wrong time. I don't recommend it, unless you mean to relocate here and not leave the island after you've been partaking of the juice for a good while.

"I call the second way the controlled method. You take the juice for a fixed amount of time, and then we give you some partially fermented pulp. That way you can choose the time and place to complete your transition."

Penelope had been squeezing Peter's hand under the table, and she nervously asked, "How long does the controlled method take?"

Bill looked at Peter for a moment. "Hmmm, for someone your size and weight...and it would take a few weeks to harvest enough fruit..." The mayor pulled out a pocket calendar and began to perform calculations on his smartphone. "If we start the first weekend in October, you'd be ready to go by the first weekend in May of next year."

Peter could feel Penelope instantly deflate—she'd been hoping this could be done on a single weekend, or by the end of the month. For his part, Peter was secretly relieved it would take a while to accomplish. He was still game, and if the mayor had told him it could be taken care of this afternoon, he would have said, "Let's do it!" But this way, he could take his time and learn as much as he could in advance.

"Well, if that's what it takes, then that's what it takes," Penelope acquiesced. "At least it'll be done in time for the wedding."

The mayor shook his head. "I haven't told you the other part of this. Whether we use the spontaneous or controlled method, once the change happens, Peter won't be back on his feet for a month. He'll have to spend most of his time, if not all of it, in the water."

Everyone could sense the panic in Penelope's voice. "Couldn't he take extra doses to speed things up or something?"

The mayor again shook his head. "We've tried various methods with earlier converts. For someone Peter's size, it takes seven months, and there's no way around that."

In desperation, Penelope made one final attempt. "What if

he starts today? That would give us a little over three weeks' head start, and Peter would have his legs again in time for our wedding."

The mayor smiled sadly at her, as he was honestly sympathetic toward her plight. "We don't keep any of the juice on hand. We have to start from scratch every time. If Peter lived here, we might be able to squeeze it in, but in order to have enough for him to take back to the city for a week or two, it's going to be a while before we have a sufficient amount ready to go. I'm sorry."

All of Penelope's hopes and dreams that had developed over the past nine days came crashing to the ground. "It's not fair. It's just not fair!" she sobbed. "I wanted to marry a merman. Not a human!"

Peter decided it would be best if he stepped out for a few minutes. After learning where the men's room was, he headed in that direction.

He heard Ilene's voice as he walked down the hall. "Penny, do you realize what you're saying? You've just insulted your mate. If a human was good enough for you to choose, then he should be good enough for you to marry."

Peter washed his hands a couple times, splashed some water on his face, and looked out the window, though there wasn't much of a view. As he slowly walked up the hall, it seemed Penelope had ceased crying. That changed the moment he walked through the door.

Penelope bolted from her chair, wrapped her arms around him, and sobbed on his shoulder. "Peter, I'm so sorry. I didn't mean it like that. I love you so much! I just wanted this for you as soon as possible. I'm sorry!"

Peter held her and made shushing sounds. "It's all right, dear. I understand. Nothing would make me happier than for us to be able to swim off on our honeymoon right after the reception, but it doesn't look like we can. The mayor is an expert at this, so let's just follow his advice, okay?"

Penelope choked back a sob. "Okay."

Bill was grateful that a crisis had been averted and peace had been restored. In his experience, some converts were disappointed that the process took so long, but he'd never seen someone this upset, and she wasn't even the person wanting to make the switch.

"Penelope, if it's any consolation, I can assure you your

mate will be ninety-nine percent mer on your wedding day, so in one sense, you'll get your wish," he consoled her. "Now, I do most of my swimming on the weekend, so I'll keep your parents apprised of things, and they can relay the information to you and Peter. If there aren't any more questions at this moment, let's go over and look at the Temple of Poseidon."

A look of bewilderment appeared on Peter's face.

"Let me give you a bit of background on the history of the Temple, Peter. Back around 1920, Christophorus Kolidakis arrived on the island from New York City. He was the only son of the Greek fishing magnate, Mikolas Kolidakis, and had been invited by the town fathers to help modernize our fishing fleet, as well as build a processing plant and cannery.

"By all accounts, he was handsome, had a natural charm about him, and was very popular with our residents, both those within the fishing community and those outside it. He was the first human many of our residents had encountered on a regular basis, and they found him very different from the somewhat frightening image the term 'human' normally conjured up." The mayor chuckled.

"Christophorus loved it here. He only left for very brief periods of time in order to return to New York to visit with his family and help handle the affairs of his father's business. He had mentioned he was planning to bring his family to the island for an extended winter holiday when his parents and sisters were lost in a boating accident off Long Island."

"That must've been horrible for him," Peter interjected.

Ilene and George nodded in agreement, and Penelope gave Peter's hand a squeeze.

"Yes, Peter. He and the townspeople were devastated by the news," Ilene commented.

"Indeed they were," agreed Bill. "As Christophorus prepared to travel home for the funerals and take the reins of his father's company, he was humbled by the town's compassion. Resident after resident stopped to offer their condolences and beg him to return to the island as soon as he was able. After two months in New York, he returned.

"The older residents still argue about how it happened or who was behind it, but Christophorus 'accidentally on purpose' learned of our true nature and was subsequently invited to become one of us. He was very moved by the outpouring of affection from the residents and decided Colony Island and joining us was where and how he wanted to spend the rest of his life."

Peter's mind started racing, wondering about the human to merman transformation process and how Christophorus had handled it. He considered interrupting to ask but decided to wait until the mayor was finished.

"Although he still made occasional trips back to New York City, he transferred as much of his company's management as was practical to Florida.

"In the mid 1930s, he sought to give back to the town that had welcomed him into its heart, and he commissioned a Greek Revival building to be used as the town hall. The name, the Temple of Poseidon, was his idea, not ours."

"Not everyone was happy about the building's design either," George noted.

"That's true," the mayor said. "Christophorus also paid for a monument to honor our residents who had served in the armed forces during the war. Additionally, it was Christophorus' generosity that funded the wildlife refuge and the buffer community across the river from the private beach. He keeps in touch to this day and has returned on a number of occasions. He's planning to visit in the spring, and perhaps he'll be here for the wedding."

"Oh—wouldn't that be wonderful?" Penelope said.

"Do you think I could talk with him about what he went through when he became a merman?" Peter inquired hesitantly. "It would be great to get some inside information on the transformation process from someone who's been through it— before I take my final steps."

"Well, Peter, you'll have to wait and see what the timing of his visit will be," answered the mayor.

Penelope was pretty glum on the walk down Main Street toward the temple, though she did perk up when the mayor unlocked the front door and they walked into the lobby.

Peter thought the lobby was plain until his eyes adjusted to the lighting. Every wall was covered with mosaics depicting sea life. There were dolphins, seals, whales, jellyfish and countless other varieties of marine life, some of which Peter had never seen before. All of them were swimming above brightly colored coral reefs or amongst gently swaying stalks of kelp and other marine plants.

The work spoke strongly of old world craftsmanship and must have cost Mr. Kolidakis a lot of money—even in terms of dollars from that era. The biggest surprise came when he looked up to the ceiling, expecting to find ordinary paint and plaster. He couldn't tell if they were mosaics or frescoes, but above him swam a host of mermaids and mermen. It was easy to pick out Poseidon and Triton, and the mermaid beside them must have been the sea god's wife.

Were the residents unaware of the treasure that lined the walls? Peter stood there in awe with Handel's "Coronation Anthem #1" playing in his mind until Bill tugged on his shirtsleeve.

They walked through the center set of doors into what reminded Peter of his elementary school auditorium. There were a couple rows of wooden folding chairs painted white in front of the low stage, and the rest was bare floor. The remaining chairs were stacked on both the stage and at the back of the auditorium. From the layer of dust on them, it appeared they were seldom used.

"George and I haven't been in here since before Penny went off to high school. We'd attend the little performances The Academy put on for the parents, but only a few of us ever showed up." Ilene sighed.

Bill shook his head. "I wish more parents were like the two of you."

Ilene was silent for a moment and then turned toward Peter. "Yesterday, while you kids were out, I went through that excellent book you gave us. It has plenty of ideas for the whole planning process, but I'm afraid that no one else on the island knows enough about weddings to be of any assistance. It's one thing to see one on TV, and quite another to actually put one on. Peter, would you help us with all of this?"

"Well, I've attended a few and was in a wedding party once, but being a guy—even a human one—really limits my experience. I'll do what I can, though."

Penelope stared out the car window for most of the ride back to the house. When she finally spoke, it was to apologize.

"Guys, I'm sorry about what happened in the meeting. I just had my hopes up too high, I guess."

"Penny," Ilene said, "We all want Peter to become one of us as soon as possible, but this may be a blessing in disguise. Even with his help, there's a lot to be done in the next eight months— not including re-doing your room. It's his too now, and you're going to need a bigger bed, for one thing. We can even clean out the storage room, and you can use that as a dressing room or something. Don't you think so, George?"

"Mmmm hmmm."

George parked the Hummer in the driveway, and Penelope ran into the house before anyone else could unbuckle their seatbelts.

"Is she upset again?" Peter asked with a worried look on his face.

Ilene shook her head. "If I know Penny, she's just realized she overlooked something very important and is on her way to do something about it. By the way, you were wonderful in that meeting. You knew when to step away so Penny could collect herself, and you knew exactly what to say to her when you returned. Every day, I understand more and more why she chose you as her mate."

Peter was too embarrassed to say more than, "Well, I try," and stepped out of the car to follow Penelope. He caught up with her in her bedroom furiously sketching designs for the makeover. "Sweetheart, this is your room. You don't have to change it just for me."

"Peter, my room hasn't changed since high school. It's frozen in time, and I've moved on. I have a mate now, and Mom's right. It's *our* room, and it needs to be about us, not some high school mermaid. All I ask is that you let me keep Mr. Splashy," she said, pointing to her stuffed dolphin. "He was my best friend as a child, and I'm too sentimental to pack him away forever."

Peter smiled and nodded. The two of them began taking measurements and discussing possible color schemes. As noon approached, Peter kissed her goodbye and left for his lunch with Carl.

The Mermaid Tavern had a half-timbered Tudor look on

the façade. The theme continued on the inside as well, and it resembled a countryside English pub. The place was almost devoid of patrons, and it was pretty easy to spot Carl once Peter's eyes had adjusted to the light. The pizza guy waved him over, and Peter slid into the booth.

"Dude! Whatcha been up to?"

Peter explained that he'd met with the mayor and the date and venue were now set for the wedding. "Penelope was pretty disappointed. It turns out becoming a merman takes about seven or eight months, and she was hoping it would be done much sooner."

"Bummer, man. Look at it this way—all good things take time, and I think this is a very good thing."

Peter and Carl ordered lunch and something to wash it down with. As they waited for their meal to appear, Peter asked Carl about his day.

"Gotta work tonight, man. I'm thinking I'll handle deliveries. It's pretty cool checking in on everyone. If someone's not doing well or needs help, I pass that on to the mayor. Anyway, after three days here, I know you're bound to have some questions for me, so let 'em rip."

Peter asked why Penelope's family—and everyone else— flashed their fins at him when they dove.

"You mean when they sound?"

"Sound? Sound like what?" Peter was confused, and not for the first time since he'd set foot on the island.

"Man, sounding is a term for when fish or marine mammals take a steep and deep dive. We fit both of those categories when we dive like that, ergo, we sound. We like the rush of it, and it's a great way to start off on a swim." Carl seemed pleased with his explanation.

"Hmmm, that's a new one on me. Okay, why does everyone flash their fins at me when they sound?"

"It's called the caudal salute. It's our way of saying goodbye. Not showing your fin is practically the equivalent of flipping someone off. Dude, the fact that everyone's showing you their fin is a sign you're accepted here even though you're human."

"That's a relief. Thanks, man. So what was it like to grow up on Colony Island?"

"Pretty much like growing up on the mainland, I guess— school, homework, hanging out with friends, watching TV—

except we spend a lot more time in the water."

"What do most merfolk watch on TV?"

"Old movies for the most part...and home decorating shows. Most mermaids don't know the governor of Florida, but they can all tell you who Vernon Yip is."

"Interesting. You know, Carl, there are a few people who think I'm starting some kind of business here."

"A few? Dude, it's all over town. Edna and Mildred have already asked me for ideas about places to go. I know Hazel wants to handle lunches, and I can provide pizzas from the South End shop when trips finish up on the private beach. This idea of yours is the best thing I've heard in years!"

Peter realized he was fighting a losing battle on this, so he steered the conversation on to more general subjects. The small talk carried them through lunch and a third beer.

It was almost mid afternoon when Carl announced, "I'm gonna to try and get a swim in before I go to work. Here's my cell number in case you have any more questions or want to order a pizza. On your way out of town this evening, honk your horn as you go by North End."

"Will do." Peter gave Carl his cell number, and the two shook hands.

"See you next time, dude!"

Peter found Ilene and Penelope sitting at the kitchen table with a small list of questions. He spent the next hour trying to answer them and dispense what little advice he felt qualified to give. They came up with a short-term action list for all concerned, and then the conversation seemed to die. Penelope looked like she had something she was reluctant to say. Ilene nudged her.

"Peter, I want to come back here next weekend."

"Of course, sweetheart. I know you want to spend some more time with your parents, and I'm sure they want to spend time with you. I'll find something to do in the city."

Ilene looked at him in dismay. "Peter, we want you to come too. You're family now. This is your home."

He was so used to being shown the door by girls' parents that this sort of invitation was difficult to comprehend. "Sweetheart, are you okay with it?"

"Of course I am, Peter. I just wasn't sure...you would want

to come back so soon."

Peter looked at Ilene. "You sure you want to be seen in the company of a known human? I mean, what will the neighbors think?"

Ilene's eyes sparkled. "Peter, if you don't mind consorting with mermaids and a grumpy merman, you're always welcome here. And don't worry about George. His bark has always been worse than his bite."

"I heard that!" drifted over from the office across the hall.

Ilene rolled her eyes and smiled. "Why don't you two go relax before dinner? It should be ready in an hour or so."

Penelope took Peter's hand and they headed upstairs. Peter peeled off to visit the bathroom while Penelope continued into the bedroom. When he was done, he walked into the bedroom to find Penelope under the covers and her clothes in a heap on the floor.

"Sweetheart, close the door and come over here. I think I know how we should spend our hour."

Peter began to undress. "I know merfolk are open about this stuff, but are you sure your mother won't mind?"

"My love, she's the one who suggested it," Penelope replied with a coy smile.

Peter looked perplexed. "When did she say that?"

Crap! She'd practically given everything away. Friday evening, her mother had passed along the mayor's suggestion that they not tell Peter about their ability to communicate telepathically, as it tended to make prospective converts somewhat paranoid. There was plenty of time to reveal it—and other things—once the transition was complete.

Recovering quickly, she said, "Sweetheart, after twenty-five years, I'm good at reading between my mother's lines."

Peter took that at face value and slid in between the sheets. The following forty minutes could only be described as a little bit of paradise. No bedroom acrobatics. No moaning matches. It was simply two people sharing their love for each other with whispers, kisses, and caresses in a place they could at last call their own.

George noticed a few tears in his mate's eyes as they watched their daughter and her mate drive off toward their home in the city, but that was her norm. They went back inside, and he cleaned up from dinner. When he finished and went in search of Ilene, their bedroom door was closed and he could hear her softly crying inside.

"Mother, are you all right?" he asked, tapping on the door. Getting no reply, he opened it to find his mate sitting on the bed, handkerchief in hand, with tears streaming down her face. "What's wrong, dear?"

"They're gone. They're both dead."

"Who's gone, Mother? What are you talking about?"

"Peter's parents. I pulled him aside before they left and asked about meeting his parents, and he told me they're both dead. He lost his father when he was sixteen, and his mother passed away just after he finished college. Aside from a brother in Seattle, he has no one. He's an orphan."

"Mother, that must have been a bitter blow to be sure, but he's old enough to be on his own now, anyway."

"George, you don't understand. A child needs a mother as long as possible. Someone to love them unconditionally. Someone to always be there for them, no matter what."

"Doesn't he have our daughter for that?"

"It's more than that, George. He needs a family. Peter is perfect for Penny. You've seen how she looks at him—how upset she was when she learned his conversion would take seven months. His mother gave us the young man who would find our little girl and bring her home. As one mother to another, I owe a debt to her, one that I can only repay by giving him a family to love and care about him. You do whatever you wish, George, but I'm going to become Peter's mother, or as much of one as I can be."

CHAPTER SEVENTEEN

The drive back to the city was a quiet one, as the day's emotions had left Penelope feeling somewhat drained. To be honest, unless there were pressing things to discuss, most of their driving time together was like this. It gave them time to be alone with their thoughts and still enjoy the simple pleasure of being with one another.

When they arrived at her apartment, Peter helped carry her belongings inside and then said, "Well, I guess I should get going."

Penelope grabbed his arm as if Peter was going to run away. "Please don't go, honey. Not unless you really have to. This weekend has been so good, I don't want to you go, not yet, not tonight."

It was hard to argue with her, and if it meant he got to spend one more night with the woman he loved, it was worth pushing the chores back in his own apartment one more day. Peter pulled out his smartphone and sent a text: "Made it home okay. See you this weekend."

A reply was not long in coming from Carl: " Awesome, dude!"

In order to speed things along, Peter brushed his teeth over the kitchen sink so his mate could have full use of her bathroom. Penelope finished first, and as she eased herself in under the covers, she felt herself begin to change with no way to stop the process.

After turning out the lights in the living room, Peter walked into the bedroom to find Penelope with her fin bunched up under the sheets. "What happened?"

"I'm not sure. It started to happen, and I was either too tired or beyond caring to do anything. I'm sorry, sweetheart."

Peter smiled and asked, "Tired but happy, huh?"

He immediately began to pull the top sheet away from the foot of the bed so the base of her tail would rest on the end of the mattress and her fin could hang free. He then draped the sheet over the rest of her tail.

"Now you don't have to stay awake waiting to change back, and I get to cuddle with my favorite mermaid."

After he pulled the bedclothes up over both of them, Penelope whispered, "Why are you so good to me?"

Peter was somewhat amused by her question. Wasn't it obvious? He was deeply in love with her. He replied, "Aside from the fact that you're my chosen mate, and I love you more than anything else, I'm going to be completely dependent upon you in about eight months. I'm taking care of you now so you'll take care of me then. Besides, who knows what I'm going to be like after I'm back on my feet? I might wind up in the same situation as you." Peter kissed her, turned so he could lay his leg over her tail, and quickly fell asleep.

As Penelope drifted off, she asked herself a now familiar question. *How did I get so lucky?*

Neither one of them was happy with the decision, but Penelope and Peter agreed they each had a lot to do in their respective apartments if they were going to go back to Colony Island late Friday afternoon. So, they spent Tuesday evening apart, getting as much taken care of as possible between barrages of texting. Neither dared call the other directly for fear of the outcome. They'd immediately drop everything and wind up in bed together. They did decide, however, to have dinner together Wednesday evening and then go in search of paint chips for their room on Colony Island. Neither needed much convincing that sleeping together that night was the best possible thing they could do, and they quickly found themselves in Penelope's bed. Who knew paint chips would lead to a repeat of Monday afternoon?

As they were lazily getting ready to settle in for the night, Penelope shuffled through the chips. They were all sea colors. "Honey, I think what I'm after is to replicate the colors I see when I wake up from my underwater naps."

"That's a good idea, Pen. We could even use a different shade for the ceiling so it'd seem like you were looking up through the water toward the sky. Remember those pictures you took with the underwater camera before...before..."

"Before we admitted we'd fallen in love with each other? How could I forget?"

"Well, we could choose a few to enlarge and hang in the room. I think there might be enough for a panorama on one of the long walls. I'll bring the laptop this weekend and we can check them out."

As Peter gathered his things in preparation for his departure the following morning—they knew they had to spend Thursday evening apart or nothing would get done—Penelope washed up and then sat on what had become "her" side of the bed.

"Peter, would you mind?" She gestured toward her legs.

"Sweetheart, do whatever you want—whatever's comfortable and makes you happy."

"Sleeping with you...like this...makes me very happy."

Peter was barely able to snatch the bedclothes out of the way before she stretched out her lovely legs and they became a beautiful mermaid's tail. She brushed her fin gently up and down his legs as he arranged the covers. Was she flirting with him? Probably. Was he falling for it? Probably.

"How long can you stay like this?"

"Around ten hours, more or less. I start to get itchy all over when it's time to get back in the water. One thing to remember is you'll dehydrate faster once you're a merman, with or without your tail on."

When at last he was under the sheets with her, Penelope rolled onto her side to face him. "Peter, I'm so sorry about Monday morning. Part of it, I think, was I was afraid you might change your mind if you didn't become mer soon."

"Pen, today, tomorrow, next year...I don't care...as long as I get to be with you. Who knows, once I'm done, maybe we can both sleep like this together."

Penelope said nothing, though when she rested her head on his shoulder and propped her tail against his leg, her opinion on the matter was clearly evident.

✱✱✱

The return to Colony Island Friday night was uneventful. Rather than a family swim the next morning, Ilene announced they were going to Edna's Home and Bath to look at furniture and then into Royston for curtains. George declared he was going swimming with the mayor and had somehow forgotten to tell anyone.

When Peter and Penelope went upstairs to unpack, they discovered the storeroom was empty, and a closet had magically appeared at the far end. Ilene had been busy.

Though Peter wished he could go run logistics for George and the mayor on Saturday, it was his connubial duty to accompany the ladies on their furniture and curtain shopping expedition. They found what they needed at Edna's, including a love seat Ilene insisted on buying. The new dressers were to go in the former storeroom, while the love seat and writing table would take their place in the bedroom. Ilene and Edna were a force to be reckoned with, and the two of them chose just what was needed to transform the upstairs into a weekend retreat for Penelope and her mate.

The curtain shopping was relatively painless, and after stopping by the home improvement store, they arrived back at the house early in the afternoon with enough paint, rollers, drop cloths, and other tools of the trade to redo the upstairs, and then some. Peter actively encouraged Penelope and Ilene to go for a mother-daughter swim so he could roll up his sleeves and get to work. With any luck, he'd be able to sneak away for a beer with Carl while the first coat dried.

He and Penelope were starting their life together, and he could actually do something to contribute rather than hang on and follow in everyone else's wake. He hoped she would realize he really was committed to the choice he'd made, and making their rooms actually feel like a home, was part of all he hoped for the two of them. With Carl's help shifting and covering the furniture, he was able to complete painting all but a fraction of the bedroom and get set up to start on the dressing room before it was time to leave Sunday evening.

By the end of the week, they had come up with a plan to settle down into a welcome and predictable routine. They would spend their weekends on the island, staying until Sunday evening at Penelope's parents' house. Wednesday night would be spent at Peter's apartment, and the other three evenings would be devoted to necessary chores and getting ahead of things at work so they could leave around 3:00 p.m. on Friday. It wasn't perfect, but it worked.

Peter expected to resume painting early the next Saturday morning, but once again, Ilene had other ideas.

"Peter, Penny and I are going shopping for her wedding dress today, and we want you to come with us."

"Ummm, that's traditionally mother-daughter-BFF only, Ilene. The bridegroom usually sits it out."

"Peter, that may be the case on the mainland, but on Colony Island, you're the only one who knows anything at all about this sort of thing. Edna gave Amy the day off so she can come with us."

"And George?"

"He's as grumpy as can be, but he'll be joining us too."

Peter made a mental note to procure some single-malt scotch to keep here on Colony Island.

The bridal salon was in a shopping center on the east side of Royston, and when the proprietress gave Peter and George the evil eye as they walked through the door, Peter knew there was trouble ahead. Storm warnings were posted when she learned Peter was the groom and not Penelope's brother or gay cousin. Still, a customer was a customer, and since it was the father who usually footed the bill, Peter was the one she aimed to cut from the herd.

The proprietress asked Penelope what style bridal gown she was interested in, and she responded that she was just getting started on her search. The lady groaned inwardly. This was going to be an hour or two of playing dress-up without a sale in sight. Peter mumbled that a mermaid style gown would be redundant, which set everyone, except George and the proprietress, giggling. They'd only been there five minutes, and the groom was already interfering with things.

So, the parade of gowns began. As far as Peter was concerned, he'd be happy with almost anything she chose. But, since Ilene and Penelope had asked for his help, he did his best and based his opinions on her facial expression, but there were very few smiles from her early on.

Penelope started with ball gowns, but quickly decided they weren't her style. Too bulky. Next she tried a few a-lines, and followed those with trumpet gowns. There were some with lace overlays, long sweeping trains, beads and sequins, and layers of tulle to give fullness to the bottoms. There were gowns with sweetheart necklines and v-necks, and low to plunging backs. They varied from strapless to long sleeves, and everything in between.

Peter smiled and told her how pretty she looked in every dress. Amy was giddy and a bit overwhelmed by the whole experience. She followed Penelope and helped pull gowns from the racks to try on. Ilene was more helpful, noting what did and did not flatter Penelope's figure, and George just sat with his arms crossed and a straight face.

The proprietress saw her opening when Penelope and Amy went back to the changing room together, and Ilene went to the ladies room. This lull in the action left George looking decidedly bored and Peter flipping through a bridal magazine.

"Young man, come with me."

She not so much led as dragged Peter out to the reception area and plopped him into a "plant chair," the infamous bench where every husband or boyfriend was planted and told to "stay," and be a "good boy," while the more important business of shopping was carried out by the women. Peter assumed his presence was making Penelope nervous or unhappy, and thus didn't complain about his expulsion.

Penelope, with Amy following, returned to the viewing area at the same time as Ilene. She was wearing one of the mermaid style gowns with a sweetheart neckline, cap sleeves, and beaded lace over satin. "Where's Peter?"

George had been hoping he'd get an emergency phone call from the mayor, or even Carl, and had paid no attention to Peter being marched out of the room. Ilene had no idea what had transpired, and it fell to the proprietress to set things straight.

"I took him out to the reception area. He didn't belong here, and now, you can choose your gown in peace."

What happened next would be recorded in the annals of the International Confraternity of Bridal Salons. The room temperature dropped thirty-five degrees as Penelope drew herself up and unleashed the full force of her icy business demeanor.

"Ma'am, that person you took out to the reception area is my mate, my protector, my confidant, my fiancé, and the love of my life. I refuse to make any critical decision without his input and will leave at once unless you bring him back *immediately*."

The proprietress quailed at the voice of doom, and Ilene was too stunned to speak. The irony of the fact she was wearing a mermaid-style wedding gown at the time was not lost on the others.

Amy was all too happy to go and fetch Peter. "Come with me. Anne wants you."

"What happened in there?"

"Let's just say someone came between a mermaid and her mate, and leave it at that."

As Amy and Peter came back out on the floor, Penelope rushed over to touch his face. "Sweetheart, are you all right?"

"I'm fine, but you really didn't have to bring me back in."

"Yes I did. It's our decision, and I want to be sure you'll be happy with what I wear on our wedding day."

Peter raised his eyebrows and quipped, "I'd be happy even if all you wore was a wet T-shirt."

Penelope scrunched her face up into a mock pout. "We'll discuss that tonight, dear…after the lights go out."

The parade of bridal gowns resumed. While Penelope wasn't totally happy with the one she was currently trying on, she felt like she was getting close. It was a trumpet shape silhouette with a sleeveless, v-neck décolletage, a satin underlay with brocade lace layer over it, and a three-foot train. As far as the proprietress was concerned, the parade was winding down.

Penelope tried on the last few dresses without a winner, and the proprietress announced she had seen most everything there was to show. The *only* exception was a dress that had shown up in a shipment just over two weeks ago, unordered, and way out of style. Obviously, the company was simply trying to get rid of the piece. It was terribly retro and most certainly was not her taste.

For Penelope, the lady had nearly ruined her bridal gown shopping experience, and she wanted no reason to have to come back to the shop again. "Let me see it."

Despite the proprietress' warnings that it was a fluke and would most likely not fit, Penelope followed the woman back to the changing room.

The general consensus amongst the bridal party was to get this over with as soon as possible and get out of there, never to darken the shop's door again. At least that was the plan until Peter saw his mate walk onto the floor in the last chance gown.

"You...look absolutely beautiful!"

Penelope was shimmering in champagne satin. The dress had long sleeves with lace cuffs and a modified sweetheart décolletage with tulle forming an illusion neckline that wrapped over her shoulders and continued down the deep cut back. A fitted bodice flared slightly at her hips, falling in a circle at her feet. Satin buttons ran all down the bodice on the back of the gown, and a lovely court train flowed out behind her. Lace appliqués adorned the bodice and were scattered about the skirt. Delicate scalloped lace, matching the sleeve cuffs, edged the entire hem. Tiny seed pearls and sequins were sewn about the lace appliqués, giving the gown just a tiny bit of glimmer.

She turned to face the large mirror located next to the dressing room and gasped. "Oh, I love it! And it fits perfectly. Do you think it's the one, Peter?"

"Yeah! It certainly has my seal of approval, sweetheart."

Penelope turned to her parents. "Mom?"

"You already know how I feel about it. George?"

"Princess, if that's the gown you truly love, then this whole morning has been well worth it. You should discuss the price with Peter, of course. It's his call."

That caught Peter completely off guard. He'd been puzzling over how Penelope could already know how Ilene felt about the gown, and then there was the thing about the price being "his call."

Ilene noticed the look of confusion clouding his face and spoke up. "Peter, it's an Island tradition that the man buys his mate's joining dress. Of course, they are rather simple dresses and usually don't run over a hundred dollars. The woman used to handle the embroidery, but now, she just hands it over to Mildred and she takes care of it. A wedding gown is far outside the tradition. George, how do you feel about this?"

George leaned over toward Peter and said, in a stage whisper, "Son, I'll take care of this for you."

Peter was not rich, but he did have a fair amount from his mother's estate. She wouldn't appreciate his spending frivolously, but she would have wanted her daughter-in-law to look her best on her wedding day...even if she was a mermaid.

"No. I really appreciate your offer, but I'll take care of it. It's the Colony Island tradition, after all."

The proprietress had every intention of making money off this deal. She had always heard the islanders were peculiar, and this bunch had ruined her morning. "It'll be two thousand, even."

Peter didn't even blink. "Hmmm. You basically got this dress for free, and you don't have to deal with alterations. Throw in...a veil of my bride's choosing, shoes, and any other accessories she might like, and you've got a deal."

The proprietress was so keen to see the back of these wahoos that she immediately capitulated.

Once everything was selected, collected, and bagged, they quickly left the bridal salon and walked over to a sandwich shop on the edge of the shopping center for a well-deserved lunch. Over dessert, Amy asked why the lady was so upset about Peter and George being there.

"Well, as I told Pen and her mother earlier, shopping for wedding dresses is usually considered to be a girls-only thing. Also, weddings are mostly about the bride," Peter said with a grin. "The guys are a necessary evil in order to pay for things and do the heavy lifting."

Penelope was not amused. "Well, that's not fair! If it wasn't for the groom, there wouldn't be a bride. That might be how humans do it, but we're different. Peter, since you're from the mainland, you probably know more about the service than anyone else. You handle that, including the music, and we'll take care of the invitations, reception, and whatever else is needed."

This was going to be a sea of change for Peter. He had expected his part would be limited to saying, "Yes, dear," and maybe planning the rehearsal dinner. As for the honeymoon, he'd probably be growing a tail about that time.

"Don't forget the formal announcement."

Ilene looked puzzled. "I thought we had already announced it."

"Well, this custom isn't as popular as it once was, but the parents usually have a photo of the bride-to-be, along with a quick bio of both her and the groom, printed in the local paper. Since Pen lives and works in the city, it should probably at least go in the paper there. I can help write it up and get Pen's portrait taken care of," Peter offered.

The announcement was the only topic of conversation amongst the mermaids all the way back to Colony Island. Penelope wasn't quite as enthused about it as Amy and her mother were, but it was part of getting married, so she decided to go along with it.

Once Penelope, Amy, and Ilene had departed for the beach and an afternoon swim, Peter decided to resume work on the rooms upstairs. He had just begun to set up in the storeroom when he heard George's voice behind him.

"Son, I was quite pleased with you this morning. Not only did you step up and honor the tradition, but you also managed to wring as much as you could out of that harpy, all while making my daughter very happy. I think she chose the right man for her mate. If you'll let me pitch in here, I believe we can wrap up a good bit of the painting today and get started on removing the furniture. The new stuff is supposed to arrive late next week."

Peter was dumbstruck. The best he could manage to say was that he'd planned to ask Carl if he could come over to lend a hand, too.

George was silent for a moment. "Son, I think Carl would really like it if you did."

On Tuesday morning, Ilene stopped by Edna's to check on the arrival date for the furniture and then walked over to the offices of the Colony Chronicle, a biweekly paper that largely subsisted on advertising and a grant from the town. What stories there were consisted almost exclusively of local interest items. Throw in some want ads, notices about garbage collection and water rates, and that fairly well covered the paper's contents every two weeks.

Ilene spoke to the girl behind the counter. She looked to be eighteen or nineteen at the most, and was probably from one of the feral families toward the south end of the island.

"Excuse me, I'd like to know if the Chronicle publishes engagement and wedding announcements."

"Whaaat?"

"Engagement and wedding announcements. My daughter's getting married."

The girl started to panic. This woman was obviously not from around here and did not have a clue about the residents of Colony Island. How a human found out about the Chronicle was a mystery, but what she was asking was absurd. The editor would know what to do about this. She yelled over her shoulder for the editor to come out immediately as she reached for the phone to call the police.

"Ilene. It's been ages since we last had a swim together. How have you been?"

Ilene glanced at the now wide-eyed girl and then replied, "Maureen, it has been much too long. I wanted to ask if the Chronicle publishes engagement and wedding announcements."

The editor gasped. "Penelope, right?"

Ilene nodded with a proud smile.

"Diana, this is Ilene Tench. Her daughter's wedding is going to be the first one ever to take place here on the island, and we're going to cover it. Ilene, come back to my office, and let's get going on this."

Ilene's next stop was the Royston News.

Peter and Penelope arrived on Colony Island Friday evening to find the new furniture delivered and in place, along with Ilene's curtains. Penelope's mother was quite pleased with herself for having accomplished so much in only five days—so pleased, that she surrendered her post dinner mother-daughter time so the kids could unpack the spare clothing they'd brought with them from the city.

When everything was in its place and all the pictures hung, Penelope and Peter snuggled on the love seat in their first "home" together—even if it was just for weekends.

"Peter, you've become a real islander, you know. The standard practice is for newly chosen mates to move in with one or both sets of parents until they or the parents decide it's time to breed. Stop that!" Penelope's mate had been nuzzling her neck and nibbling her ear. "Sweetheart, I think we need to christen the bed."

"Whatever you say, love. I'll turn down the covers if you'll close the door and get the lights."

Mom, we're going to bed early—if you know what I mean.

I do. Have a wonderful time, dear.

Of everyone in the Tench household, Ilene was the happiest of all. The family circle had been both repaired and enlarged, and everyone was under the same roof for the next two days. Life was good.

CHAPTER EIGHTEEN

When Penelope suggested to Peter that he go to bed early, she didn't need a telepathic bond to gauge his reaction. The look of horror on his face was plain enough.

Again? I have to go through the same thing as our first night here again? I thought you said once was enough!

She shook her head and mouthed the word "no." The look of relief on his face was instant.

"Mom wants to stay up a while and talk. I think she wants to rattle on about possible menus for the reception, invitations, flowers, what she should wear—you know, girl stuff."

The thought of having to sit in on that discourse was almost as bad as having to repeat their first night together on Colony Island, and he readily conceded.

Penelope sat on the edge of the bathtub, making small talk, while Peter brushed his teeth and performed the other bits of his nightly ritual. She kissed him good-night, closed the bedroom door, and tiptoed back downstairs where her mother motioned her into the office.

Once the door was closed, her father said, "Now I suppose you're all wondering why I called you here this evening."

Ilene rolled her eyes at George's rendition of that ancient joke, sat on the edge of his desk, and picked up a plastic milk jug filled with a reddish-orange liquid Penelope had not noticed before.

"Penny, this is what's going to turn your Peter into a merman. He'll have to dutifully drink this every morning for seven to eight months like the mayor said. The mayor also reminded us there are no side effects other than feeling sick as a dog for the first two or three days."

"Mother, the mayor said, 'Sick as a parrot.'"

"George, I heard him say quite distinctly, 'Sick as a dog.'"

This time, it was Penelope who rolled her eyes as she put a stop to her parent's gentle bickering.

"Okay. I think we can all agree Peter's not going to feel his best for a few days. What else did he say?"

Ilene gave her mate a look that said, "We'll discuss this later!"

"Well, Penny, the mayor told us every human he's known has balked when it came time to take the first dose. It's a pretty big step, and it seems to him to be a perfectly natural reaction. After all, you'd be hesitant too if you were going in the opposite direction. What each of us needs to do is be very supportive and understanding of Peter's situation. According to Mayor Bill, sooner or later, they all start drinking the juice, and once the first few days are over with, everything's fine. They'll complain the drink is bittersweet, or just plain bitter, but they'll get used to it after a while and will eventually almost crave it."

Penelope and her parents talked for nearly thirty minutes discussing Peter's possible reactions and their responses. Each of them wanted to be sure he didn't feel alone through all this or did not feel like a failure if it took him a while before the first sip. When they were finally done, they quietly turned off the lights, and Penelope made her way up the steps to her—their bedroom.

When she opened the door, she saw Peter's sleeping face framed in the moonlight slanting in through the window. *My beautiful, beautiful merman to be,* she thought to herself, and she was taken aback when her heart spoke to her.

"Why is it so important to you that Peter becomes a merman?"

"Well, he wants to become one of us."

"He wants to, or *you* want him to?"

"Both...I think. I want to share my life and my world with him. He's my mate."

"And what would you do if he decided not to?"

Penelope did not have an answer for that, and she brooded over it until she drifted off to sleep.

Peter awoke well after sun-up to discover Penelope was

already up and dressed. Listening to the few sounds that drifted up from downstairs, he surmised everyone was waiting to go on a family swim, and he was holding them up. Peter quickly threw on his clothes and headed down the steps. He turned left going through the living room into the dining room and discovered everyone sitting stone-faced around the dining room table.

"I'm sorry I overslept. I promise it won't happen again."

No one said a word. He pulled back a chair, angling it so both Penelope and her parents were within his field of vision. It was then he noticed the empty glass and the small pitcher of reddish-orange liquid sitting on the table.

"So, that's the stuff, huh?"

Penelope spoke with an earnest look on her face. "Dear, please know I will always love you and will always be your mate no matter what you decide to do."

Peter gave her a brief, "thank you," kind of smile and asked, "What does it taste like?"

Ilene looked at him with a bit of sadness in her eyes. "Bittersweet, dear. Sweet because you're becoming one of us, but bitter because you're losing your humanity."

"Who says I'm losing my humanity?" he questioned with a frown. "You guys are human, aren't you?"

George and Ilene could not have looked more incredulous if he'd told them the sea was made of tofu. He didn't dare to look in Penelope's direction. She was probably removing her engagement ring at this very moment. *Crap! I've gone and done it now. Feet, do your duty, because I have to tap-dance my way out of this one and fast.*

Taking a deep breath, Peter began, "Do you not have eyes? Do you not have hands, organs, dimensions, senses, affections, and passions? Are you not warmed by the same sun and cooled by the same breeze as I am?"

It was considered to be the height of rudeness for two merfolk to communicate while someone else was speaking, but on this occasion, Ilene could not help herself.

What's he talking about?

He's channeling Shylock, Mom.

Who?

Shylock...from Shakespeare's tragicomedy play, "The Merchant of Venice."

Oooohhh!

"If I prick you, do you not bleed? If I tickle you, do you not

197

laugh?" Peter continued, unaware of the silent dialogue between his mate and his future mother-in-law. "If I poison you, do you not die? If I wrong you, will you not seek revenge?"

As he paused for a moment to draw in another breath, Penelope began to feel a glow of pride—then her mate continued.

"Ever since I came to Colony Island, I have received a royal welcome. One just as warm, and yes, just as human as I could find anywhere else. The only real difference is, merfolk can do things most humans can't.

"Scientific studies have demonstrated that musical ability is inherited. Much to my mother's disappointment, those genes did not come my way. My college roommate—he's going to be one of my groomsmen, by the way—is a truly gifted musician. All he has to do at a party is sit down at a piano, play 'Endless Love,' and every girl within a fifty yard radius will dump her date to flock to the sound of his music. Does that mean he is more human than I? Or is he less human?

"The only thing that separates us is that you have different abilities than I have—and a wonderful secret—which I hope you still want to share with me. No, I'm not losing my humanity. I'm simply expanding my horizons. So now, sweetheart, pour me a glass of that merman juice so I can get this going."

George was a bit puzzled by Peter's oration, but his stoic demeanor gave no clue that he was analyzing what Peter had said. He decided to accept Peter's explanation since he saw no real difference between merfolk and humans.

Ilene needed no such analysis, because in the end, Peter's words made perfect sense. To her, this wasn't really a case of a human wanting to become a merman. No, this was simply a case of Penelope's mate—her "son"— coming home to be with his family.

Penelope carefully poured a glass of the juice, but rather than hand it to Peter, she set it on the table in front of her. With a serious look on her face, she asked, "Dear, please explain to me why you're doing this. I just want to know before you go forward with it."

Peter was rendered speechless by this request and looked thoughtful for several moments. He finally raised his head and said with a small smile, "There are four major reasons. They are all interrelated, and I can't separate one from another. The first one is, ever since the first day you reported to work, I've felt the desire and urge to protect you. We've talked about this before, so it's nothing you don't already know. However, I can't always do that if I can't go beyond the beach.

"The second reason is, I desperately want to be able to swim beside my wife and mate. I know I've got a bit of a problem with being in the ocean, but I'm not going to let it stand in the way of swimming with you. Believe me, I will overcome that fear and lay it to rest.

"The third reason is, I want to be able to take our children swimming. I don't want to have to tell them to wait until their mother comes home, or to go see if grandma or grandpa is available. They will be *our* children, and I really want to be able to do my part. Not being able to do that would kill me."

He wants to breed with me. Ever since she'd asked him to be her mate, and he'd proposed, they had not had time to sit and talk about their future. Penelope had been fairly certain he'd want to have children at some point, but there had been no discussion one way or the other. This declaration had her over the moon, and her heart was dancing.

Peter could tell from her eyes and the quickening of her breathing that Penelope was thrilled with the prospect, and he paused for a minute before continuing. "And finally, sweetheart, it's because I love you so very, very much. That's why everything I've spoken of is interconnected."

Peter paused for three or four seconds before saying with a warm smile, "Where you go, I will go. Where you live, I will live. Your people shall become my people, and your god shall become my god."

Penelope had seen her mother getting misty-eyed during Peter's speech, and now tears were starting to roll down her cheeks. Penelope took the Waiting Glass, kissed its rim, and handed to him so he would drink from that spot.

Peter raised his glass and toasted in his best imitation of a highland Scot's accent, "Slàinte mhòr!"

Penelope watched and waited for Peter to make a face or even spit out the mystical juice. He did neither and drank with apparent gusto. When he was done, he pushed the glass back toward Penelope.

"Damn, that's good! Mrs. Tench, I don't know where its reputation for being bitter came from, because it's not! This is the best thing I've tasted in a long, long time, and I'm going to look forward to getting up each morning for the next seven months or so. Sweetheart, would you pour me another glass of the nectar? One drink isn't enough."

Penelope saw the confusion in her parents' eyes, and though she was feeling a bit pixilated herself, she managed to keep her composure. Maybe the bitter bits had settled to the bottom of the pitcher. She poured the remains into the glass and handed it to Peter, expecting an even bigger look of disgust than she had before. It never came.

Instead, Peter finished the glass then moved his chair next to his mate's and gathered her into his arms whispering, "I love you."

"Well," George said as he rose from the table, "I don't know about anyone else, but I'm going to have my breakfast if you please. Mother, are you coming?"

Ilene was transfixed by what she had just witnessed and sat there gaping at Penelope and Peter.

George tapped her on the shoulder a time or two and finally had to lead her away to the kitchen.

Penelope whispered, "You didn't hesitate. Not for a moment."

"Why—were you expecting me to?"

"According to Mom, that's what the mayor said would happen, but you didn't. You drank two whole glasses and liked it. That's *definitely* not supposed to happen. The mayor told Mom it would taste bittersweet for a month or so, and you'd get used to it and eventually start to like it. I don't understand."

"Well, I'm at a loss, Pen. I really don't know what to tell you. It's delicious."

"You've already told me plenty. Those were some of the most wonderful words I've ever heard. You really do want to breed with me?"

"Yes, of course. Why wouldn't I? You know I'm coming in late on this merman thing, but I do want to see what childhood is like here. I must warn you though, our children will be going to the annual MacPherson family gathering in Scotland with us and will be dragged along to more than one set of Highland Games. And, the boys will be as much at home in a proper kilt as they will be in the sea."

Penelope smiled at the absurd thought of their children swimming out by the reef in kilts. Yes, they would definitely know about the outside world and participate in it, too. She still had a good bit to learn herself, and Peter was going to be a terrific teacher. They would learn from each other, and suddenly, life was looking to be even more wonderful than she had previously thought.

"I can't wait, but we're going to have a few years to ourselves, first. That's our future, but we need to come to terms with what happens next. I'm afraid you're going to start feeling the effects of the juice soon. I think it will feel like you have the flu for a few days, and there isn't much that can be done about it. Would you come upstairs with me, please? I have something for you I think will help."

Ilene and her George finished their meal in the breakfast nook and cut through the dining room to straighten the chairs. As they passed by the foot of the stairs on the way to their room, Ilene paused a moment, listening to the sounds of vigorous mating going on above them.

"I never dreamed that would become the most wonderful sound in the world to me."

Taking her hand, George countered, "Come along, dear. We can't let the young ones show us up. Let's go make our own noise."

Ilene closed the door to their bedroom and headed toward the den to see if her daughter was in there. As she passed the stairs, she saw Penelope quietly descending wrapped in her terry-cloth bathrobe, the new one Peter had given her. The one she adored.

"Hi, Mom. My mate's sound asleep upstairs."

"Mine too. It's so cute when they do that."

This was the first time they'd ever spoken, mermaid to mermaid, about mating, and the significance of the occasion was not lost on either one.

"Since both our mates are going to stay asleep for a while, and yours will be feeling the effects of the juice when he wakes up, why don't we have a girls' day out and spend the afternoon in the Watermans' pool. I've got the key, and we might as well use it while we still can."

"That sounds like a great idea, Mom. I'll leave Dad a note telling him where we are and to check on Peter every now and then."

"Well now, that sounds very human of you—leaving a

note. Peter must be right after all."

"Mom, at the moment, that's all Peter and I have for communicating. Besides, it's kinda fun, and I can decorate my notes with hearts and scales. We can take our cell phones, and Dad can call either one of us if something's wrong."

"Why on earth do we need to do that, Penny?"

Penelope cut her off before she could say more. "Well, Mom, remember, Peter's not supposed to know about how we communicate until after it's all over, and relying on our phones for the time being helps to keep things simple."

"You know, Penny, I would never have thought of that. It just goes to show you what a college education can do for a mermaid. You write that note, and I'll go get some towels and something to snack on."

Shortly thereafter, Penelope and her mother slipped out the back door, headed in the direction of the Watermans'.

George pulled on his trousers and left the bedroom. He saw the note taped to the door that separated the hallway from the kitchen and stopped to peruse the message. He was puzzling over exactly why he had to call them on their cell phones—the word "Call" was underlined twice—when he heard the sound of pots and pans clattering on the kitchen floor. Pushing open the door, he found Peter busily trying to re-stack the cookware and put it back in the cabinets beneath the kitchen counter.

"Hi, Mr. Tench. I was just seeing what was here. Where are the ladies?"

Glancing again at the note in his hand, George replied, "It would appear they're spending the afternoon over in Watermans' pool."

"Well, good. Mothers and daughters need time together. Are they going to be there the entire afternoon?"

"Hmmm, apparently they are."

"Great. Mr. Tench, I have an idea."

Penelope swam in lazy figure eights around the pool, the water feeling almost as good as Peter's body had felt in the bedroom. The warm glow from that morning remained with her as she recounted mating with Peter.

She had taken the lead and done everything within her power to show him how much she loved and wanted him. His response was...well...something she'd always treasure.

At this moment, she was half tempted to put her legs on and go comfort her mate, but wasn't quite sure how that would be received. She was, after all, the reason for Peter's discomfort. For the fifteenth time that afternoon, Penelope wondered why her father had yet to call. Was there something he didn't want to tell her? Was he upset that Peter thought they were human?

Was Peter actually right? They were indeed humans with special abilities? Perhaps that explained her cousin Lindsey's behavior. Both of them had gone away to university, but Lindsey had gone the furthest from the sea and had actually thrived. Indeed, she had stayed in Nebraska after she graduated and seemed to be right at home wherever she was. Reading between the lines during her visit a month ago, Penelope would have seriously believed she was interested in a non-mer. So many things to think and worry about. She had to find out how Peter was doing.

Ilene glided to the surface following her nap on the very bottom of the saltwater pool. There was a water mattress down there, and it was quite comfortable.

"Penny, have you heard from your father yet?"

"No, Mom, and while no news is good news, I'm starting to worry."

Ilene attempted to distract her by saying, "Well, from the look of things, you had some very good news this morning. I mean, about children. Had the two of you not discussed breeding yet?"

"No, we haven't had the time, and I was almost afraid to mention it for fear of sounding like that's all I really wanted from him. Some human females are like that."

"Penny, mermaids are no better, and perhaps a bit worse when it comes to such matters. It's obvious, though, that Peter would be a fool not to want to breed with you."

"Mom, Peter is far from being a fool. He's like...like....no one I've ever met, and yet, he acts like he's the lucky one."

"Dear, you are both lucky to have each other, and I'm so lucky to have the two of you. After all, he's the one who found and brought you home to me."

"Mom, I'm lucky to have you, Dad, and Peter as my family.

This has been such a wonderful change for me. You and Dad have been so accepting of Peter and the fact that he's not one of us."

"Why wouldn't we be? He's your mate, and it's plainly obvious that you love each other dearly. He's been so eager and willing to become a merman it would be difficult *not* to accept him. Penny, I think you made the best possible choice of a mate with Peter."

"Thanks, Mom. I feel the same way, myself. May I ask you a question? It's something that's been in the back of my mind for the past month."

"Certainly, dear. Ask away."

"Well…the first dinner we had together a month ago when you suggested we go through pregnancy together—did you really mean it?"

"Penny, I apologize for that. I shouldn't have brought the topic up so soon. I was just so excited over the fact that you'd chosen a wonderful mate. But, to answer your question, yes…I really meant it. We would be far from the first mother and daughter to do it. The practice has declined over the past few decades, and a lot comes down to the timing of each mermaid's life. I do know it would be a wonderful experience for me. We could even breed on the same beach under the same moon."

Penelope was quiet for a moment. She knew this sort of thing had occurred a lot in the past and still happened occasionally today, though the current trend was for best friends to do it. Merfolk were pretty much oblivious to the rest of the world when they were mating on the beach and even more so when they were breeding, so it wouldn't matter where her mother was. No doubt, living and working with humans had rubbed off on her a bit, but if she *were* to share the experience of breeding and pregnancy with anyone, it would be her mother.

"Mom, right now, I'm more concerned with getting Peter his tail, but when the time for us approaches, and if our mates are okay with it, then it's something I'd like to at least talk about."

Ilene opened her mouth to speak, but said nothing, and it looked like she was going to tear up again when her cell phone suddenly rang. The two of them left a significant wake as they streaked into the conversation pit at the east end of the pool. Ilene picked up her phone and turned on the speaker.

"Mother? Is that you?"

"Yes, George. Penny's here too. What is it?"

"Dear, there has been a change in plans. This afternoon, Peter has driven me to parts of Royston I never knew existed. He's bought a chef's outfit and all kinds of food and is now madly doing prep work in the kitchen. Apparently, he is cooking dinner for us tonight."

George's voice was muffled as he appeared to be talking to someone else. "Right," he said as his voice came back on the line. "Peter says dinner is at eight o'clock, and the two of you are to wear your best dresses. We're having Italian, and I'm supposed to be the waiter."

"Are you sure he's all right? This doesn't sound *at all* like what the mayor prepared us for."

"I agree, Mother, but he seems to be perfectly well. Perfectly sane is another matter."

After George finished up by saying he had to go and set the table, Ilene was somewhat bemused by the whole situation. Her husband setting the table for dinner? That had happened only once or twice in their marriage. Peter cooking dinner? Penny hadn't mentioned anything like that, and besides, he was supposed to be feeling poorly. And what were they going to wear? She only had one thing in her closet that would qualify as a fancy dress.

"Mom, I've got a couple evening dresses upstairs in my closet, and we're close to the same size. Should we go home and take a look at them?"

Ilene looked at the time on her phone. They would probably need two hours to take care of all the necessary details, including their hair. Thank goodness mermaid hair dried faster than other human hair. *My goodness. Did I just think 'other'?*

"Penny, we've got an hour or so before we have to start getting ready. I need to swim and think about a few things, first."

"Me too, Mom."

Penelope and her mother bypassed the back door and went in the front. Neither was quite ready to see if Peter was foaming at the mouth or had just simply gone crazy. They headed off to their respective bedrooms, and scurrying up and down the stairs ensued until it was time to eat.

When 8:00 p.m. arrived, they agreed there was no sense in stalling the inevitable, and it was time to face the music. They entered through the living room to find the dining room bathed in candlelight. There were a number of arrangements of fresh flowers scattered about, and the soft strains of a piano could be heard. George stood there in a suit and bow tie looking like a waiter in an upscale Italian restaurant.

"Buonasera, signoras. Welcome to Pietro e Georgio's Italian Villa. Il mio nome è Giorgio, and I will attend you this evening."

George's faux accent was corny, and his Italian seemed to come from an auto-translation website, but the sincerity of his efforts were unmistakable. He turned and spoke over his shoulder toward the kitchen.

"Ehi! Pietro! Our guests, they are-ah here!"

A moment later, the kitchen door opened, and out strode Peter in full chef's gear. He beamed at both Penelope and Ilene and said, "Benvenuto, signoras! Georgio, seat-ah the ladies and pour-ah the vino. Not a buon mercato. Only the best. Serve-ah l'insalata. I'll go make-ah the carbonara!" With that, he disappeared into the kitchen.

Ilene and Penelope giggled at the performance, but willingly allowed themselves to be seated by George.

And so the evening progressed. George brought out each course from the kitchen and cleared away the remains afterwards. While he did make occasional small talk, the ladies were left to enjoy a pleasant evening and quite a delicious meal. There were occasional loud noises emanating from the kitchen, followed by a stream of pseudo-Italian epithets. At one point, George and Peter engaged in an obviously pre-planned but hilarious argument on the other side of the kitchen door, followed by more pots banging and George returning to the dining room looking fit to be tied.

It was at some point after the main course that Peter emerged from the kitchen. He looked tired now, but it failed to dampen his enthusiasm. He turned toward Ilene and said, "Ah, bella donna! How you like-ah my dinner? Good, no?"

Ilene chuckled and answered with a tone of admiration in her voice, "Peter…I mean, Pietro…that was the best dinner I've ever had in my own dining room, and Georgio was very attentive and entertaining."

"Ahhh. Grazie, grazie. You make-ah my entire day. Georgio, you take-ah tomorrow off, capisce? And you, signorina.

You make-ah my heart go pitta-pat. You know, I once-ah had a fiancé as beautiful as-ah you, but she was a Sirena, capisce? I love-ah her, but she ran off-ah with Charlie the Tuna."

Peter was interrupted by Ilene sniggering.

"I talk-ah too much. I send-ah out the dolce. My dishwasher, he no show-ah up tonight, so, I do it myself. What can-ah you do, eh?"

Penelope made a touching plea to let her help with the dishes, but Peter would have none of it. "You-ah the guest. What kind-ah restaurant you think-ah this is? No! This-ah your evening to-ah relax."

He motioned to George to follow him into the kitchen. Once the swinging door had come to rest, Peter spoke to him in a whisper. "Mr. Tench, you've done very well tonight, and I really want to thank you for all you did. Take them dessert, please, and tea after that. Once the ladies are done, take them out to the living room, den, or wherever. I'll take care of the dishes."

George looked at Peter with concern on his face. "Are you sure you want to do this by yourself, son? I'd be happy to help."

"No, no. It's fine. You've done enough tonight. Go entertain the ladies. Talk about the moon, the stars, or where you want to swim next weekend. This was all my idea to begin with, so I'll clean up. Just keep them out of here for the rest of the night. I...we did this to please our mates, and they should not have to help wash dishes." Peter clapped George on the shoulder as he turned to take the deserts into the dining room.

Penelope's father had been the perfect Italian waiter—once he caught on to the whole idea for the evening—and deserved to relax. Peter simply wanted to slow down and clean the kitchen. He'd had occasional bursts of energy before, but none anywhere as sudden and long lasting as today's. The dishwasher needed loading, pots needed soaking, and after they were done, there were still the countertops and the floor to clean.

After the last item had been unloaded from the dishwasher, the last of the pots and pans put away, and the floor was sparkling clean, Peter undressed and stuffed everything in a garbage bag to be washed when he got home. Thank goodness mer families had a casual attitude toward nudity.

He quietly made his way up the stairs and into the bathroom. Penelope was not going to sleep next to a mate who smelled like a kitchen. The shower relaxed him and an exhausted Peter crawled in to bed and instantly fell asleep. He never felt the kiss on his cheek.

Peter didn't feel the kiss on his forehead the next morning, either. He woke about forty-five minutes later, threw on some fresh clothes, and headed down the stairs for the kitchen. Penelope was nowhere to be found. This being Sunday, she'd probably gone out to pick up some donuts. He poured himself a glass of the juice and was savoring it when Ilene called through the doorway to the hall.

"Peter, dear, when you finish your juice, would you please join George and me in the office?"

Well, that didn't sound good. With Penelope out of the house, he was fair game for her parents. He had probably gone way over the top last night and would most likely be told to stay in the city on future weekends. Like a condemned prisoner mounting the scaffold, he finished his juice and made his way toward George's office. Ilene bade him to close the door and sit down. *What did I do wrong? This can't be good.*

"Dear, where on earth did you learn to cook like that? I've never had such a wonderful meal."

Peter replied sheepishly, "My mom was a great cook, and a tiny bit of it rubbed off on me. You probably saw three quarters of my culinary repertoire last night, but I'm guessing that isn't why you called me in here."

Ilene slowly shook her head.

When Penelope returned twenty minutes later, the door to the office was closed and she could hear her parents discussing something or other they were going to tell the mayor. She set the box of donuts down on the table in the breakfast nook and headed upstairs to see if Peter was awake yet.

She opened the door to find him sitting on the bed, dabbing at his eyes with a piece of toilet paper. Something wasn't right, and she had to find out what it was.

"What's wrong, sweetheart? Are you okay?"

Peter wiped the rest of his tears off on the toilet paper and loudly blew his nose. He turned to look at her for thirty seconds before saying, "You know, I've never mentioned this because it makes me sound like a whiner, but I had trouble with not only girls, but their parents, as well."

Peter went on to tell her about some of his encounters with

the parents of the girls he'd dated before they met. Penelope wondered how any one person could have suffered as much as he had. His story seemed to have something to do with her parents, but she didn't dare ask and waited for it to come to a natural conclusion.

"And then six months ago, I met this amazing mermaid. Before long, she took me home to meet her wonderful parents, who have been kind to me in every possible way. I need to know just what I was doing wrong all those years."

Penelope sighed and rested her head on Peter's shoulder. "You weren't doing anything wrong, sweetheart. You just hadn't found me yet. If I'd known you were on your way, I would have swum to you as fast as I could. I think we were somehow meant to be each other's mates. But what did my parents say to you?"

Peter sighed and used the tissue one more time before replying, "Your parents…your parents have asked me to call them Mom and Dad. Your mother said she thinks of me as a son. Her son."

Penelope gasped and said, "That's wonderful, sweetheart. I'm so happy for you! But you do know you don't have to call them that if you don't want to. Your parents are gone, and I'm sure my parents would understand if you're not comfortable with that, or you feel like it would dishonor their memory."

"No, no. That's not it," Peter responded. "I'm just not sure what it all means."

Penelope smiled sweetly. "It means you're part of our family, now. It means you're one of us."

Peter looked at her in total disbelief. He was desperately trying to wrap his head around this, and his head was not cooperating at the moment. "But I've only had two…no, three glasses of the juice. I still have seven months to go."

"It doesn't matter how many you've had," Penelope explained. "Amy called me last Wednesday, and she said Mom's been calling you her son for the past three weeks. The only reason I can think of is she never found the right opportunity to tell you before now. By the way, what did Dad say?"

"Well, he said he was pleased and proud to have me for a son, and that I should stop with the 'Mr. Tench nonsense.' I'm worried about you the most, though. You've been their only child all your life. I'm afraid I'm going to come between you and your mother. How are you going to handle this?"

Penelope gave Peter a big, silly grin, and exclaimed, "With

relief! Don't get me wrong. I love my mother dearly, but you've noticed she can way overdo things at times. I'm happy as can be that she finally has someone else besides me to fuss over...especially when that someone is the person I love so much.

"So, I've got an idea. Let's go downstairs and have some donuts. When we're done, we'll tell Mom and Dad we're going down to the private beach. I'm in desperate need of some alone time with my mate."

CHAPTER NINETEEN

On Monday morning, Ilene and George arrived at the mayor's office at 9:00 a.m. Strictly speaking, it wasn't necessary, as the information could have been delivered over the phone or by email, but Ilene always preferred face-to-face meetings when important matters were involved, and there were several on her list.

Bill Marlin ushered them into his office and closed the door—another action that wasn't really necessary, since there were usually only one or two people in the town's municipal building at any one time, but he firmly believed a sense of privacy and confidentiality always helped people to open up. The citizens of Colony Island had a long history of not speaking openly about things, and if there was any way to put folks at ease, the mayor was all for it.

"Well good morning, you two. How did things go this weekend?"

George and Ilene glanced at each other, unsure who should speak. Since Ilene was the chattier of the two, George indicated with a nod of his head she should do the talking—at least for now.

"Mayor, it went unbelievably well. While Peter is a young man of very good intentions, we were all prepared for some degree of hesitation on his part—even an outright balk."

"And did he?"

"Actually, he didn't, though he certainly had every opportunity. He was ready for his first sip of the juice when Penelope stopped him by asking why he was doing this. He delivered the most touching and beautiful list of reasons for why he wanted to become one of us," Ilene paused for a moment to brush a tear from her eye before continuing, "then he drank his first glassful without a moment's hesitation."

"And how did he like the taste?"

"Mayor, that's the funny thing. He pronounced it one of the best things he'd ever tasted and then asked for a second glass." Ilene waited for Bill to say something—anything—but he was apparently too astonished to speak, so she continued. "He enjoyed the second glass as much as the first. No complaints. No looks of disgust. No anything."

Bill finally found his voice. "I suppose he was twice as sick as he should be?"

It was George's turn to speak. "Bill, as far as I can tell, it was quite the opposite. From all appearances, he felt very good and insisted on cooking a five course Italian dinner for my mate and Penelope. I was the waiter, and let me tell you, mermaids do not tip very well. He felt fine on Sunday morning and seemed to enjoy his daily dose of the juice. I plan to call Penelope this evening, but I have no doubt as to what she'll tell me."

The mayor was pensive for a moment. "Has he ever cooked before?"

"Penny told me he did hamburgers for the girls down at the private beach, and they were really good."

"Well Ilene, tell your daughter she had better hang on to Peter. He's a real catch! By the way, I meant to tell you both that creating an upstairs 'apartment' for them was a brilliant idea. I know you would have done the same for whoever she chose, but in Peter's case, having a 'home' here gives him a connection to Colony Island and will ease his assimilation. The sooner he feels he belongs here, the easier his transition will be. In fact, having that special place for the two of them may be responsible for what you observed—or didn't observe—on Saturday. Peter feels like he belongs here now, and that could have impacted how well he adjusted to the start of his transition.

"Each conversion is slightly different in one way or another. I take plenty of notes, and maybe my successor will be able to draw some conclusions from all this. Keep me in the loop as to how things go with him. It sounds like he's done with what few side effects there will be, and it's going to be plain sailing until mid-May."

Ilene and George looked at each other and again, and he indicated she should handle the next bit. "Mayor, there's something else we want to talk to you about. It has to do with Peter."

It was nearly 9:00 p.m., and Penelope was folding the laundry. It had been quite a successful weekend, and Peter was on his way to becoming a merman—her merman. He'd had his daily dose of juice that morning and had gone on to work without a problem, as happy as he could be. If anyone was having a problem, she was. She was finding it harder and harder to spend her evenings away from him, and he probably felt the same way.

Sadly, there was nothing they could do about it. They both had chores to do, bills to pay, and very small apartments. Spending too much time in cramped situations would probably cause trouble between them, no matter how much they loved each other. Penelope was calculating the amount of time until her lease was up when her cell phone rang.

"Hello, Princess! How's my favorite daughter this evening?"

"Hi, Daddy! Everything's fine, and Peter's taking his juice just like he's supposed to."

"I expected nothing less. Could you let me talk to your mate? I have a couple questions about a software package I'm considering."

"Sorry, Daddy, but Peter's over at his apartment tonight."

"What's he doing over there? Why isn't he with you?"

"I wish he was, but both our apartments are really small, and neither of our leases are up for another five or six months. We decided it would be too difficult to live together in such tight quarters all the time."

"Hmmm. I see. Well, I'll just have to call him instead. Mother sends her love."

Penelope started to panic. Her father had sounded none too happy about their living arrangements. Given the abrupt way he'd ended his call, she wanted to call Peter and warn him of what was afoot. She frantically called his number, but the line was busy.

"Hello?"

"Peter, why aren't you sleeping with my daughter?"

"Do what?"

"Why aren't you sleeping with my daughter? Is something wrong between you two?"

"Uhhh, no, Dad. If you'd ever seen the inside of Pen's apartment, you'd understand. I've seen more spacious broom closets. And sadly, even if I dumped all my computer gear and moved her in with me, we'd still need more space."

"I see. I guess there are some things that just can't be helped. Son, the next time you come home, I'd like to ask you some questions about this software I'm considering."

Peter had no sooner hung up with Pen's father than his phone rang again. This time, though, it was his mate.

"Peter, I'm sorry about Dad. He called here first, and I tried to warn you, but your line was busy. I didn't have to guess who you were talking to."

He found this whole situation rather surreal. He was all too accustomed to having his girlfriends' parents ask him, "Are you sleeping with my daughter?" In the vast majority of instances, his answer had been, "No," but they didn't believe him. It really didn't matter what he'd told them, because the end result was always the same. To have George ask why he *wasn't* sleeping with his daughter was mind-blowing, to say the least.

"Yeah, it was your dad, all right. I outlined our basic apartment situation and that seemed to satisfy him. We'll probably get grilled about it this weekend, though."

"Don't worry too much about it, sweetheart. He's really an old softy beneath all that grump."

Peter certainly hoped that was the case.

Peter was at his desk in his office and had just settled down to code another directory clean-up script for the server farm. He was already thinking ahead to his evening with Penelope—a nice meal out somewhere followed by a sleepover at his place.

Whether they mated or not that evening was inconsequential. He was going to sleep next to this wonderful mermaid, and that was enough for him. All of his plans went by the wayside when he saw a text from Penelope. The contents were short and to the point: "Peter, come up to my office as soon as you can. It's urgent!"

Peter took the stairs two steps at a time. Had Penelope lost her job? Had something happened to her parents? He flew into her office less than two minutes later.

"Peter, thank Poseidon you're here! I just heard from Mom. She and Dad are driving up from Colony Island. They're planning to stop by here around three or three thirty. What do we do?"

Peter finally caught his breath and asked, "How did Mom sound?"

"Cheery. She said she couldn't wait to see us."

"Well, that implies nothing's seriously wrong, but why not wait until Friday evening?" Peter saw his quiet evening with his mate fly out the window, never to return.

"Mom said Dad had some business here in town, and they were going to stay for a few days. He does this every once in a while to attend some seminar or other, or to meet with the brokerage firm he uses. From what I remember, though, it's usually drive up here one day, and drive back the next. 'A few days' is definitely out of the ordinary, and Mom coming along is even more so."

"The apartments. They're coming to see your apartment and probably mine, as well. What sort of shape is yours in?"

"I've been doing laundry and working on reports concerning the last fiscal quarter. I didn't clean up, because I was planning to spend tonight at your place."

Peter knew more than anyone else how much Penelope wanted to sleep with him, but the expression on her face as she realized this evening wasn't going to happen for them gave him an additional bit of reinforcement.

"Well, mine's clean…or at least 'guy clean'. How about you take a couple hours off and run home to tidy things up? In the meantime, I'll try to come up with a place to eat and possible entertainment for this evening. If anyone knows what's going on in town, it's my college roomie."

"Peter, if that's the case, I'm going to have to swing by your place. My best 'going out dress' is still in your closet. I'll take a quick look to see if there is anything out of place in your apartment."

After a quick kiss, Peter headed back downstairs to his desk. He really hated leaving Pen to handle all this, but they'd only get in each other's way if they both tried to straighten up her place at the same time. He wasn't sure why her father was so concerned about their sleeping arrangements. At the end of the day, it was just a temporary situation.

His attention shifted to contacting his former roommate, Billy King. He would be the first person Peter would tell about his engagement, and he'd have to be careful about the words he chose.

"Bill, how's my main man?"

"Pete, is that you? I thought you'd dropped off the face of the earth. It's been, what, eight, nine months?"

"Been busy, man. I'm getting married!"

"Ummm...Pete, you sure about this?"

"Yeah, I know my track record sucked in college and afterwards, but we've been together for almost six months, and her parents seem to like me, so I'm not expecting to be sleeping with the fishes anytime soon. Actually, we're getting married the third weekend in May, and I want you to be part of my groom squad."

"Pete, I'm really happy for you, man. You deserve a break after all you went through those four years. Sure, I'll be happy to do it."

"Great!" Peter exclaimed.

"Now, what else is on your mind?"

"Bill, here's the situation. Her parents are coming up here to visit on very short notice. Is there anything going on in town this evening?"

"You might be in luck. The Atlanta Ballet is at the Civic Centre for a couple performances, and I just happen to be giving guitar lessons to a girl who works at the box office."

"You giving her anything else?"

"Wouldn't you like to know? I'll give her a call to see if anything's available."

"Bill, I'm forever in your debt."

"I'll remember that! Talk to you in a few."

Peter began searching for restaurants on the way to the Civic Centre. Everyone was probably tired of Italian by now, so he looked for a place with steaks or seafood. He had just found one that offered both when Billy called to tell him his friend had found four seats in a section with excellent visibility. They were on the pricy side, but Peter was desperate for any diversion from the topic of who slept where, and he gladly took them, despite the cost.

Penelope returned to the office around 1:00 p.m. looking frazzled but confident that everything was in as good shape as could be.

They didn't have long to wait. George and Ilene arrived in the office around 2:30 p.m. Both of them seemed to be in very good spirits, and Penelope led them on the standard tour, which included meeting Mr. Williamson and a visit to the server room, where Peter had been trying to accomplish something besides worrying.

"Princess, I was wondering if we could see your apartment. Do you mind?"

Peter was right. They did want to see where and how the two of them lived.

The family first drove over to Peter's place and then on to Penelope's. After surveying their digs with a critical eye, George remarked, "I see what you meant by 'really small,' and I understand now."

Once Peter had explained the evening's schedule, Penelope's parents departed for their hotel to check in, and she and Peter congratulated themselves for dodging a huge bullet as they began to get ready for their evening out.

The four of them found their seats on the center aisle and sat down with Peter in between Penelope and Ilene. Billy was right, these were very good seats. Peter scanned the program and began to explain the different dances. The almost obligatory Act II of *Swan Lake* told part of a story, while *Valse Fantaisie* was simply about grace and beauty. They should also pay close attention to the *Pas de Quatre*, Peter's favorite. Finally, the lights dimmed and the curtain rose on the first dance.

George, they're so beautiful. So graceful. I can't believe humans are capable of this.

Mmmm.

I've seen something like this on TV a time or two, but it's sooo different watching it on the stage. And to think I've missed out on all this until now! George, can you imagine what it would be like if they had tails like we do?

Mmmm.

Penny, did you know about this sort of thing?

Well, small companies would come to campus when I was in college, and I saw them a few times. Things were starting to get really dark for me, so I didn't pay too much attention. You're right, though. We've missed out on this by living on the island.

I'll have to thank Peter for bringing us here. You should too.

Thursday's office hours were quiet for both Penelope and Peter. George was taking care of his business in town, and Ilene was most likely cruising bookstores in search of titles on ballet. When 5:00 p.m. finally arrived, Penelope and Peter took the elevator together to the lobby where her parents were waiting.

"If you don't mind, I'd like to show you some property I'm thinking of investing in," George said.

They all climbed into the Hummer, and after a relatively short drive, pulled up in front of a block of condominiums in the final stages of construction. According to the sign in front of the building, units had been on sale for a while and curtains or drapes could be seen in a number of windows.

"I hate to postpone dinner, but the office here closes at six thirty or seven," George informed them.

Once in the lobby, George picked up the key to one of the display units and they took the elevator up to the proper floor. "I wanted to show you what the interior of these units looks like. I think it's going to be a worthwhile investment."

George unlocked the door and stepped into a tastefully appointed three bedroom unit. "Of course, these are models, so the furnishings are a bit over the top, but you should still get an idea as to how good an investment this is."

George was right. With or without the fancy furnishings, it was easy to see how functional and comfortable the condos were. The master bedroom had a small bathroom attached with a shower. There was a second bathroom that was quite spacious, as well as a kitchen and living room of ample size. The second and third bedrooms, though smaller than the master, still had plenty of space.

When they finally assembled in the foyer, George asked, "What do you think?"

Peter opined that the units were going to be a good value for the money and asked how many he was thinking of buying.

"Just one...yours."

Ilene decided it was time to take Penelope by the arm and show her ideas for the kitchen and living room.

Peter's eyes bugged out. "Dad...George...Mr. Tench...I...we can't accept this," he sputtered. "It'll be years before we can pay you back. I'm sorry, but I can't allow you to do this."

George pinched the bridge of his nose and sighed. "Son, there are a few things you need to know. I have some capital gains this year I need to reinvest. Property is always a good investment, so that's what I'm going to do. You and my daughter can pay a few hundred dollars a month in rent if you like, but the main reason is, I'm doing what every good merman should do, protecting my family. That includes you, now. Family means a lot to us—a whole lot. Penelope is your mate, and you can't do a proper job of looking after her if the two of you are sleeping in two different places a mile apart from each other.

" Finally, I come to town every once in a while, and now I'll have a place to stay. The way Mother has been rattling on about ballet since last night, I believe we'll be here fairly often."

Peter was speechless. Penelope's parents had been kind enough to turn over the upstairs of their house for their weekend use, but this was beyond belief.

As the ladies rejoined them in the foyer, Peter asked, "Honey, did you know about this?" He could tell from the look on her face that she'd been as much in the dark as he, though she did seem to be a lot more at ease with what George was doing for them.

"Your unit is about six floors higher up, so you'll have a nice view of the river...and the ocean. Nearly everything is ready, and I've made one alteration. I'm reconfiguring the main bathroom so they can put in a lounging tub. When you and Penelope come home from a hard day at the office, you'll find that soaking your fin does a world of good."

There was not much Peter could say at that point, so he did the best he could to offer a heartfelt, "Thank you." He wasn't even sure George heard it, because Penelope was in the midst of hugging her father's neck.

Ilene moved next to him and touched his arm. "Dear, it'll be okay. Trust me."

Over dinner, George mentioned he and Ilene hadn't swum off this part of the coast in ages and wondered if Peter could help with logistics on the weekend. Peter was disappointed he wouldn't be going home to Colony Island.

That very thought gave him pause. When did he start thinking of Colony Island as home? He had to admit the island had become home for him to a large degree, and now that his father-in-law had given them the use of a condo, he couldn't very well say, "Sorry, not interested." No, things were different now, and he agreed to make all the arrangements.

When they got to the hotel, Peter was pretty sure he owed everyone a big apology. He'd been insistent—to the point of being obnoxious—that Penelope ride with him rather than her parents on their way to the beach. They were going to have her most of Saturday and Sunday, so why couldn't he have her for ninety minutes or so? They needed to talk about things, but now, he was so worked up the words wouldn't come. He felt like he was losing control of...everything.

George was simply doing his duty to his family, and Peter couldn't blame him for that. He just wished George would've talked to him first before springing the condo on them. Peter appreciated he was considered part of the family now, though he wished he'd done something to deserve it. Instead, he felt like he was caught in a rip tide again, being sucked out to sea and expecting to drown at any moment. What had he gotten himself into?

"Peter, I'm sorry about us not having this weekend together."

"It's okay, sweetheart. Your Dad's done...a lot for us, and we owe your parents at least this much. I'd just been looking forward to going home this weekend."

Penelope was secretly thrilled her mate was starting to think of Colony Island as home. He was starting to settle in to what would eventually become his new life, and that made everything else seem easier now. There would be challenges, pressures, and new experiences, for both of them over the coming months, but he had cleared the first few hurdles, and her father had made it possible for the two of them to be together every night they weren't at home on Colony Island.

That last bit worried her a little. Peter hadn't said very much at dinner last night or afterwards. Of course, he was as polite as ever, but there seemed to be an underlying edge to things, as if he wasn't too happy about the situation.

He was human after all, and their males probably didn't look at things the way mermen did. She was overjoyed that her father considered him part of the family, but maybe Peter didn't see it that way. Humans were funny. Maybe Peter saw it as some kind of insult. She'd have to talk to her mother about it tomorrow. For tonight, both mermaids wanted to spend time with their respective mates.

George wasn't particularly happy about being rousted before dawn and told to put on a bathing suit so he could go swimming, even though his daughter had explained to him it was a precaution she had taken every weekend with Peter.

"Daddy, Peter is doing his best to protect us. He knows more about swimming in the human world, so let's just follow his lead. Remember, what we're doing is not much different from when we swim from the public beach at home."

Peter walked them through the drill one more time as they drove toward the beach. He would park the Hummer, and they would all walk down to the water. When they got to the edge, he'd take their robes, and everyone would swim out a way before submerging. Penelope would give the swimwear to Peter, and they'd be on their way.

Penelope had plans for a bit of kissing with him before she got herself underway.

Once underwater, George struggled to get his swim trunks off. "Damn…silly…humans! You girls have it easy. All you have to do is pull a couple of strings and you're ready to put your tail on. And no, I'm not going to start wearing bikini bottoms!"

When Penelope caught up with her parents, Ilene asked, *Penny, is everything all right with Peter? He's seemed…I don't know…distant since dinner on Thursday.*

Thank goodness her mother had started the conversation. *Mom, I have a feeling it has to do with the condo. I suspect that to him, it implies he can't protect and care for me.*

Penny, that's absurd. Peter's part of our family. Doesn't he understand your father is doing what any merman would do—protect and look after his family?

Mom, Peter's human, remember? He's still stuck on land and sees all of this from the outside.

Well, he hasn't been completely human for the past week, but I think I understand what you mean. Be sure to spend all of your time on land this weekend with him. Meanwhile, I'll try and gently explain all of this to your father. Maybe the mayor will have some ideas.

Mom, I'll have no trouble with the first part.

After the couples had retired to their rooms that night, Ilene spoke with her mate. "George, you were a little upset early this morning, weren't you?"

"About having to wear a swim trunks? Who wouldn't be? It's not natural, I tell you!"

"Dear, Peter was merely trying to protect our secret. He's been doing this same thing for Penny for six months, and that's how she started looking forward to swimming again. There's no private beach here, and there are plenty of humans around."

"Mother, I've done this before, you know. I do know how to look after myself near humans."

"As I said, Peter was just doing his duty. Now, can you imagine how he felt when you told him about the condo?"

"That was totally different, Mother."

"Was it? The only real difference is, he and Penny told us about it in advance. He even got up early to fetch us donuts and hot tea"

"You're right, Mother. As usual, you're right. I'll speak to him about it in the morning."

"George, let sleeping dogfish lie. Just include Peter in future decisions that impact him and Penny. He's been trying so hard to fit in. Let's treat him like one of us."

"I'll do my best. Now, what's that noise going on next door?"

"Dear, if I'm not mistaken, the children are mating. So, while Penny is looking after her merman, I'd like to do the same for mine."

CHAPTER TWENTY

Bill leaned back in his swivel chair and closed his eyes for a moment. He had only one appointment that afternoon, and once finished, he had to drive to Feral Town and check on a house. The principal at The Academy had reported a ten-year-old boy suddenly stopped attending two weeks ago, and it was a pretty good indication the family had decided to return to the sea. If the home had indeed been abandoned, any personal possessions would be put in storage, and the house would become available for another family to use.

When he was done with that bit of business, the mayor planned to drive down to the private beach for a mid afternoon swim. From the sound of the front door opening and closing, the appointment was about to get underway.

"Ilene, how are you?"

"Mayor, I'm just like you—looking forward to the weekend. George said if you want to ask him anything, you can do it during your swim tomorrow."

Bill chuckled at that one. George was almost as closed-mouthed as a feral. "Well, I think we can get by without him. Penelope and Peter should be here in a few hours, right?"

"I'm afraid it's just Penelope this weekend." Ilene sounded thoroughly disappointed. "Peter has to work Saturday and Sunday. Penny explained what he's doing, but it's all Greek to me."

"That's too bad. I have another batch of juice she can take along when she goes back to the city. Speaking of your daughter, I called her earlier this week to get her take on things, and she told me things were going swimmingly."

"Mayor, I think she's right. Peter's doing well with the juice and hasn't shown any side effects. In fact, Penny says he regrets he can't have it with every meal, because he loves the taste so much."

Bill smiled at this, happy Peter had taken to it like a duck takes to water. "Aside from Peter's taste for merfruit juice, how's everything else?"

"Very well, I'd say. We bought them a condo in the city so they can finally live together. Aside from the very first weekend, Peter's been a joy."

The mayor looked concerned. "What about the first weekend?"

"Oh, it was mostly me. In fact, it was all me. I'm used to spending time with humans, but I wasn't prepared for a human to spend time with me. We both adjusted. Actually, it was Peter who did most of the adjusting."

A look of relief crossed the mayor's face. He wanted all conversions to go well, especially this one. "Well, Ilene, people are more comfortable around others who look and act like they do, and that applies to merfolk as well as humans. Now, do you have any questions for me?"

"Mayor, I was wondering when it's okay to start telling him about the everyday things about being a merman."

"That's pretty easy. I'd hold off on mating and hygiene until it becomes more relevant to his day-to-day life. Aside from those and communicating, I'd say tell him whatever you wish, whether he asks or not. My advice is to go easy on him, as too much new information at one time can be overwhelming. Oh, and one other thing. He's not going to be able to communicate until anywhere from a few days to a few weeks after the change. He'll need instruction, of course, from someone other than your daughter, as it can be very intense. I was thinking maybe you could be the one to do it."

Ilene felt a thrill of excitement. She'd enjoyed teaching Penelope when she was little, and now she'd be able to play a part in Peter becoming a mer. In that moment, she understood why her daughter had been so disappointed at the news the transition would take months, rather than days. She could hardly wait.

"I'll do my best, Mayor. Now, about the other matter…"

"Ah…yes. The paperwork is pretty straightforward. Since the custom has fallen into abeyance here on the island,

I've been trying to find ferals who will actually talk to me about it. As you well know, a feral never tells you anything except when it's in his interest to do so. Unless I learn something different, all we'll need is a final decision and a time and place."

"Thank you, Mayor. Oh, one other question."

The mayor hoped this would be a quick one to answer. He wanted to put his tail on as soon as possible.

"I think Peter may get more than a little nervous about all this as time goes on. Is there anyone he could talk to...anyone who's already gone through this?"

The mayor frowned at her question. He'd been hoping to avoid having to tell her this, but it looked like there was no other choice.

"Well, Ilene, humans join us for a variety of reasons. Some want to escape their old life and make a fresh start, others want to blend in as soon as possible. Whatever the case, I have to protect their privacy unless they tell me otherwise. I'll canvas the recent ones and ask them, but I'm not expecting a positive response. Furthermore, some converts like the change so much, they move offshore, and once they've gone feral, it's impossible to track them down. Nonetheless, I'll see what I can do. Now, unless there are any other questions, I'll get Peter's juice, and you can be on your way."

Penelope and Peter were having a bit of quiet time together in her office before she left for Colony Island, on her own this time, since he had to work on Saturday and Sunday.

Standing safe and snug with her back against his chest and his arms around her waist, Penelope told her mate, "Honey, I'm going to miss being with you this weekend."

Peter gently spun Penelope around to face him. "Ha! You and your mother will be having too much fun to miss me," he said with a wink and a grin. "Just remember to bring me some juice. I'm almost done with my last jug."

Penelope shot him an enticing gaze. "Come here, mister, and I'll personally show you how much I'll miss you."

Peter stepped back and wagged his index finger at her. "Before you try any of your mermaid tricks on me, here's a list of music I put together for the wedding. I figured we could use recorded tunes for this affair."

Penelope glanced at the proffered list. She didn't know too much about wedding music, or classical music, for that matter, but she did recognize a number of tunes. "Sweetheart, I'm going to take this with me to show Mom. We might have one or two local options for some of these."

"Fine with me," Peter said, smiling. "Most of them are negotiable, so if you or your mother come up with a better suggestion, let me know."

"Duly noted."

As far as she was concerned, she was happy with every song she recognized, and she could find the others on the Internet and have a quick listen. She didn't think there would be any quibbling on her mother's part.

Penelope allowed Peter to reel her back into his arms. "Now let's discuss some of these so-called 'mermaid tricks' you referred to."

Peter was all too happy to oblige.

Ilene cut through the water with Penelope at her side. She'd been looking forward to a bit of girl time, but Peter had seemed to follow along, even though he was still back in the city. Penelope had called him on her cell phone the moment she'd arrived at the house, and Ilene had heard her talking upstairs after the lights had gone out that night.

This morning, she had chatted with him from the moment they left the house, all the way down to the beach, and up to when she stood at the water's edge. Fortunately, they didn't make waterproof cell phones yet, and Penelope was forced to say goodbye and stuff the phone deep into the pocket of her bathrobe before getting underway.

As they crossed over the reef into deeper water, Ilene reflected she and George had been like that—even though he would refuse to admit it—back when they were newly chosen. Cell phones weren't available then, but they kept in constant communication as long as they were in a one-mile radius of each other. They divided their time between the houses of each other's parents until they decided to breed. Once Penelope was on her way, they moved into what was their current house.

Ilene couldn't blame her for spending so much time on the phone with Peter. Today, he was in the city, hours away, and according to Penelope, they'd been together every day, in one way or another, for over six months. As long as Penny didn't obsess over the separation, everything would be fine.

Ilene needed to be careful about obsessing over Peter, herself. She had come to think of him as her son, which was a good thing, but she didn't want to come between the two of them or scare him off.

Everything seemed to be fine on the far side of the reef, and there were no predators in sight. Even if one did show up, there were plenty of rocks, ledges, and small coral caves for hiding until it lost interest or found something else to feed on. Ilene watched a yellow fin grouper sail over the coral, a bit unusual up this way, but the warming oceans were probably causing all sorts of disturbances.

Penny, how's Peter doing without you?

Oh, he's fine, Mom. The software upgrades and installations are going smoothly, and with any luck, he'll be done by the end of today. Tomorrow, he's going to start moving some of his stuff into the condo. The bathroom's almost done, and the bed is supposed to be delivered next week. We're going to use most of our old furniture for the time being. We'll probably move in over the next two weeks.

I'm glad everything's going so well, but you must let us come and help you move. We'd be able to get it all done in a weekend.

Mom, I don't want Dad butting heads with Peter again.

Penny, he won't. Your father and I had a little talk, and everything's been smoothed over. He's just not used to the new arrangement yet, or at least he pretends he isn't. Speaking of Peter, I met with the mayor yesterday. She recounted everything they had discussed and concluded that George should leave the two of them to do the teaching when the time came.

A scene of Dad trying to educate Peter on how to mate, tails on, popped into Penelope's head and almost invoked paroxysms of laughter. She snorted seawater. A mermaid had to be careful about laughing below the surface. *Well, Mom, I had thought about asking Mrs. Troutman at The Academy if she would give one or two of her talks to Peter during the time he's off his feet. I'd sit in to give him moral support.*

You know, I hadn't thought of that. There was one other thing the mayor mentioned, but I can't remember it at the moment. In the meantime, do you feel like leaping? I haven't done it in ages.

Sure, Mom. I'll take the first watch, and when you're done, you can keep lookout for me.

Leaping consisted of building up momentum beneath the surface and then rocketing out of the water before plunging back into the sea. The more agile would perform flips or rolls during the brief time they were airborne, while the average mer was content to re-enter the water with a modicum of dignity. Merfolk usually did it when they were happy, or for pure sport, and extra care had to be taken so it was not done in front of a passing boat filled with tourists. It was also performed only a few consecutive times lest the commotion attract unwanted attention from sharks. Both possibilities necessitated the use of a lookout, as zoom lenses, binoculars, and hungry hammerheads were equally dangerous in their own way.

As the morning became afternoon, mother and daughter swam slowly toward the beach, trailed by one or two yellowtail snappers. Ilene was hoping for a late lunch—one she didn't have to fix. The diner on Main Street would be ideal. *Penny, may I ask you a question?*

Sure, Mom. Ask away.

Does Peter ever talk about his family?

Yeah, he does talk a bit from time to time.

Well, do you think he'd mind if I asked him more about his parents? I don't mean to pry. I'm just being a mom.

I don't think so. I'll bring it up with him and let you know.

That night, Penelope lay under the covers waiting for sleep to come and wishing she and Peter could communicate with each other already. Imagining herself lying safe and secure in those strong arms of his only went so far, so she did the next best thing. She texted him: "I'm alone in our bed. Missing you."

She finally drifted off to sleep only to be woken an hour later by the telltale bling from her phone: "Wish I was there with you."

After a moment's thought, Penelope replied: "So do I, but I guarantee you wouldn't get much sleep."

Another bling: "Who cares about sleep when I'm with my mate?"

Feeling safe, warm, and loved, she slept soundly until the sun rose above the sea.

Penelope and her mother sat at the breakfast table Sunday morning over tea and donuts while she explained texting with Peter was almost as good as communicating with him, and once he'd gained the special abilities of the mer, they would probably use both to stay in touch.

"I just never got the hang of it, Penny," Ilene said as she poured a second cup of tea.

Penelope passed her the small dish of lemon slices. "Well, Mom, each mode has its advantages and disadvantages. Communicating is a hands-free, no hassle approach, but it can be kind of frustrating if the recipient is wrapped up in something. With a text, you hear the bling or buzz from your phone and read the message when you have time. Texting can be tedious, but it can also be fun. At school, I knew this guy who was an amateur radio operator. He could email or video chat with almost anyone in the world he wanted to, but it was just more fun to do it by radio."

"I suppose," Ilene commented. She took a sip of her tea.

Once they made sure George was happily ensconced in his office watching an online lecture about macroeconomics, Penelope and her mother walked down to the beach for an hour's worth of swimming.

"Penny, you seem more relaxed today. Any reason?"

"Like I mentioned at breakfast, Peter and I texted back and forth last night. I know he loves and cares for me, but every so often, a mermaid just wants a bit of reassurance. He didn't say all that much, but it was what he said and how he said it. This morning, I'm happy, and I love my mate even more…if that's possible."

"Hmmm. I'll have to talk to George about texting."

Once they'd entered the water and swum out across the reef, Penelope and her mother spent most of their time with a dolphin pod that frequented the area. One of the females had a three-month-old calf with her. This was apparently the first time it had encountered mermaids, and it was not at all shy about saying hello. Penelope hovered off to the side so as not to overwhelm the youngster and watched her mother play with the new found friend. No matter what species she was dealing with, her mother was still a mom. Maybe that was the reason her mom and Peter got along so well together.

The calf's mother glided by to check on her baby and then returned to the pod, grateful for the freedom of some unfettered feeding. The calf decided that playing with two mermaids was better than one, and the trio was soon swimming together in their own little pod, shooting up to the surface so the youngster could grab a breath of air and then swimming back down ten feet below the surface.

After twenty minutes of play, the calf returned to its mother for a second helping of breakfast. Penelope's maternal feelings had been stirred, and she swam next to Ilene as another outrider for the pod.

Mom, I hope I'm even half as good a mother as you are.

Ilene felt a warm glow and replied, *Oh, you will be, Penny. The key ingredients are love, patience, and a good mate, and you have all of those.*

I'm not so sure about the patience part. I wasn't much fun to be around the past five or six years.

Penny, dear, whether you knew it or not, you were being patient. You could've settled for Anthony or mated with a feral, but you didn't. You were waiting for Peter to come your way. And, as hard as those years were on all of us, I believe the wait was worth it.

Penelope still hadn't told her mother just how black things were for her right before she met Peter, and there was really no need to at this point. Her kind and loving hero had faith in her, and now, more than ever, she wanted to love him as much as possible. Her decision about breeding was still a long way off, but she was starting to have some inkling as to how she might lean when that time came.

I'm glad you're my mom.

And I'm glad you're my daughter. Let's swim for home, dear.

As they turned to leave, the calf broke away from its mother and swam around them as if to say goodbye. Penelope would have dearly loved to play some more, but she had two appointments that afternoon concerning the wedding, and she wanted to look presentable.

She'd spent time the previous evening painting her nails, which had raised her mother's eyebrows. While manicures were not unheard of on Colony Island, most mermaids, on the rare occasions they thought one was called for, went to Bab's Kut and Kurl to get them done. However, having spent years on the mainland, doing her nails was an ordinary occurrence for Penelope.

Once home, she inspected the polish. It was still perfect after her swim, so that was one less thing she had to deal with. Time to switch from creature-of-the-sea mode into that of bride-to-be. She opened her garment bag and pulled out a tuxedo front blouse along with a very pale celery-colored suit, not nearly as formal as her suits for work, but still more than acceptable for what she had to do that afternoon. A string of sea-green beads took care of the jewelry, and heels completed the outfit.

She was mid-way through applying her makeup when a now-familiar voice spoke to her. "Wow, you're getting all dolled up for an afternoon on the island. You know you really don't have to. They're very casual with their 'dress code.'"

That was all the more reason why Penelope wanted to do it, for him and for herself. Her mate couldn't be with her, and she didn't want anyone to think she was slacking off just because he wasn't along.

Penelope pulled her hair into a low ponytail and used a scarf to tie a bow around it. The look was a bit retro, but she liked it and really didn't care what anyone else might think.

Grabbing her purse, she went downstairs and let her mother know she was going out for a few hours. While both appointments were relatively nearby, she didn't want to walk all the way in heels and thus drove her car over to Lindsey's house. She could hear her bridesmaids chatting in barely contained excitement as she walked up to the front door. All of it suddenly ceased when she stepped into the living room.

"Just who are *you* trying to impress?" snarked Cindy. "The Queen?"

Amy was quick with a retort. "You wouldn't know the Queen if you tripped over her. I will be sooo glad when Mike comes home on break from medical school!"

Coming from meek, mild little Amy, such a comment was highly irregular, but things had been changing for her best friend over the past two months, and Penelope suspected she would see a whole new Amy before too long.

While Penelope was inclined to agree with her bestie, she decided to address Cindy, instead. "I have two very important appointments this afternoon, and thank you, I wanted to look my best for *both* of them."

"She's right, you know," said a disembodied voice. "I do the same thing in my line of work. You dress up to show your respect for the people you're going to meet with."

Amy and Cindy stepped aside to reveal Lindsey, smiling at a momentarily confused Penelope from a laptop screen.

"Oh, hi, Lindsey!"

"Hey, Anne! Oops—Penelope. Sorry I couldn't come home for this, but I did the next best thing. You look really nice."

Penelope was both pleased and relieved to find Lindsey supporting her choices, even if it was all the way from Lincoln, Nebraska. Nonetheless, she had things to accomplish.

"Okay, ladies..."

"Oooh, she called us ladies," Cindy quipped.

Penelope rolled her eyes. "The custom on the mainland is for the bridal party to have a head bridesmaid known as the maid of honor, or in our case, a mermaid of honor."

Everyone sniggered a bit.

Penelope gave them each a glance that said she wanted to be serious for a moment. "Usually, this person is a sister, cousin, or best friend. Now, I have three BFFs, but I can't decide which of you it should be, so I'm going to let you decide in a mermaid of honor lottery."

Penelope removed a purple velvet bag from her purse that had once contained a bottle of her father's whisky. "In this bag are three plastic Easter eggs."

The three mermaids knew what those were. The Academy held an Easter Egg Hunt each spring as a diversion for the students.

"In one of these eggs is a note that says 'Mermaid of Honor.' The other two contain a note thanking you for being one of my bridesmaids. Don't open your egg until I say 'go.' Got it?"

All three nodded.

"Will you ask my mom to come in and choose for me?" Lindsey requested.

Her mother must have been eavesdropping, because she magically appeared in the living room doorway. One by one, the mermaids pulled an egg from the bag.

"Okay, ladies. Go!"

For the next ten seconds, the only sound in the room was that of plastic eggs popping open and paper being unfolded.

Suddenly there was a shriek. Lindsey's mother jumped up and down. "You're it! You're the mermaid of honor!" She held the note up to the laptop's camera so Lindsey could see for herself. The slight sighs of disappointment from the other two bridesmaids confirmed Lindsey's win.

I'm sorry, Amy. It was the only way I could think of choosing.

No, Anne...you did the right thing. I'm still excited to be a part of your wedding.

Amy hugged Penelope, who returned the embrace and then cleared her throat. "Okay, girls, time for the next order of business."

"Oh, so we're just girls now?"

Penelope decided that Cindy's comment was not worthy of a response. "It's not uncommon for mainland weddings to include a soloist, someone who sings the 'Wedding Song (There is Love),' 'From this Moment On,' or 'Color My World'—something like that. I'd like all three of you to sing Savage Garden's, 'Truly, Madly, Deeply,' and I made a few changes to the lyrics to fit our situation.

"Amy, your moment to shine will be at the end where I replaced the 'doo-bee do-wah' with 'come swim with me'. Everyone knows you have the best voice on the island, so that's where you can show them the talent I'm so proud of. This is my gift to Peter, so please keep this to yourselves. That means you too, Aunt Grace."

"My lips are sealed, dear."

That statement provoked giggles, since it was a well known fact that Grace Tench loved to gossip. It could be said she was Colony Island's answer to Paula Revelle. Apparently, merfolk were more similar to humans than they liked to think.

"Peter is in charge of the ceremony, so he'll contact the three of you before too long about how he thinks this whole thing should work. He'll have to know you're going to sing something, but please don't tell him what that 'something' is, okay?"

After sharing a few bits of gossip and planning a girls' day out soon to shop for bridesmaid's dresses, Penelope left her friends in order to go to her next appointment. There was some disappointment amongst them there was not going to be a group swim, but as she explained, some things simply could not be helped.

Once she was back in her car, Penelope took a deep breath and tried to regain her calm center. Amy was right. Something had to be done about Cindy for the sake of everyone's sanity. She had been a good and kind friend back in high school, even though she was a notorious flirt and a bit of a loudmouth. Her antics had kept the girls amused back in the day, but with Mike in med school at Duke, Cindy's pining for her intended mate was getting on everyone's nerves.

Mike and Cindy were what some people on the Island called "pre-chosen." As Penelope was all too aware from her own experience, everything about life changed in an instant when a couple chose each other as mates. In Mike's case, that would make his time in med school extremely difficult for him, and Cindy would be even worse, if that was possible.

Merfolk had developed an informal custom over the years, whereby a couple facing an extended period of separation or unavailability would write a letter to each other asking if they would advise them on choosing a mate at some future date. Penelope supposed that nowadays, it was an email or even a text, but the end result was the same. If the other party agreed to the future consultation, they would consider themselves to be pre-chosen or reserved. That way, each party could go and do what was necessary knowing someone was waiting for their return.

What to do about Cindy was another question entirely. The rumor was the fix was already in for Mike to do his residency at a local hospital. Even if they decided not to advise and consent when that finally happened, the proximity would be a great comfort to both of them and a huge relief for everyone else. In the meantime, she and the other girls could discuss the possibility of pooling their resources and flying Cindy up to Durham, North Carolina every now and then.

With that issue sorted out in her mind, it was time to drive over to Lilith's house. Lilith Boatwright was the somewhat imperious leader of The Colony Consort. It was not a true consort in that it was composed of two violins, a viola, a cello, and a guy who played the recorder, but they liked the alliterative name, and the community at large didn't care because almost no one on the island knew about them.

The Consort would occasionally give a performance at the town hall before a tiny audience that consisted mainly of friends and family members who had been badgered into attending. Once in a while, there would also be someone who'd wandered in to see what was going on and then wandered back out during the first intermission. Otherwise, they were without honor in their hometown and played with a small regional orchestra on the mainland most of the time.

Penelope sat in front of Lilith's house trying to dredge up enough courage to knock on the door when she spotted her walking down the street with her violin case in hand.

Getting out of the car, Penelope approached her. "Good afternoon, Ms. Boatwright. I'm Pen…"

"I know who you are. I remember you from the children's concert at The Academy. Didn't like music much as I recall, and now you're getting married."

This was going downhill fast. It was not so much the music she didn't like as it was Lilith. That was back when she was a little mermaid, and it was time to act grown-up now.

"Well…yes. My mate had…"

"He's the human, isn't he? Interesting."

That comment got Penelope's hackles up. "There's nothing wrong with being human, and he'll be one of us soon enough."

"I see…hmmm."

"As I was saying, Peter had some ideas for music at the ceremony, and I decided to ask if The Consort would be interested in performing a piece or two."

"Give me the list, and I'll mention it to the other members at our rehearsal on Tuesday. One of them might want to do something. I'll let you know if there is any interest at all. Now if you'll excuse me, good day, Miss Tench."

Less than forty minutes later, a hastily convened meeting of The Colony Consort took place in Lilith's home, where she passed around copies of the suggested wedding music. Marty, the cellist, was the first to speak.

"I'll admit there are some lovely choices here, but there are good recorded arrangements of all of these works available. I don't see why we need to get involved."

Betsy, who played both the violin and the viola, was inclined to agree with him. "Marty's right. I'm sure we could perform special arrangements of the pieces, but it seems to me a DJ would be more suitable."

Lilith drummed her fingers impatiently on the table. "You're missing the larger picture here, people. This is the first wedding that has ever taken place on the island. Half the town is already planning to go, whether they know the Tench family or out of sheer curiosity. The town hall is going to be packed." Lilith paused, waiting for the penny to drop.

It didn't take long for Marty to speak in a soft, awe-filled voice. "We're finally going to have an audience. We're finally going to have a *large* audience!"

"We're going to have a *huge* audience," replied Lilith. "Now what can we do with this opportunity?"

The other violinist's face lit up. "We can call in favors," he suggested. "The guy who plays percussion for the orchestra works at the same place I do."

"Good, Roger," Lilith said. "I think we have enough strings—though if another cellist wants to help out, I won't say no. We're going to need some horns and woodwinds. Who do we know on the mainland that we've helped out in the past?" Lilith was starting to feel a positive vibe from the other members.

"I think Ed from the Royston enclave plays the trumpet, and he probably knows a few other people who do as well. We just might be able to make this a mostly mer ensemble," Betsy's voice rang out with a tinge of excitement.

"And I'm part of a children's concert in Royston, week after next." Lilith shuddered at the thought, but her determination was clear. "I'll chat up the other participants to see if they're interested. All right, then. I'm up for a swim right about now. If any of you want to join me, we can brainstorm about other possibilities once we're underway. Don't say anything to the Tench family yet. Let Penelope squirm a bit until we're reasonably sure we can pull this thing off."

CHAPTER TWENTY-ONE

It was Ilene's shopping day. She'd have to go one more time before next Thursday, but she was rather looking forward to all the preparations.

When Penelope started high school, the family had begun celebrating Thanksgiving. Their daughter had the holiday off from school, and while the term "Pilgrim's Pride" didn't mean anything to them, it was fun to sit down for a big meal on a real holiday. Sometimes, George's brother and his family would join them, or one of her cousins would accept the invitation for a free feed, but usually, it was just the three of them. She and George had stopped doing it when Penelope declined to come home in her senior year at Florida State and the following three years when she was alone in the city.

This year, it would be the four of them, and Ilene wanted to cook a meal everyone would enjoy. Thankfully, Peter wasn't big on turkey, but there would be token slices of the noble bird so everyone could have a taste.

What really had Ilene excited was the fact that she'd have Penelope and Peter around for a whole week. They would be arriving early Sunday evening, and though she wished for an extra forty-eight hours, Penelope had said they needed to take care of a few things at the condo. Ilene had immediately understood this to mean the two of them wanted a couple of days alone in their new home. She could not argue with that, and she was pleased they'd head for their weekend home the moment they came up for air.

She was browsing the vegetable section when Samia Marinos approached her with a haughty look on her face.

Their conversation was not going to be pleasant.

Samia was the town snob, descended from one of the first families to settle on Colony Island. The family had refused to "humanize" their name, sticking with the traditional ancient Hellenic names that were usually only found amongst ferals nowadays. She thought merfolk to be superior to humans and regarded all converts—no matter what the reason—as wannabes. The argument that she, and everyone else on Colony Island, lived a much more comfortable life because of human inventions, gained no purchase with her. As far as Samia was concerned, everyone on Colony Island would be much better off in the sea. Oddly enough, the family had made no move to return there in two hundred and twenty-five years.

"Ilene, how nice to see you. I heard about your daughter. It's a shame poor Penelope had to settle for a human."

"Settle?" Ilene pulled herself up. "That's hardly the case. Peter is a wonderful boy, and Penny is so in love with him. You do know he is well on his way to becoming one of us."

"It's admirable that you're being so brave about all this, but would you have accepted him so readily if he had not agreed to do so?"

Ilene hesitated, but only for a moment. "Samia, it was Peter's idea to do this, and he immediately jumped at the chance. By the way, I would have accepted Peter whether he chose to become a merman or not."

"Well, don't you see, Ilene, you can give him some scales and a tail, but at the end of the day, he'll still be little more than a human."

Ilene had taken all of this she was going to. She fixed Samia with a gimlet eye and proudly told her, "That's perfectly fine with me. I'm a human too, and so are Penny and my mate."

Samia opened and closed her mouth a number of times like a fish out of water and then turned on her heels and stormed out of the grocery store without a further glance.

Ilene exhaled a long sigh of relief—tinged with a touch of exasperation—and finished her shopping in peace. She returned home, and no sooner had she carried the last bag of groceries in from the car than the phone rang.

"Ilene, this is Bill Marlin. You'll never guess who I've

had in my office for the past thirty minutes."

Ilene didn't have to guess. She'd hoped that Samia had taken her snit home where it belonged, but apparently, she'd decided to drag the mayor into it. With ill-concealed disgust in her voice, Ilene replied, "Samia Marinos. What did she say?"

"Well, she claimed you said you were human. Is this true?" the mayor asked with a merry chuckle in his voice.

"Yes, it is, Mayor Bill, and I stand by every word of it, though Peter can explain all this better than I can."

The mayor took a few seconds to stop laughing. "Well, you remind Peter that I'll be taking copious notes when he stops by my office next Friday. I want to get all of this down so I can use it the next time that old blowfish swims by."

It was Monday morning and Penelope and her father were heading out for a day at sea together. Ilene and Peter wanted to see the two of them off, and Penelope clung tightly to his arm, happy to be walking to the ocean's edge with her mate. When they reached the beach, they hung up their robes and towels and proceeded to give their mates a goodbye kiss.

"Race you to the water, Dad," she said after she and her mother had reluctantly let go of their mates.

"You'll never beat me, Miss Fishyface!"

Father and daughter stormed into the surf. Penelope tugged at the side-strings of her bikini bottom, and they simultaneously dove into an oncoming wave.

She surfaced further off shore thirty seconds later, waving her bikini in the air, yelling, "I won! I won!"

George surfaced a moment later, claiming Penelope had an unfair advantage.

"Round two to the ocean floor?"

George replied with, "Bah!" and sounded.

With a splash, Penelope followed her father.

"Peter, in case you're wondering, there's a place on this side of the reef where they'll leave their swimsuits until it's time to return to shore."

As Peter nodded, father and daughter surfaced together further out and waved before sounding again.

"Peter, for years, I worried she'd swim out to sea and never come back. You've given her something to come home for, and both George and I are so grateful."

Peter smiled. "Mom, how could I not help falling in love with her? I'm just amazed she fell in love with me. Seriously, I should be the one thanking you and Dad for accepting me— a human—and giving me a place to come home to on weekends. It's the first real home I've had since my mother passed away."

When it came to her family, Ilene's emotions were always near the surface, and this was one of those occasions when she wanted to take Peter in her arms and hold him as any mother would. Peter, however, was a grown man and might not take well to this from a mother-in-law, no matter how well intentioned. She fought her natural inclination to tear up and looked for another way to be motherly.

"Tell me, Peter, how are you and the juice getting along? Any side effects?"

Actually, there had been a few odd things—nothing major—that could just as well have been hypochondria as anything else. At the end of the day, none of them were worth mentioning yet. "None so far...or at least none I can think of. I haven't had any urges to sleep in a bathtub if that's what you mean."

Ilene laughed. "I slept in a bathtub once upon a time...for several days, in fact. I had some sort of flu and felt terrible. I couldn't get comfortable with my legs on and wanted to go sleep in the ocean. My mother compromised by filling the tub and throwing in a couple of salt cakes. She rigged an aquarium pump to keep the water oxygenated, and in I went and promptly fell asleep, happy as a clam. It worked so well, my mother let me stay there for the next few days, taking me out two or three times a day to change the water, and for...well...bodily functions. When I started having too much fun in the tub, she figured I was well enough to put my legs back on, and that was it."

Peter had nothing to match that story, but he chuckled at the tale from Ilene's girlhood. As they started toward home, Ilene looped her arm though his, not like Penelope, but like a mother would. Like his mother would.

Ilene read his reaction, though maybe "felt" would be a better word, and was puzzled. She was used to sensing reactions from Penny and George—it had something to do with their ability to communicate—but Peter? Most likely, it was a coincidence, or it was simply because she was starting to think of him more and more as her son, and her run-in at the market last week had only accelerated things.

Once they were home, Ilene put the kettle on and set out a plate of oatmeal-raisin cookies. "Dear, why don't you tell me what it's like to grow up human? Tell me all about your mother, too."

Peter recounted his childhood days up through his junior year in high school. He glossed over late high school and college, as he was really enjoying himself and didn't want to dampen the mood. Besides, he suspected Penelope had already told her mother about those years, and he didn't want sympathy for something that far back in his past.

Ilene contributed more stories about her girlhood as well as her own parents, now retired and living on a small island off the Brazilian coast. By the end of their storytelling, she had gathered their childhood years were really not that different.

"I'm hoping I can get word to my parents soon. They will want to know Penny has chosen a mate and that the wedding is in May. If they had electricity and lived within range of a cell tower, it would be much easier. As it is, I've left a couple messages in anticipation they'll return to shore soon and remember to turn their cell phone on."

Peter was looking for a way to make a graceful exit and allow Ilene some time to herself. "What time do you expect our wandering mates to be home this afternoon?"

"Ummm…around five or five thirty. Could be a bit later than that. Why?"

"Well, they'll probably be hungry, and this is your day to relax, so I thought pizza might be perfect tonight."

"I really don't mind cooking, but pizza sounds good. I'm going to put my tail on and soak in the tub. If you don't mind taking care of everything, I might even get a bit of a nap while I'm in there. Oh, if you see Carl, ask him if he'd like to have Thanksgiving dinner with us."

"Sounds like a plan. I'll find out where he's working tonight—maybe even have a late lunch with him. One more thing. I'm pretty sure my mother would have liked you. I'm not sure how she'd handle the mermaid part, but you're definitely her kind of person."

Penelope sailed past George, performing barrel rolls while sticking her tongue out at him. She loved swimming with her dad. Usually, her mother wanted mainly to talk—which was good, in its own way—but her father allowed her to feel the pure, unbridled joy of being a mermaid. Freedom had never felt so good.

Her father smiled at her and shook his head slowly. His little mermaid was grown up now and had a mate. The two of them would breed within four or five years, and if Ilene decided they should breed again anytime soon, he was going to be one busy merman.

George motioned his daughter over, and after she zoomed around him once or twice, she came to rest upright two feet in front of him. While it was definitely not necessary to be face-to-face in order to communicate, he'd always found that father-daughter talks went better when each could read the emotions and expressions on the other's face.

You know I won't be able to do this with you very much longer, Princess. Peter's going to have a greater claim on your time.

Oh, Daddy! Sure, Peter and I are going to be pretty exclusive for a while, but he'll be able to keep watch and practice his defensive skills while we go have a bit of fun, just like we did with Uncle Jim.

Well, now that's settled, how do you two like your new home?

It's wonderful, Daddy! Thank you! Thank you! Thank you! It's amazing to be able to go back and forth between home and home instead of back to our separate apartments. I'll probably move back here after we breed so your grandchild can grow up and go swimming every day. But, I'm not sure if Peter will want to leave the city for good. Maybe he'll just come here on weekends.

It wasn't difficult to read his daughter's sadness at that last thought. George was somewhat concerned about Peter's future, but there was plenty of time. Lots of things could still change in the interim. He could also sense his daughter's worry that the condo would largely go unused after that.

Don't worry about a thing, Princess. I'll do everything I can to help Peter. And even if you both move here, the condo will get lots of use from your mother. Right now, she's talking about the ballet and the symphony. Plays are next, and I'm scared to think about shopping trips. Speaking of Peter, how's he dealing with all this? I still feel bad about springing the whole thing on him like that.

He's really okay with it, Dad, and he really does appreciate what you did. I didn't anticipate the burden all this would be for him. While we're fairly knowledgeable about some mainland customs, he knew absolutely nothing about ours until a few months ago, and there are plenty of things that will trip him up, both now and after we're married. Please, just be sure to discuss things with him first. He'll appreciate it more than you know, and just the two of you talking will help things in general.

That's what your mother told me. If I didn't know better, I'd say that the two of you have been communicating behind my back, he said with a wink. *Princess, all of us will need to persuade Peter he's an integral part of this family, not just a supernumerary. He's your mate, and in a few years, I'm going to have my hands full with you mother.*

Mom hasn't decided already... Penelope was suddenly worried. Her mother could be overly enthusiastic at times, and this was one thing Penelope refused to be railroaded into doing. She and Peter alone would decide the when, where, and how about having children.

George immediately picked up on his daughter's concern. *No, no, no, she hasn't made any kind of decision yet, and I doubt she will for a good time to come. Believe it or not, your mother and I do talk on occasion, and while she did mention bringing up the subject with you, she had no hidden agenda or anything else of that sort. This is just like one of her many ideas for decorating projects over the years. She thinks it would be nice to do, but the chances of her ideas coming to fruition are quite often, very slim.*

Penelope wasn't totally convinced, but she visibly relaxed, nonetheless.

You and your mother can continue reinforcing the idea that Peter is one of us—with or without a tail—and I'll focus on the man to merman talk.

Penelope gave him one of those daughterly smiles that reminded George about how she had him pretty much wrapped around her tail. *Well, I'm counting on you to help turn him into a wonderful merman, just like my daddy is!*

Ilene removed her robe and sat on the edge of the tub as it finished filling with water. Here she was, a grown mermaid, a mother, and hopefully, before too long, a grandmother, and yet she still took the same delight in watching it happen as she did when she was a little girl. It was one reason why she'd lobbied so hard to get this tub as soon as they had the money.

Turning off the water and placing a towel next to the tub, she put her legs together and willed herself to change. Almost instantly, scales appeared on her hips where there had been skin, and her legs fused together. Though she couldn't see it, her bones separated into smaller segments to form a flexible extension of her spine. Cartilage sprang from the segments as her former leg muscles became tail muscles and attached themselves. There was a tingling sensation as nerves found their way through her newly formed tail, and she felt a shiver as her internal organs shifted to accommodate her true form.

She was almost done. A wave of scaly flesh began to encase her lower body. Her lower legs lengthened as the fusing and segmentation continued, and her feet morphed into a glorious fin. It only took a moment and a half, but she watched it happen with childlike awe and wonder.

Suddenly, she was a real, live mermaid, and after admiring her scales for what was probably the millionth time in her life, she maneuvered herself into the water, letting its wonderful saltiness wash over her. She was glad she'd insisted on the lounging tub in the condo so Penny and her mate could revel in the glory of their own transformations.

With Peter out of the house, Ilene could enjoy this, maybe even take the small nap she'd spoken about and not feel too guilty about his only having legs for the time being. *Soon. Soon*, she reminded herself. "Soon" applied to a number of things, like the wedding, Peter's final transformation, and the decision she needed to make before too much longer.

As she pondered the when and how, it occurred to her she'd already made that very decision last week at the grocer's and again earlier today. She whispered a prayer to Poseidon, thanking him for this blessing and entreating him to care for Peter's mother as he did for the rest of his children. In return, Peter would become flesh of her flesh and blood of her blood. He would be an integral part of her family, and she vowed she would never let him forget his own.

"Martha, thank you for the gift of your son. I will treasure him always."

Now the decision was made and the issue settled, she drifted off to sleep, thankful for this blessed peace and looking forward to her family—*all* of her family—returning home in a few hours.

The week had flown by, and time was starting to run out. Everyone had been swimming at least twice, and they'd gone as a family early Wednesday morning, with Peter taking care of the logistics as usual.

Carl Fisher had made Thanksgiving dinner a lively affair, and Peter had surprised everyone with the kelp sauce he'd been working on. Once he had it tasting just the way he wanted, he promised to share the recipe.

Now, it was Friday morning, and while Penelope and her mother were basking in the sun on the private beach, Peter was on his way to meet with the mayor, and he was not sure what to expect. He was more than a bit nervous when he rapped on the doorframe outside the mayor's office.

"Peter. Good to see you. Close the door and sit down. Your mother...I mean, Ilene has been keeping me apprised of your progress. Though, I thought since you were here, I'd get things straight form the human's mouth."

Bill cracked a wide grin at his take on this old chestnut, and Peter didn't seem to mind the attempt at levity.

"By my calculations, though," Bill continued, "you haven't been completely human for a while, now. Everything going okay? No side effects?"

"Are there supposed to be side effects? Mom...I mean Penelope's mom, asked me the same thing the other day. If I *am* supposed to be experiencing them, what should they be?"

The mayor laughed. "No, Peter. As I mentioned in September, there are no known side effects at all, other than what happens at the end of all this. It's just...well...this is the first conversion in my memory that has been so public, and I want to keep tabs on your progress for future reference. As far as the earlier ones went, we just supplied the juice and didn't see them again until the big day. I did see a bit of Ed Waterman's mate, but he traveled so much because of his business, and Gail lived in the city until a few days before she completed her transition. "

Peter relaxed. "Well, sorry to disappoint you, Mayor, but I'm doing fine."

"Good. Good. One other thing I wanted to ask you about has to do with something Ilene told me. According to her, you claim she and her family are human. Would you care to enlighten me?"

Dammit! Peter had cobbled that theory on the fly to explain why he didn't see becoming a merman to be a radical change. He'd hoped they'd take his explanation with a grain of salt and forget all about it. Apparently, Ilene had taken it to heart, and now he had to explain the whole thing to the mayor. He took a deep breath and thought to himself, *Shakespeare, don't fail me now.*

An eternity later, Peter hoped that asking a couple of questions would give him a chance to catch his breath. "Mayor, if I had decided against this, would Penelope and I still have been able to have children?"

"Undoubtedly. Look at Avery and Helen Johnson. They've had three kids and will become grandparents in about six weeks."

"Okay. And if the situation were reversed—I was the mer and Penelope was the human—would that effect things?"

"Peter, I don't see where it would. In fact, we had a case like that years ago. The merman and woman had a child together, and she made the change a couple of years later."

"Well, Mayor, being able to mate and reproduce is usually one of the criteria for determining whether two populations are the same species. At the very worst, you...I mean, we...are a human sub-species or even just a race."

Bill had been prepared to have a good chuckle, but he hadn't been prepared for this. He was silent for a long time.

"Peter, I'm going to give your argument some more thought, but I think you're on to something. I'll run this idea by The Academy's faculty as well. They're mostly PhDs, and I'd like to hear their take on things. They may want to talk to you about it."

It was Saturday afternoon and Peter sat in the den, watching college football and trying to explain the nuances to George. He readily admitted he was not anywhere near being an expert, but George seemed very curious, and he was more than willing to impart what knowledge he had.

Ilene and Penelope drifted in from the kitchen to observe the male bonding, and Ilene noted that the bulk of the commercials seemed to have something or other to do with Christmas. "Peter, was Christmas a big holiday for you when you were growing up?"

"Yeah. My mother loved Christmas, and it was the main event of the year up until Dad died. It got scaled back after that, but it was still a big day. The food, the tree, the lights, the food, the music, the family...did I mention the food? It was...well...the best time of the year at our house."

Ilene saw the mist in his eyes, heard the change in his voice, and wished they could be from the mainland—if only for a few days—so Peter wouldn't feel so lost. It must have been so terrible to lose his parents, and now he was about to lose his favorite holiday.

"Dear, I'm sorry we aren't...we don't..." Ilene, never at a loss for words, had come up empty this time.

"Mom, it's okay."

"No, Peter, it's not," Ilene said. "I'm so sorry we don't know enough about Christian practices to make you feel more at home during this special time of year."

"Thanks, Mom. But, you know, Christmas is actually two holidays," Peter said, using this as an opportunity to steer the conversation away from him. "One is the religious observance, and the other is the secular holiday—more like a winter festival, actually. If you listen to the seasonal music on the radio and in the stores, you'll find that at least half of it has nothing to do with the religious side of things. Sleigh bells, snowmen, Santa Claus—none of that is related to the birth of Christ. In fact, that event most likely took place in the spring. The holiday itself actually had its origins in the Roman Saturnalia, and there were other festivals that predated it.

"The secular festival is more about friends and family being together and sharing their love for one another. There's also an emphasis on the start of winter and our long journey back to the light and warmth of spring—which makes me wonder how Aussies feel singing about sleigh rides and snowflakes when it's the start of their summer.

"Anyone can enjoy Christmas. For example, the singer, Neil Diamond. He's Jewish, but he just loves Christmas music.

I have a good friend in New England who's Jewish, and her daughter puts a Christmas tree in her bedroom. So, enjoy the lights, the music, the food, but most of all, enjoy being with your family and friends, and tell them how much they mean to you. Saying 'I love you' to the people that matter most is the greatest gift of all."

Ilene looked at her family. "Well, I think it's high time we celebrated Christmas around here. Peter, would you help us, please?"

"Sure Mom, I'd love to."

"That's the family spirit!" She turned and headed back to the kitchen, humming a slightly off-the-tune version of "Frosty the Snowman" as she went.

George leaned toward Peter. "Don't flatter yourself, son. She's been trying to find an excuse to celebrate Christmas for *years*."

Once George had followed his mate to the kitchen, Peter looked sheepish. "Is all this okay with you, Pen? I don't want to force something on you and your family."

The look on Penelope's face said it all. It was the same sparkle of sunlight on water that had warmed his heart from the beginning.

"Of course! You've shared so much of our world, we should share some of yours as well. I think the four of us are really starting to come together as a family, and I know it makes Mom happy. I get to spend my very first Christmas with my merman-to-be, and that makes me very, very happy too." Penelope took Peter by the hand and led him upstairs.

It was late on Sunday afternoon when the family had their now traditional early dinner so Penelope and Peter could drive back to the city and not get in too late. They had driven to the private beach at the south end of the island that morning so George and Ilene could go for a swim and Peter and Penelope could have some time in the water together.

It had been a wonderful week for all concerned, and now it was winding down. They were all relaxing and enjoying a snack in the dining room before the kids headed back to the city.

"Peter," Ilene said, "I'm going to have to ask you to take

the lead on the food and decorating for Christmas. I will do whatever you need me to do, but I'm new to all this."

Penelope leaned in closer. She needed to hear every bit of what her mate had to say on the subject.

"Well, Mom, you don't have a tree, but I can take care of that, and the lights. Do you have any seashells lying around?"

Ilene's face brightened. She just might have something to contribute, after all. "I've got a box of them I planned to clean up, polish, and sell to the tourist shops on the mainland."

"Great! We're going to need the smaller shells—no conchs, abalone, or large whelks—so we don't weigh down the tree branches. At the same time, we don't need the teeny, tiny ones either. They'd be too small to see. You'll need to take a hand drill and make a small hole at the top of each one. Run a loop of fishing line through the hole and tie it off, and you'll have a Christmas tree ornament. I'll pick up some of the traditional glass ornaments so we have a good mix. Now, do you happen to have any dried starfish?"

"No, but I know where I can find some." Ilene was starting to get excited now.

"All right. We can use a large one on top of the tree and any smaller ones can be used as ornaments. We'll also need something to go under the tree, and that means presents. To keep things reasonable, I'm going to suggest that we all get one gift for each person. Nothing too expensive. Just something you think the other person would like and you want them to have."

Everyone nodded in agreement, though Peter didn't check under the table for crossed fingers.

"I have some of my mother's recipes, and we can look them over next weekend. I know we can get a lot of stuff in Royston, but I'll do my shopping during the week and bring it with me. Once I'm here, I hate leaving the island."

Ilene reached for George's hand under the table. *He loves it here. He loves us!*

It would appear so, Mother. It would appear so.

CHAPTER TWENTY-TWO

Penelope dozed in the car for most of the ride back to the city. Ordinarily, Peter would have missed their post-weekend conversation, but tonight, he welcomed the opportunity to collect his thoughts and develop a plan for the next three weeks or so. *I'll call it Operation Mer Christmas.*

There was a lot to do and not much time in which to do it. Aside from all the shopping he was going to need to do in order to stage Christmas for a family who had never truly seen the holiday, he was also going to have to come up with ideas for Christmas presents. Penelope would be fairly easy, but her parents were another matter entirely.

The other unspoken question had to do with what, if any, *was* their religious outlook. Peter had heard exclamations such as, "For Poseidon's sake," or "Thank Poseidon," but were they simply a linguistic convention of their society or an expression of something deeper?

He had spent almost eight months with Penelope without noticing anything he would consider to be a religious observance of one sort or another, but maybe it was the kind of thing that was done in private. Peter didn't consider himself to be religious in the ordinary sense of the word, and he was certainly not trying to peddle anything to Penelope or her parents. He simply wanted to share some of the customs of the season with his merfamily.

Penelope's head lolled and she began to softly snore. Peter guessed if you could comfortably sleep underwater, you could probably sleep anywhere.

Why was he planning to do all this Christmas stuff in the

first place? Well, aside from wanting to do something for his mate and her parents, he guessed he was doing it for himself as well. When he was a kid, Christmas was something to be looked forward to...even six months out. His father's passing changed all of that, and his mother was just not up for the big celebration. In fact, their Christmas celebrations had declined each year until she died—a sign she'd been losing interest in living.

After she was gone, there was no close family to celebrate with, and certainly no girlfriends, either. After almost ten years, he was due for a good holiday celebration, and now that a mermaid had turned his life around, he wanted to have some sense of normalcy.

That led to another reason. By this time the following year, he would either be a merman, or he would be dead, a thought that continued to nag him. If the latter was going to be his fate, then he wanted to make his final Christmas a good one.

Penelope woke up, at least somewhat, when Peter turned the car into the condo's parking garage. She mumbled something about having to get her bags, but Peter was insistent about taking care of things himself. He guided her into the elevator and up to their floor, and once inside their unit, steered her into their bedroom, where he quickly removed her clothes and tucked her into bed.

Once he'd retrieved their luggage, Peter was too wired to go to sleep and instead sat down at his PC and began to do some research. He laid out all the things that needed to be done by Christmas—a lot more than he'd originally thought—and scheduled them via a spreadsheet. After that, he ordered his baking supplies online. There was no way he could even begin to equal his mother's kitchen prowess, but he could do a few things, nonetheless.

Next, he made a list of things better purchased locally. With luck, he would have a tree, lights, and decorations in hand when it was time to return to Colony Island.

"Peter, do we really need all this stuff to celebrate Christmas?"

It was late Friday afternoon, and he was loading the last of their luggage into the back of the SUV. He straightened up and closed the back hatch to the vehicle. "An easy answer is both yes and no. We don't really *need* much, if any, of this to celebrate the holiday. I just wanted your mother to get a real taste of things. If you think it's too much, we can leave some of it here and I can return it next week."

Penelope suspected he wanted something out of his past to hold on to, and she really couldn't blame him. His world had been turned upside down ever since that Sunday afternoon back in April, and in six months' time, it would be turned upside down once again. Still, it was sweet that he was doing all this primarily for her mother's sake. Just one more reason for her to love him.

"No, dear, it's all fine with me. Remember, I've never had much to do with Christmas other than to participate in the high school chorus' holiday concert. I'm looking forward to this as much as Mom is."

During the trip to Colony Island, the two of them brainstormed over what to get her parents. For Ilene, it would have to be something pretty or useful, maybe both. George, on the other hand, would be a very tough nut to crack.

Peter's plan for Saturday was going well so far. He had all day to get the main decorating done while Penelope and her parents were out on a long swim. Putting up the Christmas tree and stringing the lights on it was the easy part and was accomplished within an hour after they left. It was the exterior lights that promised to be a bother, and they were true to their word. Of course, he could have enlisted George's help, but Dad was a complete neophyte and would have made the whole job longer and less fun.

Peter began to feel kinship with squirrels as he went up and down an extension ladder for the rest of the morning and well into the afternoon. The objective was simple: outline the front of the house in white fairy lights, wrap the columns supporting the roof of the front porch, and weave the remaining lights into the low hedge that ran along the edge of the porch. There were power cords to deal with and remote control units to install. By the time he'd placed the last electric candle in the windows, he was worn out.

After Peter tested the remotes, as well as the lights themselves, he was finally was able to put his feet up. His sense of accomplishment lasted all of fifteen minutes before his cell phone rang. The sun was setting and Penelope called to tell him they were back on dry land, would pick up a few things at the market, and be home in less than thirty minutes.

Following a mad dash to pick up the boxes and wrappers, Peter sat down on the front steps and waited. George's Hummer soon pulled up in front of the house, and Peter walked out to help unload the groceries. The family was turning to head inside when Peter hit the switch.

The lights of Christmas blazed forth for the first time ever on Colony Island, and he cringed, waiting for someone to ask what the hell he thought he was doing.

Instead, there was silence, finally broken by Ilene's soft statement. "It's so beautiful. Peter, did you do all this? By yourself? For us?"

"Yes, ma'am."

Ilene kissed Peter on the cheek. "Thank you, dear. Thank you." She smiled at her daughter. "Penny, you've chosen very, very well. Always be sure you yourself are worthy of your mate."

George nodded at him and followed his mate up the front walk and into the house.

"Worthy?" Peter queried.

Penelope smiled. "It's Mom-speak. It's her way of saying, 'You'd better not do anything to run him off.' I'm inclined to agree with her."

A good kiss was moments away from taking place when they were interrupted by the approach of their neighbor from across the street.

"What's going on here? What's with the lights?"

Penelope beamed at him. "It's Christmas, Mr. Chandler. My mate did all of this while we were off for a swim today."

"So that's what Christmas looks like. Hmmm."

More and more of their neighbors began emerging from their houses and walking over to gaze at the light show. Since Mr. Chandler showed no sign of going back home yet, she figured he would do just as good a job of explaining things to everyone else and tugged on Peter's arm to follow her inside.

For the rest of the evening, there was a parade of neighbors, people from two streets over, and just plain nosy merfolk in front of the house. George quipped that they'd missed the perfect opportunity to sell souvenirs and refreshments.

The following day was reserved for decorating the tree and planning Christmas dinner. While it was not intended to be a fancy, over-the-top meal, Peter hoped it would be a memorable one. He spent a good part of the morning huddled with Ilene, discussing various dishes and poring over one of his most prized possessions—his mother's recipe box. He didn't quite have her skill and flair for cooking, but with Ilene's help, he was confident they'd be able to somehow muddle through preparing the dinner.

Following lunch, everyone gathered in the living room. Since he'd promised to show Christmas to his new family, Peter wanted them to share the fun and frustration of trying to get the ornaments to hang just right on the tree. After watching Peter help Penelope place the starfish at the top, George decided to sit the rest out but promised he would emerge from his office when they were finished.

Ilene brought out the seashell ornaments, which she had done an astonishing job of making, and the decorating began in earnest. Once the shells were hung, along with the store-bought glass ornaments, Peter went upstairs to retrieve a special box of his own.

When his older brother had packed up the house prior to selling it, he'd divided the Christmas ornaments—at least the ones worth keeping—between the two of them, making sure each had their favorites. Carrying a sealed box labeled "X-mas," Peter returned to the living room and asked Ilene if he could add some ornaments from his childhood.

"Of course you can, dear. This is your home too."

He reminded Ilene and Penelope that they did not have to go in a prominent place on the tree—an instruction the two mermaids immediately ignored.

When he reached the bottom of the box, he found three oddly shaped pieces shrouded in tissue paper. He unwrapped the first one and gasped. "Wow! I forgot about these. On our way home from the beach the summer I got caught in that rip current, my mom insisted we stop at a Christmas shop. I found three ornaments I liked and bought them with my grass cutting money. They hung on our tree for a couple years, and when Dad got sick, we started scaling back on our decorations. I'd completely forgotten about them."

Resting in Peter's hand was a painted glass figurine hanging on a thin wire hook.

CHAPTER TWENTY-TWO

"By Poseidon—it's a mermaid," Ilene said in wonder.

"You liked this all those years ago?" Penelope beamed.

"Yeah," Peter answered, glad they seemed excited and not upset about his past purchase.

Ilene studied it carefully. "Hmmm. Beautiful, but somewhat stylized, I would say."

"That's because the people who make these things don't know what you guys really look like."

"*We*, dear. They don't know what *we* really look like."

The second ornament he unwrapped was similar, but the third one caused Peter to tremble—for there in his hand was an exact likeness of his mermaid mate.

Ilene shared his astonishment. "Penny, it looks just like you!"

Penelope took the ornament from Peter's hand. "Hmmm. It does look like me. They even got my tail right."

"What are the odds?" Peter shook his head. "Honestly, sweetheart, I wasn't stalking you or anything."

"I know that, dear," she laughed. "By the way, I think the whole thing is really sweet."

"Pen, I can tell you this. I spent every last cent I had so I could take this ornament home with me that day."

"That's why I love you so much. Hang it up on this branch so you'll be sure to see *me* whenever you walk by, and *I* can keep my eyes on my mate."

George chose that moment to emerge from his office to admire their handiwork. "Well, it looks like we've got Princess Fishyface hanging on the tree. I don't see any mermen, Peter."

"Gee, Dad, I'm kinda into girls, you know…"

Penelope giggled and gave him a kiss.

"We'll have to have one of you hanging up there this time next year. Mother, what's for dinner? The children will need to be on their way back to the city before too long."

The company Christmas party was Mr. Williamson's way of thanking his employees for all their hard work during the year and was usually held in a downtown hotel's ballroom with a live band, an overwhelming buffet, and an open bar. It was also his way of impressing clients, both potential and current, as well as schmoozing with board members and suppliers. It was, therefore, not unexpected, when he corralled Penelope and Peter and brought them to the corner of the room where the big boys—and girls—were sitting.

"Ladies and gentlemen, I would like to introduce you to our new comptroller, Penelope Tench. This bright young man next to her is our systems administrator, and her fiancé, Peter MacPherson."

There was a smattering of "Congratulations," "Pleased to meet you both," and other formal acknowledgements. Peter found it a bit jarring, as he'd grown accustomed to being introduced as her mate. In spite of this, he immediately acknowledged who the star of this show was and settled back, prepared to beam with pride at the mermaid who loved him.

It didn't take long for Mr. Williamson to get into top gear. "Miss Tench has been with us for almost nine months now. Our former comptroller announced his retirement the very day she reported for work as his assistant. Luckily for the Harriman Company, she immediately stepped up and has not looked back ever since. In my opinion, she has the finest financial mind I've run across in all my years in the business, and I sincerely believe we are lucky to have her on board."

Penelope blushed at the attention and blushed even more as plaudit after plaudit was laid at her feet. She wore a velvet cocktail dress in a very deep blue—something Peter had suggested she buy because it would look so good on her. It had taken little convincing that this was the perfect dress, and Peter had surprised her with a necklace comprised of multiple cords of fine gold rope. His gift was a stunning finishing touch.

Peter's reaction was somewhat different. The more she blushed, the hotter he became under the collar. What right did these men have to stare at her like that? None of them had any business at all even *thinking* about sleeping with the woman who was his, and his alone.

His immediate impulse was to grab her, kick out a window, and climb to the top of the bank tower next door, swatting at a swarm of bi-planes as he went. It was this last bit which convinced him he should get out of there before he embarrassed himself and made a muck of Penelope's career. Excusing himself, Peter fled to the men's room and locked himself in the furthest stall from the door.

His heart was racing and his blood pressure seemed to be going through the roof. Peter loosened his bow-tie and shed his

Black Watch tartan dinner jacket. He shook, shivered, and finally emptied the contents of his stomach into the waiting toilet. Once the purge was complete, he sat on the stall floor, trying to calm his body and its raging emotions. What the hell was going on? What the *hell* was wrong with him?

He had no idea how long he was in there. Men came and went, and still he sat there, until finally the world shifted back into focus, and he was able to reign in his emotions. Peter left the stall, splashed cold water on his face, and tried to make himself as presentable as possible, or at least look like he was simply a hearty partier.

After leaving the men's room, it wasn't long before he ran into Penelope.

"Peter, where have you been? I've been looking all over for you! What's wrong?"

The truth was, there was definitely something wrong, but what? How could he explain his heightened emotions and jealousy without looking like he'd lost his mind? If he didn't understand it, there was very little chance of her understanding it. Peter hated fibbing to his mate, but it was the only way he could shift attention away from himself. "I'm sorry, sweetheart. Something I ate must not have agreed with me, and I didn't have time to explain."

"Oh, baby. Are you sure you're okay? Let me take you home."

"Pen, I'll be fine. Just let me sit down somewhere and have a soda or something. If you need to go and be sociable, don't let me stop you. All I want is a couple of dances with the mermaid of my dreams before the evening's over."

Neither Penelope nor Peter was up to driving to Colony Island after the party, and going the next morning would take a significant chunk out of the day. Even though it would be the first weekend they'd missed going home since Labor Day, after calling Ilene and George, everyone agreed they could skip it and use the time to catch up on things like Christmas shopping.

The Christmas party was the informal signal that the work year was all but done at the Harriman Company. The following week, almost all regularly scheduled meetings were cancelled for what remained of the year. Senior management began departing on pre-holiday golfing vacations or Christmas cruises. Members of the rank and file began taking comp time to go shopping or to pad out what remained of their annual leave. On the other extreme, Paula Revelle clocked triple time and a half during this period, which always paid for a winter cruise to Barbados.

By the end of the week, the company looked like a ghost town, and no one would have been surprised if they saw tumbleweed rolling down the aisles between the rows of cubicles. Even if a staff member took more time off than was their due, they had little chance of being caught, because there was no one on hand to witness their transgression.

Of all people at the company, Mr. Williamson minded this sort of thing the least. He knew any extra time taken off would be more than made up during January and February. As long as the lights were on and the phones were answered, his employees more than deserved time with their families.

Peter and Penelope departed for Colony Island on Friday and planned to stay there until the day after New Year's. They would both be able to telecommute, which assuaged any residual guilt they might have had. Besides, this was Penelope's first Christmas, and she wanted to spend as much time as possible with her family.

Once they arrived, sneaking Christmas gifts into the house was fairly easy, as they had intentionally kept the size of their gifts small, and therefore, easily concealed. The main transporting involved handling the fruits of Peter's holiday baking as well as spare ingredients in case reinforcements were called for.

Ilene could've easily played the role of a mother in a Norman Rockwell painting, welcoming her children home for the holidays. As far as Peter was concerned, this was one thing he really needed. It was good to feel welcomed home. He missed his mother and father dearly, but circumstances being what they were, Colony Island was just as good.

For the next few days, Ilene and Peter continued to collaborate on Christmas dinner. He suspected she'd been surfing holiday websites, and those suspicions were confirmed when he heard "I'll Be Home for Christmas" and other seasonal tunes emanating from the stereo. "Jingle Bells" and "Winter Wonderland" seemed a bit out of place in Florida, but Ilene didn't appear to mind at all, and Peter was convinced he'd created a monster, albeit a very happy one.

When Peter wanted to try a couple last minute baking projects, Ilene organized family swims or shopping expeditions so he could have the run of the kitchen. When he began to fret about how much food they were preparing, Ilene suggested they invite Carl for Christmas dinner. Peter was all for having his friend join them, but Carl had the day shift at North End and would not be able to come until after 6:00 p.m.

Throughout all of this, Penelope was ecstatic. She felt like a human. It was not that she disliked being a mermaid; she simply wanted to feel normal and not like some sort of aberration. Having her mate and family to share this holiday time with was another giant step toward reconciling her life in the sea with her life on land.

Christmas Eve finally arrived, and Penelope finally understood Peter's assessment that the anticipation was almost better than the actual holiday. The presents were all arranged under the tree, and as the evening wore on, it became apparent that the one present rule was more honored in the breach than in the observance, as each family member contrived to pass through the living room and surreptitiously stash an additional gift, or two, or three, in with the official ones. After Penelope and Peter went to bed, they held each other quietly before drifting off to sleep, listening to the sounds of "mice" scurrying about downstairs.

Penelope awoke well after sunrise on Christmas morning and struggled to keep her tail under control. Her father had mentioned he and her mother might go for a swim that afternoon, and she was plotting a private session with Peter in the Watermans' pool. It would most likely belong to someone else by this time next year, so she and Peter might as well make the most of it, especially with her parents off on an excursion.

Penny, are you awake?

Of course I am, Mom. Peter's still sound asleep, but I'm so excited, I'm going to break out in scales at any moment.

Well, don't do that yet, dear. As soon as Peter's awake, give me a thought and then come on down to the living room.

It took some effort to rouse Peter, which was understandable, since he'd been running around nonstop since Thanksgiving weekend. Penelope coaxed him into his bathrobe and almost went downstairs in her natural state before he reminded her of the oversight.

Peter punched the button on his remote to light the Christmas tree, and they were on their way. Penelope steered him into the living room where her parents waited.

"Well, I don't have the mind for math that Pen does, but even I can see there are way more gifts than there should be."

Ilene feigned a look of displeasure. "Don't be such a grinch, Peter. We had fun Christmas shopping, didn't we, Penny?"

Penelope nodded vigorously and bounced up and down on the balls of her feet. Given the grinch comment, even Peter had to admit Ilene had done her homework.

"Before we have breakfast, there's one present you have to open, Peter, dear." Ilene motioned to the oddly shaped gift in front of the tree, swathed in what appeared to be an entire roll or more of wrapping paper.

Wincing at the thought of all the trees that had been sacrificed for this moment, Peter tore gingerly at the paper until a wooden table chair was revealed. On its back was painted the name "Peter."

"There are three more like it in the breakfast nook, and each has a different name. Now grab your chair, and let's have a bite to eat!"

The exchange of gifts that morning was one of the nicest Christmases Peter could remember. The presents were thoughtful items the recipient could use and probably would not have expected.

Peter gave George a bottle of twenty-one year old single malt Scotch and a faster router than the ancient apparatus he currently used. He'd splurged on Penelope's gifts, which included a pair of diamond earrings. His mate may have been from the sea, but she could outshine the best of them on land.

Ilene's gifts were the "mom" kinds of things, like perfume and dressing gowns. Penelope had somehow located scented salt cakes that Ilene could use for her naps in the lounging tub.

Peter was touched by George's gift to him. It was a dive watch, the expensive kind, with plenty of bells and whistles.

"You'll be needing this before too long, son. Speaking from experience, the minutes quickly turn to hours when you're out for a swim, and if my daughter is anything like her mother, it's best you not be late for dinner."

Peter had aided and abetted George's shopping for Ilene,

and she was thrilled to receive a coffee table book on the great ballets, three DVDs of ballet performances—including *Swan Lake*—and two tickets to the Miami Ballet's spring gala, which were accompanied by a strong hint she and Penelope should attend together.

Although Ilene seemed like she might be the "socks and underwear" type, Peter need not have worried. She presented George and Peter each with a silver merman pendant on a chain and a necktie in the MacPherson tartan. Her gifts to Penelope included her great-grandmother's pearls to wear on her wedding day and a silver mermaid pendant. Penelope immediately insisted that she and Peter swap necklaces.

George was the recipient of a silver rope bracelet and a coffee table book on Hummers. George later confided to Peter that mermaids liked to decorate their mates, so he might as well get used to the fact that he'd receive necklaces, bracelets, etc., more often than not.

After a round of hugs and thank yous, Ilene headed to the kitchen to get Christmas dinner started. George followed with a sprig of mistletoe in his hand, intent on being shooed out of there and into his office as quickly as possible.

Penelope reached under the tree and withdrew one last gift. If she'd waited until they were alone to give him this, then it must surely be special. Peter pulled away the wrapping paper to find a simple necklace of turquoise stones.

"Honey, I know most human guys don't wear necklaces, especially ones like this, but I want my mate to look like a real merman. That's your favorite color, isn't it?"

Peter nodded mutely, nonplussed by such a simple gift apparently having such meaning to Penelope.

"Here, let me put it on you, and you can wear it for our swim this afternoon...as long as that's the only thing you wear. By the way, Dad plans to offer the annual prayer of thanks to Poseidon at dinner. Don't worry, there's nothing you'll need to do. It's as religious as we ever get."

Promptly at 12:30 p.m., everyone was seated around the dining room table. George rose to speak, and Penelope and Ilene held Peter's hands under the table. It was quite touching as George gave thanks to Poseidon for both their life in the sea and on the shore, as well as the many simple blessings they had enjoyed over the past year.

"We heartily thank you for heeding our prayers and safely

returning our Penelope to her family and her home by the sea. Finally, we are all thankful for the gift of Penelope's mate, Peter. We ask that you watch over and protect him and guide his steps as he makes his way to your holy sea."

Ilene and Penelope squeezed Peter's hands under the table as this simple gesture of acceptance and inclusion caused his eyes to mist. He supposed it had to be the juice doing this to him. Perhaps it was, but there was a greater force at play here. It was that of their love for him.

An hour later, one and all were more than full from a Christmas dinner for the ages. Ilene suggested they save dessert for that evening when Carl stopped by. There were no dissenting voices, though George was of a mind to steal one or two of the gingerbread mermaids Peter had baked.

Once the cleanup was underway, Penelope suggested, or rather, insisted, that her parents go for their afternoon swim, as her mother deserved a break after making such a wonderful dinner. With George and Ilene off, Peter and his mate made short work of the dirty dishes, and once the dishwasher was swooshing along, the two of them shed their clothes, grabbed their robes, and headed for the Watermans' pool.

As they were lazily treading water, Peter playfully asked Penelope which she liked the more, their condo or their rooms on the upper floor of her parents' house.

"Well, the condo is our haven in the city, and our place upstairs is our haven by the sea. As long as I have you, I'll love them equally. In five months or so, the sea will be our haven, too, and that will be the best wedding present a mermaid could ever hope for. Now take a deep breath and let's see how long we can kiss at the bottom of the pool."

Peter wrapped his legs around her, and Penelope easily ferried him to the water mattress on the bottom. He was pretty comfortable staying under for long periods, but still, humans had their limits. As he began to fidget and exhale, Penelope gave him a lung-full of air, and that somehow made her want to kiss him even more passionately than before. If they kept on doing this long enough, they would find themselves racing to get back to their room in time to properly mate before Ilene and George returned. To Penelope, that seemed like a wonderful way to finish off the afternoon of her first Christmas.

CHAPTER TWENTY-THREE

The day after Christmas began with Peter seeing the Tench family off for a morning swim. The previous day's over-indulgence was still with them, and Ilene and George were more than happy to skip breakfast and hit the water.

Penelope herself protested that Peter should come with them, but he declined. Christmas Day's kissing session in the Watermans' pool hardly counted as "exercise"—even if you included the post-kissing mating session in their bedroom.

Peter had his own reasons for opting out. One was, they had not had alone time as a family in a while. What they had done for him over Christmas dinner was touching, but Peter supposed he would always feel like something of an interloper. The years of rejection and exclusion had taken too much of a toll on him.

The second reason was, Peter needed to get Carl up and on his way once he regained consciousness. Carl had stopped by after work the previous evening, expecting a light dinner with friends; instead, he'd walked in to Christmas evening with desserts, wine, and quite a few presents for him to open.

Carl had been overwhelmed by the sweet food, and after helping polish off the leftover wine from Christmas dinner, as well a bottle or two that had been opened for some mysterious reason or other, he was out like a light. There was nothing to do but make him comfortable on the couch in the den and call it a night. Ilene had checked on Carl before leaving and reported he was still blissfully asleep.

Peter woke him and helped him to his car. Their arms were encumbered with presents such as T-shirts, a cap that read "Surfer Dude," a fancy beer cooler, and a CD of Jimmy Buffet's greatest hits—and leftovers, including a large, covered plate of treats. Despite Carl's protestations to the contrary, it was obvious he had already bitten into one of Peter's gingerbread mermaids.

Carl exclaimed with a shake of his head, "Dude, you guys shouldn't have done all this for me!"

"My man, you more than deserve it."

After planning lunch for later in the week, Carl climbed into his jeep and drove off, still shaking his head.

On December 27th, things in the Tench household began returning to normal. Penelope and Peter were seated at the table in the breakfast nook where she was working on the fourth quarter financial statement and he was cobbling a Perl script to analyze the source of the spam messages that had been bombarding the Harriman Company of late.

Ilene was watching them and could not have been happier. Here was her family, her very own, wonderful family, together, under one roof, and she now easily understood why Christmas was important to so many humans. The fact that she was able to appreciate this was to her, just one more argument to bolster Peter's conviction that merfolk were human too.

Even though they were working on separate laptops across the breakfast table from each other, Ilene noticed there was something going on between her daughter and Peter. She contrived to peek over her daughter's shoulder as she went into the dining room and returned. Though Penelope was indeed working on her report, she also appeared to be conversing with Peter via some sort of chat feature.

At first, Ilene thought it perfectly ridiculous to do that from only a few feet apart and expected this would end when they were able to communicate the mer way, but the more she watched, the more delight she saw in their using this method. It was a simple pleasure, and Ilene suspected there were more things merfolk could learn from humans.

After lunch, more wedding planning began in earnest. Some items had already been taken care of, such as the time, the ceremony venue, attire, etc. Peter had been working on the ceremony but had yet to write the vows and the pledge for the exchange of rings. The afternoon was to be taken up planning that most delicate of functions, the reception.

"Do we really have to have one?" George complained.

"Well, Dad, not really. We could just have a receiving line, shake everyone's hands, and send them on their way. Of course, some people would be *slightly* disappointed if there wasn't anything to eat," Peter offered jokingly.

"We can't have that, can we?" Ilene already knew what she wanted and was biding her time.

He chuckled. "I'd advise against it. We could have a reception with light refreshments. Punch, cookies, and wedding cake. That might work for a morning or early afternoon wedding, but the last I heard, we wanted the ceremony to be later in the afternoon, and that has us pushing up on dinner."

Penelope had decided to hold her peace during this discussion. She'd never attended a wedding, while Peter and Ilene had. Factor in her dad being asked to pay for the reception and the voice of reason told her to sit this one out.

Ilene decided to lay her cards on the table. "Why can't we have a sit down dinner with music and dancing?" She had attended the weddings of two of the library ladies' daughters, the only weddings she'd ever been to, and for Ilene, they were the gold standard.

"Mother, you do know this thing is taking place in town, and everyone's invited," George noted. "There is absolutely no way in *hell* I'm going to pay to feed every blasted mer on this island. What do you think I'm made of? Money?"

Peter saw Ilene's chin quiver and sensed this was going to go rapidly downhill unless he intervened quickly. "I have a compromise that might work. Why not limit the reception to close friends, family, and business associates. They'd be the ones we'd actually send printed invitations to. And, so no one is completely left out, we can set up a tent on the front lawn of the temple to use directly after the ceremony. We could serve lemonade and squares of sheet cake there to those not invited to the reception. It would cost a bit, but nowhere near as much as feeding the entire town."

"Humph. Now what's this about business associates?" George was still upset. It would take a bit more to pacify him.

Penelope saw her opening and leaned over to whisper in her father's ear. Suddenly, his face brightened. Seeing it was apparently safe to continue, Peter speculated on possible reception venues.

George looked out the kitchen window for a moment or two and then said, "Leave the reception venue to me," as he disappeared into his office.

Planning continued on, and several possible menus were put together, each containing one or more items of seafood caught by the town's fleet. Peter insisted they support the local economy as much as possible.

When they began to run out of steam, Peter asked Penelope, Ilene, and George to each draw up their own list of potential guests for the reception. Meanwhile, he'd take his list of potential caterers and start making calls. He was deeper into wedding planning than he really cared to be, but this was for Penelope. *So, damn the torpedoes. Full speed ahead!*

George's wedding guest list included a fair number of people he had dealings with on the mainland, while Ilene's included the ladies from the library. Penelope's had a few of the women she worked with, and Mr. Williamson. Other than his brother and old roomie, Peter's list was nonexistent, so he added a couple of guys he worked with, though they were flagged with an "E" for "Expendable." When he finished entering all the names into a spreadsheet, he noticed there was going to be a sizeable human contingent. *Interesting.*

Over the next few days, Penelope had used her daughterly wiles on her father, and he had finally stopped complaining, not that he had a chance to begin with. Now, George simply glowered and muttered, "Damn human nonsense," whenever he crossed Peter's path.

Peter's old worries about George's speargun resurfaced, and he mentioned the situation to Penelope as they relaxed in the Watermans' pool on the afternoon of New Year's Eve. The pool had become a sort of haven for her, where she could put her tail on, swim, and be alone with Peter—her three favorite things to do.

"Don't worry about Dad. This is his way of dealing with things. He has to spend money, so he might as well have some fun grumping about it. I did a little research online about wedding costs, and we're actually letting him off pretty easy. He also probably realizes you'll be a merman in less than five months and he'll lose the opportunity to complain about humans. Just ignore him, sweetheart.

"By the way, we have a New Year's Day tradition in our family. We get up early and go for a swim as the sun rises. Since this is the first New Year's Day I've been home for in years, I want to be a part of it. We won't be out all that long, so you don't have to go this year if you don't want to."

Peter usually liked to stay up to watch the ball drop in Times Square, sleep in until it was time for the Tournament of Roses Parade, and watch wall-to-wall football for the remainder of the day. Penelope was now handing him a get out of jail free card, but if he took it, it would look like he didn't want to participate in family activities. The fact that they had celebrated Christmas with him cinched it.

"Sweetheart, if you don't mind, I'd love to come along for the ride. When you guys return to the beach, I can have breakfast waiting for you."

"Honey, I'd love that. But I don't think the donut place is open on New Year's Day."

"Don't worry—I wasn't planning to serve donuts. I want to make breakfast from scratch."

As it turned out, everyone decided to sit up with Peter to watch the ball drop, and once the champagne he'd bought was polished off, they all headed for bed and as much sleep as they could squeeze in before dawn.

They arrived at the private beach about fifteen minutes before sunrise, and while everyone stretched and tried to wipe the sleep from their eyes, Peter scurried around, setting up his equipment.

He was about to light the stove when the sun finally peeked over the horizon, and George said, "Let's go!"

Peter walked down to the waterline to see them off, and when Ilene was waist deep, she turned to him and said, "Well, come on! You're part of this family, too."

As Peter shed his robe and waded in after his mate, Ilene surfaced. "You two spend as much time together as you like. We usually just swim in the immediate area for an hour or so, and there's no need to catch up with us. I'll make sure Mr. Grumpytail behaves." With that, she flashed her fin, and he and Penelope were alone on the water's surface.

"Sweetheart, thank you for coming along this morning. I know you're stuck on the beach one more time, but it means a lot to Mom and Dad, and me as well."

As Penelope snuggled into the crook of his neck, Peter noted, "Why wouldn't I come? As for being left on the beach, someone has to stay and fix breakfast, don't they?"

Penelope simply smiled, put her mouth over his, and pulled her mate beneath the surface for an underwater kiss. When they finally came up for air, they swam in closer to the beach, and she watched as Peter waded to the shore. Penelope waved, turned, and after flashing her caudal fin, disappeared beneath the waves. It was time for Peter to light the stove, put the kettle on, and get to work.

He'd finished his cooking and was enjoying a cup of tea when Penelope appeared on the surface and waved at him. Time for him to play "hostess" and pour their tea. The family came ashore and slipped into their robes, the very same ones Peter had gifted them during his first weekend on Colony Island, and happily reached for their mugs.

Once everyone had adjusted the beverage to suit their taste, Peter asked, "What will it be, apple or strawberry?"

"Apple or strawberry what?" Ilene asked.

"Apple or strawberry crepes."

Everyone wanted at least one of each, which Peter had anticipated, and he began preparing each individual plate. He could tell from the looks on their faces that the crepes were a big hit as he dug in to one with apples.

George and Ilene were slowly finishing theirs and discussing the mundane business of domestic life when Peter put his empty plate down, opened his robe, and did his best imitation of a flasher in front of Penelope. Not to be outdone, she opened her robe and responded in kind. The two quickly found themselves face-to-face with the fronts of their robes wrapped around each other in a warm and loving crepe of their own. There was nothing overtly sensual about it, just the simple pleasure of skin-to-skin contact with one's mate.

Peter whispered, "You know what? We're getting married this year."

Penelope crinkled her nose and replied with a giggle in her voice, "Yeah, I know. You know what else?"

Peter shook his head.

"You're going to become a merman this year!"

He refused to let his worries kill the moment and kissed her full on the lips. It was a private bit of joy that their lifetime together would officially begin in less than five months.

The following weekend, Penelope and Peter returned for their usual visit and to help take down the holiday decorations. By late afternoon on Saturday, most of the stuff had been packed away and things had settled down enough for Peter to begin working on the actual wedding ceremony.

The service itself was pretty easy to plan, but the vows were going to call for his creativity. He glanced across the breakfast table at Penelope and smiled. She was reviewing the list of family and friends invited to the reception, just like a human bride. The adjective stopped him. *Human.* He could see no difference between her and any other bride. In fact, he preferred the mer version of a bride-to-be. His mate wasn't hung up on having this or that a certain way. She simply wanted to ensure everyone attending had a good time.

Peter did, on occasion, have to explain things to her, but that helped make all of it so much fun. It was now up to him to make the service a joyous and memorable one. He opened an envelope from the mayor and found a note that read:

> Peter,
>
> Here are the traditional vows between merman and mermaid as spoken at our joining ceremonies. You may add additional promises, pledges, etc., as you see fit. However, it is customary for the man to speak his vows first and for the maid to give hers second. I ask, therefore, that the first word of your vows and the last word of Penelope's vows to remain unchanged.
>
> Bill Marlin

That seemed like a fair request to Peter. He'd done his best over the past four months to hew closely to island customs and traditions. After all, he was the outsider asking to join them, and he saw no need for their wedding to be any different. He pulled the sheet marked "Peter's Vows" from the envelope and began to read.

Hmmm...protect, love, honor, cherish, and care for. That should be easy to conflate with the "Book of Common Prayer." Peter wanted to use bits from the 1928 Episcopal "Book of Common Prayer" as a nod to his late mother. She'd loved the poetry in that edition so much more than the 1979 revision, and except for a few words, it was his choice as well. He wasn't quite sure if Penelope would like it, but he was determined to be flexible and take things one step at a time.

Peter turned to the sheet marked "Penelope's Vows." *Love, honor, cherish, care for, and...OBEY? Holy crap!*

"Pen, we have a problem. I can't let you say this."

Penelope made a mark on her list and looked up. "What, sweetheart?"

"Honey, the last word in your vows is 'obey.' I can't let you promise that. No way!"

Penelope put down her pencil and gave Peter one of those "I mean business" looks, the kind that told him he'd already lost the battle. "Peter, I have to say 'obey.' I want to say 'obey.' I *insist* on saying 'obey.' It's non-negotiable."

"But, sweetheart...why?"

"Honey, grab your jacket. Mom! Peter and I are going for a walk on the beach."

Ilene responded from the den. "That's fine, dear. Don't stay out there too long!"

"We won't! Come on, Peter. Let's go."

Peter felt like he was being marched out behind the woodshed, and what was coming next was not going to be pleasant, but he decided to hold his peace and wait until after she fired the first volley.

He jammed his hands into the pockets of his windbreaker as protection against the icy blast that was sure to come. Penelope threaded her arm though his as they walked toward the beach. Maybe it wasn't going to be quite as bad as he thought. When they stepped out onto the sand, Penelope turned to walk south, deeper into the heart of Colony Island. The symbolism was not lost on Peter.

"Honey, there are a couple of reasons why I both have to and want to say the word 'obey.' You said you wanted to breed with me. Well, I want to breed with you...very, very much, but merbabies can be a handful. Just ask Mom. They are mobile at an earlier age than humans, and besides being able to travel horizontally, they can also travel vertically— there are no playpens in the sea. Especially when we're underwater, our child will require most of my attention. The ocean is a beautiful place, but it can also be very dangerous."

"I can easily understand that idea," Peter said. "But I don't understand what it has to do with the word 'obey.'"

"Well, dear, there are plenty of predators who will look at a merbaby as a tempting appetizer and a distracted mermaid as a tasty meal. This is the main reason we practice serial parenting. Each merbaby grows up as an only child because we are then able focus all our attention on raising and protecting that child without the distraction of a second one. If a mermaid has a daughter, then she might breed again early so she can teach her all about looking after a merbaby before her daughter chooses a mate. You'll see that more in the ocean than here on the island, but it's still not that uncommon.

"Anyway, you have a part to play in all this, sweetheart. It's your duty as my mate to protect us, and if need be, sacrifice yourself so our child and I can survive. If we're in danger and you order me to take our child and swim the hell away, or duck into a cave, or hide under a ledge, I have to immediately obey you. Since I'll follow your instructions without question, you'll be able to focus your full attention on the threat and not be distracted, wondering if I have obeyed your orders. If you don't make it, I will mourn you for the rest of my life, but this is the way of things in the ocean. It's the way things have to be."

Peter looked out at the water. The sun was beginning to set, and the waves were touched with gold. *Oh Stranger, tell the Lacedaemons, we lie here obedient to their word*, Peter mused. He thought he hadn't said it aloud, but Penelope asked what he meant, so he explained about the ancient battle of Thermopylae and how 300 Spartans were ordered to hold off a massive invading army at all costs.

"Sweetheart, life would not be worth living without you in my world, and I'd do anything to make sure you'd survive. Yes, I will agree to that vow, but only in *that* context."

Penelope smiled fondly at Peter. Yet again, he'd shown her that she'd made the right choice in a mate. "Sweetheart, my vow includes everything, not just that context."

"Honey, don't say that. You have a wonderful mind. You're a smart, independent woman, and you shouldn't even consider obeying everything I say just because you vowed it."

Penelope looked up at him with doe eyes that would have put a harbor seal to shame. "Not even in the bedroom?"

"Well...I guess that can be negotiable."

She threw her arms around him and hugged for dear life. "Peter, if you don't know by now, I love you so much!"

Penelope had won the argument, and whether Peter liked it or not, her vow included most everything. When she really wanted something, she usually got her way.

Peter realized no merman who truly loved his mate would ever call upon her to obey him in anything other than a dire situation. Now, what he really wanted to know was just where Penelope's flash of inspiration had come from.

"Is there anything else you're holding back from me, Pen?" Peter intended to say this with a smile on his face and a chuckle in his voice, but it all fell flat the moment the words left his lips.

Penelope was silent for a few moments. She had been dreading this, but the mayor's instructions had been pretty explicit. How was she going to explain without hurting him?

"Peter, there are things I haven't been able to tell you. Not because I was afraid or didn't want to, but because the mayor told us not to. It's not that anyone is trying to hide anything from you, and I can't think of any item that is truly earth shattering. It's just that there are some things that are difficult or impossible to explain until you're one of..."

No! She refused to say that. It was getting harder and harder to think of Peter in a "become one of us" context. He'd been dutifully drinking the juice every day since the beginning of October, and according to the mayor, he would be past the point of no return by the end of January. If he quit taking it now, he would probably pass away well before the inertia from drinking the juice took him to the point where he would completely transition to being mer. By February 1st, however, there would be enough momentum from the juice to eventually make him a fully functional mer.

"I mean, until you have a tail of your own. Try to think of it this way. Let's say I don't have legs and won't until I finish eating a whole bunch of pomegranate seeds. How do you explain the concept of walking to me?"

Peter was silent. She had him there. "I see your point, Pen. But are you saying there is nothing at all you can explain to me now?"

"Of course not, sweetheart. The mayor told Mom back in November that other than a handful of really important things that require a tail to understand, we can begin explaining pretty much everything to you. I've just been too scared to say anything about it. Can you forgive me, my love? I'll tell you almost anything you want to know."

"Honey, there's no need to ask forgiveness, and I really didn't mean for my question to come out that way. You should be the one forgiving me. Honestly, I can't think of anything to ask other than one question. I will tell you, though, if I survive all this, I'm going to volunteer to help the next human after me. There has to be a better way to do this."

Apparently, they were both feeling vulnerable. Penelope held on tightly to Peter's arm and looked up at him. "Well, dear, I'm ready. What's your question?"

Taking a deep breath, Peter asked, "What about...you know...mating? Do you, I mean do we...do it without legs?"

Spoken like a true man. Spoken like the man she loved. Spoken like her mate. Obviously, all men, mer, or otherwise, were the same, and she laughed out loud.

"Yes," she confirmed.

"How? And is there a certain time we're able to do it?"

"We can mate in the water or on the beach, and whenever we feel like it, though on the beach under a full moon is quite romantic from what I hear. As for how, I'm going to ask one of the teachers from The Academy to explain it all to us. I've never done it, and my memories from school are pretty vague. We're both going to be virgins for this, and I think it's so wonderful that we get to share our very first mer style mating with each other."

While the thought of sitting through another Sex Ed lecture did not appeal to Peter—he'd had enough of those along the way—at least the material would be different.

It would be the final flourish to the start of their life together, and if he really was going to become a merman, he was glad Penelope would be there, waiting for him. As he held her in his arms, Penelope was thinking the same thing.

$$\star\star\star$$

"Pen, I'm meeting Amy and Cindy to go over a few details for the service. I should be back soon, sweetheart." It was early Sunday afternoon, and Peter only had a few hours before they'd need to head back to the city.

"Okay, Peter. I'm helping Mom with some stuff anyway. Say hi to the girls for me." After a goodbye kiss, Penelope disappeared down the hallway and into her mother's room.

Peter was thankful that Ilene had agreed to engineer the diversion without asking too many questions. All he had to say was, "It's for the wedding," and she became a willing accomplice.

Peter was a few minutes late when he knocked on Amy's door, but she didn't seem too concerned and ushered him into the living room where Cindy waited. After running through the logistics of the prelude and the service itself, Peter decided it was time.

"Ladies, I was hoping the two of you would assist me with something for Penelope." Peter couldn't help but notice Amy had been hanging onto his every word and now looked like doing anything he asked would be the greatest honor in the world. He'd have to keep an eye on that. "Now, I know she has asked you to perform some sort of song or something as a surprise for me."

Amy looked thoroughly distraught and almost on the verge of tears. "We're not supposed to tell you. It's a surprise, and Anne swore us to secrecy."

Peter sought to calm her trembling lower lip as quickly as he could. "It's okay—I'm not here to ask about what she's planning. I don't even want a hint. I just want the two of you to help me surprise her too."

Both mermaids visibly relaxed at his words.

"The song is a duet, and I'd like you to perform it after 'Canon in D.' Lindsey will have left the stage and be on her way to the front of the building for the processional, so this will give her some extra time to get there and maybe take a breath or two."

Amy and Cindy nodded to indicate it was a good idea.

"The song is the one we danced to after we both realized we'd fallen in love with each other."

"Awww, that's so sweet! Of course we'll do it. Right, Amy?"

Peter was somewhat taken aback by this. He'd always

thought Cindy was something of a smart mouth, and this was entirely new to him. He supposed the face she showed to her girlfriends was different from her public one. He handed the mermaids a copy of the words and music along with a CD containing the melody that a friend out in Utah had sent him.

After perusing the material for a few moments, Cindy asked, "This looks pretty easy, but will we have any accompaniment?"

"That's the next item on my list, ladies."

With that, he said goodbye to the bridesmaids, who had already begun practicing, and headed to Lilith Boatwright's house. Luckily, she was at home, and she invited Peter inside.

"We are looking forward to your wedding, Mr. MacPherson. I suppose you want to change the music?"

Peter had to admit this mermaid was sharp. He didn't know how, but she had read his intentions like a book. He couldn't back away now.

"Ummm...I would like to add a piece, if you wouldn't mind." Peter handed her the score. "It's based on Jean-Paul-Égide Martini's 'Plaisir d'amour,' written in 1784."

"I'm well aware of that, Mr. MacPherson. Well aware."

"Ummm...okay. Two of the bridesmaids will be singing a duet. It's my gift to Penelope."

"She is a lucky young mermaid, Mr. MacPherson. Now, how much accompaniment would you like?"

"One violin, ma'am. Just something to carry the melody."

"I see. Well...I will play the accompaniment myself. Ask the bridesmaids, Amy and Cindy, I believe, to get in touch with me concerning a rehearsal. Now if there is nothing else, I must resume my practice."

Peter felt like he'd walked into a shark's lair, been considered as a dinner entrée, and then been summarily dismissed. As he closed the front door behind him, he heard the strains of "Can't Help Falling in Love" emanating from Lilith's music room.

CHAPTER TWENTY-FOUR

Peter elbowed his way through the front door with a sack of groceries in each arm. He balanced on one foot and used the other to push the door closed. "Mom? I'm home!"

Ilene's disembodied voice wafted up the hallway from the kitchen. "I'm in here. Did you get everything?"

"Yep!" Peter made his way to the kitchen, set the grocery bags on the counter, and leaned forward to receive the obligatory motherly peck on the cheek from Ilene.

"Thank you, dear. I appreciate all you do for me...for us. By the way, Ellen paid you a very high compliment today."

"You mean Mrs. Gar from next door?"

"Precisely. She stopped by for a visit while Penny was still here, and she said you had done such a remarkable job of fitting in. The only thing that tips her off is your hair."

The hair thing again! The de-facto style for the mermen of Colony Island to wear their hair long and in a ponytail was a bit of a sore subject. The exceptions were usually guys who had jobs or businesses on the mainland or those for whom having long hair would prove a hazard in their line of work.

On more than one occasion, Ilene and Penelope had expressed their desire to see Peter with a ponytail and offered him advice on how to care for it. Mainly in order to please them, he'd been letting his hair grow out for the past few months. It had reached that annoying stage where it was long enough to bug him but too short to do much with it.

Peter sighed to himself. "Well, that was nice of her."

"It certainly was, dear, and it's certainly true. You have blended in without a problem, almost as if you were born here. The only rough spot was your first night under this roof, and I am so, so sorry about what happened."

Ilene spoke with a tear in her eye, and it was quite evident where Pen got her habit of repeatedly apologizing for things that had almost been forgotten. This had been going on for months now, and Peter decided it was well past time for him to take a hold of this mermaid by the tail.

"Mom, I'm the one who should be apologizing. I ruined a memory for you, one that I know you must have looked forward to for years. I'm the one who is sorry."

That did it. Ilene was on the verge of crying. "Dear, don't ever think that! I'll always treasure that memory of you and Penny."

Peter sought to change the subject before things got out of control. "Speaking of Penelope, where is our bride-to-be?"

Peter was relieved to see Ilene beam at the sound of those words. *Crisis averted!*

"She went to the public beach for a swim just before you got home. If you hurry, you can still catch her."

Peter knew his chances of finding Penelope still on the beach were slim to none. At the very most, he might see her caudal fin as she sounded, but hurrying after her would at least allow things to settle down at the house.

He gave Ilene a kiss on the forehead. "Thanks, Mom!" Peter made his exit out the back door, crossed Mr. Waterman's side yard, and turned left on the next street over.

Colony Island's public beach ran the length of the island from a block or two south of the harbor to a quarter mile north of the private beach. Most of the enforcement and signage was confined to the first mile of the northern end. Humans were passively discouraged from going to the public beach by "No Parking" signs along Beach Street, the road that ran next to the woods and dunes bordering the beach. Visitors could, of course, park along Main Street and carry their beach gear the five to seven blocks to shore.

There were a number of private ordinances regulating the residents' use of the beach. For one thing, they were prohibited from hauling out and basking on the beach. In other words, no tails. If residents wanted to go for a swim from the public beach, they were supposed to wear a swimsuit and go straight into the water before changing. No caudal fin salutes or anything like that—a rule not always observed, especially if the beach was empty.

The town's three-man police force regularly patrolled the blocks closest to the beach to make sure the residents' casual approach to nudity was confined to the private beach...at least during daylight hours. The town had erected roofed kiosks along the path from the street to the sand so residents could hang robes and towels before heading for the water. In exchange, the police turned a blind eye toward those who left *all* their clothing at the kiosks and streaked or strolled their way to the water, provided, of course, they first confirmed the coast was clear.

To be sure, it was a pain in the tail fin, but following the rules meant the residents had easy access to the sea, and the town didn't have to draw attention to itself by forcibly keeping the non-mer off of the beach. The few humans who occasionally made their way to the public beach had a relaxing and enjoyable day in the sun without a clue they shared the sand and surf with merfolk.

Peter covered the last few yards of paved road and stepped onto the path that led toward the beach. There was a break in the woods at this spot, and he was soon making his way through the dunes toward the strand.

As he came out onto the beach, he saw a beautiful woman standing with her hands in the pockets of a white embroidered bathrobe, looking out to sea. He didn't need to see her face to know she was his fiancée. The way the offshore breeze tugged at strands of her brown hair. The way the diamond studs he'd given her for Christmas caught the light of the sun. Her legs. The way she carried herself. If the breeze had been right, he would've known her by her scent—the mixture of salt air and beach morning glories would have told him instantly.

Peter didn't hesitate to come up behind her, put his arms around her waist, and whisper, "Where have you been all my life?"

Penelope leaned to the side so she could turn her head, kiss his cheek, and reply as she pulled his arms closer to her, "Right here by the water's edge, waiting for you."

It was one of those perfect moments, so rarely achieved and so quick to pass. "I thought you would've been way out there by now."

He could feel her smile and hear it in her voice when she

whispered, "Sometimes, my love, it's just as satisfying to contemplate the sea as it is to swim in it. Besides, I knew my mother had sent you down here."

Peter pulled his head up and asked, "How did you know your mother sent me?"

Penelope stiffened slightly as her breath hitched, and she answered somewhat hesitantly, "I told her to send you down if you got home within ten or fifteen minutes after I left. I felt your presence nearby and waited for you to get here."

"Is this another one of those mermaid things?"

"Maybe, yes. Maybe, no," she said with an enigmatic smile.

Generally speaking, proximity sensing was something shared between mates, their children, and immediate family members. In all other instances, one could sense another mer was nearby but would have no idea as to who it might be. It was probably connected to how they communicated at sea. Penelope had never heard of it happening between humans and merfolk, but here it was. And it was not just because they had chosen each other as mates.

She could tell when he was near well before that wonderful Friday night, and probably even earlier than that. Maybe she had already made her choice long before they found they loved each other. Penelope was not going to waste her time trying to sort this one out. All she knew and cared was it *was*, and they *were*. She had successfully dodged a bullet concerning how she knew her mother had sent Peter down to the beach, but she'd have to be more careful for the next couple of months.

Peter began to scan the beach on both sides of them. They were alone as far as he could tell. "I hate to break this up, but now is the perfect time for you to get in the water. No one's around, and I have to go talk to a certain person."

Penelope sighed. Of course, he was right. He was her mate and was simply doing his duty to protect her from harm. Still, the timing sucked. Nonetheless, she managed to put a smile on it. "I think what you're doing is wonderful."

"Well, we'll see how he reacts to the idea."

Peter held her robe as Penelope undid the tie and stepped out of it. His breath caught as she turned and began putting her hair into a ponytail. "Sweetheart, you become more and more beautiful as each day goes by."

Penelope glanced at him and smirked. "Don't be silly, Peter. If anything, I love my mate more and more every day."

"After the wedding, are you going to refer to yourself as my mate or my wife?"

"Both. I want it all, and I want all of you, too." Penelope pressed her perfectly bare and perfectly beautiful body against him, savoring his warmth.

Peter felt himself burning up. Ideas, almost commands, began to take shape in his mind. Thoughts that told him to throw his clothes off and carry her into the sea. Swim with her. Mate with her. She'd shift to her tail on the way to the water, and he'd dive in after her and swim, and it would be oh so good.

"Love, I'm going to tell Mom our bedsprings will be singing tonight," she said in a perfectly sweet and yet perfectly sultry way.

What? Peter was grateful for the distraction. Something to focus on beside what was going on inside his head. "Honey, I'd love that...but we have to get up extra early tomorrow to drive back to the city. Isn't that going to be pushing things a bit?"

"All the more reason to be on time for dinner." Penelope reached up, kissed him, and ran toward the water.

She dove in, and Peter could see the scales starting to appear on her legs as they disappeared into the surf. A minute or two passed, and Penelope reappeared about fifty yards off shore. She waved, blew a kiss in his direction, and sounded, making sure to show her tail fin as she vanished beneath the waves. Another ordinance violated, but who cared?

After a few minutes of looking out to sea, Peter sighed and turned to make his way back between the dunes. He stopped to hang her robe and towel on a kiosk, and out of the corner of his eye, thought he saw her fin further off shore. By the time he turned his head for a better look, it was gone.

Penelope glided along just above the bottom, headed for deeper water. This was the first time she'd swum alone since choosing her mate, and she didn't like it at all. Indeed, she almost wanted to sit on the ocean floor and sob.

Whenever she had gone for a swim during the intervening months, it had always been with her family or friends, and they had provided enough distraction and companionship for her to not mind, too much, leaving Peter on the shore. It was okay for them to be apart while shopping with her mother or running errands, but this felt so different, and she felt so sad. Penelope suddenly understood why mermaids would so willingly quit the sea to be with their human. She shot up to the surface to see Peter one more time.

He was leaving the beach as her head emerged from the water. She wanted to swim to shore at top speed just to be with him, but instead, she remained where she was. Penelope knew he had to attend to a matter concerning the wedding.

Their wedding! Her hand automatically went to her engagement ring, which she wore on a chain around her neck when she was in the water. Peter had told her it was okay with him to leave it at home while she was on a swim, but she was adamant about keeping it with her.

Holding the ring between her fingers served to remind her she had a mate, and within three months, he would join her in the sea. Suddenly, she was a mermaid on a mission. Her mate was on his way to her, and she wanted everything to be perfect for him. She sounded again, feeling quite happy this time, and swam south along the island side of the reef. She wanted to see if her special place was still there.

Ever since visiting Colony Island for the first time, Peter had come to consider the town and its people as his own. Mrs. Gar was right. He was definitely fitting in.

He pulled into the gravel lot that separated South End Pizza from Avery Johnson's grocery store just as the neon "Open" sign in the window flickered off. Peter tapped on the door, and a smiling Carl let him in.

"Dude! What are you doing down here all by yourself?"

"Penelope went for a swim, so I thought I'd see what you were up to. We can hang out some other time if you've got plans of your own."

"No way, man. I was going to go for a swim myself. How about I grab some cold longnecks and we go to the private beach for a while."

"Fine with me, but we're gonna take my car. Otherwise, you'll swim off somewhere and leave me stranded."

"My man, would I do something like that to you?"

Peter grinned and gave Carl a soft punch. "Of course! I

know you too damn well, my friend."

Carl laughed as he headed toward the beer cooler. A few minutes later, they were ensconced in Peter's car with a six-pack of longnecks on the seat between them.

"So, Carl, how's your love life these days?"

The normally ebullient Carl mumbled, "Okay, I guess."

"Carl, I can tell something's up, and I'm not going to pry. But, I've been at rock bottom because of women before, and while our situations and backgrounds are different, I can still listen. Just give me a call whenever you feel like talking about it…even if I'm back in the city."

"You'd do that, man? For me?"

"Of course! What are friends for?"

While he was not exactly bubbling over, Carl seemed a lot happier, and the conversation switched to idle chitchat and lame jokes until they passed through the gate of the Colony Island Beach Club and pulled into the parking area.

Carl stripped down and headed toward the water. Peter changed into his bathing suit and followed with a couple of towels, the six-pack, and a bottle opener. After setting his burden down on the sand, Peter watched Carl dive into the waves and surface a few moments later. Carl held his hand up and then disappeared under the water, showing his caudal fin as a parting salute.

Peter wondered if he'd ever be as casual about this as Carl and everyone else was. Probably not. Most everyone on Colony Island was born to this, and he would be, now and forever, the new kid on the block. He appreciated all that Penelope and her family were doing to allow him to tag along, but he was afraid this would always be the case. He'd always be a tag-along. That is, if the conversion even worked.

Maybe he was being paranoid, but he sensed a general unease beneath the surface of each congratulatory hug or handshake. Was there something he wasn't being told? What would happen if this transformation thing didn't work, or worse yet, he barely survived—if he did indeed survive at all?

And what had happened up the beach with Penelope? He'd never felt anything like that in his life! An overwhelming urge to run into the sea and swim. They had promised him that other than the first few days, there would be absolutely no side effects from drinking the juice. Well, he'd not had the standard spell of being under the weather. In fact, he'd felt great for days afterward. So why was he feeling these strange urges *now*? Was this a warning sign things were going to go south? The only thing he knew for sure was he needed to apologize to Pen when he got back to the house.

Carl was the only one who never seemed to show a bit of doubt. It appeared that to him, all this was a regular occurrence, and everything was going according to plan. Maybe Carl's outlook was the right way to go—to not worry about any of it and simply carry on. Until something changed, he had a part to play and a duty to ensure that Penelope had the best wedding a mermaid could ever hope for.

The breeze switched around to the southeast, and it began pushing the waves further onto the beach. Carl rode one in and hauled out onto the wet sand, curling his tail around him. Peter carried two longnecks to the shoreline and opened the bottles.

He was about to sit down when Carl stopped him by saying, "I hate to be rude, dude, but would you mind taking those swim trunks off?"

"What's wrong with them, and why does everyone keep telling me to do that?"

"There's nothing wrong with the trunks, man. They just make you look...I dunno...like a human."

Peter grinned as he slipped off his still dry trunks and asked, "Well, isn't that what I am?"

Vigorously shaking his head, Carl replied, "Not to me, dude, and not to a lot of us around here. You've been drinking the juice for over five months, and you're more like us than one of them. Hell, as far as I'm concerned, you became one of us the second you and Anne chose each other as mates."

Peter was deeply grateful for the acceptance and vote of confidence, and he decided not to debate the fact that Carl and everyone else on the island were just as human as he was.

As Peter settled on the wet sand, Carl noted, "That's a one hundred percent improvement, man. By the way, how are the wedding plans going? I don't know much about these things, so feel free to enlighten me."

This was all going to be easier than Peter had thought. "Well, I'm still trying to choose my third groomsman. The groomsmen are...you know...the groom's supporters, the friends he wants beside him on that day of days."

"Yeah, I kinda get the picture. My cousin had a couple of

his best buds stand with him at his joining ceremony, and his mate had her best friends standing alongside as well."

"Yeah, same concept. Well, I have my brother as my best man, and my college roommate as number two, but I wasn't sure who to pick for number three. I was thinking about it last night, and it occurred to me that the solution is right here on Colony Island. The one person, the one friend, who welcomed me from the beginning and has always given me good advice. My brother represents my family, my old college roomie represents my past, and this person from Colony Island is going to represent my future."

Carl nodded his head, curious to learn who Peter could possibly be referring to.

"Carl, that one person is you, and I'd be honored for you to be my groomsman."

Carl looked away for a moment, and when he turned back to face Peter, his eyes were moist. "I've never been in human wedding before...you want me to be a part of yours?"

Peter nodded yes, and Carl swallowed hard as a tear rolled down his left cheek.

"Your...wedding..." he said absently. "No one has ever wanted me to be a part of something like that. You've got yourself a deal, man. I'm the one who will be honored to stand there with you." He smiled, and from his lounging position on the sand, gave Peter a firm handshake.

"Thanks, Carl."

"No, thank you, man. So, what do I have to do?"

"It's pretty easy. You just have to rent a tux—it's actually called a morning suit for a wedding before six. They're a bit more stylish, and I want to look my best for Pen. Then, just be at the rehearsal and rehearsal dinner, have a few drinks with the guys and me afterwards, and sober up before bed so you're not hung over the next day when you help seat people before the wedding."

"Sounds easy to me, but what's with the sobering up thing? Do these dinners really get that rowdy?"

Peter chuckled. "No, the rehearsal dinner is pretty tame. I figured since I'm not having a bachelor party, we guys could go to the tavern and have a few beers."

"Dude, I've heard a bit about these bachelor things, and there is no way you're not going to have one. I'll close North End for the evening, and we'll have the first bachelor party ever on Colony Island! Is it okay if I invite some of the guys?"

Peter was genuinely touched by Carl's offer. "Sure, as many as you want. They're all going to be my neighbors soon, so I might as well get to know them."

"Awesome, dude! Leave everything to me."

A large wave washed up on shore and swept its sea foam around them. As the water receded, Peter grumbled, "Great! Now I have wet sand in the crack of my ass."

"Dude, that's the beauty of being a merman. You don't have an ass-crack!"

CHAPTER TWENTY-FIVE

On this particular Friday, George decided to get a jump on the weekend and go for a swim. By mid-morning, he had taken care of everything he intended to, and the stock market had been flat for the past week. Not much chance of anything happening, and there was precious little he could do about it anyway. Besides, the stock market crash of 1929 had happened on a Monday and Tuesday.

He asked Ilene if she would care to join him, but she declined the invitation, saying she had too much to do before the kids arrived early that evening. Besides, with her mate out of the house, she just might get everything accomplished sooner, and she could then snag an afternoon nap in the lounging tub. It was a win-win situation. She waved goodbye from the kitchen door and then set about getting the house ready for those most welcome of visitors, Penny and her mate.

Ilene finished her planned chores as well as some additional ones in record time, allowing her to linger over tea and a cookie in her kitchen. This was where she truly belonged, and Penny's return home had made her time there in to a joy to be savored once more.

Not for the first time, she thanked Poseidon for the gift of Peter. This small act of gratitude guided her thoughts along a different path—one that could be more easily traversed through the medium of a long soak in the lounging tub.

She was napping in that very tub when George returned home and slipped into the shower to wash up from his day at sea. By the time he turned off the water, she was wide-awake.

As George left the shower stall, Ilene called him. "Honey,

could you come here and talk with me a bit?"

George instantly knew which of them would do the most talking, but he loved his mate and good-naturedly walked in and sat in the chair, *his* chair more often than not, and waited to hear what was on her mind.

"Dearest, how was the ocean today?"

"Just as good as it always is," he replied. "I see you've enjoyed a quiet afternoon here at home."

"My mate is so observant and notices everything. I think I'll keep him."

This loving sarcasm had its foundation in the fact that when George was preoccupied, Ilene could remove all the furniture in the house and replace it with a couple of lawn chairs, and he wouldn't notice a thing until dinner time rolled around.

George had his own little digs held in reserve. He might be a merman, but he kept his powder dry. He nodded his head and waited for her to continue.

"Dear, I dropped by the mayor's office yesterday to pick up some more juice for Peter, and Bill told me everything was ready to go. The only thing left is for all of us to sign the documents. He suggested we could do it a week after the wedding, right before...well, you know. Bill thinks it would make the day more special for him, and us, and we could make a little ceremony out of it. I'm inclined to agree, but I think we should tell Peter and Penny in advance.

"What's wrong with waiting until the day?" George was in a relaxed mood after his swim and was reluctant to stir things up so early in the weekend.

"Well, what if he says no? What if he balks and says he doesn't want to do it, any of it?"

"At that stage of the game, he won't much choice. It's going to happen eventually whether he wants it to or not."

"George, that's not what I mean. We're going to spring this on him at the moment he's the most vulnerable. We don't know how he's going to take it. We don't know how Penny is going to take it. We could tell her in advance, but that would open an even bigger can of worms. We run the risk of turning the day he's been looking forward to—the day we've all been looking forward to—into a shambles.

"Dear, he's going to be nervous enough as it is, and we're going to ask him to make a totally unexpected decision. It's asking for trouble. It's asking too much...of all of us."

At this point, Ilene was waving her fin in the air, flicking drops of water at George and the rest of the tub room. He was still reluctant to stir things up unnecessarily, but his mate had a valid, inescapable point. The last thing he wanted to do was spoil things for his daughter, or his wife, or even Peter. He had grown very fond of his daughter's mate and looked forward to the time when he could start teaching him defense tactics and do merman kinds of things together.

"Well, Mother, what do you suggest we do?"

"Honey, I want to tell them both this evening, after dinner. If things go wrong, we have a number of weeks in which to smooth things out. I want both the wedding and Peter's final transition to be happy, joyous occasions, and a little bit of upset now can prevent a lot of upset later on."

This was one of those times when he would have to concede defeat and admit his mate had the best solution. At least he'd had an enjoyable day at sea. Hopefully, he might be able to salvage a bit more of the weekend before it was over.

"Mother, you are absolutely right. We need to take care of this as soon as possible, and I'll do what you need me to if it means there will be happiness for all of us at the end of this road."

Ilene smiled at George. Her wonderful mate was on-board, and it was time for her to be magnanimous. "Thank you for listening and giving me your considered opinion, darling. I could not have come to this decision without your constant love and support. You are my protector in many more ways than one. Now, if you'll hand me some towels, I'll put my legs on, and once I've given you the kiss you so rightly deserve, we can get ready for the kids' arrival."

Home has never felt so much like home as it does now, Penelope mused as she and her mate worked as a team to wash and dry the dishes. She had noticed that Peter and her parents had become very comfortable with one another, and she was so grateful for it. Office gossip had informed her this was not always the case, at least in human families, with some spouses suffering through threats, abuse, and humiliation from their partner's parents. Those marriages usually didn't last too long. Yes, Penelope was very, very lucky...and happy.

Her thoughts were interrupted when Ilene asked the two of them to come into the dining room once they were done with the dishes—there was something she and George wanted to discuss.

"I wonder what this is about," Peter whispered.

"I have absolutely no idea. Mom seemed to have something on her mind during dinner, and I think it's wedding stuff. She probably wants to tinker with the reception menu again."

They finished up their task and found George seated at the head of the table with Ilene on his left. Penelope took the chair to his right hand and Peter sat next to her, turning his chair so everyone was within his line of sight.

Ilene hesitated for a moment and then began to speak. "Peter, hardly a day passes that I do not commend your parents to Poseidon's care and give thanks to him for sending you to us. George and I have both said this many times, but you would not believe how glad we are that Penelope chose you as her mate. George and I have given this a lot of thought, and we have decided we want to adopt you as our son."

Ilene saw Peter's jaw drop and his face assume a look of utter disbelief. She wanted to maintain the momentum before things got out of hand. "It's an old custom of ours meant to bind families together. Each would adopt their child's mate as their own son or daughter. It didn't always happen for various reasons, but it was done often enough for us to be aware of it, even though we've lived here on land for over two hundred years. The practice seems to have fallen into abeyance, but we discussed it with the mayor, and he is more than happy to help us."

Penelope seemed to have been in shock at the announcement, but she suddenly leapt from her chair, hugged her father, and then kissed him on his cheek. Next, she went to her mother and embraced her, crying, "Thank you. Oh, thank you!"

"Pen, I'm lost at sea here. Wouldn't you technically become my sister?"

Penelope placed her hands on the backs of her mother's and father's chairs. "No, silly. When you asked me to marry you, I became yours, forever and always, and we'll still be husband and wife. The adoption just means that my parents want to make you theirs, too. You're not lost at all—think of it as being found and brought back to shore."

"Peter," Ilene added, "we're not trying to come between you and your family or supplant them in any way, but sadly, they are no longer with us. We would simply be acting in loco parentis on Colony Island. It would have no legal standing on the mainland, but here, you would become flesh of our flesh and blood of our blood, and both George and I would very much like that."

Penelope took Peter's hand. "If you feel uncomfortable with this, we...they will understand. Mom and Dad are doing this out of their love for you—not to come between you and the memory of your parents."

Peter asked if he could have a moment and then rested his forehead in his hand. Just when he thought he finally had things figured out, they threw him another curve ball, and this was one from way out in left field. How should he respond to this?

He thought of his mother and father. Their love had been strong, but their bodies had failed them. Peter loved his parents, and their memories would always endure, but they were gone now, and there was nothing anyone could do to change that.

Now, here were Penelope's parents, wanting—asking—to pick up where his parents had left off. They wanted to give him a family. Something to ground him. Something to come home to. Peter had never thought of himself as adrift in the world, but in fact, he was, and the rejection he'd endured the past eight or nine years had only made his situation worse. He had no idea how his older brother felt, but Peter suspected it was the same. Was marrying Penelope and joining her in the sea a rejection of his family and all he had been?

There was only one answer he could give to this latest thing to rock his world. Peter raised his head, looked at the three of them, and took a deep breath. "If you really do want this, then...yes, I'd be honored."

Ilene was out of her chair like a shot and nearly ran on her way to his side of the table, where she gathered him into her arms and began to sob.

Peter kissed her forehead and whispered, "It's all right, Mom. It's all right."

George rose from his chair and put his hand on Peter's shoulder. "Son, you should know by now that your mother can get a bit overwrought when it comes to her family. You also know I'm not much on words, but I am proud to be your father. We'll have a proper tail on you in no time." George put his hands on Ilene's shoulders and said, "Mother, I think we ought to let our children have some private time together."

She nodded, and after kissing Peter's cheek, she put her arm around her mate and walked into the kitchen. It was obvious they needed a bit of private time of their own.

Now, it was Penelope's turn to hold her mate. "Dear, thank you. Thank you. This means the world to Mom. Dad too, though he probably won't admit it."

"Pen, I don't know what to say. I'm overwhelmed."

"Sweetheart, you don't need to say anything. If you can't tell, I'm thrilled. You've helped make my wish come true."

Peter looked at her quizzically.

"This is like choosing a mate. Once everyone agrees, it goes into effect immediately. You're now part of my family...our family. And that selfish wish I had in September is going to come true after all. I'm going to marry a merman."

"It wasn't a selfish wish at all, honey."

"Yes it was, and I'm still so sorry I hurt you, though I really didn't mean to. It was just...well, now we've done an end run around things, thanks to our parents."

Peter chuckled. "I never thought I'd hear a mermaid using football metaphors."

"We're full of surprises! Seriously though, Mom and Dad were really, really touched that you accepted them."

Peter was totally confused. "Accepted them? I thought that had happened months ago. What did I miss?"

"Nothing really, sweetheart. You all accepted each other pretty quickly—quicker than I would have imagined. As the weeks went past, Mom discovered just what you mean to me...and her. Dad too. They've wanted to tell you for a while now but never found the right moment, and they weren't sure how you'd take it."

Peter was totally baffled by all of this. He'd always assumed that Penelope and Ilene had this kind of mother-daughter thing going on, but this was too much, and he quickly became suspicious. "I thought you said you had no idea what this was about."

Damn! He caught me! Penelope had to figure a way to extricate herself from another one of her slip-ups. He only had less than two months to go, and it was difficult for her to see the harm in telling Peter everything now—especially after he'd just agreed to the adoption. On the other hand, everything could go south when he discovered they'd been talking behind his back. No, it would be easier to explain once he had the ability to communicate telepathically himself.

"It was just some odd things that Mom had said over the past few months. Nothing significant on their own, but everything fell into place after we sat down at the table."

That was close! Penelope was getting tired of covering lies with more lies—especially when it involved her mate. *Now, to distract him.*

"Honey, our parents have retired to their bedroom to celebrate by...well, you know. I think we should go upstairs and do the same."

Peter was still suspicious. "How do you know that?"

This time, she was prepared. "Because I heard them whispering about it in the kitchen. Didn't you?"

Peter looked at her blankly.

"Honey, I'm starting to think our hearing must be more acute than humans.' I guess it's something we take for granted, but it won't be long before we have a better idea."

That, at least, made sense to Peter and explained some other situations as well. "I'm sorry, Pen. You're probably one hundred percent right about everything. It's just, this evening has been a confusing one for me."

"Another reason we should go upstairs. You know, I have some ideas on how to take your mind off all this."

The following morning, they were all at the private beach for a preplanned family swim. All through the night, Penelope held Peter close as he tried to figure out what exactly he'd gotten himself into. Eventually, he'd come to some sort of reasonable conclusion and fallen asleep, content in the fact that Penelope was cuddled next to him.

Now, as the sun began to climb higher in the morning sky, the two of them stood side by side with their arms around each other. The only things standing in the way of full dermal contact were Peter's board shorts and T-shirt. As a general rule, he was excused from the "requirement" to strip down when he was doing a drop off.

While the family was usually off like a shot, they vacillated on this particular day, walking in and out of the water as if they were loath to get underway.

"What's the deal with your parents?" Peter quietly asked. "You guys are usually long gone by now."

"I was afraid of this," she whispered in reply. "It's supposed to be a *family* swim, and they don't want to leave a member behind."

Peter took Penelope by the hand and led her to where her parents were making nervous small talk with each other. "Mom, Dad, what's wrong?"

"Oh, Peter. This is new territory for George and me. We want you to go with us, but you can't."

"It's all right, Mom. Somebody has to get our lunch. Tell you what—when you come back here at noon, Penelope and I can spend some time together in the water," he suggested, knowing it was a solution that would please everyone concerned. Swimming with his mate was something he looked forward to more and more with every passing weekend.

Penelope bounced up and down on the balls of her feet, excited at the prospect of spending some more time acclimating Peter to her native environment.

"Peter, dear, you always know just the right thing to say. You're absolutely right. Penelope, give your mate a good kiss so he can get going."

It was actually several long kisses before Ilene intervened to give Peter a motherly hug and a peck on the cheek and told him they'd look forward to seeing him soon.

Having placed their order at the deli, Peter strolled into North End Pizza. Carl had assigned some cozies to be used only for deliveries to the Tench household, and Peter wanted to return the ones from Friday's dinner.

"Dude! It's good to see you."

"Hey, Carl. You too." He set the cozies on the counter, and Carl took them to the back room.

When Carl emerged, he said, "Congratulations. I told you, you were one of us. Now it's official!"

Peter had long since given up on trying to figure out how word got around so quickly on the island. He took it as one of those unexplained mysteries of life amongst merfolk.

"Yep, that's what they say. Ilene, I mean, Mom, told me at

breakfast there were some papers everyone has to sign, but they want to wait until after we get back from our honeymoon. There's too much going on with the wedding right now. Once we take care of that, it'll be officially official."

"That's great, man."

"Thanks. Speaking of the wedding, could I ask you to make accommodations for my other two groomsmen? I bet you're the best person to find good rooms at the same motel."

"Pete, I'm all in. Give me their names and cell numbers, and you can consider it done."

Penelope floated upright in the water, her head resting against Peter's shoulder. The pair required only the mildest swish of her caudal fin to keep their heads above the surface. Her tail muscles must have been getting stronger, because Peter seemed lighter and lighter as the weeks had gone by.

They had started with a game of tag after lunch, which quickly devolved into, "Let's see how many times I can fin-slap my mate and get away with it." The answer had turned out to be "Very few," before he'd caught up with her ten feet below the surface. Okay, she hadn't been trying very hard to get away, but ten feet was pretty impressive, especially when his first impulse had been to kiss her rather than immediately claw his way back up for air.

At the moment, they were in water eighteen feet deep, but Peter didn't appear to mind at all—so different from his first visit to Colony Island. He had become more and more comfortable in the ocean, and Penelope was so proud of him.

The sea was so placid, only a gift from Poseidon could have made it so. Peter's strong arms and legs were wrapped around her, and she felt safe—oh, so safe. Keeping them both afloat was easy and relaxing. She could do it forever, as long as her mate was with her. Life was oh, so good, and she was oh, so happy.

It was a shame it couldn't last. Her mother had informed her that the afternoon would be curtailed somewhat in favor of some spur of the moment grocery shopping.

Penny, dear, it's time to come to shore.

Aw, Mom. Do we have to?

Yes, you have to. Now hurry up.

Oh, all right. We're coming.

Penelope whispered to Peter that Mother had called time on their bliss, but he didn't respond. He was asleep. Actually asleep in the ocean. She suddenly understood Peter's feeling of confusion from Friday evening. Yes, he'd made great strides over the weeks and months, but this? She'd try and figure it out later. For now, she had to concern herself with getting her mate back on to the beach.

"Peter? Peeeter!"

"Hmmm?"

"Time to wake up. Mom's ready to go home."

"Ummm, no problem."

He yawned and kissed her on the head before lazily swimming toward the shore. She watched to see if he'd panic, but there appeared to be no trace of it. She planned to have a good talk with her mother about his sudden behavior change while they were out getting groceries.

Peter had hoped for a day of peace and quiet before heading home that evening, but his plans for a walk along the beach with Penelope were shattered when Ilene put him to work vacuuming right after breakfast. He wasn't quite sure what was going on, but the impressive list of chores would occupy his time through lunch, if not afterwards. Penelope and her mother confined themselves to the kitchen, where the rattle of trays and instructions indicated they were preparing a significant amount of food for some purpose or other.

Peter had just finished polishing the dining room table when Ilene and Penelope began laying out a spread of hors d'oeuvres, cheese and crackers, cupcakes, and cookies, and set a punchbowl on the sideboard.

His mate had disappeared back into the kitchen as Ilene asked from the far side of the table, "Petey, would you go upstairs and change? Our company will be here any minute."

Petey? He hadn't been addressed that way since he was a kid. In fact, the only one who addressed him as such in later years was his mother, and now his mother...no, his second mother...was going to call him that as well. *Penny and Petey.* He could live with that. Easily.

"Sure, Mom. I'm on my way now."

The smile on Ilene's face was one he would remember to

his dying day.

The doorbell rang as he was on his way back downstairs, and Peter became the self-appointed doorman welcoming all and sundry. The mermen headed instinctively toward George's office, where the tinkle of ice cubes and glasses could be heard, while the mermaids gravitated toward the dining room. Penelope had been drafted as assistant hostess, so it looked like Peter wouldn't be able to ask what was going on. He found out later the guests included George's family as well as Ilene's, some neighbors he had seen during his comings and goings, and a few old friends of the family.

The doorbell had stopped ringing and a happy buzz of voices could be heard throughout the house when Grace Tench, Lindsey's mother, approached and pulled him into a hug. "Peter, welcome! Your mother is so happy."

Ooookaaay. That was probably to be expected from Penelope's aunt, but when one of the neighbors said something in a similar vein, and James, George's brother, mentioned he didn't acquire a new nephew every day and was proud to have one in the family, the light bulb suddenly clicked on. Him…it was *him* they'd come to see. He really was an honest-to-goodness member of the family. He quickly slipped down the hall to George's office, fortified himself with a dram of single malt Scotch, and then waded into the crowd.

While Penelope was covering for her mother as hostess, Grace joined Ilene in the kitchen.

"It's so wonderful, don't you think?" Grace commented. "He fits right in. You'd never guess for a moment he was human."

"Dear, from my experience, we are more like them than most of us care to think. In fact, I don't use that term much anymore. It's not an 'us' versus 'them' kind of thing like we were taught. I'll ask Petey to explain it to you some time."

"You know, I heard one of the teachers from The Academy say something similar the other day. Oh, by the way, Samia Marinos says you've completely lost your mind."

Ilene looked at Grace with an ear-to-ear grin. "Good! Now I know I'm doing the right thing."

CHAPTER TWENTY-SIX

Peter returned to the condo after completing the list of errands that had caused him to leave work early. Penelope had come home on her own, and that worried him—not that she couldn't go to and from work by herself, but because he wasn't with her. He'd been getting these feelings for a couple of months now. Actually, he'd had them ever since day one, but they had become sharper, more nagging ever since December, and the last thing he wanted to be accused of was being over-protective.

Mermaids intrinsically loved their freedom, and trying to shelter them too much could sour a relationship in record time. The unanswered question was, where exactly was the boundary, and how would he know when he was about to cross it? Even more puzzling was the fact that he somehow knew all this stuff and had these nagging feelings, too. At the end of the day, it was probably due to the simple certainty that the wedding was six weeks away, and he loved his mermaid so very much.

Peter left his purchases on the table in the foyer and strolled into the living room to find Penelope relaxing in the wing chair reading a book. What was unusual about the scene was, she was totally naked with her trail resting on the ottoman, and the book had absolutely nothing to do with weddings, honeymoons, or creating a love nest.

After a quick glance at his watch, Peter said, "I hope you haven't been waiting long."

Penelope gave her mate one of those radiant smiles that sapped his will and turned his legs to jelly. "I left a little early and decided to get comfortable. How were your errands?"

"Mission accomplished, dear. I'm guessing you want some time in the tub?"

"Only if you come sit with me. We'll only have to do this for a little bit longer."

While Peter had the urge to tell her, "I only live to serve you," he stifled it as usual and simply said, "I'm on it, sweetheart," instead.

He turned on the water in the lounging tub, tossed in a couple salt cakes, and monitored the temperature until the water level was high enough to properly soak his mate without soaking the floor as well. He gently lifted her from the chair, and she rested her head on his shoulder and loosely curled her tail around his legs—not enough to hobble him, but enough to let him know she was completely his and he was hers.

Peter took a deep breath. *Dammit, woman! Don't you know what this does to me? Now I'm going to have to go take a cold shower in the other bathroom.*

He carried her like the precious cargo she was, down the hall and into the master bathroom. He knelt to lay her in the water, and as it washed over her scales, she uttered the same sort of sigh one hears when the cork is gently eased out of a champagne bottle.

Great! Now I'll have to do push-ups as well.

Penelope looked at him curiously. "Don't think I don't feel it too, love, and I plan to fix our mutual problem once I'm done in here. The wedding's coming up fast, and we both know what happens after that. I think the two of us are going to need frequent stress relief from now till then."

Peter was not inclined to argue at all and asked, "Wine, my dear?"

"Mmmm, you certainly know how to treat a mermaid right. Yes, please."

He strode toward the kitchen, grinning to himself about how she'd had him wrapped around her tail for nearly a year, and he was enjoying every minute of it. When he returned with two glasses of Chardonnay, he grabbed some towels and pulled up a low stool.

After a few minutes of chitchat, they'd caught each other up on all that had transpired over the past three hours. It was then that a mischievous grin crossed her face. "I hear someone

I know is being called Petey now."

He rolled his eyes and shook his head. Of all the things Ilene had to tell her daughter. "Yep, that's the way it seems to be. I haven't told her my mother used to call me that."

Penelope sat up in the tub, flinging small droplets of water over the edge. "Honey! I'm so sorry. I'll talk to her about it this weekend."

"Pen, she's my mother now, too, and she has every right to use that term of endearment. After all, she calls you Penny."

"Yeah. I used to hate, hate, hate my name and made most of my friends on the island call me Anne. You know, since we've been together, I've come to enjoy and even love my first name. I just wish I hadn't been mean to you and forced you to call me Penelope instead of Anne when we first met. I thought you were the enemy back then, and I didn't want to feel anything but sheer annoyance with you. I'm really sorry I hurt you like that."

Penelope's smile vanished, and her face clouded with what Peter predicted as a ninety-five percent chance of tears within the next few minutes. He knew what was coming after that too. She was going to apologize—again—as she had on a monthly basis since the end of last June. Like mother, like daughter. She had to stop beating herself up like this. He had forgiven her many times over already.

"It's all right, dear. I know I bit your head off a time or two. It's okay that I was the enemy."

"No, Peter. I was the real enemy—my own enemy—and I wanted to hurt you, when actually, I was really hurting myself. I prevented myself from hearing what I most wanted you to call me."

Penelope had buried her face in Peter's shoulder. She began to sob, wrapping her wet arms around him. When you were in love with a mermaid, you became used to getting wet.

"It's okay. It's okay, sweetheart," Peter shushed. "What did you really want me to call you?"

"Penny!" she said with a loud sob. "I wanted you to call me Penny so badly."

She was really upset now. Her tail proved her agitated state, and her fin threw water everywhere. Peter knew her father called her Princess or Miss Fishyface, and that was one path he did not want to tread, in the same way he would never call George, Daddy. Dad and Sir were enough for him, so why shouldn't it be the same way with her mother?

"But that's what your mother calls you, sweetheart. I definitely don't have a right…"

"Yes, you do. You do if I want you to, and I messed things up so much. I'm so sorry!"

"Sweetheart, I'll call you Penny if you really want me to…and you can call me Petey if you'd like to, but only when we're at home."

Penelope raised her head in mid-snivel. "That's not much of a restriction, sweetheart. Wherever and whenever I'm with you, I'm home."

Peter's stomach twisted, and it was all he could do to keep his emotions in check. He was only a hair's breadth away from bawling too, and it was time to give up.

"Well, dear," he said, taking a deep breath, "I don't know about you, but I hope we'll always be together, so call me Petey whenever you want."

"Really?"

"Yes, sweetheart. Really. And one other thing…we don't have to do anything after this. You're too upset."

"Petey, I want to more than ever, now."

Penelope flexed her tail against the side of the tub in order to almost instantaneously leverage herself out and on top of Peter, who suddenly found himself pinned under 125 pounds of wet mermaid. Her lips were on his as her fin repeatedly slapped the bathroom floor, and she tried to scoot the lower end of her tail under and around his lower shin, but his legs were shorter than her tail, and there was not much for her to latch onto.

Making a pouty face, she joked, "You're no fun without a tail!"

"Sorry, Penny. This model doesn't come equipped with one."

"Well, it'll have one soon. But that doesn't matter right now, because once I'm done with you here, I'm going to put my legs on, drag you to the bedroom, and start all over again. Resistance is futile!"

It was now the end of March and they'd only known

each other for about seven months, but Peter was Carl's main man, his best friend, his bro, and Carl was not ashamed to say it. Peter had been his friend since the moment he walked into North End Pizza, and by the time they sat down to lunch together three days later, they were old buddies.

Peter was the only one on the Island who'd wanted to hear about his problems with the feral chick he'd been seeing—was still seeing, in fact—and Peter had asked him to be a part of his wedding. A human had asked him to be a part of his wedding. Carl had never thought there was anything particularly wrong with humans, but apparently, they weren't much different from mer in many respects.

Then, there was Anne. She'd told everyone they could call her Penelope now, but she would always be Anne to him. He liked her and always had, but they were just two different people, good friends instead of mates. He didn't know if anyone besides him could see it, but Peter was perfect for Anne—absolutely perfect—and it was almost as if they had been made for each other. No…they *were* made for each other, and Carl felt privileged to know them both.

Carl had always thought of Peter as one of them, and now he truly was. He had mer parents, and Carl was pretty sure the adoption went much deeper than the somewhat ceremonial adoptions that took place amongst ferals. About the only thing remaining was to issue Peter a proper tail.

It went without saying that Peter and Anne would be pretty exclusive when they went for swims—they more than deserved that—but once he branched out from his family, Carl hoped he would be one of Peter's first swim partners. And now, Carl wanted to throw the best bachelor party possible for his good buddy.

He pulled out his phone and dialed the first number on his list. "Billy, this is Carl Fisher, one of Peter's groomsmen. I wanted to talk to you about your motel arrangements for the wedding weekend and the bachelor party…"

It was mid April and the weekend of Penelope's bridal shower. Actually, it was the weekend of her second bridal shower. The bridesmaids had organized one at Amy's house—because it had the most room—a couple weeks earlier, but many more mermaids wanted to attend than they were prepared for, so they'd decided to host party two at Lindsey's house for those who were left out of round one.

In the meantime, there had been gossip about some mermaids who'd attended the first one and were planning to attend this one as well. The bridesmaids were having the time of their lives planning and hosting the showers and were secretly hoping they might even get to do party number three.

The gifts ranged from practical, to sentimental, to frivolous. Besides things like kitchenware and towels, there were beautiful seashells—often quite large ones—in the form of decorations, necklaces, and bracelets. Penelope figured some of the simpler ones would look better on Peter, and she daydreamed about how handsome her merman was going to look. There was even one she planned to insist he wore beneath his shirt on their wedding day.

The shower was tomorrow, but tonight, two naked—or nearly so—individuals walked into the Tench home.

Ilene looked up from tidying the den and gasped, "Daddy! You got my voicemail!" She rushed to meet him in the entryway.

"Ilene, we swam here as fast as we could. Are we in time?" the older merman asked.

"In time for what?"

Ilene's mother stepped inside and answered for him. "In time to stop the wedding! We're going to take Penny back with us. A few months at sea, and she'll forget all about this...human. There are some lovely boys off the coast of Brazil, and she doesn't necessarily have to choose a ginger for a mate, if she doesn't want to."

Ilene frowned as she began to tremble. She was on the verge of becoming very upset with her parents. "Mother, Penny is in love with this young man, and I'm very fond of him myself."

Ilene's father was now quite cross with his daughter and laid into her. "Ilene, you've been spending far too much time amongst humans. I told you that job at the library would come to no good, and I was right. You've completely lost your mind because of it."

Penelope had heard the commotion and providentially chose that moment to come down the steps. "Hi, Grampy! Hi, Grandma! What's going on?"

Her grandfather grabbed her roughly by the arm. "You're coming with us, dearie. We'll wash this wedding foolishness out of your lovely young head and set you up with a boy from down our way. There are plenty of eligible mermen in the sea, Anne. You don't need to consort with a human to be happy."

"Nobody is taking my daughter anywhere!" George had left his office and was now glowering at his father-in-law. "Pops, he's a fine young man and smart, too. Besides, he has merparents."

"A human with merparents? That's impossible! I suppose you'll tell me next he's planning to grow a tail."

"I will do just that. He's becoming one of us and is less than two months away from having scales of his own."

Ilene's father looked incredulous. "Rubbish! I've never believed all that balderdash about turning humans into merfolk. It's just a fairy tale someone invented. He'll never be one of us. It's impossible."

Describing her father as hardheaded was an understatement. "Well, that really doesn't matter. We're all human anyway."

Ilene's parents looked at him as if he were mad. "George, all that time in front of your computer has addled your brain!"

"He's right, Daddy. We are human," Ilene agreed. "We just have extra abilities. Peter has merparents because…because…we've adopted him. Peter is our child just as much as Penny is."

Penelope flashed a smile of gratitude at her mother.

"That's absurd! I'll talk to the mayor tomorrow. He'll straighten all this nonsense out. Just you wait and see."

"Daddy, he's the one who drew up the papers for us."

Things seemed to have reached an impasse when the front door opened.

"Oh—hello, everyone!" Peter had not expected to be greeted by a congregation of merfolk in the entryway. "Um, sorry I'm late. We hit a snag migrating one of the servers to the latest release of Ubuntu and wound up going into overtime." He closed the door behind him and walked over to embrace Ilene. "Hi, Mom. It's good to be home again."

Ilene said nothing. Her warm smile and look of motherly love and affection said it all for her, and the feelings behind it were quite evident for all to see.

"Dad, how's it going?"

"Better, son, now that you're here."

Peter glanced around and pulled Penelope to him from the grasp of her startled grandfather. "Sweetheart, it's been a long twenty-eight hours. I've missed you so much!"

Peter lifted her off her feet. She was almost five inches shorter than he was, and she had come to love being lifted off the ground by his strong arms. It made her feel like she was floating in the sea.

Penelope said nothing to her mate. She just planted her lips over his and kissed him as if he'd been away for a year. When they finally came up for air, Peter gently set her down. Then he noticed the fuming couple staring at him. He seemed to grow a foot taller right there in the hallway.

"Hello...I'm Peter. Is everything okay here?" The protective impulse was coursing through him again, and for once, he didn't mind. In fact, he reveled in it.

Penelope's grandfather instantly recognized the baleful glare of a merman in full protective mode and shrank back.

It was George who spoke up. "Son, these are Ilene's parents, Raymond and Ethyl Merman. They want to take my princess home with them and find her a more suitable mate."

"I see. Well, she can go with them if she likes, or she can stay here. Either way, it's her decision," Peter declared in no uncertain terms. *And I have a feeling I know what she'll do.*

"Well, Anne?" Raymond prompted cautiously, thankful this Peter person wasn't wielding a trident. Where did they find him, anyway? He wasn't a merman, but he certainly acted like a merman, and not a particularly happy one, either.

Penelope suddenly realized she had been correct, way back on Labor Day weekend. She and Peter had much more strength together than apart, and she was ready to do something she would never have otherwise dared to do—talk back to her grandparents.

"Grampy, first of all, you and Grandma can call me Penelope from now on. Since I met Peter, I've really come to like my first name. Second of all, I'm sure you remember the rule, right? No one, absolutely no one, comes between a mermaid and her mate."

Her grandfather was aghast. "You...you mean you actually chose this human as your *mate*?"

Penelope slowly nodded with a stern look on her face. Peter pulled her closer, and she willingly melded to his side.

"Actually, sir, we chose each other. I'd like to think, in a way, we chose each other the Sunday afternoon we met, in April of last year." Without even looking at her, Peter sensed the happy glow coming from his fiancée that told him he'd said exactly the right thing. "Now, if there are no further questions, please excuse me. I came to claim my bride."

Peter threw Penelope over his shoulder in a fireman's carry and started up the steps. He was doing exactly what she'd been silently hoping he would, and she grinned as she wiggled the fingers of one hand in a gesture of farewell.

"Bye. We'll be down in a bit...or not."

Peter smacked her bottom and she both squealed and giggled. He set her down on their bed, and Penelope immediately began tearing at his clothes.

"Sweetheart, take me *now*. I've wanted you ever since you walked in the door!"

Peter only grunted in reply. He was too busy trying to kiss her and undo her blouse and bra at the same time. To Penelope, that grunt was one of the sexiest sounds ever, and she felt like she was only a step or two away from a spectacular orgasm.

When they were completely unencumbered, she lay back on the bed and motioned him to climb on board for the ride of his life. As Peter gently and lovingly eased himself into her, Penelope gave a joyous shout.

"Sweet Poseidon, you feel so good inside me. Don't hold back, honey! Give me everything you've got!"

Peter was confident that although the vocalizations were largely theatrical, the sentiment behind them *definitely* was not. He gave a loud groan and settled in for a vigorous session of mating.

The activity upstairs was plainly audible downstairs. George looked longingly at his mate. *Mother, are you thinking what I'm thinking?*

Ilene smiled at him in a loving way. *I certainly am, and we will do just that, as soon as I deal with my parents.*

"Well, I think that's settled now," she said with a smirk. "As you can see, we're a little short on space at the moment, but I'm sure Grace and James will be happy to have you stay with them this weekend," she informed her mother and father. "You're welcome to stay with us when the children go back to the city, though. As for the wedding, you're also welcome to stay for the event, or you can both return home. It really doesn't matter to me, though I do know Penny would dearly love to have you there on her wedding day."

Her parents just stood there gaping at her.

Ilene walked down the hall and retrieved two spare bathrobes from the closet. "Here, you can borrow these, and George can drive you over to Grace's house. Don't take too long, dear. I'll be more than ready by the time you return."

George dropped Raymond and Ethyl off in front of his brother's house and gunned the engine for the return trip. The fact that he and his brother had chosen sisters came in especially handy at times like this. George would give James a call in the morning and fill him in on all the details. Right now, he was needed back at home.

Ilene's father muttered to his mate as they mounted the steps to the front porch. "Hopefully, we can at least enjoy a bit of sanity over here."

Ethyl readily nodded in agreement.

As they approached the front door, it burst open, and Grace squealed, "Mummy! Daddy! Ilene told me you were on your way over. It's so good to see you!"

As Grace led them upstairs to the guest room, her father cleared his throat and asked, "Well, my dear, what do you think about that absolute madness at your sister's house?"

"Oh, it's wonderful, Daddy. I'm so excited! We're holding a bridal shower here tomorrow afternoon, and you know what? Your granddaughter is going to be the bride's mermaid of honor!"

Grace's father stopped on the stairs and stared at her in disbelief. Penelope marrying a human, Lindsey the mermaid of honor—whatever that even meant—and both his daughters in full support! What sort of hell had they stepped into? Was everyone on Colony Island completely crazy nowadays?

Early the following morning, Penelope slipped out of bed, tied on her bikini, and headed downstairs to find her mother closing her own bedroom door behind her. Grabbing towels and robes, they quietly went out the back door and headed for the beach.

"I think we've got about an hour before your father wakes up, Penny."

"Peter should be out for at least that long. Mom, I'm really sorry about talking back to Grampy last night."

"Penny, dear, I love my father, but he's an old mossback. Your own father can be stubborn, but at least he changes his mind when the facts don't support his notions. No, you did the right thing and told him what he had to hear, whether he liked it or not. I was so proud of your father last night, and as for Peter, I think we've got a proper merman on our hands."

Penelope smiled, thinking she'd had a merman of her own for just over a year now, but said nothing.

"And then, what Peter did. That was the most romantic thing I've ever seen. I'm so glad you belong to him."

"Mother, you of all people should know, Peter and I don't subscribe to those old-fashioned ideas."

"Penny, you know what I mean. If you haven't noticed, Peter worships you."

Penelope certainly knew what her mother was talking about, and the warm feeling that surged through her almost felt like her mate was holding her in his arms. Almost.

Things were very different in the other Tench household that morning. Grace had been up before the sun and presently had some sweet treats for the shower that afternoon baking in the oven.

She was taking a break in the kitchen when her father walked in. Grace had hoped he would sleep a little—well, a lot—longer, but apparently it was not to be. He was awake, alert, and ready to pick up exactly where he'd left off Saturday night.

"Grace, you can't tell me you approve of all this wedding nonsense. If my granddaughter hadn't met that blasted human, none of this would be happening. None of it!"

"Daddy, I will thank you not to speak of my nephew that way."

"Grace, don't tell me you've fallen for all this adoption nonsense too?"

"It's not nonsense, Daddy. I have a nephew now, and

he's the best thing that has ever happened to Ilene's family. I'm thrilled those two young people are going to have a wedding, and right here on Colony Island, where it belongs...where they both belong."

"But you and Jim have done perfectly well all these years without a wedding."

"Daddy, James and I wanted a wedding, and so did Ilene and George, but you said no. You said a joining ceremony would do just as well, and I don't doubt that if you'd had your way, there wouldn't even have been a joining ceremony."

"Merfolk in the sea don't do that sort of thing. I don't see why any of it is necessary on land either."

"Well, times and things have changed, Daddy. There are plenty of mermaids here on the island who would stay out of the ocean for a year if they thought they could have a wedding in return. What you want is not always what your children want. When we're old enough to choose a mate, we're old enough to do things to suit us, not you. My niece is the envy of over half the mermaids here on the island, and if you can't at least be happy for her, then I suggest you swim back to Brazil."

Her father decided to make a tactical retreat and headed back upstairs, but not before grabbing a few cookies on his way out of the kitchen. He resolved to stay upstairs during the afternoon's whatever-it-was, and they would swim home tomorrow or the next day. Maybe he'd stay for a week or so in order to speak with the mayor, but he was definitely swimming home as soon as he could.

When the time for the bridal shower neared, Grace loaned her mother a dress so she would at least be presentable, but Ethyl remained upstairs, hoping the mermaids she heard coming through the front door were there to rescue her granddaughter from...from...all this. As the chatter, giggles, laughter, and applause at the guest of honor's arrival drifted up to the guest room, it was obviously not a rescue mission, but a social gathering.

After fixing her hair, Ethyl quietly crept down the stairs in order to learn what all this was about. "All this" seemed to be very confusing. Grace introduced her mother to some of the mermaids in hopes of keeping her away from Penelope and ruining the afternoon with an outburst of some kind.

Grace had to go answer the phone, and her mother was suddenly left on her own. She was trying to find an exit route when she heard the voice of her other granddaughter.

"Granny! Granny! I'm over here. Turn around!"

She turned but still could not find her granddaughter until one of the visiting mermaids stepped to the side. There she was, looking out from the screen of a laptop.

"Lindsey! What are you doing in that box? Why aren't you in the room?"

"Granny, I had to stay in Nebraska this weekend, so I decided join the fun through a video call."

She had no idea how a video call worked, but that wasn't going to stop her. "What are you doing in Nebraska? It's on the Pacific Ocean, isn't it?"

Lindsey sighed with exasperation but tried not to let it show. "Granny, Nebraska is where I went to college. It's where my job is and has been for the past four years. Nebraska is in the middle of the country, miles and miles away from any ocean."

"What? You've given up on being a mermaid?"

"No, Granny. There are some lakes in the vicinity where I can swim when the weather's warm, but otherwise, I save my swimming for when my job sends me to either coast, which it does quite a lot."

The idea of a mermaid willingly living so far away from the sea was inconceivable, but she wasn't going to let that stand in the way of her interrogation. "When are you going to choose a mate?"

"Soon, Granny. There are one or two boys out here I've got my eye on."

"You mean there are mermen out where you are?"

"No, Granny. I'm the only mer out here. The boys are all human."

Amy came over and asked if she could talk to Lindsey about some wedding things. Lindsey's grandmother waved goodbye and left the room in a daze.

As she retreated to the guest room, she resolved not to tell her mate that his other granddaughter was considering choosing a human as well. The mere thought of that would surely kill him.

CHAPTER TWENTY-SEVEN

Ilene's parents didn't depart on Monday or Tuesday, or after the end of the week. Ethyl resigned herself to the fact there was nothing that could be done to stop her daughter's folly, especially since she was aided and abetted by her other daughter, and decided to stay and help Ilene pick up the pieces when it all came to ruin, as she knew it would.

Raymond was a different story. He arranged for an appointment to see the mayor on Friday and spent his time mustering arguments and counter arguments. Bill called Ilene to see if she could tell him what was up, and she related the whole affair from start to finish. She became a bit weepy at the end, and the mayor tried to calm her fears by reminding her that he was responsible for maintaining public order and that Colony Island's finest would do everything in their power to make sure her father made as little mischief as possible. Ilene hated being at odds with her father, but her children, both Penelope and Peter, came first, and there were plenty of other mermaids with children of their own to back her up.

Bill made his own plans, and when the appointed hour on the appointed day arrived, he was ready to rumble. Actually, it wasn't much of a contest. For every argument Raymond presented, the mayor responded with a convincing—at least to a rational merman—counter argument. Regarding the adoption, Bill had one of the teachers from The Academy, who had been Grace's playmate, incidentally, educate Ilene's father on the history of such things, and that the significance of the act really depended on the two parties.

Given his daughter's seemingly limitless affection and

Peter's loss of his mother at the appalling age of twenty-two, it was only natural this adoption was more literal and less ceremonial than they usually were, and the community respected that bond. The rumor that Peter intended to take the Tench name for his middle one had more than sealed it as far as everyone else was concerned.

When Raymond tried to call him out on the "absolute absurdity" about a human becoming one of them, the mayor called in one of Mr. Merman's closest friends from his younger days who revealed he had once been human and had become mer about a year and a half before they'd met.

Bill responded to the wedding argument by saying the joining ceremony was simply a much abbreviated version of human wedding customs, and he was honored to officiate. The couple could have gone anywhere else, but they chose to have their ceremony on the island with their family and friends in attendance.

The coup de grace came when Bill reminded Raymond that his office as mayor was ultimately responsible for maintaining the peace on the island and that he was prepared to have him occupy one of the cells at the police station until after the wedding, honeymoon, and conversion if necessary. Once Peter was back on his feet, Bill would happily issue Peter a trident and advise him to settle any grievances at sea.

The memory of Peter on the Friday night they'd met was enough to convince Ilene's father to give up and submit to the inevitable. The mayor offered Raymond and his mate the use of a newly vacated bungalow until after the wedding. The bungalow was near Feral Town and on the route of regular police patrols.

Raymond returned to Ilene's house about the same time she announced Penelope and Peter should be on their way from the city by now and would need their room back. Ethyl and her mate gathered up the few things that had been lent them for the duration of their stay and declined Ilene's offer to chauffer them to her sister's house. At least by walking, they would have privacy en route. Raymond related the details of his meeting with the mayor to Ethyl. He finished by saying it wasn't their Colony Island anymore, and they would swim back to the waters off Brazil on Monday.

Ethyl halted mid step. Her mate had been telling her what to do for more decades than she cared to count. If he wasn't so stubborn and pigheaded, things might be different for them today. His telling her that they were swimming home on Monday had pushed the wrong button.

"Raymond, Colony Island is changing and has been changing all along. When we were knee-high to a duck, there were only a few telephones on the island, and we had to hand crank them, yet you brought your cell phone along in the waterproof bag when we swam here.

"I was astonished to learn about Ernie, but his mate was the nicest young mermaid you could wish for. I knew her family, and she's most likely the reason Ernie became one of us. This adoption business still has my head spinning, but our daughter really dotes on Peter, and he was protecting our Anne's secret from the very beginning. Apparently, I have a grandson now, and in a few years, I'm going to be a great-grandmother."

Raymond drew a breath to speak, but Ethyl shook her finger at him.

"Not a word, *dear*. I've decided to stay and help out where I can, at least until after the ceremony, and maybe longer. You can swim home if you like, but if you stay and wind up in the jail, don't expect me to come and visit you. Oh, by the way, I'm tired of swimming back and forth between here and Brazil. From now on, I'm going to fly."

Penelope's impending wedding was celebrated in the city as well as on Colony Island. The ladies at the Harriman Company threw a shower in her honor at Mr. Williamson's downtown businessmen's club that included most of the people on her floor. It was a fun affair and served as a counterpoint to the way things were done for the first two bridal showers ever on Colony Island. As was to be expected, there were some duplicate gifts, but much less than one would have thought—except for the seashells, of course. Some of the shower gifts were used in the condo, while others were destined for their future home on the island.

Penelope was having a hard time deciding exactly where "home" really was. She spent five nights out of seven in the city at the condo, but the two nights on Colony Island were absolute heaven. She finally came to the conclusion that the island was her "real" home, where her heart would always be, but the condo would also be a home as long as there were salaries to earn and bread to put on the table.

Peter had adopted her home by the sea without the slightest bit of urging from her or her parents, and that made Penelope love him all the more. They would probably put the Christmas tree up in the condo this year, helping to make it the spot where their lives touched the human world.

Peter was still unsure as to what lay in store for him after the honeymoon, but he would definitely be hard pressed to surrender all associations with the world in which he had lived for twenty-five years and retire to life on the island and its environs. Who knew—life just might return to pretty much normal once it was all over. If the truth be known, Penelope would have been hard pressed as well, especially as she had begun to think of herself as at least part human.

Not unexpectedly, Penelope was the guest of honor at a third shower on the island a couple weeks after the first. It took place at the very end of April, and though the numbers were somewhat diminished, every mermaid who wanted to participate finally had their chance. Nonetheless, there were a few who boasted of attending all three events, or at least two of them. It was all part and parcel of the wedding fever that had swept across the island. It was driven, to a large degree, by a series on wedding etiquette and customs that had begun appearing in the Colony Chronicle, sponsored by Edna's Home and Bath, as well as one or two other shops in town, that might serve as a source of wedding and shower gifts.

Maureen was all too happy to have something to publish besides plans for new sewer lines or the fishing forecast for the coming season. Something was starting to happen on Colony Island, and copies of the Chronicle began to disappear from the newspaper vending boxes as soon as they were distributed.

Throughout all of this, Penelope was the perfect bride to be. Although it goes without saying that nearly every bride wants her day to be as perfect as possible, Penelope's version of perfect was rather flexible. When she was told by the florist in Royston that the type of flower she wanted to use for her bouquet and floral decorations was hard to find at that time of year, she didn't demand they be shipped in via air freight from Madagascar. Instead, she decided on a more easily obtainable substitute and declared it to be even better than her first choice.

When it came time to order paper products for the reception, scale patterns were popular that year, and Penelope had the clever idea to find things in a color that matched her own scales. When no such offerings were found after a reasonable search, she settled on a scale pattern with a turquoise background, Peter's favorite color.

Penelope was actually thankful things had worked out this way because the whole day was supposed to be about the two of them, not just her. She took on a more than reasonable share of the planning duties, and her bridesmaids had to beg to be given things to do. Penelope refused to be a Bridezilla, and drama was not allowed.

Her attitude extended to other things as well. While Penelope did have a professional photographer in Royston do her bridal portrait, she knew of a woman on Colony Island who dabbled in the arts, and she commissioned her to take a second series of photographs of her in the wedding gown...with her tail on. These were to be special gifts to her bridesmaids, her parents, and most importantly, Peter.

Other preparations included taking her gown to Mildred's for an extra bit of embroidery. At Penelope's request, Mildred merged the mermaid and merman logos that adorned the Tench bathrobes and modified them so that the two were holding hands. Her gown had a very short train, and Mildred embroidered the design on it in white silk thread. A few inches above this, Mildred also embroidered the family crest from Peter's robe. In all probability, no one would notice these two items, but Penelope knew they were there, and it helped to make her gown, and the approaching day, even more special.

It was finally May. The days leading up to the wedding began to fly past, and the time soon arrived for Penelope to take the two weeks prior off from work. She hadn't thought she'd need that much extra time, but Mr. Williamson insisted on it, reminding her she would most likely pay that time back, and then some, at the end of the company's fiscal year.

The ladies in her department gave her a big send-off and

promised to be there on her wedding day. That evening, she said goodbye to the condo for the coming five weeks, and she and Peter drove separate vehicles to Colony Island for the weekend. She would not return to the city until she was Mrs. Peter MacPherson.

Peter planned to work eight or nine days more before saying goodbye to the Harriman Company. Most of his work in preparing for the wedding was done, until the day before the event, and if anything came up in the interim, Carl promised to either take care of it himself or ask one of the guys at the shop to do it. As far as Peter was concerned, if he had been an only child, Carl would have been his best man.

The nights he spent in the city away from Penelope were not easy for Peter. It was a comfort having her sleeping next to him, not only because of her sweet-smelling warmth, but because it meant he could hold her close and protect her.

He had stopped worrying about this compelling urge. Mermen were very protective of their mates, and he was...well...mostly merman now. He still didn't think of himself as one, but there was no denying he had a wonderful mermaid to have and to hold.

As he would drift off to sleep each evening, Peter would think of her eyes and her smile looking up at him from the water, and of her sitting at the water's edge with her tail curled around her. He could feel the warmth of the sun on her shoulders, and the taste of her mouth on his, as she pulled him below the surface to kiss until his air ran out.

Lately, all of his dreams about her involved water in some way, and Peter never bothered to think why this was. It was only natural, though. Penelope was his mermaid, his mate, and he slept each night holding her pillow against his chest.

If Peter had wanted, he could have said his goodbyes to everyone in the office on the same day Penelope left to prepare for the wedding, but there was one thing that necessitated staying in the city, and it had all begun during a check-in meeting with the mayor in early March.

"Well, you two," Bill had said, "your big day is not too far off now, and there's one thing I've been meaning to ask the both of you. What do you want me to wear for the ceremony? I've done joining ceremonies in a T-shirt and shorts and in trousers and a white shirt, and for more than one ceremony down at the private beach, I wore nothing at all. Since your ceremony is easily the fanciest one to date, I've got a suit I can get dry cleaned, if the bugs haven't eaten it up."

Penelope and Peter had told him they'd need to cogitate on this a bit, and after due consideration, they had come to a decision. As the mayor acted as a magistrate and adjudicated small claims—disturbing the peace cases, etc.—they had concluded that he was a sort of judge. Therefore, he was to wear a judicial robe. Peter had thought, given that Bill was the mayor of Colony Island, he should also have a chain of office to add an extra bit of dignity to the occasion.

Since most of the residents had welcomed Peter with open arms, the robe and chain would be their gifts to the town for use in future ceremonies and public events. They had been ordered in advance of the wedding date and finally arrived a couple days before Peter was to depart for the wedding.

Penelope kept herself busy during the two weeks leading up to the wedding, since the busier she was, the less time she had to miss Peter. They did text and call daily, but that came nowhere close to the feeling of being by his side.

One of the very first things she did was confirm their honeymoon accommodations. Peter felt guilty about not taking Penelope to the Caribbean Islands, or someplace like that, but the mayor and her parents agreed the couple should stay close to home, given what was to occur the day after they returned. Since Penelope knew much more local fare than Peter did, it fell to her to make the reservation. He would have no clue as to exactly where their honeymoon would be spent until they got there.

Meanwhile, Amy decided to search the Internet for human wedding activities in addition to bridal showers. She found one tradition she thought Penelope and all her girlfriends, including herself, might enjoy—a bachelorette party. She researched how humans threw one and then discussed it with Lindsey and Cindy.

They decided to wait until after the mermaid of honor flew in from Nebraska for the wedding. This limited their outing to only a few possible nights, but Tuesdays happened to be ladies night at the club two exits south of Royston. A group of buff human males just happened to be scheduled to perform the Tuesday before the wedding.

On the prior Thursday afternoon, Ilene sent Peter the following text while he was at work: "Petey, call me ASAP. Mom."

Peter took the steps two at a time up to Penelope's empty office, where he could have a modicum of privacy.

When Ilene picked up, he skipped the greetings and said, "Mom, what's wrong? Is everything okay?"

"Petey, dear, everything's fine. This is the first time I've ever sent a text message. Did I do something wrong?"

Peter wanted to tell her that her message scared him half to death, but he didn't. "Well, it's just that you've never sent me a text before, and it sounded urgent. What's up?"

Ilene apprised Peter of the plans for the girl's night out the following week and the fact that she and Grace had been invited to go along. Once she'd hung up, Peter wasted no time in calling Royston Limo Service to arrange for the mermaids to be chauffeured to and from the club. He couldn't be there himself, but he wanted to keep Penelope safe on her designated night to party it up.

Penelope, Lindsey, Amy, and Cindy were less interested in the buff male strippers than they were in the reaction of the human female spectators, who were constantly whistling and hollering at the dancers and trying to see who could be the first to stuff money in their G-strings. One would think these women had never seen a man with his clothes off, or most of his clothes off, anyway. Admittedly, the men were good looking, each with an eye-catching set of abs, pecs, biceps, and so on, but the younger fishermen on Colony Island were just as handsome, and they had tails too.

After the third round of drinks, the mermaids settled in and enjoyed the show for what it was, even cheering the dancers on. Through all of this, Penelope daydreamed about Peter being one of the dancers. He wouldn't get quite the cheers from the humans the other dancers did, but they couldn't see what she saw, and if he could flash a few scales her way, she'd be the first to toss her panties at him.

By the end of the evening, most of the mermaids were

somewhat sloshed, though no one was out of control and flashing their fins at the strippers. Still, Peter had been smart to provide the limousine, and Penelope felt so grateful to have a fiancé like him.

When he arrived on Wednesday evening, she wouldn't be able to drag him into the sea, but their bed upstairs would be closer and almost as good.

The morning after his arrival, and enthusiastic reception, Peter hit the ground running. There was a lot to do in the next forty-eight hours, and it began with picking up his order at the carpenter's shop. The first was a custom made set of steps to be butted up against the temple's low stage, so Amy and Cindy could make a smooth and dignified descent during the procession. The other item was a simple stand, painted white like the steps, with openings at the top to hold the bridesmaids' bouquets upright while they sang.

Once these were dropped off at the Temple of Poseidon, he drove over to Royston to pick up the wedding clothes for George and the groomsmen. Penelope had insisted on buying Peter's suit, and he already had that on hand. Later that afternoon, he was to drive to Tampa to collect his brother at the airport and deposit him at the motel Carl had chosen. In between, he grabbed a quick swim with his mermaid.

The Friday before the wedding was an even busier day for the couple. They barely had a quick kiss before Penelope left to run errands with her mother. Peter packed his bags for the honeymoon and departed for the motel outside of Royston so he'd be there when Billy arrived.

As he was leaving, Peter saw George in the Watermans' side yard, personally overseeing the erection of the tent for the main reception. He didn't need to ask. If his father-in-law had to pay for it, he was going to make damn sure it would be set up properly.

On the way back to Colony Island from running errands, Penelope spied Peter's SUV in the motel's parking lot and managed to whip in without being rear-ended. She left her mother in the car and ran up the stairs to the second floor. Her proximity sensing was working perfectly that afternoon, and she automatically knew which room was his.

Peter came to the door and pulled her inside. Fifteen seconds later, his brother, Jim, found himself outside the room with a "Do Not Disturb" card hanging from the doorknob.

Ilene laughed and waved Jim over to the car. "Sorry, but I'm afraid we're dealing with an unstoppable force here. Don't be too mad at your brother. It was Penelope's idea to stop by. By the way, I'm the mother of the bride. You must be Peter's brother, if family resemblances are anything to go on."

"Nice to meet you, Mrs. Tench. It's okay—I've kinda done this to him a time or two over the years. I'm just glad to see him happy for a change."

"Please, call me Ilene. We think of Peter as our son, and since you're his brother, that makes you family too."

While waiting for her daughter's return, she continued to chat with Jim. *Such a nice, well-spoken young man. I see it runs in the family. He's different from Petey in a number of ways, and yet he's the same. Martha MacPherson, you never cease to amaze me…*

After Penelope returned to the car twenty-five minutes later, they said goodbye to Jim and headed toward home.

As she pulled out onto the road, Ilene asked the bride-to-be, "Did you get what you came for?"

Penelope regarded her with one of those "Do you really need to ask?" looks. Then she confided, "Mom, I can't keep my hands off my mate…not that either of us mind, but it seems to be getting worse the closer we get to the wedding— and maybe even more, the 'change' next Saturday."

"Are you feeling nervous, Penny?"

"Not really, Mom. Actually, it's a strange kind of calm to tell the truth. It's hard to explain. I'm excited about what's going to happen in twenty-four hours, but I'm not anxious. Peter has put a lot of effort into making tomorrow special for me…and special for us. Maybe the fact that we're already each other's mates has something to do with all of this."

"You could be right, dear. By the way, I saw that Petey's brother isn't wearing a wedding ring. He's going to be quite the catch. Do you think he and Amy might be good together?"

Penelope rolled her eyes.

Three and a half hours later, a visibly relaxed Peter arrived at Town Hall with his groomsmen in tow to find the bride and her party already there. At Carl's suggestion, Peter had worn his kilt, and Jim had managed to squeeze into

Peter's spare one.

Inasmuch as he had organized the ceremony, Peter did most of the talking during the rehearsal and instructed everyone, including the mayor, as to what they were supposed to do, where they were supposed to be, and when they were do this and that. After some additional words from the mayor, everyone trooped over to the diner on Main Street, and Penelope and her mate seemed to be joined at the hip.

While there were fancier and assuredly better places for the rehearsal dinner in Royston, Peter had wanted to keep things local as much as possible, and the only ones who appeared to be nonplussed by the venue were Peter's brother and his college roommate.

The diner usually closed at 4:30 p.m., but both the management and staff were happy to stay open for the island's first rehearsal dinners. On a small table sat portraits of their late parents, and once everyone had found a booth or a place at the counter, Peter rose to speak. "I'm sure most of you know that over the past nine months, I have come to think of Ilene and George Tench as my parents. With their kind permission, I would like to talk about my birth parents, who, sadly, could not be with us this evening."

Jim nodded his head in agreement.

"I can't speak for them, but I do know they would have fallen in love with my bride and her family, and their home by the sea. I also know they would be thoroughly pleased to host this gathering and to greet each and every one of you. So, on behalf of James and Martha MacPherson, I welcome you to our rehearsal dinner and hope to see you all tomorrow afternoon at our wedding."

Jim began a round of applause in honor of their parents and in celebration of his brother's approaching ceremony. The room was filled with a solemn joy, and Ilene dabbed at a tear or two.

The small, informal venue allowed Peter and Penelope to easily move about and speak to everyone. Lindsey's parents had been invited as guests, and this gave Ilene a chance to learn how Raymond and Ethyl were getting along. According to Grace, their usual bickering had quieted down, and she had the distinct impression that their mother had said or done something to put Raymond in his place. If they could just behave themselves for the next thirty hours, all this just might go off without a hitch.

Eventually, things began to wind down, and it was time to depart. The mermaids had planned a quiet evening in Ed Waterman's pool, and Carl was not so subtly trying to move Peter along to the bachelor party.

The bride and groom enjoyed a protracted kiss in front of Town Hall before going their separate ways. Peter loaded the guys into the SUV and drove them to North End Pizza.

A hand-lettered sign on the front door indicated they were closed for a private party, but there were a good number of people inside nonetheless. The cooks and waiters broke into cheers and applause when Peter and his groomsmen entered, and the rest of the guests applauded politely but seemed more focused on trying to figure out why the groom and best man were wearing skirts. After shaking Peter's hand, the cooks slowly began preparing pizzas for those who had not attended the rehearsal dinner.

Carl took Peter around and introduced him to the rest of the guests, some of whom he'd met before or knew by nodding acquaintance. Most of the tables had been arranged in two lines, one for the buffet, and one for the groomsmen. Carl bade the humans sit down and motioned to Anthony, who brought a tray covered with a white cloth and set it on the banquet table before them. With great flair and showmanship, Carl pulled back the cloth to reveal three bottles of single-malt Scotch—the really good stuff—that was more than old enough to vote.

"Dude! We got a little something for you to drink."

Peter was incredulous. "Carl, do you know how much each of these bottles cost?"

"Indeed I do, man. But since this is a very special occasion, I thought it would be awesome for you to have some of this stuff to wet your tail with."

Peter immediately caught the joke, but it went way over the heads of Jim and Billy. *For once, I know something my brother doesn't!*

"And for everyone who'd rather swim with the fishes, we've got a couple kegs of special suds here tonight," Carl announced with a nod toward the best man.

The groom's party and the guests were well into their first round of drinks when Peter heard a familiar noise outside. Carl opened the front door and motioned somebody to come in. A moment later, a bagpiper strode in playing "MacPherson's Rant."

Peter glanced at Billy, who suddenly looked away and studied the paneling along the far wall. Peter and Jim linked arms and danced around in a circle, and most of the mermen concluded that human guys in skirts were crazy.

Since Peter was to be married in less than twenty-four hours, Jim called for "Highland Cathedral." With a couple of drams in him already, Peter broke down in tears listening to the stately tune, regretting for a moment not to have used it for Penelope's processional. Maybe if they ever had a daughter...

The piper turned out to be from just outside the city and down for a weekend's worth of fishing. After a few more tunes, plus a slice of pizza, he departed for his motel.

Fueled by alcohol and pizza, Peter and Jim stood on their chairs and sang—in their best Scottish accents—a somewhat intoxicated, off-key version of "MacPherson's Rant." They crooned sentimentally the song written about a member of their family awaiting execution in Scotland in 1700.

It was then the mermen attending decided human guys in skirts were plain crazy.

Carl himself was feeling no pain and mentioned things were going to have to wrap themselves up before long. Peter and Jim took that as a sign to stand on their chairs once again and serenade the gathering with their high school alma mater. The high school that the locals attended used the same tune for theirs, which led the assembled mermen to give voice and decide that human guys in skirts weren't quite so bad after all.

In the spirit of keeping the peace and preventing a disaster at the next day's festivities due to over imbibing, at about 11:45 p.m., as previously arranged, the party was "raided" by officers Bud Waters and Bubba Shrimpton. They "arrested" the humans, none of whom were hammered, though they were close to it, and loaded them into the squad car—but not before confiscating a couple large pizzas, fresh from the oven, as "evidence."

Bud drove the guys back to the motel, and Bubba followed in the SUV with Carl in the passenger seat. The three mermen were able to put the three humans to bed, and then the officers said it was high time for them to return to the station house and "examine their evidence."

CHAPTER TWENTY-EIGHT

It had finally arrived. It was here. Penelope's wedding day had dawned—and by 8:15 a.m., the joint was jumping.

First came the arrival, one by one, of the bridesmaids, who each thought the door to George's office was the perfect place to hang their gowns while they crowded around the breakfast table and Ilene played short-order cook. There was the usual gossip that was the standard bill of fare whenever the four mermaids got together, and Ilene was able to add a few tidbits of her own. The commotion was already starting to wear on George's nerves, but he was determined to hold out for as long as possible.

It was soon decided the bridesmaids should have an impromptu rehearsal of the song they were to sing that afternoon. Amy dashed home to get her old boom box in order to play the CD, and she returned in record time.

They squeezed in two complete run-throughs and a few tweaks before Babs Fishman, a slender, middle-aged mermaid with ebony hair, arrived from the Kut & Kurl, promptly at 9:30 a.m. with an assistant in tow. As a general rule, most mermaids on Colony Island did not wear makeup. The only exception was on special occasions, and all in the bridal party agreed Penelope's wedding day was one of them.

Apparently, they weren't the only ones thinking that way. Babs and all of the operators at her shop had been working almost non-stop for the past forty-eight hours to accommodate mermaids who had never seen the inside of a styling salon but suddenly felt they needed their hair and makeup done in order to attend the wedding.

Once the commiserating was done, Babs and her assistant

began to lug in portable hairdryers, makeup cases, bottles of shampoo, and other hair products, much of which was stashed in George's office, because both the dining and living rooms were full of gifts, and the den was reserved as a chill out zone.

Hair, nails, and makeup were to be done over the next four hours, with a second assistant scheduled to come over as soon as there was a break at the shop. The kitchen was the pre-wedding beauty salon, and when they weren't running up and down the stairs, the girls were all crowded into the small room, giving running commentaries.

It was all too much for George, and after his daughter had been asked for the fiftieth time if she was nervous, he decided he'd had enough. He quietly collected his wedding clothes, shoes, and a few other things, and sought shelter at the Watermans', where Ed waited for him with cigars and a bottle of Scotch.

Peter awoke in the motel around 8:00 a.m., slightly hungover, but not in the state his brother was in. At least Peter was not making love to the toilet. After his brother's stomach had emptied its entire contents, Peter steered him into the shower with Carl's help and turned on the cold water.

Peter barely noticed the chill, but Jim was another matter. He yelled, bellowed, and cursed Peter's descendants unto the seventh generation. Once the water had worked as much of its magic as it was going to, they steered Peter's somewhat more sober sibling out of the bathroom, forced two aspirin into him, and put him on the bed to sleep it off.

"Check on him around eleven. If he's not up already, try to get some coffee into him. How's Billy?"

"Out like a light, but in better shape. He didn't drink as much."

"Carl, you had more than your share last night, but you seem to be feeling better than any of us. What's your secret?"

Carl gave Peter a shifty-eyed look and dramatically glanced around to make sure no one was listening. "Dude, it's easy. I drink like a fish!"

Peter gave Carl a high-five, and in vain, tried to contain his sniggering. Luckily, Jim didn't wake up.

"Okay, Carl," Peter said in a tone that let him know it was

time to get down to business. "The wedding's at three o'clock, so we need these guys to be presentable and at Town Hall by two fifteen. But first, for some unfathomable reason, I need to take a quick swim. After that, I'll grab some donuts and be back here as soon as I can."

The sign on the gate of the motel's pool said that it didn't open until 10:00 a.m., but that didn't stop Peter. He hopped the fence and dove in without hesitation. The water felt cool, but not unpleasant, though he could have done without the chlorine. A necessary evil, he supposed.

Peter swam the length of the pool before surfacing. The underwater makeout sessions with his mate had really helped his lung function, not to mention his confidence. He was not about to swim the English Channel, but his trepidation in open water had all but vanished. He really owed her a lot, and for more than just the swimming. He'd finally found someone to love who actually wanted to reciprocate. And man, did she reciprocate!

If anyone said she was merely pretty, they needed their eyes checked. As far as Peter was concerned, Penelope was the most beautiful woman both above and below the sea's surface. He wanted to spend the rest of his life with her, and he was going to do something about that this very afternoon.

She needed, and wanted, his care and protection, and Peter planned to do something about that the following Saturday. Actually, he was more nervous about that than saying, "I do," in less than seven hours.

Peter's musings were interrupted by a catcall from the second floor walkway overlooking the pool. "Hey, Aquadude! I have a couple of ideas for you!"

Peter slowed and then stood up in the shallow end of the pool and grinned at Carl. "Yo! Bro! Lay 'em on me!"

"Man, you're the one getting married this afternoon, yet you're doing all the work."

"Hey, you're working too. You're babysitting those two wasted groomsmen."

Carl shook his head. "You may be right about that, but here's my idea. You take another twenty or thirty minutes in the pool and then come up here to take your shower. While you're doing that, I'll do the donut run, and we can both take it easy until it's time for you to pick up the flowers and take them to the house."

Colony Island didn't have a florist shop. Up until this point, there had been no weddings, and funerals were quiet affairs for the most part. The florist Penelope and Peter were using had never heard of Colony Island, and when Peter pulled out a map and showed him, the florist wasn't sure his driver would know how to get there or arrive in time.

In a bid to stave off any further arguing or having to find another florist, Peter had volunteered to handle the delivery himself. He'd just use the SUV and keep the air conditioning turned up. That would save the delivery costs, but he did want to charge the florist an aggravation fee.

"Well, if you don't mind, man. Be sure to pick up some OJ while you're at it. We need to get those two rehydrated and un-hungover in the next three hours so they can start getting ready. What was the other idea?"

"It was for you to take your clothes with you when you deliver the flowers and get dressed at my place, rather than driving back and forth. It would save you a lot of hassle, and I can get those two showered, fed, dressed, and ready to roll. I have plenty of experience rousting drunken mer... uh...customers and getting them out the door."

"Carl, you are a gentleman and a scholar...well, a scholar... Okay, you're a great dude, and I appreciate it."

Peter did appreciate it. Carl's plan gave him more time in the water and a decent break before it was time to play delivery-boy. He owed Carl big time!

The bride and her attendants had just gone upstairs so the assistant could get started on their nails and makeup. Ilene was in the kitchen having Barbara put the finishing touches on her hair. After that, she'd slip into her dress and join the makeup waiting line, saving Penelope for last.

"Ilene, I heard Samia Marinos has let it be known Penelope is not going to say all of her vows, because no mermaid in her right mind would vow to obey a human, even if he had a tail, which Peter clearly does not...and don't shake your head like that! I'm trying to finish up here."

The doorbell rang, and Babs went to answer it. Upstairs, her assistant was doing Amy's nails.

Cindy looked out the window. "That must be Peter with the flowers. His SUV is out front."

Penelope, who was in a remarkable state of undress, jumped up from the bed. "Peter? Maybe he can come up and sit with us for a few minutes!"

"Anne, you can't go see him like that! You're not even supposed to see him at all before the wedding. It's bad luck."

Lindsey was adamant that Penelope adhere to the traditional human wedding custom, and both Cindy and Amy were in agreement...for once. Not only had the bridesmaids insisted Penelope hew to tradition, but they had also probably invented a few new ones along the way.

Penelope's face fell as she heard her mate's SUV start up and drive away. Amy attempted to console her. "Don't worry, Anne, you'll see him in a few hours."

"I know. I just wanted a couple minutes alone with him," Penelope grumped, ignoring the fact that the girls had forgotten to call her by her first name.

Cindy intended to have the last word on this. "Yeah, right. You'd be all over him like suckers on a squid, and we'd never get the two of you apart."

The rest of the bridesmaids, and even Babs' assistant, were inclined to agree.

Peter headed for the Temple of Poseidon after dropping the bouquets, a corsage, and a boutonnière off at Penelope's house for all the ladies and George. The bridal bouquet was cascading with white and several shades of turquoise lilies, roses, and mums. The bridesmaids' bouquets were round and small with the same color scheme and flowers as Penelope's, but the maid of honor's bouquet also had turquoise and white ribbons trailing down. Ilene's corsage had turquoise and white roses, and George's boutonnière was the same as the groomsmen's—a single turquoise rose.

He was almost dying from not having been allowed to go inside to see his mate, but Peter had to honor the tradition of not seeing the bride before the wedding.

Peter swung by to drop off the corsage for the mayor's wife on his way to the town hall. There was more traffic on Main Street than he'd ever seen, and it got heavier as he neared the temple. The parking places directly in front of the building were cordoned off with orange safety cones, and Peter stopped to move one so he could pull in to one of the spaces. That was enough to bring all traffic in both directions to a dead stop.

With the remaining boutonnières and floral arrangements in hand, Peter turned up the front walk to the temple, and Main Street traffic, bicycles included, resumed its slow crawl as the residents gawked at what little was going on. Once Peter was inside, the main focus of interest was the crew setting up the marquee for the refreshment tables.

Peter took the flowers into the auditorium. The arrangements were full of the same flowers in Penelope's bouquet, along with a variety of greens and both turquoise and white daisies added. After setting them down, he turned, expecting to see four of five chairs on the low stage for the musicians, and instead saw enough chairs for a small orchestra. Astounded, he walked to the edge of the stage.

Lilith Boatwright walked in carrying her violin case, and Peter knew she could shed some light on the situation. "What's going on here? I thought there were just five of you."

"Ahhh, Mr. MacPherson, so good to see you," she said with a smile—an actual smile. "We are not quite as provincial as the rest of the inhabitants here. All but one of us gives music lessons on the mainland and performs from time to time with the regional orchestra, as well as other ensembles. This is the first wedding here on the island, and the first time we've ever had an audience larger than five people, so we decided to call in some favors, twist a few arms, and here we are—The Colony Chamber Orchestra."

Peter was somewhat flabbergasted. "Does Penelope know about this?"

"No, and I hope you won't tell her. All of the music and accompaniment is going to be live."

Peter nodded numbly and managed a, "Thank you."

Lilith began to arrange her sheet music on its stand, and Peter watched the workers setting up the folding chairs and cordoning off the area where the invited guests would sit with white ribbon. There was not much more he could do.

The bouquet stand was in its place on the stage, and the temporary stair steps he had commissioned were butted up against the foot of the stage, ready to be used by Amy and Cindy. Peter was nervous enough for himself as well as Penelope. All this was either going to be a brilliant success, or...he didn't want to think about the alternative.

A glance at his watch told him it was time to head to Carl's apartment and change. Hopefully, all of his careful planning would come to fruition, and his mermaid would have the dream wedding she deserved.

Penelope's nails were done and Ilene's makeup was in the final stages when Lindsey, Cindy, and Amy paraded down the stairs and into the kitchen having just donned their bridesmaid dresses. For her three best friends, Penelope had chosen a knee-length sleeveless organza dress in turquoise. It had a fitted scoop neck bodice and a full skirt with a white satin ribbon around the waist that tied in a bow at the back. They were all wearing matching pearl jewelry—earrings, necklaces, and bracelets. Their shoes were white satin slip-ons with kitten heels.

At that moment, George returned home and loudly announced the limousine had arrived. Just like for the bachelorette party, this had been Peter's idea. While Town Hall was theoretically within walking distance, Peter didn't want Penelope's day marred by ruined hair, makeup, or shoes, and trying to load the bride and her mother into George's Hummer was a non-starter. The limo was expensive but necessary to his way of thinking.

Babs still had to put Penelope's face on, and the bridesmaids were starting to fidget. Ten minutes after George's announcement, Ilene decided to limit her daughter's stress by suggesting Lindsey, Cindy, and Amy go on ahead to Town Hall. If they arrived a bit early, they could do a final run-through of their music.

The girls dutifully trooped out the front door, and Ilene headed downstairs to finish dressing. Penelope decided that once her makeup was done, she'd wait upstairs until it was time to go. There was no sense in going downstairs just to pace back and forth.

Peter stood on the temple's front porch greeting those who were arriving for the ceremony. He and his groomsmen were wearing three-piece dove gray suits with matching top hats and light turquoise ascot ties—and Peter looked sharp.

He had just briefed Officer Bud Waters about escorting Lindsey from the stage door around to the front of the temple once her part in the musical program was done. With the mob of merfolk standing around outside, there was too much of a chance she'd trip or break a heel. Bud was built like a linebacker and was perfect for running interference.

As Bud headed inside to review his route, a noble looking elderly merman, accompanied by a mermaid in her late teens, approached Peter. "I understand you are the lucky young man. My name is Christophorus Kolidakis, and this is my granddaughter, Valarie Kolidakis. She is planning to attend the University of Miami in the fall, and I brought her with me to show her my hometown."

Valerie's classic Grecian beauty was stunning, to say the least. She was destined to break many a heart until she found the right merman.

"Peter MacPherson," he said as he shook the merman's hand and nodded to the young mermaid. "Mr. Kolidakis, I'm honored to have the two of you as our guests today," Peter said with forced composure. This was the man he'd been silently hoping to talk to but doubting he'd get to meet. "If there is anything we can do to make your time with us more enjoyable, please let us know."

"Son, seeing my gift to Colony Island being used for a wedding is more than enough joy for me. Maybe my granddaughter will have her wedding here when she chooses a mate."

Valarie blushed and bumped her shoulder up against her grandfather's arm, leading Peter to speculate there might be another wedding on the island in a few years' time.

"Perhaps Valarie will even settle here someday. Nothing would make me happier. I love this town and the merfolk who live here. "

"So do I, sir," Peter said. "Everyone has done so much for me over the months since I first visited."

"Ah, yes—they are by far the warmest, most openhearted members of our kind I've ever run across. Would you like to hear one of my favorite stories about the people of Colony Island?"

"Of course," Peter encouraged.

"Well, as you may know, my family was originally from Greece, so when in the fall of 1940, Italy invaded Greece, followed by Germany in the spring of 1941, I felt it was my patriotic duty to join the resistance. It was September of the following year before I had settled my affairs here, said my farewells, and was ready to leave from the beach just a few blocks away from here. Do you know what happened next?"

"No, sir."

"The town's fishing fleet escorted me out into the Atlantic, and each boat was flying both the Greek and American flags." Christophorus wiped the tears from his eyes and continued. "After the war, I donated money for a monument to honor all those from Colony Island who'd served in the U.S. Armed Forces. The people here insisted my name be included even though I'd fought with the Greek resistance."

"Wow. That certainly sounds like the wonderful people I know here. They honored you well, sir. If you don't mind my asking, what happened while you were in the Mediterranean?"

"Not at all." His voice was shaky at first but became stronger as he mastered his emotions. "The merfolk off the Greek coast didn't want to get involved at first, but the depredations of the Nazis could not be ignored. Together we disrupted Axis shipping by attaching limpet mines to the hulls of their vessels. Some ships sank far out at sea. Others sank at their docks, and they never knew who was behind it all.

"It was during that time I met my dear Marturia. After the war was over, we settled on a small island in the Aegean. I wanted to come back here to Colony Island to live, but we mermen will do anything for our mates. She would be here with me today, but I am about to become a great-grandfather again," he said with a touch of pride in his voice. "She has vowed to come with me the next time I visit."

"Congratulations, sir. And I would be honored to meet Marturia someday."

"Thank you, Peter. Perhaps we'll have more time to talk at your reception. Come along, dear. We mustn't preoccupy the groom any longer."

Valarie smiled, and the two went inside. Peter was more than eager to speak with Christophorus during the reception. Maybe he would finally learn something about what was supposed to happen seven days from now.

Just then, the limo carrying Penelope's bridesmaids pulled into the reserved parking space in the front of the temple. Peter waved as they emerged, and seeing them in their formal attire reminded him of his beautiful bride in her satin wedding dress.

The moment was rapidly approaching.

The limo returned and had been parked in front of the Tench house for barely a minute before George arrived at the foot of the stairs and loudly called up to his daughter. "Princess, time to go! We're going to be late!"

Ilene appeared at his side. "Dear, the bride is supposed to be late. It's tradition."

George muttered to himself, "Not if I have anything to say about it." Once more, he looked up the stairs and called, "The driver is waiting for us!"

Penelope's voice drifted down from her room, "Coming, Father," a response calculated to delude her dad into thinking he was actually in charge of things.

There was the rustle of satin on the carpet upstairs, and with Babs' assistant helping with her gown, the most jaw-droppingly beautiful mermaid George had ever seen began her descent. Was this really his daughter, or was it the physical embodiment of Amphitrite? He couldn't be sure one way or the other and stood transfixed with his mouth agape.

"George, close your mouth. You look like you're feeding on krill." Her daughter looked every inch the princess her husband had always said she was, and Ilene wanted to weep tears of joy.

Gathering up her skirts, Penelope Tench was escorted by her father from the house she had grown up in, and made her way into the limousine that would take her to her wedding, and her mate.

Bubba Shrimpton's patrol car appeared out of nowhere with lights flashing and led the limousine onto Main Street. The roadway was thick with both cars and bicycles that pulled to the side when Bubba turned on the siren. He rarely got to do this and was loving every minute of it.

As the limo approached the Temple of Poseidon, Ralph Delamar, Colony Island's Chief of Police, halted traffic and allowed the limo driver to pull into the reserved space in front of Town Hall.

The driver lowered his window and asked, "Haven't these people ever seen a wedding before?"

"Mister, you don't know the half of it," Ralph answered.

Penelope was taken aback by the throng of merfolk in front

of the temple, and as Ralph came around to her side of the limo, she lowered her window and asked, "How am I going to get through all these people? My mate…" Penelope caught herself. The human driver could hear every word, so she continued, "…my fiancé is waiting for me."

You can take the mermaid out of the sea, but you can't take the sea out of the mermaid, Ralph thought to himself. He grinned and replied, "Ma'am, as soon as Bubba parks his patrol car, the three of us will escort you and your parents inside."

When everything was ready, the driver opened her door, and Penelope stepped out to face two dozen camera phones, chronicling her every move. The human wedding photographer elbowed his way through the crowd and went to work as Penelope and her parents fell in behind the police officers and headed up the walkway to the temple steps. She visibly relaxed as the crowd broke into polite applause, and as Bud and Bubba held the doors open, Penelope made her way into the lobby.

Once inside, she realized the happiest moment of her life was about to take place. Overflowing with joy and love for Peter, Penelope could not help but communicate her feelings. *Sweetheart, I love you, and I can't wait to become your wife!*

Ilene turned to her and said, "Well, I'm sure everyone in the place heard that!"

Penelope hardly noticed, because there was a fairly faint and fuzzy reply. *Penelope…? I can't wait to become your husband. I love you, too.*

Penelope tapped her mother on the shoulder and whispered, "I heard him, Mom. Peter answered me!"

"Penny, you know that's impossible. You're just overwrought."

Penelope was unconvinced. She *knew* what she'd heard.

The mayor stepped out of the small room at one end of the lobby dressed in the judicial robe and chain of office the couple had given him, which conferred more gravitas than a plain business suit ever could.

"Well, is everyone ready?" Bill asked with a smile. "Peter is sitting just on the other side of that wall. I suggest all of you stay out of sight from the center doors until it's time to make your entrance. If we're all set, I'll give the go-ahead."

The mayor exited through the door to the side aisle, sat next to Peter, and whispered, "The bride has arrived."

Somehow, Peter already knew that, though he was still

puzzling over how.

The musicians completed the short piece they'd been playing, and at the mayor's signal, the young man sitting at the electric piano started the drum track to accompany his playing, and the bridesmaids began to sing—with new lyrics for the chorus:

> I want to stand with you on an island,
> I want to swim with you in the sea,
> I want to lie on the beach forever,
> For together we'll always be.

It wasn't quite the way Peter remembered the chorus to Savage Garden's "Truly, Madly, Deeply." He recognized Penelope's handiwork, and her friends sang with such entrancing beauty, Peter would have gladly steered his sea kayak onto the proverbial rocks.

He knew this was Penelope's gift to him, and as Amy closed the song with the soaring, angelic call to "Come swim with me," Peter felt the unmistakable urge to follow his mate into the sea. He only hoped Penelope would like his gift to her half as much.

The strings played the opening strains of Johann Pachelbel's "Canon and Gigue in D" as Carl rose to escort Ilene to her seat and then helped Billy put the runner in place.

Through all of this, Peter noted how entranced the merfolk in the congregation were—not just by this piece, but indeed, all of the music comprising the prelude. Heads were nodding in time to the melody, and it was if they'd never heard music before, never listened to voices singing or instruments playing. This was something else he would have to figure out later.

As "Canon in D" wound down, Lindsey entered the lobby and smiled at Penelope, who mouthed, "Thank you," in return. Penelope waited for the opening of her wedding processional but instead heard Lilith's violin begin "Can't Help Falling in Love with You."

As Amy and Cindy joined in with the other strings, Penelope fought back tears. She didn't want to ruin her makeup, and yet it was hard not to cry. Peter loved her. He *really* loved her. Lindsey smiled again at her cousin. Mission accomplished.

After a pause, the musicians began the second minuet from "Handel's Music for the Royal Fireworks." It was time. The mayor and the groom's party made their way down the aisle and took up their positions facing the main entrance to the auditorium. When their turn in the processional arrived, Amy and Cindy, holding their bouquets, descended the steps to move into place on the bride's side of the aisle.

As Lindsey was waiting in the doorway to make her entrance, Penelope and her father realized that in just a few minutes, their worlds would change forever.

In that last nervous yet intimate moment, George turned to Penelope. "Princess, you look so beautiful today."

Penelope executed a lovely straight-backed curtsey, saying, "Daddy, thank you for being my father."

George—gruff, stoic, George—fell apart and silently offered a prayer of thanks to Poseidon for his daughter, and for the fact she had chosen a human for her mate, for if she had not, he would never have felt this way at an ordinary joining ceremony.

The music gathered itself for the stateliest portion of the minuet, and all eyes were on the doorway of the center aisle, awaiting the bride. Only one person saw the look of rapture blossom on the face of the groom as he beheld his love, his future, and all that went with it. She was the most beautiful mermaid on land or in the sea, and she was smiling. She was smiling at him.

The memory of Penelope in the gown at the bridal salon paled in comparison to the vision before his eyes, and that vision was walking toward him—toward their life together. Penelope had seen the look on his face, and it swept away all of her jitters and reminded her once more, she had made the right decision under the dock that Sunday afternoon.

Father and daughter reached the end of the aisle and stood next to Peter as the final bars of the minuet were played. Penelope peeked around her father's left shoulder to give Peter a smile of love and adoration.

The mayor signaled the congregation to be seated, and once the shuffling and creaking of chairs ceased, he asked, "Who gives this maid to be married?"

George responded in a firm and steady voice, "I do," and with that, he relinquished his duty as Penelope's primary protector. He kissed his daughter on her cheek and then turned toward Peter, first exchanging a handshake, and then embracing him with the whispered words, "Poseidon bless you, son."

George guided Peter to stand beside Penelope, who then took his proffered arm. The father of the bride slid into the seat beside Ilene, who dabbed at his tears in wonder at this rarely shown side of her mate.

Penelope gently tugged Peter's arm down so she could interlace her fingers with his and rest her head against his shoulder. This is where she wanted to be for today, tomorrow, and the rest of her life.

Then, Bill began his homily, remembering to use only the initial "T" for Peter's new middle name, Tench, as there were humans among the guests in attendance. "Family, friends, citizens of Colony Island, we have come here today to witness the joining of Penelope Anne Tench and Peter T. MacPherson together as a couple, as mates, as husband and wife. In preparing for this joyous occasion, I have come to know both of them very well, and I can truly say, Penelope will do anything for Peter, and Peter will do anything to be with Penelope."

The mayor continued on, speaking of how marriage was a joining of two kindred spirits and unions such as this were the foundation of life on Colony Island, and indeed, any civilized society.

Penelope and Peter heard none of it. The mayor and everyone in Town Hall faded into the background. Only the two of them were left, standing side by side, together, as one. There was no one to see the loving glances they stole or the happiness they shared. No, it was only they, and they alone, forever.

The rest of the world suddenly began to intrude, as the mayor spoke in his most solemn voice, "Now is the time for the exchange of vows and the exchange of rings."

The majority of those in attendance, both inside and outside, were mermaids who had not only come out of curiosity, but because of something more. Penelope was a mermaid who had chosen a human as her mate, and her mate had chosen to become one of them. Penelope was no longer a friend, niece, or cousin. On this day, she was a sister—every mermaid's sister—and attending this sister's wedding became a point of honor for every mermaid, no matter how old or young.

In this moment, every mermaid who had ever wished for a wedding, and every mermaid who wanted one in the future, stood in a wave that rolled to the rear of the auditorium and broke upon the back wall. Their mates and boyfriends—some of whom had been wishing all this would be over so they could go for a cold beer or a swim and some of whom were secretly touched by the moment between bride and groom—were lifted to their feet in the tidal surge, and their partners held their hands to keep them afloat. For those who had the eyes to see it, the wave continued on, out through the doors and windows, and across the entire island, until it finally reached the sea. The world of Colony Island had changed, and it would never be the same again.

"Peter, are you prepared, of your own free will and accord, to give your vows to Penelope?"

"I am."

"Then please do so."

"I, Peter T. MacPherson, do hereby vow to take Penelope Anne Tench as my mate and wife, for now, for always, and until the end of time. I furthermore promise that I will protect, love, honor, comfort, care for, and cherish my mate in both sickness and in health, and forsaking all others, for as long as we both shall live."

"If there is a ring, would you place it on her finger?"

Peter's brother reached into his pocket, and without pretending he'd misplaced it, gave Peter the white gold, milgrain-edged wedding band that matched Penelope's engagement ring, along with a gentle pat on his shoulder.

"Penelope, I give you this ring as a token of my neverending love and my enduring commitment to share my world, and all that is in it, with you, now and for always." After slipping the ring on Penelope's finger, he gently raised her hand and kissed it where the ring now rested.

Penelope's heart raced. This was totally unexpected, yet brought back memories of her kissing Peter's first glass of juice.

"Penelope, are you prepared, of your own free will and accord, to give your vows to Peter?"

"I am."

"Then please do so."

"I, Penelope Anne Tench, do hereby vow to take Peter T. MacPherson as my mate and husband, for now, for always, and until the end of time. I promise I will love, care for, comfort, honor, cherish, and obey my mate, in both sickness and in health, and forsaking all others, for as long as we both shall live." With those words, Penelope had put herself completely in Peter's hands.

Rita Scales was watching the ceremony through the open

window and sent a text message to Samia: "She said obey."

"If there is a ring, would you place it on his finger?"

Lindsey reached around Penelope to give her the white gold band with a Greek key design, symbolizing infinity and unity, for Peter, and in doing so, revealed her tears and a sniffle from Amy behind her.

"Peter, I give you this ring as a token of my neverending love and my enduring commitment to share my entire world, and all that is in it, with you, now and for always."

Then Penelope's heart spoke to her. "Do as you did for your father."

Holding Peter's hand, Penelope executed another straight-backed curtsey, and as she rose, she saw that Peter had bowed to her, and his eyes were shining.

Billy whispered to Jim, "What was that? What just happened?"

Jim whispered out of the right corner of his mouth, "I don't know."

Carl wanted to tell them it signified a son and daughter of Poseidon taking each other as mates but kept his peace.

Rita sent another text message to Samia: "She curtseyed to him."

She chuckled to herself. If that didn't irk Samia, nothing would.

Penelope was so joyously happy, she wanted to put her tail on and let her merman carry her in to the sea—but now was neither the time nor the place.

The mayor was smiling. "Do you, the family, friends, and residents of Colony Island, vow to support, care for, and protect this couple as they swim through life's unresting sea?"

"We do."

The mayor was glad he could communicate his prompts to a selected claque of merfolk who would take the lead in this response, though he still wasn't sure why everyone had stood up earlier. The humans in the congregation were somewhat confused by the sea metaphors but figured since it was an oceanside town, it must be some sort of local thing.

"By the power vested in me by the citizens of Colony Island and the State of Florida, it is my happy duty to declare you husband and wife," the mayor proclaimed, and then in a whisper, added, "You're on."

Peter took Penelope in his arms as she took him in hers.

Their kiss was soft, sweet, and as wonderful as their "official" first kiss on that first morning in her apartment, all those months ago. She was his mate, his wife, and his forevermore.

Penelope wasn't sure if she heard or felt him say, "I love you," but this was the happiest moment of her life, and she felt a few scales appear beneath her gown before she could rein them in. *Not yet. Not yet!*

The kiss lasted so long yet was over so quickly. Nonetheless, they had a lifetime of kisses to share, and they were just getting started.

Peter took Penelope's hand, and as they turned to face the congregation, the mayor announced, "Citizens of Colony Island, I present Mr. and Mrs. Peter T. MacPherson!"

There were loud cheers and lots of applause as Lindsey handed the bouquet back to her cousin, and the musicians struck up Jean-Joseph's "Mouret's Rondeau." They were now officially official, and as the trumpets sounded and the tympani rumbled, Peter escorted the love of his life up the aisle. They were both walking on air.

Once they were in the lobby, Penelope took Peter's face in her hands and kissed him deeply, her tongue searching his mouth as if she wanted to take him into her, body and soul. That would have been perfectly fine with him, except then he remembered there was the small matter of the receiving line to attend to.

Penelope reluctantly broke off the kiss. "Peter...as much as I never want to stop, we have guests to greet very soon."

He didn't pay much attention to the timing of her comment, since he had just about given up trying to explain all the coincidences and odd occurrences over the past months. Part of it was most likely due to the fact they spent so much time together, and as for the rest of it, well...he guessed the more he hung around with mermaids, the more odd things that were bound to happen. He wondered how odd he would feel in a week's time, and that thought set off a nervous flutter in his stomach.

Any opportunity for further pondering this conundrum was cut short when Ilene let go of George's arm the moment they entered the lobby and ran toward them, squealing. Peter stepped aside, as he was sure she wanted to embrace her daughter, but instead, Ilene altered her course a bit so she could envelope both of them in a motherly hug.

"You were so beautiful. Both of you looked so beautiful in there. I'm so happy we're a family!" After kissing the newlyweds, she stepped back and regarded Peter with a maternal eye. "Petey, your mother would be so happy." Ilene took a deep breath, pulled herself up, and added, "Both of your mothers are so happy today."

If it had been possible for Ilene to pull his mother's spirit from the ether and waltz her around the lobby, Peter was sure she would have done it. Instead, she looked over her shoulder and called, "George! Come here and give your children a hug."

He ambled over and kissed Penelope on the cheek, saying, "I love you, Miss Fishyface. You looked like a true princess in there."

Peter stuck his hand out for a man to man handshake and suddenly found himself clapped on the back and pulled into a bear hug. "I'm so happy you chose each other, son...so happy!"

Peter wondered if George needed an emergency dram of single-malt Scotch, but the wedding guests were lining up, so he and George took their places and began shaking hands.

The musicians swung into a lively number designed to keep the receiving line moving, and Peter nodded Carl over and whispered, "Tell the orchestra they're welcome at the wedding reception. We got extra food, just in case. And don't let anyone from the wedding party wander off. We have pictures to take right after this."

Carl was only too happy to run these errands for his friend. Someone finally needed and appreciated him.

Following a seemingly endless photo session that involved every possible combination of wedding party members, the photographer from Royston called time, packed his gear, and headed off to the reception. Penelope and Peter shared a lingering kiss in the lobby before walking out onto the steps of the Temple of Poseidon.

Peter's idea was to send the rest of the wedding party on to the formal reception so the two of them could have an extra bit of private time before the evening's celebrations got underway. To his gratitude and delight, Carl already had things well in hand and was directing them to the limo, two by two. Peter really was going to need to find a way to thank Carl properly. His efforts had been way over the top.

There was still a sizeable crowd on the front lawn of the temple, and Peter's idea to include an informal reception for the islanders had definitely been a smart one, and from the looks of things, there would be few—if any—leftovers. After spending a few minutes alone to soak everything in and reflect on the fact that they were now husband and wife, he guided his bride to the refreshments tent, where slices of sheet cake and cups of lemonade were ready to be served.

An appreciative round of applause erupted as they approached, and Peter and Penelope entertained their audience with the customary ritual of feeding each other some cake and drinking lemonade via intertwined arms.

Suddenly, Penelope was surrounded by a bevy of mergirls wanting to see her gown and look at her bouquet. One around the age of ten walked over to Peter, looked up and down at his wedding attire, and asked if he would marry her when she got old enough. Peter had heard about "the old ways." Was this how it started?

Their turn in the limo arrived at last, and the happy couple drove off to waves and cheers from the merfolk on the lawn.

CHAPTER TWENTY-NINE

After giving the driver a substantial tip, Peter helped Penelope out of the limo. George and Ilene waved to the bride and groom from the Watermans' front porch, and as they mounted the steps, a distinguished looking merman came out the front door to join them.

Penelope squealed, "Mr. Waterman!" and ran forward to embrace him. "Thank you so much for letting us have our reception in your yard."

"Penny, Gail would not have had it any other way. She would have been so pleased to see you married. You know, we had a wedding of our own, once upon a time."

Penelope beamed and introduced Ed to her mate.

Following handshakes and congratulatory words, he continued. "As you've probably heard from your parents, I'm relocating to California, at least for now. While I can never replace Gail, I have found a mermaid out there who's had a similar loss, and we've chosen each other as mates. Because of that, I've decided to turn my house over to you and Peter. I know Gail would have wanted the two of you to have it."

George noted, "And I reimbursed him for part of the indoor pool. That way, I get to use it too."

Penelope was speechless, though she could tell by the smiles on her parents' faces that this had been in the works for some time.

"As soon and Elaine and I have found a home and settled in, I'll send for the furniture I want to keep. The rest belongs to you two."

Penelope was bouncing on the balls of her feet, and Peter

was still trying to collect his thoughts and figure out how to express his gratitude.

"Just think," Ilene chimed in enthusiastically, "you've got your very own house on the island now!"

"Mr. Waterman—thank you! Thank you very much," Peter said. "If you need any help with moving, let me know. Having our own house here will be amazing, and your generosity is truly appreciated."

They shook hands, and then Peter turned to Ilene. "Mom, is this your way of getting rid of us?"

"Oh, no. That's not it at all! We want you to stay with us as long as you can, but this way, you can set up a home office and decorate at a leisurely pace, so when we're ready to breed, you two will be all set!"

Ilene had a look of bliss on her face, and Penelope was regarding him with an enigmatic Mona Lisa smile, so Peter made a mental note to find out exactly what all this "we" business was with regard to breeding and why Ilene was so excited about the whole thing. He also decided to find out about it sooner rather than later.

As for Mr. Waterman's house, the way real estate worked on Colony Island made sense for people who might suddenly pick up and go to sea for a few years, or permanently, but it still took some getting used to. In the meantime, Peter would simply have to grin and bear it, just as he had since last Labor Day weekend.

Peter swept Penelope up into his arms and carried his bride across the threshold of their new home. From the looks on everyone's faces, apparently this was one tradition that was completely unheard of on Colony Island.

The interior layout was not too unlike the house Penelope had grown up in, though Ed and his wife had slept upstairs, next to the smaller room reserved for the baby that never came. Downstairs was a home office, a spare bedroom, and the kitchen, which was being used as a staging area by the caterers.

Once Penelope had taken off her veil, the couple exited through the back door to the pool area, which had also been commandeered by the caterers. Bubba Shrimpton was relaxing by the door with a sandwich and a cold beer, looking forward to the prospect of an extra shift's pay for keeping tipsy merfolk out of the pool. There were too many humans at this gathering to risk exposure of any kind.

For an inter-species gathering, the reception was a brilliant success. Not a single guest from the mainland would ever have guessed they were amongst people who sported a fin and scales in their spare time.

Surprisingly, the merfolk seemed to be quite comfortable eating and dancing alongside so many humans in one small space. The DJ that Peter and Penelope had worried over so much turned out to have the magic touch when it came to choosing crowd-pleasing favorites for a diverse audience, and although mer mostly danced with mer, they enjoyed the music, and hardly a human thought anything was amiss.

Amy was quite taken with Peter's good-looking roommate who had escorted her up the aisle and even overcame her shyness to ask Billy to dance. She let him make most of the small talk, and though she wanted to ask for another dance later that evening, Billy was off schmoozing with the rest of the wedding party as well as the guests. It was just as well, she thought. He was a human, after all, and unlikely to ever come to Colony Island again.

One person Billy did not get a chance to dance with was Cindy. Mike had come home for the wedding, and Cindy was not about to leave his side for an instant. He brought the not unexpected news that he would be doing his residency near home, and that had Cindy over the moon. Mike was due to receive his medical degree in less than a month, and Cindy huddled with him to discuss the timing and logistics of her trip to Durham for the event.

The only thing that distracted her was the library ladies asking Penelope if she still enjoyed being a mermaid. Her disarming answer of, "Yes, but only on weekends," had Cindy in stitches.

The dinner itself was wonderful, the champagne flowed, and the usual toasts were offered. Despite the information on wedding day etiquette that had accompanied the invitations sent to those from Colony Island, there were several residents who tried to offer toasts of their own until they were told to quiet down by their mates.

The best man's toast consisted of wall-to-wall jokes, most of them at Peter's expense. In the end, Jim spoke of how much he envied Peter and his new bride and wished them a lifetime of happiness. Jim's threats to recount childhood incidents never came to pass.

After his touching conclusion, the formal five tier wedding cake was ready for the couple to make the first cut. It was white cake with turquoise cream filling and white frosting, decorated with turquoise and white roses and a pair of dolphins for the topper. They did another round of feeding each other before the cake was cut and served.

There was, of course, the "official" first dance by Penelope and Peter, though they had been seen in each other's arms, swaying to the music, several times before dinner had been served.

George bowed to his princess before taking her out for a turn on the dance floor.

Much of Ilene's dance with Peter was taken up with her saying how happy she was. "I never even dreamed this could happen," she sniffled. "Thank you, Peter. Thank you for all the happiness you've brought to our family."

He had come prepared with an extra handkerchief for her to use.

Peter had been trying to maneuver himself closer to Mr. Kolidakis all evening without success. He did wind up dancing with Valarie, but he really wanted to speak with her grandfather about what was going to happen to him a mere seven days from now. The clock was ticking, but he was having no luck at all. The last he saw of them, Christophorus and Bill Marlin were walking off together out into the night.

As the evening wore on, Penelope danced with her mate in the same yard she had played in as a child, and the memory of Gail Waterman was a silent but welcome companion. It seemed as if the party had just gotten started when the time came for them to depart on their honeymoon.

Lindsey let Amy attend the bride as she changed out of her wedding gown and into her traveling clothes. Though she had been thrilled to be the mermaid of honor, Lindsey felt the title should have gone to Amy, even if Penelope had not wanted to choose one friend over the others. The honor of sharing those last private moments with the bride was one that Amy more than deserved.

When Penelope returned to bid her family and friends farewell, Cindy was sitting in Mike's lap, and it was blatantly obvious from the lip-lock that they would head for the beach within minutes of the bride's departure, even though the celebration was scheduled to run for another hour and a half. Penelope instructed Amy to tell the amorous couple they were free to use her parents' house as a place to change as well as a source of bathrobes and towels. Returning them in good condition was her only request.

It was now time for the bride to toss her bouquet, and Cindy was persuaded to come up for air long enough to participate in the tradition. The bridesmaids dutifully assembled, along with a few mermaids who really weren't quite sure what this was all about. Penelope tossed the bouquet over her shoulder. The flowers were batted around like a game of beach volleyball until they finally found their way into Amy's hands. Lindsey explained to Amy what catching the bouquet meant, and she turned beet red.

When it came to the garter toss, Peter was too busy dealing with catcalls from his groom squad to enjoy the beauty of his bride's leg. This mermaid, who regularly swam naked and thought nothing of it, was suddenly very shy about exposing too much.

Once Peter had the garter in hand, he did a perfect imitation of a pitcher checking the runners on first and third base before winding up and throwing a scorcher right across home plate and into his brother's mitts.

After stopping in front of Gus's Garage to divest the SUV of the soda cans tied to the rear bumper, the newlyweds continued on to their honeymoon destination. The streamers and signs attached to the vehicle could stay where they were for the time being.

When they reached a cluster of old-fashioned tourist homes at the south end of the humans' resort, Penelope directed Peter to park in the small lot that served them. He half expected to see a bolt of lightning arc across the sky followed by thunder and organ music played in a minor key.

"See that chain link fence on the other side of the house next door? That's the northern end of the Wildlife Preserve. On the other side of the street, the fence runs behind the houses for just over a block. All the properties in this cul-de-sac belong to Colony Island and are occupied by our kind. It's mostly retired merfolk who run these establishments, and they keep an eye on things so tourists don't wander into the preserve and eventually end up seeing things they shouldn't. Since the main resort area begins five blocks north of here, things stay pretty quiet down at this end."

She was right about that. When Peter stepped out of the car, he could easily hear both the waves on the beach and the cricket frogs in the marsh. Taking the two small bags they'd packed for their wedding night, Peter and Penelope walked past the floodlit sign that read, "Mermaid's Rest Bed and Breakfast – No Vacancy." There was nothing like hiding in plain sight, but Peter hoped the reservation was still good and that the "No Vacancy" didn't apply to them as well.

Peter knocked on the door and it opened slightly to reveal an older woman who took one look at the couple and then turned to yell back down the hallway, "Emma! They're here! They're here!" The door was flung open as the woman moved faster than Peter would have imagined and threw her arms around Penelope.

"Congratulations, dear! Congratulations. You were such a beautiful bride. Come in and let me show you the pictures I took," Margaret offered.

Peter heard, "Mine were better!" before being nearly bowled over by Emma. "Such a handsome merman you are! Where were you when I was younger?"

Both Penelope and Peter were dragged through the door, and once it had closed behind them, they were subjected to the full appreciative scrutiny of the two grandmotherly mermaids.

"You two looked so happy up there. Such a perfect couple," commented Margaret. "I'm going to tell my great-granddaughter to let her girls have a wedding if they want."

The downstairs looked like an ordinary Edwardian home that one would see in period movies. Emma motioned the couple over to the guest register, and flipped to a blank page. "This page is for you, and you only. I'm going to paste in a few pictures to remember your stay with us."

Once the newlyweds had entered their names, Emma remarked, "Margaret, look. She signed it as Mrs. Penelope Tench MacPherson."

"Oh, that's wonderful. I wish more mermaids would add the surname of their mate after their own like human females do. It's a sign we simply need more weddings on

Colony Island. Now let me take you upstairs to the bridal suite. Of course, we've had a few brides stay with us before, but this is the first time the bride and groom have been merfolk. I'm so excited!"

Emma raced ahead to open the door for them and lead the couple into a warmly lit room with fresh flowers on the dresser and bedside table. "We got these especially for you. Nothing is too good for our first merman and his mate."

Peter was finally able to get a word in edgewise. "Well, I appreciate that, but I'm afraid I'm still just a human."

"No, you're not. Your parents are merfolk, so that makes you a merman. Your tail is the only technicality, and even that will be resolved in a week's time. You're a merman, Mr. MacPherson, and I won't entertain arguments to the contrary," Emma insisted.

Penelope smiled and said, "You ladies are so sweet about all this, but we really don't—"

Margaret stopped her. "Yes you do. We are the ones who are honored by the two of you choosing to spend your honeymoon here. Now, we'll have no other quests in the house from this evening until your departure on Friday. That way, you won't have to worry about making noise, or your clothes, and after sunset, you're free to go for a swim without having to dress for the occasion. Emma, let's leave these lovely young people alone, now. I'm sure they have things they want to do."

After Emma and Margaret made their way downstairs, Peter looked at Penelope with a quizzical expression. "Do you think they'll be downstairs…?"

She sat down on the bed. "Yeah, probably. Their mates are gone now, and at their age, they probably don't want to try and find another. Hearing us might give them a chance to remember when they were young and in love. According to Mom, you and I gave our parents a big nostalgia trip. I honestly don't mind them listening. In fact, I'm proud of my mate and what he does for me."

Peter wondered if he was less a lover and more of a performing monkey but kept that thought to himself as he removed his toiletries from the bag and placed them in the en suite.

He was pulling the rest of his things out to put in the dresser when Penelope cleared her throat and asked, "Well, what do you think?"

He turned around to see his wife wearing white stockings with lace tops held up by a white garter belt. A lacy white bra and thong completed the ensemble.

"Wow!"

Penelope released a shy giggle. "I'm glad you like it. It was kind of fun to wear this under my gown today."

"You've been hiding this from me all day?" he teased. He walked to her and placed his hands on her hips after tracing the lines of the lace on her body.

"Yep," she responded with an alluring smile.

"Clever girl," he said, giving her a kiss. "But as beautiful and enticing as you may look in that, my favorite is still skin and scales."

"Correct answer, sweetheart!" She pecked him on both cheeks. "Still, though, even if we've been each other's mates for the past nine months, tonight I feel like I'm completely and finally yours, and I wanted to look special, just for you."

"That you do, honey," he acknowledged with a fond look and another kiss. "Speaking of skin and scales, you're more than welcome to go for a swim while we're here. I won't mind."

Penelope looked crestfallen. "Two weeks ago, I had planned to stay out of the water until you could be under it with me, but things just didn't work out that way. First, there was the girls' evening in the pool, and then I had to take Mom for a swim early this morning because she was so full of nerves. It didn't help, by the way. So, that plan went out the window. I still want to spend all my time with you this week, though the two of us in the water together after sunset sounds rather nice. Hmmm…I'm going to have to think about that."

Peter "unwrapped" his beautiful wedding night gift, and soon they were nestled in bed with the lights off.

"Well, was it worth it? Was it as wonderful a day as you had hoped?" he asked.

"Petey, it was so much more than that. The ceremony, my father, you… I felt like a beautiful princess marrying a handsome prince. You're my husband as well as my mate, now. I love you so much, it's hard for me to find the words. When I got to the temple this afternoon, I… Did you know I was outside? How did you know?" Penelope almost gave it away, but Peter seemed not to notice.

"Sweetheart, I just knew. I'm not sure how. I just felt that I loved you, and I couldn't wait to become your husband. Look, I'm just a guy, but it was a special day for me too."

It was a plausible explanation, but Penelope was not entirely convinced. She would be so glad when she didn't have to hide this from her mate anymore.

"Well, I suppose we should get some rest." Peter kissed her cheek and whispered, "Good-night, sweetheart."

"What? You're going to sleep?"

"Well, I know it's been a long day for you, and I thought that since we've…well… I thought that you might appreciate some rest more than…"

Peter sounded deflated. They'd made love so many times over the past nine months, he thought she might want to opt out on the post-nuptial version and get some sleep instead. There was always tomorrow.

"Oh, no, mister! My day hasn't been any longer than yours. I married you this afternoon, and I'm going to get what I came here for. So now, my sweet husband, mate, and love of my life, shut up and put out!"

The following morning, Penelope awoke to her husband's handsome sleeping face and understood the reason behind her pre-wedding inability to keep her hands off him. She was worried she might lose Peter on Saturday and wanted to mate with him as much as possible, just in case. As she gazed at him, she told herself everything was going to turn out all right—she was going to have her merman with her and swim off into the sunset. At least, that's what she hoped would happen. She shook her worries off, determined to enjoy their first morning as husband and wife.

When they got downstairs, Margaret and Emma gave both of them knowing looks and big hugs. Another of Peter's assumptions had been challenged and changed. He was tired of living in a world where people pretended that sex didn't happen. It was a really wonderful fact of life to be enjoyed by all. This was so much better than the human world.

Wait! Did he really think that? He had referred to life before Penelope as something that was now somewhat alien to him. Peter guessed they were right after all, and he'd truly become one of them. Change was good.

They lingered over breakfast while the two ladies took pictures of them with their camera phones and argued over who'd taken the better shot. Penelope didn't mind—she was on her honeymoon with her mate, and absolutely nothing could bother her. She was pretty sure Peter felt the same way. The little ways in which he touched her hand, her arm, her knee, conveyed as much as communicating telepathically did, and she couldn't wait for the two of them to have that option—as long as he didn't stop touching her or holding her in his arms.

Penelope was ready for round two, and she felt a walk on the beach together might help set the mood. They left their sandals on the front steps and strolled along the waterline. Although the chain link fence ran across the beach and into the water, it looked easy enough to get around. She was sure Margaret and Emma kept an eye on the fence, and she was pretty sure it would be okay for them to enter the sanctuary, as long as no one else was looking.

There was a spot where the beach curved away and out of sight that might be perfect for a romantic afternoon. *Hmmm...a beautiful mermaid caught and brought to shore, where she is ravished by a handsome human, who follows her back into the sea.* That definitely had possibilities...she decided she should find a distraction before her imagination ran away with her.

"Sweetheart, are you excited about this coming Saturday?" Penelope queried.

"Huh? Excited? Nervous is probably more like it. I mean, I'm looking forward to having a tail of my own. It's just getting to that point I'm nervous about."

This was not quite the answer Penelope had been hoping for, and the concern showed on her face when she asked, "Why? What's wrong?"

"Nothing and everything, if you want to know the truth. Let me see if I can explain it. You've been what you are ever since you were born, and so have I. Now, I'm about to step across the divide and be what you are for the rest of my life. The problem is, there's no one I can talk to who has already done it. No one. I understand the mayor's rationale for protecting their privacy, but it doesn't help me. He says there's nothing to be concerned about, but he can't speak from firsthand experience.

"I'm really looking forward to swimming with you, but I'm going to be more than a bit worried until that happens. I can say one thing, though. I've done all of this out in the open—at least as far as Colony Island goes—and I plan on volunteering to speak with anyone who comes after me, because there has to be a better way of doing this. Honey, I'm sorry if I've ruined things for you. I know you're looking forward to this, and I am too, believe it or not. I just wish I didn't have the nervousness to deal with."

Penelope wondered why no one seemed to really understand Peter's dilemma, or had anticipated it. She gave him a smile. "I think I sort of have an idea as to how you feel, and I know what you want to do is a wonderful goal. In the meantime, I'll try to provide some distraction. Would going back to our room and mating help?"

That sentence had Peter's blood surging. "It definitely wouldn't hurt," he joked. "But I think we're both going to need some fuel, first. Let's walk up the beach and find a place for an early lunch. Afterwards, I'll take you up on that idea of yours, and then we can follow it with an afternoon nap in each other's arms."

In the following days, a handsome human ravished Penelope twice, though their attempts at dialogue and role-playing went out the window the moment Peter carried her out of the water. Peter suggested that once he was back on his feet again, they could swap roles, and Penelope's eyes lit up like the Fourth of July. They spent the rest of their honeymoon taking walks on the beach, swimming, and mating.

They spent each evening after sunset alone in the water together. It was such a blissful five days, Peter was reluctant to leave on Friday morning, and it wasn't just because of what was to happen the following day.

"It's been so wonderful having you children stay with us," Margaret gushed after they had snapped photos with every conceivable combination of the four of them.

Peter offered—for the fifth time—to pay for their stay, but was once more steadfastly refused.

"Mr. MacPherson," she said in a formal tone, "it has been our honor to have you and your wife here."

"She's quite right, you know," Emma added. "We've enjoyed your visit so much, and it has made us feel at least fifty years younger. Peter, I know everything will go well for you tomorrow, so there is no need to worry. And as for you, Penelope you made a truly beautiful bride. It was such a thrill to be at your wedding, even if we had to watch through the windows of Town Hall."

"I think it was more fun to do it that way than to sit inside. Now, Peter, Emma's right. You'll do fine. We want the two of you to swim up here for a visit soon so we can see that tail of yours."

This would've continued indefinitely had it not been for a paying guest arriving to spend the weekend. After another round of hugs and a peck or two on their cheeks, the couple climbed in to the SUV and drove home to Peter's destiny.

CHAPTER THIRTY

The day Peter was to become a fully vested merman dawned. It had finally arrived, and he was doing his best to maintain a calm demeanor. On the whole, he was succeeding, but just barely.

Things were quiet in the Tench household, and that was a relief, considering the way things had been the week before the wedding. At 3:30 p.m. that afternoon, he would be married a whole week, but would he still be alive?

Things were supposed to get underway at some point after lunch, but Ilene had been deliberately vague as to exactly when. "Whenever the mayor is ready," had been her reply, and Peter was sure that was a little white lie, because the mayor favored punctuality, at least as far as his workday was concerned.

Following their return from their honeymoon, he and Penelope had spent the afternoon ferrying wedding and shower gifts over to their new home. Peter was still coming to terms with the idea that he now had a house on Colony Island.

Mr. Waterman had cleaned out the upstairs bedroom, as well as the home office he'd shared with his wife. Her clothing had finally been bundled up and taken to a nascent charity shop to be named Gail's Place in her memory. Besides giving Islanders a place to drop off as well as buy used clothing, it would also serve as a source of apparel for newly arrived feral families. All the proceeds would be put into a fund to aid residents down on their luck.

Although Peter and Penelope planned to live and sleep

at their parents' for the foreseeable future, they did want to take advantage of the extra space they now had to set up their own home office and auxiliary closet. Over the past year, Penelope had suddenly "discovered" clothes and shoes and had subsequently begun making up for lost time.

Penelope would also make use of the bedroom, bathroom, and kitchen while Peter was off his feet, and because of that, she and her mother were off buying sheets and groceries. Peter couldn't live on donuts the entire time he was confined to the pool.

George was busy in his office, so Peter decided to stroll along the beach for a while and walked off toward the shore humming the melody to Hysterium's song from "A Funny Thing Happened on the Way to the Forum" as the lyrics about remaining calm ran through his head.

The beach had its usual soothing effect on him, and he wondered what it would be like to swim and sleep in the ocean like Penelope. That was, of course, if he survived the change. If for some reason he didn't make it, at least he would have been Penelope's mate and husband, and that was honor enough for any lifetime.

Ilene and Penelope's shopping trip also included a quick meeting with the mayor to check on any last minute details.

"As I believe I've already mentioned," Bill said, "this is not an instantaneous change like we're used to when we go for a swim, so there's no need for the entire family to be there for the duration. As you requested, we will have the formal adoption ceremony to start things off, and once that's done, you can give him a hug and a kiss and then go back over to your house. I'll call George when it's time to put Peter in the water, and you two can come back once it's all over."

"Mayor Bill, while I appreciate what you're trying to do here, George and I want to be there the entire time."

"Me too." Penelope vigorously nodded.

Bill shook his head. "Ilene, please. The initial stages can be extremely disturbing to someone who has not witnessed the change before. I'm quite used to it, so it doesn't faze me a bit, but for your sakes, please don't stay."

"Bill, I've spoken with George about it, and he agrees

with me. Peter is our son, and we intend to be there. We're not going to abandon a child of ours simply because something may be unpleasant."

Penelope added, "He's my mate, and he's going through all this to be with me. I should be with him for everything."

Bill saw it was a lost cause and sighed. "Okay. I really can't stop you, even though I wish you wouldn't. Wear your bathrobes. You'll all be in the water at some point, and Peter will most likely want a bit of company when it's done. We'll get underway at three o'clock."

A knock on the Tench's door at 1:45 p.m. gave Peter palpitations, but it was just the postman delivering a package for George that required a signature. At 2:30 p.m., the phone rang. It was the mayor asking him to come over to the Watermans', now the MacPhersons', pool. Ilene and Penelope hugged him like he was going away on a Polar expedition and promised they'd be over there at 3:00 p.m.

Peter's mom—his birth mother—had employed her love of literature when he was a child and often used a quote from Shakespeare as he made his way out the front door, less than enthusiastic about going to school. "And then the whining schoolboy, with his satchel and shining morning face, creeping like a snail unwillingly to school."

Peter did not currently boast a shining countenance nor was he whining, but he did identify with creeping like a snail. He entered through the pool area and continued on to the kitchen, where he found the mayor waiting.

"Peter, good to see you. I hope you're excited about the next stage of your life."

Peter was less than excited about what could well be the last stage of his life but simply smiled and sat down in the chair after the mayor motioned for him to do so.

"Peter, just a couple things before you go upstairs to change, and they both have to do with your options. The first is, you can choose not to do this today and simply go on drinking your juice until the change happens spontaneously. The second is, your parents—I mean Ilene and George..."

"Mayor, I consider George and Ilene to be as much my parents as my original ones. There is no need to differentiate.

Now, let's get this thing done."

"Peter, I'm glad to know you have found both a home and a family here. I can say your parents really love and care about you, as do quite a few of the other residents here, if last Saturday is any indication. But returning to the topic at hand, your parents, along with your mate, have asked to remain with you through the entire transformation. You may, of course, ask that this process remain private, and I'm sure they will understand."

Peter looked at the mayor and wondered if this was going to be something like an execution. "No, I'm perfectly fine with them being here, if they want to be. I'd be lost without them."

"I see," Bill said with a touch of disappointment. "Very well. If you'll go up, undress, and put on your bathrobe, I'll set things up and greet your family. Just wait here until I come for you."

Peter took his time changing, but the mayor was apparently still not ready for him by the time he returned to the kitchen. He sat, fumed, and twiddled his thumbs while the clock advanced further and further from 3:00 p.m.

Finally, there was the sound of female voices out by the pool, and about five minutes later, the mayor stuck his head through the door. "Peter, it's time. Come with me, please."

Peter followed him to the pool area where his family stood, wearing bathrobes, next to something that looked like a gym mat, a table with a small thermos, a scallop shell, and a manila folder resting on top. He tried not to look at Penelope too much. He had to be brave, and thinking of his wife would only weaken his resolve.

"Folks," Bill began, "I apologize for the delay. The mat was heavier than I remembered. Now that we're all here, let's get started. Our first order of business is to witness the official adoption of Peter T. MacPherson as the child and son of George and Ilene Tench. Peter, do you consent to your adoption by George and Ilene, to become flesh of their flesh and blood of their blood, forever after, and to both love and honor them as if they were indeed your birth parents?"

"Your Honor, I hereby solemnly consent to my adoption by George and Ilene Tench, whom I love as if they were my birth parents. I agree I will both willingly and happily become flesh of their flesh and blood of their blood, forever after, and both love and honor them as I did the parents of my birth. Furthermore, I would like to declare that henceforth, I will take the Tench name as my own middle name." *I'm not half bad at winging all this. I just hope I can keep it up.*

The mayor then turned and asked, "Ilene and George, by adopting Peter, do you pledge to love and cherish him as you would your own natural child? Furthermore, do you consent to his request concerning the use of 'Tench' as his middle name?"

Ilene's eyes were misty. "Yes, of course. How could I not? He's my son," she said with her warmest motherly smile.

George nodded his head in agreement. "Yes, I do."

That was all he intended to say, but everyone could sense there was a lot of emotion moving beneath his usual reserve.

"Very well. Would you each sign the instruments on the table before you in the places indicated, please."

Both Ilene and George stepped forward and signed the documents, and Peter did likewise. The mayor then signed as the witness.

"These proceedings are complete. Congratulations. Peter is now officially your son."

Ilene threw her arms around Peter and whispered, "Welcome home, son."

"It's good to be home, Mom."

Knowing that Ilene's emotions might get the best of her, George came over to collect her. "Son, I'm glad it's official, now." That was as much as he was going to say.

Penelope was elated. This was more proof Peter was right where he was meant to be, with her and her family. She hugged her mate and smiled warmly at him.

Ilene sniffled, "Peter, we've got something for you to see after this is over."

"Okay, Mom," he said. *If I'm still alive at that point.*

There was just one more item left, and the mayor wasted no time in getting to it. "Peter, this is the moment you've been waiting for."

Yeah, right.

"All you need to do is drink the contents of this thermos, and the final stage of your transition will begin. I should advise you that you'll be unconscious through the entire process, and you won't know anything has happened until you wake up. As a precaution, I ask that you remove your jewelry. Once you're done, remove your robe, and stand on the mat."

Penelope stepped forward with the scallop shell in her right hand. Peter took off his chains and crest ring but hesitated when it came to his wedding ring.

It's okay, sweetheart. I understand. It's only for a little while.

Yeah, I know. I just hate taking it off. It's the first thing that goes back on when I'm done.

And I'll be the one to put it on your finger, just like I did a week ago. I love you, Petey.

And I love you, Penny. Don't worry about me. I'll be fine.

Peter squeezed her left hand, kissed her on the cheek, and then took his place on the gym mat.

Just then, something dawned on Penelope, something that made her eyes open wide. Their conversation. It hadn't been verbal. They had communicated telepathically! He wasn't supposed to be able to do that yet. Something was wrong here, *very* wrong.

Peter looked at Penelope questioningly for a second before the mayor's voice distracted him.

"Peter, here's your final dose. Drink up."

Penelope wanted to yell, "Stop!" but the word froze on her lips as Peter gulped down the contents of the thermos.

The mayor was about to ask him to lie down but never got that far because Peter immediately collapsed. Ilene gasped in shock, and Penelope rushed to his side, knelt down, and put her one hand on his chest and the other on his forehead.

Though the mayor was slightly annoyed, his voice didn't show it. "Ilene, Penelope, this is perfectly normal. George, would you help me move Peter to the center of the mat? This happened a bit sooner than I would have thought, but it is simply part of his transition."

Penny, do think Peter's all right?

I hope so, Mom. Dear Poseidon, I hope so. Penelope began to twist the belt of her robe into knots.

What happened next seemed to contradict the mayor's words. Peter's body began to tremble, and the tremors increased their intensity as the seconds passed. His limbs began jerking spasmodically, his legs twisted at impossible angles, his eyes opened wide as his mouth gaped open and shut like a fish, and a howl seemed to emanate from deep inside him.

Ilene was visibly horrified, and George stood there, as stoic as ever. Penelope cried his name repeatedly while trying to hold him steady to no avail.

It looked as if thousands of minute worms were writhing under Peter's skin, as a fine mist seemed to hover around his body. Peter's body bucked out of Penelope's control and rolled over. His vocalizations resonated into the mat as Penelope began to weep. She was watching her husband die right before her eyes.

Ilene clung to her daughter, struggling to comfort her as Peter rolled back over, drool cascading from the corners of his mouth. The tremors slowed and ceased for a moment before resuming. When they did, they were confined to his hips and below, and Peter's skin began to mottle.

There was a second pause, longer than the first. Then his legs began to stretch, twist, and deform, and the mottling of the skin on what had been his legs became deeper. His scalp twitched as his hair grew longer, and a beard sprouted along his jawline.

There were a few more convulsions, and then Peter was still, a protracted sigh streaming out from his open mouth, his eyes open and unseeing.

"It's all my fault. He's dead!" Penelope sobbed, burying her head in her mother's chest.

Ilene was on the verge of collapsing, herself. She was convinced her son had been taken from her.

Starting about 4:00 p.m., a small crowd had begun to gather at North End Pizza and slowly grew as the hours passed. Somehow, everyone knew what Peter was going through, and Carl couldn't blame them for wanting to be somewhere with someone.

Except for a few deliveries, business was almost nonexistent. There were a few orders for appetizers, and Carl had the wait staff serve free tea and soft drinks.

The streets of Colony Island never saw much vehicular traffic, but it was absolutely dead out there, as if the entire town was holding its breath. *Nothing to do but wait.*

Peter was lying on the back seat of his father's car as they traveled home late at night, watching the streetlights flash by overhead. Dad must have sped up, because the intervals between flashes grew shorter, and they soon became a continuous stream as if they were driving through a tunnel on the interstate. Suddenly, it all went black, and Peter could still feel himself moving forward, though he couldn't tell how fast or if the direction was up or down. Eventually, he could see a reddish dot in the distance, and as it grew closer, the color intensified.

Great. Just great. I'm on my way to hell!

As his field of vision increased, the red deepened to burgundy, and Peter suddenly found himself floating down into some sort of temple or palace. Once his feet were finally on the floor, ground, or whatever, he looked around, unable to comprehend his surroundings.

"Where the hell am I?"

"Welcome, Peter," a musical feminine voice echoed in his head. "We have been expecting you."

Peter turned to look where he thought the voice was coming from and saw a woman with reddish-blonde hair wearing a peplos walking toward him alongside a rectangular pool surrounded by a sea of flowers—beautiful, beautiful flowers. The woman smiled graciously as she walked between the columns of the temple, or palace.

"What is *that*?" Peter knew he was being terribly rude, but he couldn't help but point at the scene behind her.

"Oh, that? What you are seeing is the palace gardens at our home in Αἰγαί. We are not really there at this moment, but I like to keep the view with me."

"I wish my mother could have seen that. She loved gardens and flowers," Peter said with a wistful note.

Peter could hear the smile in the woman's voice. "She did? I will have to speak to my husband about it. Maybe we can arrange something. Anyway, he is busy at the moment, so he asked me to greet you."

"You seem to already know my name, but I'm not sure who you are."

"Well, for now, you can say I am just a friend. Come with me." Taking Peter by the hand, she led him to a corner of the garden where a bench sat with a hairbrush resting on it. Picking up the brush, she bade him sit. "It is not your fault, but your hair is a tangled mess. Let me take care of it for you."

Peter suddenly noticed that his hair was a bit thicker and reached his shoulders, if not beyond.

As he sat there under the almost hypnotic spell of having his hair brushed, the woman asked, "Peter, what sort of tail would you like?"

Peter instantly remembered he'd been in the middle of turning into a merman, however many hours, days, or weeks ago that was. He didn't know that he had a say in things like this. "I guess I'd like one like Penelope's, or at least a manly version of it."

He could feel the woman's smile wash over him like a wave as she replied, "You truly love her, don't you?"

"Yes. Yes, I do. Very much."

The brushing slowed, and he began to feel drowsy.

"I think that is a very good choice. I know Ilene will be pleased by it. Now, lie down on the bench and rest. You are almost finished."

The woman kissed Peter on the forehead, and he slipped into a dreamless sleep.

Bill walked onto the mat and closed Peter's eyes. Certain her mate was dead, Penelope threw her arms around him to hold him one more time, but the mayor stopped her.

"He's fine, Penelope. This is normal. Just wait and see. He'll be all right. We just have to get him into the water."

The mayor left and came back with a cloth stretcher. "George, would you help me lay Peter on this?"

After his body was resting on the stretcher, Bill asked Ilene to put her tail on and receive Peter's body when he and George lowered it into the pool. Once Peter was in the water, George shucked off his robe and joined Ilene.

"Peter will have neutral buoyancy all the way to the bottom, so it should be easy for you to lay him on the water mattress."

Penelope watched her parents slip beneath the surface with Peter. She wished everyone would drop the charade. Once they came to their senses and realized Peter was gone, she was going to have to do something with his body.

While most merfolk were either buried at sea or cremated, Penelope would never be able to bring herself to do that to her mate and would probably lay him to rest in one of the tiny cemeteries that dotted the island in out of the way places. Somewhere she could visit.

When Ilene and George returned to the surface, the mayor directed them to swim into the conversation pit before he addressed the Tench family as a whole. "This is why I asked you not to stay for the transformation. It can be extremely frightening if you aren't prepared. I know it seemed to go on forever, but if it's any comfort to you, it took less than half the time it usually does. At this point, all we can do is wait. Don't worry, Peter is doing well."

Penelope did not believe him. *Any sign of life, Mom?*

I couldn't tell, dear. I did kiss his forehead and smooth his hair out. It's beautiful, Penny.

The mayor sat down in a poolside chair, pulled out his e-reader, and settled in for the wait.

After sitting by the pool staring at Peter for what seemed like hours, Penelope couldn't stand seeing him so lifeless any longer. She went inside what was supposed to be their new home and arranged the plates and serving pieces for a dinner she was certain would never take place.

She checked the iced tea and sodas in the kitchenette. They were nice and cold for all the good that would do. She asked, but no one wanted anything. Other than a sip or two of tea, she didn't want anything, either.

Bill remained in his chair reading as the shadows outside lengthened. Every half hour or so, he'd get up, walk to the far end of the pool, peer down into the water, and return to his seat. The sky was gloomy when he called everyone over to the conversation pit to address them again.

"There are a few things all of you need to know. When a convert first wakes up and realizes they're underwater, they'll shoot out of the water like a rocket, especially when they see their tail. So, you need to be prepared for that. Peter won't want to get back into the water and will wind up sleeping on the mat, and this is where you three will come in.

"You'll need to keep Peter hydrated with a bucket of water every so often. Most of us can stay out for at least six to eight hours with our tails on, if not more, but new merfolk aren't that lucky, so no one will get much sleep for a few days until Peter gets used to things. Don't let him foul the water. Teach him how to use the mer toilet as soon as possible. If you haven't explained hygiene by now, please do so immediately. I'll let you decide who gets to do that."

A waste of time as far as Penelope was concerned. Peter wasn't ever coming out of the water under his own power. Her parents talked quietly together, but Penelope didn't want to join in. She just wanted to be alone.

It was dark outside. Penelope stood on the edge of the conversation pit, compiling a mental list of a few miscellaneous things she would need when they finally retrieved Peter's body from the bottom of the deep end.

Bill walked over to her and said, "Penelope, your mate is asleep on the sea bed. Go and awaken him to his new life."

Penelope slipped out of her robe and grabbed a couple ponytail holders, one for her, and one for Peter. Her mate was going to at least look decent when she brought his body up.

She pulled her hair back as she walked down the steps and slipped into the water. Her legs gave way to her tail, and she circled the pool once on the surface before slipping beneath it. She wanted a few more minutes of hope, however false it might be. Penelope continued to circle, dropping a foot or two each time but keeping her eyes shut.

When she found enough courage to open them, Penelope had the shock of her life. There, just below her, was the most beautiful merman she'd ever seen. And if the gentle movement of his tail fin was any indication, Peter was alive!

She adjusted her buoyancy and swam to his side. Penelope settled on the water mattress next to his shoulder and curled her tail so she could touch her mate with her fin.

She wanted so badly to take Peter into her arms, hold him close, and weep tears of joy. But she didn't do it because of an overwhelming fear he would instantly vanish—or worse, she'd wake up from this dream to find a twisted, lifeless corpse lying before her.

After staring at him for what seemed like an eternity, Peter's eyes still hadn't opened, and she could not put it off any longer. Gathering all of her courage, Penelope leaned over

Peter, gently kissed his lips, and listened. It was like searching for a station on an old radio. There was something like static, something that sounded like Amy talking to her mother, and then she heard it crystal clear.

Penny? Is that you?

Yes, sweetheart. It's me. I was so worried about you!

Penelope trembled, and the water surrounding her seemed agitated. Her mate was alive...and he had a tail!

Dearest, I thought I heard you coming. Where am I?

On the water mattress at the bottom of the pool. Our pool, sweetheart.

I thought so, he said, his eyes still closed. *I'm actually very comfortable down here, you know. Okay, now for the big question. How do I look?*

Petey, you're so beautiful. You even have the same fin and scale coloration as I do.

Good. I asked for it to look like yours. I hope Mom approves.

Penelope was taken aback. How could anyone ask for their tail to look a certain way? Who would he ask? She decided it must have been something he dreamed while he was out of it. Still, the fact that their tails were identical was puzzling.

Do you want to take a look?

Peter opened his eyes and gazed up at her. *You're absolutely beautiful, Penny. I couldn't ask for a prettier sight.*

That's not what I was talking about, silly. I meant your tail.

Oh, yeah. Definitely.

Penelope helped raise Peter to a semi sitting position, expecting him to take look at himself and go off the deep end. To her surprise, Peter merely flipped his fin a couple of times and flexed his tail. He had only one word to say.

Cool!

As Peter lowered himself back down onto the mattress, he reached out with one arm, grabbed Penelope, and pulled her into his embrace and a long, achingly soulful kiss. Their underwater practice sessions over the past nine months had not been wasted. In many respects, this was the best kiss they'd ever shared, and Penelope had to fight hard to resist the overwhelming temptation to curl her tail around his, because once she did that, there would be no stopping, and she so wanted their first time together to be on the beach under a full moon. Fortunately, or unfortunately, as the case may be, her mother supplied the solution to the quandary.

Penny, is he all right? What is going on down there?

Penelope broke off the kiss and looked up toward the conversation pit where her parents were gently treading water. Ilene had ducked beneath the surface to find out what was taking so long.

Mom, we're having a moment together. Okay?

Peter could easily feel her irritation over this interruption.

Well, hurry up. I want to see my son!

Okay, Mom.

Peter was bathed in the resentment that a petulant child would express over being called inside because it was too dark to continue playing outdoors.

Petey, dear, I'm afraid we have to go up to greet our parents.

It's okay, honey. Could I have a couple minutes to get used to swimming with a tail first?

Penelope knew it was going to take well more than a few minutes, and until he learned how to control his buoyancy, she feared he would land on the pool bottom, hard. Nonetheless, she owed him for all he'd been through to reach this point. After using the second ponytail holder to pull his hair back into a sloppy ponytail, she gave him the go-ahead.

Peter was wobbly as he rose and circled the water mattress, but on the second orbit, he was doing much better, and on the third pass, he was dead brilliant. Teaching Peter to swim was going to be easy peasy.

He hovered in the water and held out his hand. *Time to go see Mom and Dad.*

They swam to the conversation pit at little more than a snail's pace.

I can go faster if you want.

Penelope smiled at him and shook her head. This was their very first swim together, and she wanted it to last as long as possible.

CHAPTER THIRTY-ONE

Penelope imagined what her first swim would be like if she were in Peter's fins. Surely, she would have surfaced about eight or nine feet away from her parents and then splashed her way over to them. Not particularly graceful, but much safer for a raw recruit. From Peter's angle of attack, it was obvious he wanted to try and come up right in front of them. She decided to let him go through with it, as experience was the best teacher. Besides, they all needed something to laugh about after the horror of his transformation.

What happened next astonished her. At precisely the right moment, Peter pulled up, his body checking any further forward motion, and with an ordinary flick of his fin went straight to the surface in front of Ilene. It was Penelope who almost ran into her parents. Where was he getting this stuff?

"Hi, Mom! Sorry I'm late, but I couldn't help kissing Pen."

Ilene pulled him into a motherly hug. "Peter! We were so worried. Thank Poseidon you're all right!"

Peter's eyes widened. He was quite accustomed to Penelope hugging him sans clothes, but a bare-breasted embrace from Ilene? Having a tail was easy—it was this kind of thing that was going to take a while to acclimate to. In the meantime, he was not going to say one word about his discomfort to anyone. He loved his second mom too much.

Ilene held Peter at arm's length to study him. "Son, just look at you." She sighed, turned Peter's head toward George, and added, "Dear, see how good your son looks with a beard and ponytail? I wish you'd let your hair grow out."

George rolled his eyes and shook his head. He was never

going to hear the end of this. He reached over to Peter. "Mighty good to see you with a tail, son."

Peter was starting to feel a bit embarrassed because Penelope's parents were favoring him with all the attention.

It's okay, dear. You deserve all the attention at this moment, Penelope told him. He could even sense her smile.

Peter was glad he and Pen had this way to communicate now, but he worried he might never have a private thought again. Was he really that transparent?

Bubba Shrimpton sat in the corner at North End Pizza, eating his calzone and sipping an iced tea. The officers working the second shift on Friday and Saturday usually made it a point to stop in and have dinner either here or at the Mermaid Tavern. The tavern usually had some good apple pie, and that would be his dessert in an hour. Although Colony Island was usually a quiet place, and its citizens well behaved, things occasionally did get out of hand on weekend evenings, and a member of the police force stopping by for a meal usually helped keep the peace.

Things were abnormally quiet this Saturday evening, and Bubba was pretty sure of the reason. He took special note when the phone rang up front.

Carl was animated as he took the order, and suddenly there was a flurry of activity by the ovens. "That was the mayor. The usual order plus an extra sausage. Be generous with cheese and toppings. Tony, go dig out the special cozies. Let's go, people. They're gonna be extra hungry tonight!"

The wait-staff had been starting to bring up a handful of dinner orders, but they were all put on hold until this one went out. Bubba finished his dinner, ambled up to the register to pay his check, and then walked outside. He stood in the open door of his patrol car as he watched the pizzas come out of the ovens and go into their boxes after slicing. Two minutes later, the Pizza Guy walked out the front door with the order.

"Carl. Follow me."

Carl nodded and climbed into the delivery jeep as Bubba slid into his patrol car. Bubba turned on the light bar, gunned the engine, and hit the siren. The front and side windows of North End Pizza were crowded by faces watching a pizza delivery with a police escort.

This was the second time in eight days Bubba had used "blues and twos," and he loved every minute of it. The three or four cars on Main Street scooted to the side of the road, and the procession turned onto Tenth Street.

Halfway down the street, Bubba stopped in the middle of the road, and Carl hopped out of his jeep, walking as fast as he could toward the mayor, who was holding the door to the swimming pool open.

Peter swam into the conversation pit and after two attempts was able to seat himself on the bench and properly curl his tail around him. It felt both weird and normal at the same time, and that made the experience strange in its own right.

Penelope grabbed her hairbrush from the side of the pool and sat next to him. "Sweetheart, turn your head away from me." She hoped he would keep his hair, at least for a while, and proceeded to neaten up his ponytail.

"Penny, I had long hair in college, you know."

She sighed, "Oh...well...okay." She stopped brushing.

Peter could easily sense her profound disappointment. "If you want, you can take care of it for me, as long as I get to take care of yours in return."

Penelope felt a warm rush course through her. When she was a child, some of her most intimate moments with her mother had come during mutual brushing, and the fact Peter was open to doing the same with her helped Penelope begin to put away her bad memories of his transition.

It suddenly dawned on her why her mother had been nagging her dad to grow his hair out for years. She wanted to share that experience with her own mate.

"Deal!" she said with sunshine in her voice.

She had just finished putting the ponytail holder back on when Carl walked in with the delivery.

"Dude, what happened to your legs?"

Peter turned toward him. "My man! You're a godsend. I wanted to ride my bike down for some pizza but something went wrong," he quipped.

"Peter, it looks to me like something went *right*. You doin' okay?"

"Yep, or at least that's what everyone tells me. Hey! Don't forget, we're going swimming together as soon as they let me, and I'm bringing the beer."

"It's a deal, dude. Good lookin' tail you got there, and you're really rocking the hair and beard. I have to get back to the ranch, but I had to come make sure my main merman was copasetic."

After handshakes all around, Carl headed back to the jeep and gave Bubba the thumbs-up before they went their separate ways.

A few minutes later, Carl walked back into the shop and climbed onto a chair. "Hey, everybody! I just saw Peter, and he looks great."

There were cheers and applause. The dam had broken, and orders for pizza and beer poured in from the crowd. Overall, it was a very profitable night for North End Pizza.

Once her parents and the mayor had left for home, Peter had wanted to swim some laps around the pool, and after thirty minutes, they'd finally grown tired and settled down on the mattress in the deep end rather than swimming up to the surface as Penelope had expected.

This behavior was so unlike what the mayor had prepared her to expect. He had also mentioned along the way that Peter would not be able to swim very well at first, but her mate seemed to have rapidly caught on. Peter still had some things to master, but he was already as good as a lot of merfolk who had been born this way. She could remember a couple kids at The Academy whose swimming skills were more like blundering through the water than anything else.

Now that the timer had turned the lights off, she was reveling in the feel of Peter's scales against hers and decided to ask a few questions before they went to sleep.

Peter, do you remember the conversation we had when you took off your wedding ring?

Yeah, that was kinda weird. What was going on?

Honey, we were communicating, just like we're doing now. What's really strange is, you weren't supposed to be able to do this until after you got your tail.

The two compared notes on the strange occurrences, like

just before the wedding, in the soaking tub at the condo, and all the way back to the afternoon they first met. Even accounting for coincidences, they had nonetheless been communicating in a rudimentary way for a very long time.

Why this had happened was an unknown, as was the fact that he seemed to be a natural at swimming with a tail. Penelope decided to save all this for a talk with the mayor, and after sharing a long, sweet kiss, she watched Peter drift off to sleep as if they were in bed together back at the condo.

Penny, are you still awake?

Yes, Mom. What's going on?

I just wanted to remind you that your father and I will be happy to come over and spell you when you get tired. We can't let Peter dehydrate, you know.

Mom, we're at the bottom of the pool, and Peter's asleep.

Ohhh? How did you convince him to do that?

I didn't, Mom. It was his idea, and now he has his arm around me and is holding me the same way I used to do with Mr. Splashy. It's the best feeling in the world…well, maybe the second best.

Okay. Let us know if you need any help.

I will. Good-night, Mom.

Peter yawned and stretched as he awoke the following morning. He'd gotten used to the sensation of water rushing in whenever he opened his mouth and easily pushed it back out. As for the salty tang that was left, it tasted normal to him, just like fresh water did on land. It was simply a minor adjustment that was all but forgotten now. He glanced over at the underwater "toilet," a flexible, flanged hose not unlike that of a vacuum cleaner's. There was a constant suction in the hose, and all Peter had to do was to place the flange over the slit protecting his cloaca. The wastewater would go through a filtration process and be returned to the pool as perfectly clean saltwater.

Penelope had shown him how to use it last evening, and it was definitely going to take more than a bit of getting used to. So what did they do in the open ocean? Swim behind a conveniently placed sea fan? Peter was facing a brave new world of bodily functions.

He swam some lazy laps and figure eights around his new environment, which already felt like an old environment to him.

Peter was reluctant to go to the surface, but he supposed he should find out where Penelope was and poked his head above the rim of the pool.

Positioned up against the legs of a poolside chair was a whiteboard with the message, "Gone for donuts. Be back in a bit. Love you!"

Sweet. He might be a merman now, but his appetite was still very much human. Maybe he could talk Pen into making some chili in the next day or so. Pushing back from the side of the pool, Peter sounded, just like he'd seen Penelope do many times. It was just a simple surface dive where a mer bent at the waist and then straightened their tail by giving an upward flip of their fin. He descended quickly with little effort and tried to imagine how his fin looked as it slipped below the surface.

Damn, that felt good!

He'd probably get tired of being in the water sooner or later, but for now, his impulse was to stay submerged—except to eat donuts.

Penny? Are you awake? Is it okay for me to come over?

Penelope's not here. She went out for donuts, but she should be back shortly.

Who is this?

Uhhh, Peter.

Peter took the ensuing silence for an implied acknowledgement and resumed swimming for thirty-five seconds until the door to the pool area was flung open and Ilene marched in.

"Just what do you think you're doing? That's a private link! I use it to communicate with my...child...ren...oh..."

Mom? Are you okay? Penelope asked. She had returned with the donuts and what looked like the Sunday paper just in time to see her mother stuttering as she stared at Peter.

"Petey, I'm sorry," Ilene said, her chin quivering. "I just wasn't expecting...and I was so looking forward to teaching you." Ilene dove into the pool to find a private place to cry at the bottom.

Peter motioned for Penelope to stay where she was.

Mom. Mom! He caught up with her and pulled her into his arms.

She was bare-breasted like yesterday evening, but that didn't seem to matter much anymore. He was beginning to understand why merfolk thought humans acted strangely about nudity—nakedness was natural.

Ilene, you're the best mermom a guy could ask for.

Ilene chuckled at Peter's newly minted word and looked up at him. *Really, Petey?*

Peter could not help but smile. *Really, Mom. Really. You know, Penelope and I can't figure out what's going on, but I've heard every communication between the two of you since I woke up yesterday evening. Don't think you can't teach me anything, though. I need to learn how to do all of this the right way. If Pen tries to give me lessons, I think my mind will drift to other things. For all I know, everyone in a three-block radius is hearing what I say. Mom, will you please teach me?*

Of course, son. You know I will.

After breakfast, Ilene sent her daughter grocery shopping in Royston so she'd be out of range. Peter asked her to pick up a beard trimmer and some ponytail holders for him. The knowledge that her mate indeed planned to keep his beard and long hair for the time being put a song in her heart and a few things of her own on the shopping list.

Peter and Ilene worked on lesson one of mer communication while she was gone.

"Well, Mom, I guess you and Pen need to develop a private link between the two of you, now that I've come into the mix."

"Petey, don't say that like it's a bad thing. I'm going to keep using this one to communicate with both of my children. Though I may set up private links with each of you as we get closer to Christmas. We don't want to spill the beans about the gifts, do we?"

"Mom, you want to do Christmas again?"

"Boy, do I! I had so much fun, and even Mr. Grumps enjoyed it, though of course, you'd have to twist his tail for him to admit it. Remember during the wedding ceremony when you and Penny talked about sharing your worlds and everything in them? Well, you've shared your world with us, and I hope we've shared our world with you."

"Mom, I have a tail now, and I like to sleep underwater. What do you think?"

Ilene laughed. "Well, I want to go on sharing until there's just one world that holds us all."

"Okay, guys, enough with the love fest. Lunch is going to get cold!" Penelope had returned from her shopping expedition and was trying to look annoyed with her hands on her hips and her foot tapping.

"What did you bring us?" Peter asked, trying to imitate Penelope's tone of mock seriousness.

Chinese takeout. I even brought some for Dad, and he's on his way as soon as he can tear himself away from the PC.

Penelope obviously had a private link with her father. It made sense to Peter.

Penelope laid out the containers next to the conversation pit and pulled up a chair to sit in. George arrived a few minutes after that and decided to keep his daughter company. He pulled up a chair since he was already planning a swim in the ocean later that afternoon. Ilene and Peter swam over to join them.

As everyone dove into to their meal, Penelope spoke up. "I ran into Carl over at the shopping center in Royston. Everybody at North End says hello. He also mentioned the ovens and kitchen need maintenance on Wednesday, so I was thinking of throwing a small pool party since they're going to be closed all day. I know Peter's going to want a bit of company after almost five days of being stuck in the pool. Besides, it'll be our first opportunity to entertain."

Peter swallowed his mouthful of kung pao chicken and said, "That sounds great, sweetheart, but there's not much I can do to help."

"You're not supposed to do anything, silly. You're the guest of honor."

After lunch, George headed back home so he could wrap up some business before taking his afternoon swim, and Penelope disappeared inside for a bit. Ilene confided she was looking forward to an afternoon at home to herself and swore Peter to secrecy about the fact that some of his father's old underwear and socks were going to magically disappear.

They were discussing the possibility of another communication practice session the following day when Penelope walked into the pool area wearing a smile and a pretty—if somewhat small—bikini. Peter's head swiveled, and his eyes locked on to his mate.

Whoa! Lookin' good, Pen!

Penelope blushed, and Peter experienced the same protective, "This is my mate and no one else's!" feeling he'd had at the Christmas Party.

Peter! You've seen me in a bikini before. Plenty of times.

Yeah, but back then, I was more concerned with getting you in and out of the water as quickly as possible, so I didn't have much time to enjoy the view.

Penelope would never quite be able to forgive herself for the way she had treated Peter back then, but his forgiveness had allowed her to substitute that with fond memories of the early weeks of their courtship.

Today, though, the rationale for the bikini was totally different. *Sweetheart, we have some work to do today. You need to begin strength training. With you stuck here in the pool for most of the next four weeks, your muscles are going to atrophy. When we finally hit the ocean together, I want your scaly ass to be in topnotch shape, both for swimming, and as eye-candy, if you know what I mean. Now, I'm sure you remember what we did to get you comfortable with being in the water. Well, this time, you're going to be the one keeping the two of us afloat. The bikini is to keep our bodies from getting any ideas. Got it?*

Peter nodded his assent and Penelope dove in and swam over to where he was—not as gracefully as she normally did, but legs just weren't the same as a tail. She wrapped her legs around him just above his hips, and Peter suddenly rode low in the water. He stepped up his fin action, and the two of them were head and shoulders above the surface.

"Pretty good, sailor. Now, here's a bit of incentive." Penelope pressed her lips against his, and her mouth opened.

They momentarily sank down in the water, but Peter soon figured out how to swim and kiss at the same time. Valuable training for their lifetime in the ocean together.

Ilene decided this was the perfect opportunity to make a quiet exit and shifted back to her legs to walk back home.

Penelope finally came up for air and smiled at her mate. "You like this?"

Peter's grin told her everything she needed to know.

"Question, Pen. Can you still breathe underwater when you're wearing those gorgeous legs of yours?"

"Of course, silly, and so can you once you get those manly legs back."

Penelope had not wanted to tell her husband too much about her capabilities before his transition, as it seemed to her she would be saying, "I can do this and you can't." Now, though, it was high time for her to start filling him in on his new capabilities.

"Your legs are a different story. When you jump into the

water, your natural instinct will be to put your tail on and swim around. You're going to have to concentrate in order keep your legs. It will eventually become second nature, like what I'm doing, but it will take practice."

That evening, after an hour or so of swimming and kissing, the two of them were cuddled together on the water mattress just after the lights had gone out. Now that the excitement was over, and he was one of them, questions about Peter's immediate future had started to come to the surface.

Sweetheart, once you go back to work two weeks from now, what am I going to do about food?

Penelope didn't want to think about leaving him on Colony Island, but if her mate couldn't be with her in the city, knowing that he was here at home was the next best thing.

Mom will be taking care of you. She can't wait! You're going to be her sicky-wicky wittle boy.

Peter smiled to himself, as it was the same thing his birth mother would have done for him. *The mayor said that starting next week, he'll get a few guys together and haul me down to the private beach every other day or so. At least I'll get to see something besides the bottom of this swimming pool every now and then. Also, we'll be able to have our first real swim together before you go back to work.*

That brought up a topic Penelope had been dreading. *Peter, the full moon is next week. How do you feel about...well, give me your honest answer.*

Peter found himself in a no win situation, but he was going to try and make the best of it. *Penny, the thought of having to get a bunch of guys together so we can go mate, and then having them hang around until we're done, doesn't exactly thrill me. If you were leaving for Australia on a two-month trip, I'd say, 'Let's do it.' Otherwise, unless you really want to, I'd rather wait until the next one.* Peter mentally cringed. He was expecting to be doing damage control in a second or two.

Sweet Poseidon! That's a relief. I hate having to wait five weeks, but I'd prefer we did it on our own, too. Having our first time under a full moon is supposed to be the most romantic thing in the sea, but plenty of mer have saved that experience for the right time instead of trying to squeeze it in at an inopportune moment.

Pen, if you can wait, so can I. But as soon as I get my legs back, I'm going to drag you upstairs.

Not if I tackle you on the living room floor, first.

Penelope began to drift off to sleep, thinking of mating

with her merman no matter where it might be. They were very happy thoughts.

Things settled into something of a rhythm over the next few days. The strength training sessions with Penelope were quite successful. By Wednesday, Peter could keep the two of them afloat for well over ninety minutes without feeling the least bit tired or sore.

She'd begun to explain more of the ins and outs of being merfolk. The more detailed bits—including sex and being a merman—would have to wait until Beth Troutman from The Academy could come by and teach Peter the facts of life. She remembered from her own experience that Beth was well versed when it came to explaining merboy bits, which was good in and of itself, because she knew her father wouldn't be of any help at all.

Then, there were the training sessions with Ilene. After Monday, they had become a little bit of practice and a lot of chatting. Ilene had shown Peter how to set up a link between himself and someone else, and now they had their own private line of communication.

In practice, the number of links merfolk had was rather small, with most of them confined to family members and close friends. For everyone else, there was the sort of party line arrangement used for face to face, or nearly so, communication. On the whole, merfolk these days preferred cell phones or simply talking one-on-one. Communicating telepathically was mainly reserved for the sea and occasional short messages on land.

Peter seemed to have come from the factory with a built-in link between himself and Penelope, as well as the one Ilene used for her children. He supposed he might also have a built-in link with his father, but George seemed to be in no hurry to test it out.

Penelope used the fact she had to spend time out of the water to run errands as the cover for a meeting with the mayor. She briefed him on Peter's progress as a merman, his natural swimming ability, his total comfort in being underwater, and the fact they had been able to communicate after a fashion even before his transition and immediately after he woke up.

The previous evening, when they had their private time

together, Peter told her about his dream, or hallucination, during the transition, and she retold the story to Bill as best she could. He seemed to be particularly interested in this, saying that most converts reported seeing a woman who simply said, "Welcome," or something like that, but he had never heard of an account so vivid and detailed.

There were certainly a lot of oddities that bore watching, but in the end, the mayor told Penelope that most likely, there was probably nothing to worry about.

Penelope and her mother spent a good part of Wednesday afternoon getting things ready for the pool party. Since there was nothing he could really do to help, Peter spent most of that time swimming laps. It was not going to be one of those over-the-top kind of affairs—mainly hors d'oeuvres, hot dogs, and hamburgers.

George had been drafted to handle the grill, which meant he got to spend most of his time outside, sipping Scotch and talking with his brother. The guests mainly consisted of the crew from North End Pizza, Lindsey's family, Amy, and a few other friends of Penelope's family.

Amy was there to check out Peter's tail and send photos to Lindsey, who had gone back to Nebraska after spending as much of the week following the wedding in the water as she could. Her mother hinted about some big news to come, but when pressed, she admitted she was in the dark about specifics.

The novelty of the pool was the obvious draw for most of the guests, since getting to put their tails on and swim in a pool was a real novelty for all but Peter's family. There were only one or two other private pools on the island, and they were not as large or deep as the one Ed Waterman had built. The town's plan to build an indoor community pool that would give injured mer a place to convalesce, and serve as a training facility for newly minted mer, as well as kids, had been on the books for a long time but had never gotten beyond the initial design stage.

Penelope and Ilene chose to remain on their feet for the duration and join Peter, and hopefully George, for a family swim after most of the guests had gone home.

Carl had been one of the early arrivals, and he had immediately shucked his clothes and jumped in to see Peter. They had spent some time under the surface together and were now treading water in the far corner, animatedly talking about whatever it was mermen talked about when they got together. It looked like there was a real bromance going on, and Penelope was happy for both of them.

Peter now had a tie to someone on the island, outside of the family circle, and Carl had gained a new bestie. Carl, the Pizza Guy, was everybody's friend on the island, which really meant he was nobody's particular friend. Penelope hoped this was one more step toward normalcy for him, and she was almost positive that he and Peter had set up a communication link straight away.

It was the end of what had become a normal day. Penelope had slept in following the previous evening's exertions, and if Peter had access to legs, he would have fixed breakfast for his wife. Somehow, though, breakfast in bed ten feet underwater wouldn't quite be the same as it was back at the condo. He needn't have worried, as Ilene was very keen to start looking after her convalescing child and brought over breakfast for the both of them.

By bedtime on Thursday evening, Penelope felt their time together rapidly flowing into the bottom of the hourglass. They had returned from their honeymoon, and a week from tomorrow, she'd leave for the city in order to open up the condo after nearly five weeks away. Certainly, there would be chores to do and groceries to buy over that weekend, but she wished she didn't have to leave so soon.

Peter, when do you plan to come back to work at Harriman?

That's a good question, Penny. I spoke with Mr. Williamson before my last day there, and he told me the old buzzards on the board weren't too happy with his end-run around their opposition. I'm going to be on call in case of an emergency, but he doesn't think I should report for work until after Labor Day. He says that'll give the guys in my old department a chance to adjust to the new world order and give the old buzzards a chance to find something new to grouse about. I'll spend a good part of the summer setting up home offices for us here at the house and at the condo.

Sounds good, Penelope replied.

Yeah. Also, I plan to come up to the city a few days after I get my legs back, but the mayor suggested I stay close to the water for a few months and put my tail on once a day and work up to twice a day. The lounging tub will be a big help, but I'll be in and out of town all summer. I'll do my best to make sure I'm with you as much as possible, but I can't be in two places at once.

This wasn't quite what Penelope wanted to hear, but the reality of the situation could not be denied. Peter needed the job more than they needed the money. She wanted him to be by her side every day, but it was pretty obvious Peter would be bored sitting around the condo waiting for her to come home.

They would still be together a lot over the summer, and she didn't doubt Peter would miss her. He had to do this for them, their future, and everything else in their world. Looking at it that way, things were nowhere near as bad as they seemed. Peter was right. And who knew what tomorrow might bring?

CHAPTER THIRTY-TWO

Late on Friday afternoon, Peter sat with his tail curled around him in the pool's conversation pit looking at his e-reader and sipping a soda. His fin tapping against his back somehow brought a sense of comfort to him in almost the same way that Penelope's fin did—just one more thing for him to figure out in the coming weeks and months.

If he had his way, he'd be doing this at the bottom of the pool, but the technology for a waterproof e-reader had yet to be invented. Besides, it would be a pain to have to surface every time he wanted a sip from his can of soda.

Penelope and her mother—his mom too, now—had gone to Royston in search of fabric and curtains, two words that brought terror to the hearts of men. Poor George had been dragged along on the shopping expedition, and they wouldn't be back until early evening. Until then, Peter was a merman on his own, and he was enjoying the solitude. At least he had been enjoying it until he reached for his soda and succeeded in knocking it over and spilling all but a small amount on the concrete deck.

Great! Just great!

He'd ask Penelope to start leaving a small cooler next to the pool where he could reach in and get a fresh drink, but that was tomorrow, and he was thirsty now. He could, of course, drink the pool water if he had to. It was filtered and purified, after all, but it didn't appeal to him. There was nothing else to do but go and get another can.

Peter climbed out of the pool and walked over to the kitchenette adjoining the pump room. Nothing worthwhile in the mini-fridge, so it was on to the kitchen. There were cans of his soda in the fridge and chocolate chip cookies in the jar. Once he was provisioned with food and drink, he headed back to the pool area and walked down the gentle ramp onto the concrete deck.

Halfway across, Peter stopped and looked down. *Feet! I have feet!*

This wasn't supposed to happen for another three weeks at least. He felt the urge to go and get back in the water, but caution kept him where he stood. The fact that he'd lost his tail and not noticed was worrisome enough. There was no need to compound the situation by trying to get his tail back without thinking things through first.

Peter's robe was still hanging on the peg where Penelope had placed it a week ago. He wrapped himself in it, grabbed his e-reader, and sat down at the café style table next to the pool. Nothing else to do other than wait for everyone to get home so they could figure out what had gone wrong with his tail. That gave him plenty of time to think.

Peter sat at the poolside table staring at his e-reader. He wasn't comprehending much, but at least it seemed to keep his mind occupied as well as slow down time itself. He had thought things through from every angle he could come up with and still reached the same conclusion—a conclusion he didn't like or want at all.

Unfortunately, there was nothing to do but prepare to have his heart torn out by his own hands. Right now, drowning almost seemed like a viable option. At this moment, he felt hopeless, and letting go of his life seemed so much easier than doing what he needed to do. Doing what he had to do. Outside, thick grey clouds began to move in ahead of an approaching front, further darkening his mood.

Penelope and her parents walked in the pool entrance from outside, laden with shopping bags. She started to say, "Honey, I want to show you these curtains I found," but stopped after, "Honey, I …" and stared at him, her mouth opening and closing with nothing more coming out.

George and Ilene were doing the very same thing, and the three of them looked like a trio of goldfish staring out through the side of their bowl.

Ilene was the first to recover her ability to speak. "Dear, why do you have legs? What happened to your tail?"

Before Peter could find the words he had so carefully rehearsed, the three Tenches all began to talk at the same time.

"Are you all right?"

"Didn't you like being a merman?"

"Can you shift back to your tail?"

"How did this happen?"

"When did it happen?"

"What are you going to do now?"

"I think we should call the mayor!"

"Do you want us to call the mayor?"

"What are we going to do?"

Suddenly, George and Ilene stopped, and the only sound to be heard was that of Penelope starting to weep.

Ilene asked Peter to tell her exactly what happened from the very beginning as George took Penelope aside, saying, "There, there, Princess. It will all be all right soon."

Peter started at the beginning and told her everything that had transpired since they left for Royston. The only thing he didn't mention was his attempt to turn his legs back into a tail. He had tried it after repeatedly arriving at the same sad conclusion about his future. Peter had returned to the pool and it was a dismal, dismal failure. He saw no need to clutter the conversation with even more depressing news.

Ilene looked disheartened and went over to comfort Penelope. It was George's turn to ask what had happened. Peter gave him the same rundown he'd given to Ilene.

After he was done, George pulled Ilene aside, and following a brief huddle, from which the word "mayor" was heard several times, the two of them walked quickly into the house. Through the door, Peter could see George on the kitchen phone. He finally hung up, and half a minute later Peter heard a bang as the front door slammed shut. Ilene returned to stare mournfully out the back door at the pool.

Peter walked over to where Penelope stood. How he hated having to do this. But there was no way around it.

Halfway through telling her what had happened, she began removing her clothes. "Peter, there's no need to tell me any more. It won't affect what has happened. We need to concentrate on how we're going to fix this. The first thing we need to do is to get you back into the water."

"Pen, that's not going to work. I've already tried, and look at me. Do you see a tail? I should probably wait to talk to the mayor, but it's only going to be a formality. For whatever reason, the conversion didn't stick, and I really doubt there's anything that can be done now. I've failed as a merman."

"Don't say that! There has to be an explanation. There has to be a way to fix this. Maybe you didn't drink enough of the juice."

"Penelope, stop. It didn't work. It's over... And I can't be your mate anymore."

Penelope gasped at that jolt and began to tremble. "P-P-P-Peter..."

"No, Penelope. Don't. I'm still a human and always will be. A cripple who can't go where you go. We thought there was a definite end in sight, and it has ended, but not the way we hoped. I'm sorry—I'll always be a cripple, and none of you will want to put up with me for the rest of my life. Plus, you're going to live seventy to ninety more years than I will. Do you really want that? I'd be an increasingly feeble old man, while you'll still be so youthful. Do you really want to go through that? You'll want to choose a new mate, but you won't because I'm still around, hanging on."

"No, Petey, I never want anyone but you. We promised forever, remember?"

"Pen, I know, but I won't be able to fulfill my vow to protect you because you'll have to leave me behind when you go anywhere in the sea. I know your parents want to breed again before too long, and they won't be able to substitute for me because they'll have their own concerns and worries with their second child. You'll have to find someone, but who? Some unattached merman from around here? You'll wind up having a mutual attraction to each other because the two of you swim together so much, but you won't be able to take the next logical step because I'm still your mate. And if you do mate with him, are you ready to handle the guilt?"

"Sweetheart, I'd never, ever to that to you. You're overthinking all of this."

"Penelope, I know you're so loving and loyal, but time and circumstances will wear anyone down. Besides, we have to be realistic. I won't be able to fulfill my duty to our children because I'm stuck on shore. I won't be able to take them swimming. I'll only be able to be a real father to them half of the time or less..."

"Peter, please," Penelope said. "We can move inland.

We can raise our children as humans. No one will have to know."

"Pen, do you want to rob them of their birthright, their heritage, just because I couldn't be what you needed me to be? I know *I* can't do that. And what about you? You're a mermaid! The sea is your life. Sooner or later, you'll want to slip away to get your tail wet. It's only natural that you would. But when it's time to come home, will you want to? Do you really want to go through that conflict?"

Peter's face was contorted in agony, and he looked nothing like the man she loved. Penelope closed her eyes for a moment and took a deep breath. She knew he was right about that part, but she refused to acknowledge it aloud.

"And if you take our children to see their grandparents, I'll have to worry you won't come home because you're *already* home. Your real home. Your natural home. You can live and work in the city five days a week, but you're still tied to the sea in so many ways. No, sweetheart, I can't do this. I can't let *you* do this. I'd never be able to forgive myself."

Peter covered his face with his hands in exasperation and despair. Penelope could feel waves of anguish emanating from him, and judging by his action, he could sense every bit of hers as well. At times like this, being able to communicate telepathically was a real bitch.

"Is this really what you want?" she asked, barely able to contain her sorrow.

Peter looked as if he'd been stabbed in the heart. "God, no! There is no way on earth I would ever want or ask for this, but this is what has to be. It is what *must* be." Tears began to stream down Peter's face. "I have to move inland, as far away as possible and as quickly as possible. And I can't tell you where I end up."

"There has to be another way," Penelope murmured.

"No. This is the only way we'll be able to move on. I have to go someplace where I'll never see or hear the ocean again or stand at the water's edge. If I put just one foot in the sea, I'll wonder if you're out there swimming at that very moment. If I watch a couple strolling on the beach, I'll wonder if you've found a new mate. I'll wonder if he's good to you. I'll wonder if you're happy. If I see kids collecting shells, I'll wonder if your first child was a boy or a girl and what they're like. If I even see a picture of the sea, I'll get a painful glimpse of what it's like to be what you are.

"Pen, I wanted too much. I reached too far, and now I'm going to have to pay the price. You've told me so many times that I'm the one who restored your love for the sea, your joy at being in the water, and your happiness in being a mermaid. I guess my role was to give your life back to you, and now that I have, it's time for me to make my exit."

Penelope ran toward the pool crying, "No, no, no, nooo!" and dove in. She swam straight to the bottom and after circling a few times, settled onto the water mattress, her tail curled around her body and her head buried in her arms.

It's not fair! It's just not fair! she sobbed as her tears contributed to the salinity of the pool.

She had been patient. She had chosen a mate, a man she dearly loved. He had jumped at the chance to become a merman, and he had dutifully done everything that was required of him in order to become one of them. So why had Peter suddenly been rejected?

Why had this final bit of happiness been snatched from her so abruptly? Why was everything crashing down around her? *Why? Why? Why?*

The worst thing of all was that Peter was probably right about their situation, and that made it even worse. It was no consolation he would suffer as much as she would.

When a merman tangled with a shark to protect his family and the shark won, the pain and agony of death was intense but relatively brief. Peter's pain, agony, and grief would continue on for decades. Sacrificing one's self was a step that was never taken lightly, but it was one taken without a second thought and at a moment's notice.

Peter was being a merman like all those mermen who had gone before him. Doing what was expected. Doing what was necessary. Doing what he couldn't help but do, and the pain it brought would not be short. It would continue on and on, gnawing away at his very being until he died. A shark attack would be more merciful. Peter was a merman sacrificing his life, his life and his happiness, for the sake of his mate and the children they'd never get to have.

Ever since the first morning of their honeymoon, Penelope had felt the faint, almost imperceptible stirrings of the urge to breed. She now had a mate and a husband, and she had been very, very happy that morning. Her body had simply ticked off another two items on its checklist and was signaling her she ought to breed relatively soon. Penelope had so wanted for Peter to be the one to breed with her, and she would have joyfully borne his children. Not any time in the immediate future, mind you, but at some point, say four or five years from now.

This disastrous setback had really shaken things up, and she had no intention of breeding with anyone but him. How long she would be able to hold out, though, was another matter entirely.

She had always wondered how much truth there was to the stories that teenage mermaids told each other. Those stories about mermaids unable to find a mate, coming ashore, their bodies literally glowing crimson from their breeding flush, in search of a suitable partner, and repeatedly mating with him over and over again until the flush began to subside and the reproductive mission was accomplished. The mermaid would then return to the sea, and the poor human— if he survived at all—would try to follow her and either drown or lead a miserable life beside the sea waiting for her return. In all probability, she never would.

She had done a bit of research while at the university and found that humans had almost identical legends, so there must be some truth somewhere to the stories, and they were not simply cautionary tales told to remind young mermaids they should not wait too long before choosing a mate. She was not going to let that happen to her. No matter what the outcome of this setback might be, Penelope was bound and determined for Peter to sire at least one of her children.

At that moment, she held out little or no hope for a happy outcome from this catastrophe, but at least she now had a plan going forward. Peter may not be able to be one of them, but his child would be, and as long as she had breath in her, Penelope would tell Peter's descendants about the wonderful human who was their ancestor—that was if she could stop crying long enough to finish the story.

Meanwhile, she would fight as hard as she could to keep Peter in her life, no matter what the odds were. As soon as possible, she would seek out Helen Johnson to ask her how she and Avery had been able to make things work and get her advice. Something just had to go right in her life. It just had to!

Penny, are you okay? Do you want me to join you down there?

Mom, I just want to be alone right now.

Penny, I can understand some of what you're going through, and I feel like I've failed my son, somehow. We shouldn't have gone shopping this afternoon. We should have stayed with him. I don't know if it would have prevented this, but at least we'd know we hadn't shirked our duty by going to Royston.

Mom, do you know what Peter said to me? Do you understand what he's planning to do?

Yes, dear, it is one of the plusses and minuses of sharing a link with my children. The negative bit is that I heard the whole thing. The positive part is you don't have to relive it in order to tell me. Just like you, I'm going to need some time by myself to grieve on my own, but don't worry, dear. You can stay down there for as long as you want. At the same time, I think you should know the mayor just arrived, and he's going to talk with Peter.

Peter had watched Penelope run across the concrete deck and dive into the pool, showing her caudal fin just before it disappeared beneath the surface. Such a beautiful and graceful return to her natural element.

He was going to miss watching her do that. He was going to miss falling asleep with her underwater. He was going to miss...everything. That thought made him shake even harder. Right now, he wanted nothing more than to collect his things, say goodbye to Mom and Dad—no—Ilene and George, apologize for wasting their time, and thank them for everything they tried to do for him.

If he got on the road soon, he could put a couple hundred miles between him and Colony Island before he had to stop and rest. He couldn't tell them where he was going, because he didn't know, and he certainly wouldn't tell them where he finally wound up—it would be too easy for Penelope to find him, if she would even want to. Once he broke the news, George and Ilene would want to see the back of him as soon as possible, and Peter couldn't blame them.

He was about to head into the house, the house that would never be his home again, when George arrived with the mayor in tow. Though Peter felt talking to the mayor wouldn't help matters—what was done was done—it couldn't hurt things either. He'd say goodbye to Bill and thank him for everything. After that, he would hit the road before the urge to stay, the urge to return to the water, caused him to make things even worse than they already were.

For Penelope's sake, he needed to make a quick, clean break. Giving her even a glimmer of false hope would be terribly cruel, and he'd already failed her so badly. No, he had to go as soon as the niceties were taken care of.

The mayor stopped a few feet away and gazed at Peter's legs as if he was trying to find a stray scale or two. After a minute or so, Bill came forward and grasped Peter's hand.

"How are you holding up, son?"

"Well sir, I've been better—much better."

The mayor shook his head. "Peter, would you mind if I asked you some questions? I'd like to understand what happened and see what I can do to solve your problem."

Peter knew that talking would solve nothing, but his mother—his human mother—had raised him to be polite. He was determined not to let her down, not like he had let his family and friends here on Colony Island down.

Peter nodded his assent, and the mayor said, "Good. Good. Could you find me a notepad somewhere? I'd like to take some notes as we talk."

Peter turned to walk up the ramp into the house. He was tempted to keep going but instead returned with a legal pad and a pen. Everyone was watching him as he closed the kitchen door behind him, including Penelope, who watched from the pool.

Peter clamped down hard on his thoughts, hoping not to give her any inkling of what was running through his mind. George and Ilene were sitting on the wrought iron bench near the conversation pit, and they too were trying not to show any emotion. Walking across the concrete deck, Peter joined Bill at the round table in the corner near the pump room.

"Thank you, son." He tore off two sheets from the legal pad and wrote a heading at the top of each one.

Peter didn't look to see what the headings were. He didn't want to see. He just wanted to get this over with.

"Now, please…tell me how it happened."

Peter gave essentially the same account he'd given individually to George, Ilene, and Penelope. There wasn't much to add to his earlier account, just a few minor details here and there, nothing that affected the story or added to the body of evidence. When he was finished, the mayor jotted down a last note or two.

"Peter, tell me about today, prior to losing your tail."

"I woke up beside Pen on the water mattress this morning, took my daily laps before breakfast, didn't really want to surface, but did to have breakfast with Pen. After that, I swam some recreational laps that were more maneuvering exercises than anything else, while she cleaned up the dishes. Penelope came back in a bikini—a new one—and we did some strength training, plus a bit of kissing.

"Ilene came over with some sandwiches for lunch, and while Penelope went to change for their afternoon shopping excursion, Mom and I went through some exercises in communicating, even though she said I didn't need them.

"Once the ladies departed for Royston with George, I took a short nap on the bottom, swam a bit more, and settled down to read. Overall, it was a normal day compared to any in the past week."

"All right," Bill said. "How have you felt about this new aspect to your life, prior to this afternoon?"

"Mayor, it has been absolutely wonderful from the moment I first woke up underwater, until I discovered I had my legs again. My only regret is that the whole thing didn't happen to me sooner. I really wish I'd been born this way. I've had no complaints other than over the past day or two, I've felt a bit confined and restless. Honestly, I've really been wanting to go into the sea. I needed to swim, I mean, *really* swim with my mate."

The mayor's arched eyebrows relaxed when he heard Peter tell about his desire to swim with Penelope. Maybe it was the full moon coming up in a few days. Maybe not. It was hard to say. Merfolk did get a bit restless—a bit aroused—a day or two before the full moon, but that usually happened amongst the newly chosen or younger population. Older merfolk—himself included—were more settled and only took to the sea at that time to celebrate an anniversary or cap off a nice evening together. Otherwise, their lovemaking was confined to the bedroom or underwater during the day.

On the other hand, Peter was still pretty young as merfolk went and very new to life as a merman. Being cooped up in the pool for a week and having the full moon in the offing, easily explained everything.

"That sounds all right to me. How have you felt about the entire transition?"

It was now that Peter recounted all of the odd, off script things that had happened since his first sip of the juice. Things like the juice tasting wonderful from the very beginning, his craving for a second glass, not being sick at all, the side effects he'd felt during the last three or four months, apparently being able to communicate with Penelope in the minutes before their wedding, definitely being able to communicate with her from the moment he woke up rather than after four or five days of hard work, and the fact he was perfectly comfortable and happy underwater from the very first moment of awareness.

The mayor already knew about Peter's hallucination while he was unconscious but said nothing as Peter recounted his experience. Finally, Peter shared about the uneasiness that had haunted him after the first month or two.

"Foreboding is not all that unusual, and while the vision you recounted far exceeds the norm, I see nothing wrong with it. Tell me what you'd most like to do at this moment."

"Mayor, I would most like to do what I know I can't do. I want to jump in the pool, put my tail on, and hold my mate, my wife, close, and tell her everything is going to be fine—which it plainly is not."

There were a few more questions, but at the end of it all, the notes under one heading extended onto multiple pages while the other heading had a very few short notes, each one followed by a question mark. The mayor asked if he could make a few calls from the house phone and left Peter sitting there, feeling like he was under a microscope.

Penelope paced back and forth in the pool, as much as anyone could when they had a tail rather than legs. Peter had been talking and gesturing with his hands for what seemed like hours, and her parents, who were still sitting on the wrought iron bench, now gave her a brief smile. What was taking so long?

She wanted her mate. She wanted her Petey so badly, but he just sat there looking dejected. Penelope wanted more than anything to communicate with him, but she didn't dare. She might learn something she desperately didn't want to know. The lights in the pool area flickered a time or two, adding additional drama to a situation that didn't need any more.

Whether he knew it or not, Peter had invoked the final word in her wedding vow to him. That word was " obey." If she had been threatened by a great white shark, Penelope would have instantly done whatever he'd instructed. He would be risking his life to save her, and it was her duty to do exactly as he said. But, as much as he was trying to protect her now, "obey" was quickly replaced by "no." Peter was her husband, her mate, and it was her duty to stay with him, no matter what happened.

Finally, the mayor emerged from the kitchen. He was shaking his head. He sat down with Peter, and their conversation became more animated. Now Peter was shaking his head. It didn't look good at all, and Penelope was on the verge of tears when Peter stood up and removed his robe.

Peter noticed the lights flickering and wondered if there was something wrong with the circuitry in the pool area, but it really didn't concern him anymore. This wasn't his house to worry about anymore.

After what seemed to be a lifetime, the mayor made his way down the ramp to the pool deck, sat at the table, and shook his head. "Peter, I've spoken with every convert, recent and otherwise, I could think of. There were a couple I couldn't get hold of, but the consensus is, there is nothing out of the ordinary with your transformation, other than your getting your legs back after one week rather than the standard four or five. Most of the items that were out of the ordinary have happened before, though no more than one or two of them have happened to a single convert.

"It looks as if you simply experienced everything. The extremely early competency in communicating and the initial taste of the juice were the only real standouts, and even so, they shouldn't be enough to affect your tail. As far as I can tell, there is no known reason for you to have lost it. I wish I could offer more insight or consolation, but I'm at a dead end. The only thing I can say is, Penelope is still your mate...and your wife."

Now it was Peter's turn to shake his head.

"I'm sorry, but I can't be Penelope's mate any more. She deserves a merman to breed with, one who can carry out the duties required of a chosen mate. One who can be there for the children. One who can protect his family. I'm just a cripple now, and no mermaid should have to deal with that, especially Penelope. As soon as we're done here, I'm going to get my things and hit the road so she can start to put all of this behind her as quickly as possible."

The mayor suddenly looked very aged, like an old man who had lost his only friend. "I was afraid of that. I think you're wrong about this, but there's nothing I can do to stop you. Leaving may very well be the best thing for all concerned. I just don't know. Before you leave, though, would you do one thing for me? It may sound like a futile endeavor, but would you try just once more to get your tail back? If nothing else, it will give your mate...I mean, give Penelope and her parents a sense of closure."

Peter sighed. He'd been hoping to avoid doing this, but it looked like he had no choice but to try. "Well, I do owe them at least that much, but how do I do it when I've never done it before?"

"Peter, it doesn't require ruby slippers or fairy dust. It's something that is just as natural for a merman as wanting to protect his mate. All this time, the water has been calling you. I can tell it has, just by looking at you. Peter, you have to *act* on that call. The water is calling you home, son. It's time for you to go and swim with your mate, be a part of life in the sea. This may be a long shot, but it's the best and only one I can offer you."

Peter stood and removed his robe. Yes, he had felt the water's call and wanted to follow it, even though he suspected he was just trying to escape all this, rather than heeding the call as a merman. He was going to do this for his mate, and he would subsequently suffer this final humiliation. After that, he could leave with a clean conscience.

The thought of this being his final night on Colony Island somehow brought him to the memory of his first night here, and the passionate scene in Penelope's bedroom. With a tear in his eye, Peter fondly remembered her saying, "Give me everything ya got!" He loved Penelope and always would, and that fact alone required he give this his all. Peter was determined. He was going to give this one last attempt his best effort, and then some.

Penelope instantly understood what Peter was about to do and swam out of the way. He was still her mate, and she would be there to comfort and console him, both now and in the future. She'd be there with him, no matter the outcome, and no matter what he thought he should do.

Where you go, I will go.

She glanced at her parents, still sitting on the wrought-iron bench. Ilene took George's hand and held it tightly.

Peter appeared to be deep in thought for a few moments and then ran toward the edge of the pool on the deep end. As he gained momentum, he started to raise his arms above his head in preparation for his dive. He was half a stride away from the pool's edge when all the light vanished, and suddenly, it was pitch black.

There was a sound like a pop, and Peter yelled, "What the hell?" This was quickly followed by the sound of the largest belly flop in history.

"Peter!"

Penelope swam furiously in a diagonal line toward the deep end but reached the far corner without locating him. There was absolutely no ambient light, and while she could see much better in the dark than humans, she still needed something to work with. She swam in ever decreasing circles around the deep end, but it was as if her mate had vanished from the face of the earth. Penelope was in full panic mode.

Peter! Where are you?

Bubba had just walked through the back door of the station house after flipping the switch for the emergency generator when the mayor's call came through.

"Police Station," he answered.

It wasn't much of a police station, because Colony Island didn't have much of a police force, and it was all because the town didn't have very much in the way of serious or even semi-serious crime. There were three officers on the force, and three jail cells at the station. One of those cells, one was used for storage, and the other two were mostly used for residents who'd had too much to drink and needed to sleep it off. A desk, a few chairs, and a closet full of equipment rounded out the station's contents.

"Ah, hello, Mayor. I was just about to call you at home when the lights went out. I heard on the scanner that some drunk driver hit a pole on Royston Road, and they needed to cut the power in order to make repairs. Sorry, sir. I guess those county boys were a bit slow in getting the word out that the cut was imminent. Nah, the guy's okay. Airbags."

Bubba was never much for words and would elaborate only when the situation demanded. This wasn't one of those.

"Yeah, they should have it fixed by morning. You're welcome—have a good evening, sir."

With that, Bubba hung up and pulled his dinner out of the microwave. Bud was supposed to come on duty at midnight, and a moonlight swim sounded like just the thing to do before he went home to his mate.

I'm down...here. I don't...

It was very faint, very faint and weak, but Penelope didn't need to ask who was communicating with her. She sounded, and after swimming back and forth above the bottom a few times, she ran into a hand. *His* hand.

Sweetheart! Are you okay?

Yeah...think so...just so tired.

Here, wrap your legs around my waist and I'll take you to the surface.

Can't...do that.

Why? What's wrong?

I don't have...legs...

Penelope ran her hands down his torso and across the point where skin blended into scales. She ran her hands over his scales, both fore and aft, and felt for his fin for a long moment.

She then shot up to the surface, launched herself out of the water and performed a back-flip while yelling, "Whooo hooo!"

Penny! What's going on? Ilene asked.

He's back! It's back! Peter's tail is back!

Penelope swam to the bottom and slipped her arms under his. *Come on, honey. Let's get you onto the water mattress.*

Mmmm…okay.

Peter was no help at all, but she was still able to move him without too much effort and soon had him sprawled across the water mattress. She took him into her arms.

Sweetheart, I was so worried, so afraid I'd lost my mate and my dear, sweet husband. To hell with the full moon! Peter, please mate with me right now. Right here.

I'd love to….no energy…need to sleep.

With that, Peter fell into a deep, dreamless slumber. It was at this point that Penelope finally understood. Peter had used every bit of energy he had changing back, probably much more than was necessary, and now he was paying the penalty.

When he tried to regain his tail earlier, it had been either too soon, or he hadn't known how much he had to put into it. This time, though, Peter had put all of himself into changing. Changing back for her. Changing back to be with *her.* She continued to hold him and stroke his hair as he slept.

Peter woke, grateful to be underwater where he belonged. Nine feet above him, he could see sunlight streaming in the door and windows on the east side of the pool. He should have thought to grab his dive watch while he was on his feet yesterday.

What time is it? he asked no one in particular.

It's breakfast time! Time for you to rise and swim and stretch your fin! You have twenty minutes to get your tail in here to eat your breakfast.

Uh huh, was the most creative response he could think of at that moment. He pushed off of the water mattress and began to slowly circle the bottom of the pool, rising six to eight inches with each circuit. It appeared his reluctance to break the surface was still with him. He had no problem pushing his head or fin above the water, but it was his natural inclination now to stay submerged…even if it was a bit dull in the pool.

Eight minutes, sweetheart.

Slave driver!

I heard that. You snooze, you lose. It's your stomach.

Peter kept any further thoughts to himself and dove

toward the bottom of the pool, gaining momentum as he went. He picked up even more speed in a long, sweeping turn near the far end and rocketed upwards, breaching the surface and leaving the water entirely until he landed with as loud a splash as he could manage at such an ungodly hour.

Ha!

Ha, nothing. I'm cooking the last of your bacon right now. Soft fried, just the way you like it. But, I don't know how long it will last, Penelope taunted him. *If you want to show off, it'll have to be later. Much later.*

Defeated, yet somewhat turned on, Peter smiled at his wife's wit, swam toward the steps, and walked right out of the pool. It was amazing how that worked! A few seconds ago, he had a scaly tail with a caudal fin, and now he stood on his own two feet as he dried himself with the towel Penelope had left for him on the wrought-iron bench.

You're welcome.

He wrapped himself in the terry cloth robe she'd also laid out for him and walked into the kitchen just as his mate put the last strip of bacon out to drain. She was wearing that silky robe from her trousseau, and she looked like an angel.

Peter needed to apologize. He had to apologize. He so wanted to apologize, but just how did someone apologize for something like yesterday? "Honey, about yesterday...I..."

Penelope wiped her hands with a dishtowel and instructed, "Peter, sit down, and I'll serve you breakfast."

Peter sat at the table, and his mate laid a plate of eggs, hash browns, and strips of bacon before him. As she poured him a glass of orange juice, she smiled one of those "everything's gonna be all right" kind of smiles.

Penelope pulled her chair around and sat next to him, resting her hand on his upper leg. "Sweetheart, you don't have to say a word. If anything, the fault was mine. If I'd paid attention, I would have seen all the signs that indicated you were still one of us. You kept picking up my thoughts, even though I wasn't really trying to communicate, and I was picking up your feelings.

"The biggest sign of all was what you were saying. It was classic merman, if you didn't notice. You were ready and willing to sacrifice your life with me so I would still be able to bear children and raise them as merfolk. It was my survival and the survival of our kind you were most concerned about, no matter how much it broke your heart. We still have a few years ahead of us before it's time to breed, but when it is, I can't wait to carry your child.

"Thankfully, a merman hasn't been called upon to sacrifice his life for his mate around here in over a century, but yesterday evening, I saw what you would do if that was necessary. I want you to know that I'm honored to be your mate. Honored and grateful. Do not, I repeat, do not ever believe, even for a second, that you're not one of us because you weren't born this way. You've shown me, and everyone else, you're a true merman."

Penelope's hand had slipped over to the inside of his thigh, and it was becoming harder to focus. Still, there were things he needed to tell her.

Peter took a deep breath. "I...don't know what to say. I was just trying to be me and do what was right."

"Dear, you're a merman. You're *my* merman. Being yourself is being a *merman*."

Peter sighed. "I need to apologize to your parents...I mean Mom and Dad. I'm so sorry. They must hate me now."

"Absolutely not! Mom heard most everything last night. She knows what you were doing and your reason for doing it, and she understands. Even Dad said it was what he would have done if it'd been him. Do you know what upset Mom the most, though? The thought that she was going to lose you as a son. Dad felt the same way. You are their child now, and you are my mate and husband. All of us love you so much, and we want to have you with us always."

Peter was dumbfounded. He was expecting to be read the riot act, or even told that Penelope didn't want him to protect her anymore. Nonetheless, here he was, half a day later, being showered with praise when he had originally expected to be packing his bags.

He mumbled, "Thank you, but I still think I need to go over there and talk to Mom and Dad."

Penelope's face looked like he had just given her a bouquet of roses, and she said with a smile, "The mayor called about half an hour ago, and..."

"He's up pretty early."

"Peter, it's after ten. You slept for almost twelve hours."

"Oh. Well, I still want some more time in bed," he quipped while stifling a yawn.

"We'll get to that in a bit. Anyway, he said you've probably had the ability to change for a couple of days now, maybe for the entire week. It takes longer to complete a cycle for the newly converted, and he thinks maybe you gave up trying before your body was ready to shift back again. He's never seen anything like it, but you should probably be safe as long as you rest in between legs and tail, and vice versa. I told him you'd report in tomorrow."

"Okay. But I feel like there's something else you wanna say. What is it, Penny?"

"Well, there's a full moon in three days, and especially after almost losing you, I don't want to pass up the opportunity for us to mate mer style. But before that, you're going to need some solid sleep out of the water today so you can sleep in the pool again tonight."

"I like the sound of that," Peter said gratefully. He leaned over to give her a kiss.

"Tomorrow, we can go for a swim in the ocean and check out some possible beach front locations that we can use. In addition, I'm going to call the teacher who handles Mer School to see if she can give us *both* a quick run-through on the birds and the bees from a mer perspective."

Peter chuckled at this, imagining them sitting at tiny desks while listening to a lecture complete with diagrams.

Penelope seemed too focused to notice. "Now, so you can easily go back to sleep, here's what we're going to do. While you finish your breakfast, I'm going to go upstairs and take a quick shower. After you're done, I want you to come up and take one, too. Spritz on some of that cologne I like, and join me in the bedroom. I'm going to make sure you sleep like a log today, and you're going to make sure I have enough of you to tide me over until the full moon."

While Peter certainly wasn't opposed to this plan, especially not the last part, he wasn't used to being bossed around like this. But here he was with his mate, his wonderful Penelope, telling him what to do—and he didn't mind at all.

CHAPTER THIRTY-THREE

After his long nap, it had been strange to wake up, walk out of the water, and go put on regular clothes. Penelope told him it would probably be all right if he spent the coming night in bed rather than in the pool. He was grateful for the news, but at this moment, he kinda wanted to spend tonight underwater. He'd probably get over this eventually, but it was, nonetheless, a far cry from the way he'd felt a year ago when he got antsy just putting his big toe in saltwater.

Now, he was on his way to the Tench house to apologize to George and Ilene. Penelope told him more than once their parents understood everything and were fine with it, but that was not enough for Peter. There was room in his heart to love two sets of parents, and while he would always keep a candle burning for James and Martha MacPherson, they belonged to his past, while George and Ilene belonged to the here and now. It was important to him, anyway, that he squared things with them, as they were the most important people in his life, after Penelope. They had truly become his parents.

"Mom? Dad?" Peter opened the back door and inhaled the scent of home. If he could have his way, he'd go upstairs and take a nap in the bed he'd shared here with his mate. He wasn't sure how the sleeping arrangements would sort themselves out, and his new house deserved to be lived in after being empty for so long, but he didn't want to give up their rooms upstairs, not just yet.

He heard George talking on the phone and a rustle in the hallway as Ilene walked into the kitchen. A look of surprise flashed across her face, followed by a look of combined joy and relief. "Petey! Thank Poseidon you're all right. I was so worried about you. The mayor told us we needed to give you and Penny some time alone to rest and recuperate, but she kept me updated on how you were doing. Are you really okay?"

"I'm fine, Mom. I came over to apologize for putting you and Dad through all that the other night. I'm so sorry."

"Petey, we were all caught off guard by what happened, but you don't need to apologize at all. We heard most everything, and we understand what you were going through. You know, when merfolk are upset or in distress, we seem to automatically want to use the common link, so there's a communication tip for you, dear," Ilene explained as she put her palm to Peter's cheek.

"See! I told you there was a lot about communicating you could teach me," Peter noted, his face brightening—but it soon clouded over again. "Mom, Dad, I'm so ashamed of what I was planning to do...to leave Pen...and you," he said sheepishly.

"Petey, it meant a lot that you would willingly sacrifice yourself for your mate. Your father and I are so proud to have you as our son. I don't care that you were born on land. When I saw you and Penny had the same tail, I knew instantly you were truly meant to belong to us."

"I agree with your mother." George had hung up the phone and walked into the kitchen. "I was proud of you, Peter, as proud as if you were my son from birth. Mother's right—you were meant to be with us."

"I...I...I was going leave you..." Peter stammered.

"I know, son, but we wouldn't have let you go. We couldn't let a child of ours do that to himself, and we would have sorted things out one way or another. It may have taken a while, but you're one of us, and don't you forget it.

"Now, before I go and try to sort out some mainlander's sorry attempt at day trading, I wanted to tell you that your uncle and I have been talking about giving you some training this summer. James has a shark suit he climbs into, and a rubber-tipped trident. The three of us will go out near the reef, and James and I will teach you some defensive and offensive moves." George clapped Peter on the back and then returned to his office.

"Dear, Penny tells me you're going for your first swim in the sea today. As your mother, I'd like to do that with you, but I think you and Penny ought to do this on your own. The two of you more than deserve that experience with each other. Tomorrow, the four of us can go for a family swim...a real family swim this time. We can do it in the morning so you'll have time to rest up for tomorrow night."

Peter knew what Ilene was referring to. "Yeah, Mom. I'd really like that."

Peter sat in the passenger seat, enjoying the sun and the breeze as Penelope drove her car south toward the private beach. From the feeling in his stomach, he was either excited about his first time in the ocean, hungry, or both.

His wife flipped the turn signal and pulled in to South End Pizza. They had just opened for lunch, though the lunch crowd—if you could call it that at this end of the island—had yet to arrive. They walked through the door to find Carl behind the counter, setting things up.

"Sweetheart, I'm going to pick a place for us to sit. Order some calzones and chat with Carl for a bit."

"Dude! It's good to see you back on your feet again."

After some small talk, Peter placed the order.

Once it had been sent to the kitchen, Carl leaned across the counter with a somewhat conspiratorial air. "Man, I understand you had a bit of trouble the other evening."

Peter was chagrined that news of Friday's events had leaked, but it was to be expected—he now understood how word could get around so quickly. "Yeah," he said abashedly.

"Dude! You're a legend in this town. No one's ever been man enough to do that," Carl whispered. "There are guys all up and down Main Street who wanna shake your hand, and there are people you wouldn't recognize who claim they knew you were one of us the moment you first set foot on the island. And mermaids—man—if you weren't already chosen, you'd be swamped with offers to breed. Anne is considered to be the luckiest mermaid on the island, hands down."

Peter glanced at his mate, who was sitting in a booth, looking out the window. "Carl, I'm the one who's lucky. Lucky to have her. Lucky to be here among you. Lucky to be a merman."

Carl regarded Peter with a knowing smile. "Look, before I go hurry your order along, I think you should know one of my drivers also works at Colony Moving and Storage. He told me Samia Marinos is giving up her house, putting everything in storage, and returning to the sea."

"Oh, crap! I didn't mean to chase anyone off."

"Don't worry, dude. She'll be back in a couple years, or even a couple weeks, I guarantee it. I think your mom would be interested to hear this, though—if your Aunt Grace hasn't already told her. I mean, that woman…"

"Carl, that's why I say we're all human. I have one just like that at the office. Tail, legs—it doesn't matter. By the way, Pen is driving back to the city Friday evening to open up the condo and get things in shape before she goes back to work next Monday. I'm going to join her for a few days around the middle of the week. Do you wanna hit the water on Saturday? Don't forget who's bringing the beer."

Carl gave Peter a fist-bump and grinned. "You're on, man!"

It wasn't any sort of race, but Penelope was ready for the water well before Peter was—one of the advantages of wearing a simple wrap skirt if you're a mermaid. As she waited for him, she saw the mayor coming out of the water.

"Petey, I'm going to go say hello. You can join us when you're ready."

Penelope met Bill half way across the beach. They'd only been chatting a minute when Peter ran over to them and said, "Hi, Mayor Bill. I don't mean to interrupt, but Pen and I have been waiting a long time for this swim."

"Hello, Peter. I completely understand. Go on and swim with your mate. Penelope, we can catch up later."

"Thanks!" Peter kissed his wife, said, "Ready, sweetheart?" and sprinted toward the waves after she nodded and gave him an encouraging kiss.

She watched her husband run towards the surf. A lot had happened since Labor Day weekend. He had changed, and so had she. Her family had changed, and it was all for the better. Peter looked so cute trying to get into the water as fast as he possibly could.

Then it dawned on Penelope that this was the moment she'd been waiting for. It was the moment she'd longed for. It was the moment she'd thought would never come, and yet, here it was. It was time for her to join her mate in the sea. She absentmindedly waved goodbye to Bill and dashed toward the surf, close behind her mate.

What happened next caused her jaw to drop and made her stop in her tracks at the water's edge. She saw—or thought she saw—the image of a woman in the waves, opening her arms in welcome as Peter entered the water.

"D...di...did you see that? A woman. In the waves with Peter," she called to Bill as he made his way up the sand.

"Uh, sorry. My back was turned. Nothing about that husband of yours surprises me anymore, though. "

Penelope shook her head. The stress of the past few days must have really been getting to her. But, it was time to shake it all off and enjoy every second of this experience. With a giggle of excitement, she dove in, and it seemed it was the fastest she'd ever put her tail on. Once she reached deeper water, Penelope rose to the surface to locate her husband.

Peter surfaced in front of her, and she curled her tail around his as he enfolded her in his arms. She uttered a small gasp—the same gasp she gave when he first entered her all those months ago. Back when he chose her. Back when she became his mate. Penelope undid his ponytail and ran her fingers through his hair, as Peter's mouth found hers, and he pulled her beneath the waves.

A couple can kiss for only so long before it's time to come up for air—both literally and figuratively. They broached the surface, and Peter held her in his arms as she rested her head against his shoulder.

Mom was right. I do belong to him. Every hair, eyelash, and scale. And he belongs to me. I'm a mermaid in love with my merman. The one I will breed with when the time is right. The one I want to be with forever.

Penelope looked up at Peter and said, "Let's go for a swim."

He kissed her on the forehead before they sounded.

Swimming hand in hand was harder than it looked. She'd seen her parents do it, and she'd watched couples do it when she was in high school, but she'd never had a chance to try it until now. Well, she had done it a little bit with Peter, but the pool at home wasn't really designed for swimming in formation. It called for a bit of practice, and they wound up swimming in circles and bumping into each other, which she actually rather enjoyed. Goodness gracious, he looked sexy with his tail!

Penelope found herself becoming very turned on—not that

she hadn't been plenty of times when she was in the water with Peter—but now, there was something she could actually do about it. *Dear Poseidon,* she thought to herself, *give me strength! Just until tomorrow night.*

They finally seemed to sort things out, and she led Peter deeper and closer to the reef. The water was unusually clear, as if someone had made an extra effort just for Peter's first swim in the sea.

As they approached the reef's edge, she could feel her mate's emotions sweeping over her. She just hoped her dear Peter could sense her own feelings of joy.

Oh my God! Peter said. *It's...it's...so...beautiful! I never would've believed it, no matter how many times you told me. You might think this is sorta lame, especially coming from a guy, but...I feel like I'm part of all of this. It's like something running through me. Something telling me I'm part of the water, the coral, and the fish. I feel like I belong here. Like I've come home.*

A song of joy flowed through every part of Penelope's being. *Peter, you are a part of all this. Darling, you belong here. You're a merman, and your home is the sea.*

Penelope curled her tail around his—she was getting good at this—and held Peter close. She briefly contemplated staying with him in the sea forever, but home, friends, family, and food called her back to reality. She was a child of the sea who enjoyed the land, and she had the best of both worlds.

Come on, dear. Let's explore the reef.

Fish, hundreds of fish of all kinds and colors, swam around them. The fish were not in a tight school, but simply milling about. The couple got underway with slow strokes of their tail fins, and some of the fish darted off, not in a sort of swim for safety response, but seemingly getting underway themselves. The fish followed the mermaid and her mate in a kind of escort, some peeling off and immediately being replaced by others.

Penelope noticed the smaller fish were swimming very close to Peter, almost caressing him with their pectoral fins as they glided along his body—the body with that really sexy, scaly ass. She had observed fish do something vaguely like this before, but this time it seemed like it was a sort of act of acceptance. If she didn't know better, it would appear they were welcoming him home. The mayor had asked her to keep notes on Peter's progress, and this was going in the book as soon as they got back to the house.

They continued to swim alongside each other, occasionally jogging to the left or right to see if the fish would stay with them. They did.

Petey?

Peter responded to her communication with a lazy, *Mmmm hmmm?*

Before I go back to the city, I'm going to take you to this fantastic sea grass meadow I know, and we're going to have a nice, long nap. If I did it today, we'd probably sleep until sunset, and it'd be too dark to check out some water front property.

Huh? Peter didn't quite make the connection.

Peter, I want to find us a safe and secure beach location where we can mate tomorrow night.

Ohhhhh! I get it. That sounds good to me. Got any ideas, Pen?

Just a few. Back when I swam these waters almost every day, I wasn't exactly in the mood to check out possible mating spots. I figured if I ever decided to breed, I'd just find a convenient feral, do it underwater somewhere, and get it over with.

Sweetheart? I'm sorry if I said something wrong. The last thing he wanted to do was dredge up Penelope's bad memories.

Honey, you didn't. That was then. This is now, and I'm married to a wonderfully handsome merman I adore. And you know what? Tomorrow night, I'm going to mate with him on a beach under the full moon. So let's get swimming!

Penelope and Peter bade goodbye to the fish, who seemed to realize what the couple was about to do and quickly returned to their normal routine of finding food and trying to avoid being eaten.

Mermaid and merman shared an underwater kiss and got down to business. They went south to look at a couple of locations then turned north to see what the shores of the wildlife refuge looked like.

Their heads and shoulders were bobbing on the surface with only a bit of fin action from each to keep them there when Penelope commented, "Peter, I really like that spot to the south, but I'm not sure about what's behind those trees. I'd hate to swim down there only to discover there's a bunch of lights and people on the beach. Up here is probably our best bet. For our first time, I want us to be truly alone, nobody else around. Just you, me, the sand, the waves, and the moon."

Peter pulled her close. "That sounds perfect, but I really don't care where we are as long as I'm there with you."

"Peter, stop doing this! Stop making me want to pull you under the surface and mate with you right here and now. All you have to do is touch my fin with yours or brush your scales against mine, and I start to lose control. Hearing your words only makes it worse."

Peter knew how much tomorrow evening meant to her, and he felt the call too. "Okay, sweetheart, here's what we'll do. We'll take a leisurely swim back to the private beach, and when I say leisurely, I mean it. Then, we'll stop by the house, change clothes, and go to Colony Burgers for a bite to eat. When we're done with our night of Sex Ed, we can keep with the theme and go home to...take the edge off of things. Then, a good night's sleep will have us ready for tomorrow night."

"Yes, my sweet mate."

"This will go on for one to three hours, sometimes longer. When it comes to breeding, however, it's under an hour. Why? Because you're both on a mission, and there's a deliberate urge to complete it so you can return to the water and safety. Now, this is the first time for both of you?"

Penelope's head bobbed up and down, but Peter was too much in shock to do more than tilt his head once toward the instructor.

Beth Troutman appeared thoroughly delighted with their answer. "I think that's wonderful! I've kept my eye on the weather, and you should have absolutely perfect conditions for your first mating."

Peter's jaw was on the floor in astonishment as Penelope asked a very specific and detailed question about the breeding process.

"You're absolutely right, Anne—I mean Penelope. I'm sorry, I still remember you as a student," Beth commented.

Penelope was now looking at Peter with a predatory gleam in her eye. *Tomorrow should be...interesting. And very fun.*

"Mr. MacPherson..."

"Please, call me Peter." If there was one thing he'd learned, people on the island tended to use first names most of the time. Honorifics like Mom, Dad, Mr., or Mayor were used to indicate a special status. If a stranger was involved, it was an invitation to a less formal relationship.

"Very well, Peter. Judging by the look on your face, I can see you're surprised to learn how mermen and mermaids mate. If you're looking for additional clarification, the best I can do is to recommend an article on the grunion fish. Much of our mating behavior seems similar to theirs, though happily, ours takes longer, and we get to decide how often. This leads me to another point, the difference between the way mer and non-mer mate. Now don't get me wrong, human style is very popular. It's pleasurable, more convenient, and fun! However, there's more that you have to get 'right' for it to be successful.

"As for mer style, while the positions are limited, our piscine side seems to naturally take over. We run on autopilot, much like our breeding behavior. Just remember, with human sex, you share your bodies, but with mer sex, you share yourselves, and nothing else around you matters. There could be other couples within ten feet of you, but you'd never think twice about it. We're simply creatures of the sea doing what our instincts call us to do.

"Now, that should about cover it. There's plenty more we could go into, but it usually takes some education on anatomy, biology, and such. The Academy offers courses on the aspects of mating such as the ones presented in our after school program, and you're welcome to attend them. In the meantime, I'll be here to answer any questions or concerns you may have once you have successfully mated."

Peter thought he knew most everything about sex with Penelope, and she certainly had never complained, but this was a whole new ball game. *Penny, you knew about all this?*

Yes, dear, it was one of the details I couldn't tell you. It's just one of those things you can't comprehend without having a tail. I really hated to keep things from you, but explaining it before you were completely one of us would've blown your mind.

Blown my mind? It would've fried it! Peter could appreciate her reasons for keeping mum on this subject, and he was grateful that she'd remained true to her word.

"Beth, I have a general question. Why? I mean, why did you do this for us?"

She smiled broadly at Peter. "It's because you are important to us—to our town and its people. As I am sure Penelope has told you, sex is very important to merfolk. It allows us to enjoy our lives and allows for mates to truly connect with each other. You know, I attended your wedding, and I saw what everyone else did. The two of you have something truly wonderful—something that's impossible to describe. What you have is so precious. It's our duty to make sure that holy spark continues and is passed on to your children. The two of you are part of our future, and it falls to the rest of us to make sure our future happens."

Peter looked slightly uneasy. Yes, he felt like the two of them had something special, but knowing that everyone could see it and felt compelled to do something with it made him feel a bit uncomfortable. His mate appeared to be relaxed and seemed perfectly at ease and happy with what she was hearing from Beth. *Must be another 'mermaid thing,'* he thought to himself.

"All that leads me to something I've wanted to ask *you*. We, The Academy, would like you to speak to our students about what it's like to be non-mer and what it's like to become one of us. You would be an Adjunct Professor of non-mer studies as well as help with our information technology classes. The Academy has a greater role than simply teaching kindergarten through eighth grade and overseeing those who are home schooled. It is our mission to gain and preserve as much knowledge as possible about our people, our society, and the world around us."

Peter sat up straight. This sounded like something he could do—a way he could feel useful here on the island.

"Most faculty members here hold at least one advanced degree, and we hope you will pursue one on the mainland when time allows. Nonetheless, we'd like for you to address next year's graduating class, and in return, accept an honorary degree, a Doctor of Piscine Letters."

Peter could feel the waves of admiration and pride emanating from Penelope as he struggled to speak. "I...uh...well...I, I don't really deserve such an honor."

"Peter, we believe you more than deserve it. That theory of yours about merfolk being human has changed a lot of the thinking, not only here at The Academy, but on the island, as well. Your mate and her family had the honor of being there when you first presented it. You are an important part of our community, and you are entitled to the recognition."

Peter was overwhelmed. Penelope was over the moon.

When Peter opened his eyes, it was not quite dawn. Penelope was still asleep, dreaming happy dreams, though he wasn't sure how or why he knew—he just knew they were.

Last night had been wonderful, something to remember. It had been building all day, and after the Sex Ed session with Beth, they had raced home for a joyous session of their own. Now, in the early morning light, before the evening's full moon, he could feel something else beginning to build, something calling to him. It was subtle, but it was there. He didn't think it would interfere with the family swim planned for later in the morning, but this evening after sunset was another issue entirely.

Yesterday evening's news gave him something to ponder while waiting for his mate to open her eyes. So much had changed for him over the past year. So much had changed over the past thirteen years. They hadn't been easy ones, that was for sure. All the rejection by all the girls and their parents still stung. He had probably tried too hard, but he'd just wanted to be normal. He'd just wanted a sense of belonging.

Now, here he was—a new home, a new life, and a new place—with people who accepted him, people who wanted him. He had a wife he worshiped. He probably didn't deserve her, but she loved him fiercely. He had parents again. Two people who cared for and loved him. And, he was a merman.

After yesterday in the ocean, he knew he could never go back to who he was before. There was nothing wrong with being non-mer, but this seemed to suit him so much more. Sure, there was danger in what he was now, and he would have to be constantly on guard to protect the secret, but he was up for that.

One thing was certain: Colony Island was a place of contradictions, and even being a mer was a contradiction in its own way—half human, half fish. There were residents who almost never went to the mainland, except to attend high school, and yet there was also an educational institution on the Island with PhDs who taught kindergarten through eighth grade. There were ferals who were seldom seen north of Feral Town and long-time residents who had jobs and careers on the mainland. Peter had fallen in love with one of those professionals, which was how he'd come to be here. Simply amazing!

As the sun began to creep over the horizon, a quotation came to mind. "The stone the builders rejected has become the cornerstone." Well, he would certainly dispute the notion he was a cornerstone of any kind, but still, he was a rejected stone that had finally found the place where it belonged. Growing a tail was one of the best things that had ever happened to him.

Peter? Penny? Are you up? Are you awake?

G'morning, Mom. I'm awake, but Pen is still asleep, I think.

Well, I thought we could all have a pleasant family breakfast together before going for our swim.

Sounds great, Mom. Can we make it in thirty minutes or so? I need to kiss the princess in order to awaken her.

That's fine, dear. Your father's awake, but he's glued to his PC screen, and it'll probably take most of that time for me to tear him away from it. See you in a little while.

Okay, Mom. It was so easy talking to his mer mother, just like talking to his birth mother.

Penelope yawned and stretched. "I caught some of that. What's up?"

"Breakfast at Mom and Dad's in half an hour, with our swim afterwards."

"Okay."

Peter leaned over to kiss his wife awake.

"Mmmm, that's nice. I was having the most wonderful dream. There was you, and there was me, and there was the ocean, and we were so happy."

"Sounds great. Are you saying we aren't happy now?"

"Absolutely not! We're living the dream, sweetheart."

"Got time for a question, Pen?"

"Sure. I'm all yours."

"I'm not trying to sound ungrateful or anything, but I was wondering if you knew exactly why Mom and Dad adopted me. I mean, beyond what they've told me."

"Wow, that's heavy for whatever time it is in the morning. Actually, it's pretty easy to grasp if you grew up as a mer. As you've probably gathered, we live a very long time. That includes you too, now. It's one of Poseidon's many gifts to his children. Anyway, we usually have our parents with us for over a hundred years. For someone like you to lose your parents so young was a tragedy. Mom believed you deserved to have living parents, and Dad agreed with her. Finally, Mom fell in love with you, just like I did. And I know Dad did too, even though it would be hard to get him to admit it.

"They saw you for who you really were, and what you were, and you were everything they wanted in a son. You were no mere son-in-law, and the adoption was to make you part of their life and world."

Peter mulled this over for a minute or two. His question was pretty much answered, even though he doubted he deserved that sort of love. Probably best at this point to steer the conversation onto a different topic.

"Any other gifts from Poseidon I should know about?"

"Well, there's the greatest gift of all—and most mer don't even know how it works. That gift allows a mermaid to have the human she loves with her always and forever."

Peter pulled her close, and she snuggled against him. They just had to go out and sleep in the sea, and soon!

The minutes quickly slipped by, and it wasn't long before it was time to head over to their parents' house for breakfast. Peter pulled on some lounge pants and a T-shirt, while Penelope crawled into a way over-sized T-shirt that read "Florida State XXXI."

With all the necessary bits covered—not that anyone would have minded or even noticed at this ungodly hour—they declared themselves fit to stumble over to Mom and Dad's for breakfast.

On the way there, Peter stepped on something in the grass. As he hopped around, he decided yard project number one would be to pave the path between the two houses.

CHAPTER THIRTY-FOUR

No one was more excited about this morning's outing than Penelope. Family swims had been a regular routine for her up until age thirteen. After that, her interest in the outings had waned. Teenagers!

As her gloom had deepened, her participation had ceased altogether. The last two or three times were during her years at the university, and the experience had become so painful for her parents, they'd stopped asking her to go with them. Then, when Penelope returned home back on Labor Day weekend, she had chosen a mate and was suddenly eager to participate in family swims again. It was a downer her new mate had to stay behind, but Peter had made the best of things, and his logistics had become an important part of the outings.

This was going to be a red-letter day, as her mate was going to come with them for the very first time. Penelope was still trying to sort out whether to refer to Peter as her mate or her husband. Since they were married now, she supposed she ought to refer to him as the latter.

Ilene was bouncing along with a spring in her step. She was taking her children for a swim, and nothing could rob her of the joy this moment provided. Even George was in a good mood—for George.

The family reached the kiosk and began hanging up their towels and removing their robes. Peter was at the end of the procession, and once they'd strolled out on the beach, George turned around asked, "What in the hell is *that*?"

All eyes were on Peter, who was wearing a shorter than

usual men's sarong in dark blue with a white Polynesian pattern.

"It's a beach sarong. The Polynesians call it a lava-lava, and there are other names out there as well. I tried finding one in a tartan print with pleats in the back, but they were out. I figured this would be an easier off and on in the water than board shorts."

Penelope closely eyed her mate. "Hmmm, I think I like you in a skirt. We'll have to take a look at your wardrobe."

Peter rolled his eyes.

"I mean it, love. You look hot!"

George looked Peter up and down. "Son, could you get me a couple of those? I want to win the race into the water against Fishyface one of these days."

As the men stood discussing the relative merits of the garment, Penelope kept eyeing Peter, and then Ilene interrupted.

"Well, what are we waiting for? I want to get my tail wet!"

There was a dash to the water, and soon there were four caudal fins saluting the shore. Peter wore the sarong until they reached the spot near the reef where they could stash their beachwear, and the swim began in earnest.

Ilene swam up between Penelope and Peter, taking their hands in hers, the way a mother would, and led them up and over the reef. While Peter's first instinct leaned toward an, "Awww, Mom!" sort of moment, he stifled it. His mother simply wanted the joy of swimming with her children, and he was not about to deny her that.

After a while, Ilene let go of her children's hands and swam forward to take that of her mate. Penelope and Peter dropped back a bit so both couples could have their space and then picked up from where they'd left off the previous day. The party swam like this for a while until the loving communications between Penelope and her mate necessitated pausing for a kiss. She curled her tail around his as he pulled her into his arms.

Peter thought, *She looks so beautiful with her hair floating behind her. Everything around us is beautiful. If this is heaven, sign me up!*

Ilene sensed they weren't being followed and paused to turn around to see her children in each other's arms. *George, look at them. Don't they look happy? So in love with each other?*

I'll grant you they do, Mother. Indeed they do. By the way, James tells me your father is talking about swimming home on Saturday. Your mother is going to have to swim back with him because she left her passport down south. No plane ride home for her. Also, Grace told James your mother's making noises about moving back up here for at least part of the year. Don't know how your father feels about all this, though, George finished.

Dear, my parents are joined at the hip. Where one swims, the other is sure to follow. Do you think we can nudge them into the water on Friday before Penny heads back to the city? Maybe once they see what a fine merman Peter makes, and how much Penelope loves him, they'll settle down and admit we have a true match here.

I don't hold out much hope, but it's worth a try. If they fume and fret, the kids can swim off for some alone time. They'll probably do that, anyway.

Penny? Petey? You need to save something for tonight, dears. As soon as the two of you can take a break, let's show Peter what leaping is all about.

Five minutes, Mom. I just need five more minutes, Penelope pleaded.

I need five more minutes myself, Peter added, *so I guess that adds up to ten.*

Around noon, the family decided it was time to go home and eat. Their lunch was pretty basic, cold cuts and cheese on rye with chips on the side, and George filled the time pontificating about leaping. His oration had less to do with speed and angles of attack and more about dealing with possible predators and tourist boats. Peter correctly guessed his training had begun.

Once the meal was over, Peter readily admitted to his family that although getting a tail and sleeping underwater was great, he really missed being at home. "Mom, would it be okay if Pen and I took a nap upstairs?" It had been well over a week—and seemed even longer—since they'd slept in their room there.

Ilene beamed as if he had given her a big bouquet of roses. Her children wanted to sleep under her roof again, and she was happiest when she was being a mother. "Of course! I changed the sheets while you were living in the pool, so they're nice and fresh. Why don't you both go upstairs, have a shower, and take that nice long nap together. The moon won't be up until after nine, and I'll wake you with plenty of time to have something to eat before you go and mate."

The afternoon came and went before Penelope and Peter began to climb out of dreamland. It was strange, but he had the feeling they'd been communicating in their sleep. It left him with a sort of warm, comfortable feeling, and it was just one more thing he needed to find out about.

Whatever it was that called him early that morning was much stronger now. It wasn't insistent, but nonetheless, it was drawing him in the same way the moon draws the world's oceans to it. Would it be something he would feel at every full moon, or was it simply because he was a newly minted merman with a mate whom he loved? He'd have to talk to her about this too when everything settled down.

Glancing at the love seat, Peter saw fresh towels, clean bathrobes, and two pairs of flip-flops waiting for them. Ilene had not been idle while they slept. She had mentioned this morning when they were getting ready for the family swim that there would be no need for them to wear bathing suits beneath their robes that evening. It would be plenty dark before the moon rose and unlikely any non-mer would see them as they crossed the beach. Even Colony Island's finest tended to look the other way on nights like this.

Penelope softly stirred. A bleary-eyed look at the clock radio told her it was past 6:30 p.m.

Peter leaned over and kissed his wife. "Time to get up, dear. Time for us to get ready."

Penelope smiled up at her merman. "It *is* time, isn't it?"

Peter nodded and smiled warmly at her.

"I was hoping so." She lifted the sheets and sat up as she put her feet on the floor.

She seemed to be filled with a quiet excitement and anticipation, and Peter hoped he would be able to stay even half as cool, calm, and collected as his mate was. Penelope stretched, stood up, and padded her way to the bathroom. Peter followed suit when she returned, and when he came back, she had just finished putting her hair into a ponytail.

"Here, let me do yours." She brushed with slow, deliberate, loving strokes.

When his hair was up, Peter stood, drew her close, and whispered, "Are you ready?"

"I've been ready since the moment I first saw you."

They put on their robes and flip-flops, grabbed their towels, and slipped down the stairs. They turned left to go through the living room and dining room en route to the kitchen, but Peter stopped them short when he saw the mantle above the fireplace. The portraits of his mother and father from the rehearsal dinner were displayed front and center.

Ilene came up the hallway and said, "I hope you don't mind. Your family is now part of our family, too. I like to think had they been given the opportunity, both of your parents would have been fine mer, just like their son was meant to be."

From that moment forward, his mother's spirit lived on in Ilene, and Ilene lived in his memory of his mother. While Peter had been young when his dad had begun to slip away, he was fairly certain both his father and George would have easily and grumpily co-existed.

The last wound had finally been closed, and it was now healed. Tonight, Peter and Penelope would mate, and he could see children, grandchildren, and great-grandchildren stretching out before him in the years to come. He and his wife would soon pass their parents' light on down through the ages.

Peter put his arm around Ilene, and as he gazed at the mantle, he whispered, "Thanks, Mom."

Penelope added, "That's really sweet of you, Mom. I'm proud to be your daughter."

"And I'm proud of both of my children."

The sun sank beyond the trees, and the first stars began to peek out. It was time, and as the newlyweds turned to leave, Ilene and George rose from the dinner table.

"Your father and I want to walk you two down to the beach."

The Peter MacPherson who had entered this house on Labor Day weekend would have been appalled that Penelope's parents had wanted to see them off, but that man no longer existed. Peter Tench MacPherson, husband and mate of his beloved Penelope, and son of George and Ilene Tench, believed it proper and right for their parents to do this. He felt the warm glow of love and appreciation from his mate course through his very being. She heard him and understood.

As they started across what was now properly called the MacPhersons' side yard and turned toward the beach, George pulled Peter aside. "Son, I know you're a merman through and through, but sometimes, we have to yield to experience. This is going to be your first night swim, but my princess is an old hand at this sort of thing. Defer to her, do as she asks, and you will both fulfill your duty."

Peter clapped his hand on his father's back in acknowledgement of and appreciation for his counsel.

As they approached the kiosk, George told them, "Keep on going. We'll hang your things up after you leave."

They all walked out onto the sand, and Peter and Penelope removed their flip-flops, knocked the sand off, and stuck them in the pockets of their robes. Then George and Ilene held the shoulders of their robes as Penelope and Peter slipped them off. Next, it was time for hugs and kisses.

They turned toward their parents, and George supplemented the man to man handshake with a pat on the back and the whispered words, "I'm proud of you, son. You're my kind of merman."

Ilene held her daughter saying, "Penny, I'm so happy for you." She took Peter's hand, and said, "I'm so happy for both of you. Have a wondrous and joyful mating tonight."

Penelope slipped over to hug her father and receive his blessing while her mother held Peter's cheek in the palm of her right hand and whispered, "Petey, take good care of your mate. Give Penny the happiness she deserves, and she will give it back to you, tenfold."

"I promise, Mom." Peter held her tight, for he was hugging two mothers at once.

As the moon rose from the sea, Penelope and Peter looked at each other, turned, walked hand in hand into the surf, and dove beneath the waves. A few minutes later, the pair surfaced further off shore, waved at their parents, and after a brief kiss, sounded.

"Well, Mother, they're off. They couldn't have asked for a more perfect evening."

"I know, George. I'm so happy for them. This evening reminds me of our first time, all those years ago."

"We can always swim a couple miles down the beach..."

"George, you certainly know how to keep a mermaid in love with you. Yes. Let's." They left their clothes hanging in the kiosk and ran toward the water.

Penelope lost herself in the steady rhythm of her tail as they swam north. She was excited, but not in a giddy way. It was more of a serene expectancy. She knew and understood what was before her, and the fact she was on her way to mate with Peter at the edge of the sea filled her with a tranquil joy. She had waited for this moment all her life, and now it was upon her. She just hoped her mate wasn't frightened or having second thoughts.

Peter? Are you all right? You haven't said anything since we left the beach.

Who, me? I'm great. You have all the experience here, and I didn't want to distract you.

You'll never distract me, sweetheart. I'm good with swimming at night, but as for what comes next, I'm as inexperienced as you are, aside from the Practical Mating course Beth Troutman taught in Mer School.

Practical what?

Mating, my love. It was all about locating and selecting a secure location, safety, getting on and off the beach...stuff like that.

What was the exam like? No, don't tell me.

It was sort of a practicum. We went through all the before and after steps. Uncle James showed up in his shark suit, and some of the guys screamed like twelve-year-old girls. The mermaids screamed like they were twelve years old, too—they just had more experience.

Peter chuckled at the screaming joke, but then he remembered the shark prank. *Great, Penny. Now you have me thinking of the opening scene from " Jaws."*

That's why we're down here instead of up near the surface, Petey. Merfolk are good at sensing sharks, and trust me, the area is clear tonight. Anyway, I'll tell you more when we get up there, so just relax and enjoy the swim.

Peter had forgotten to put his dive watch back on, so he had no idea how long they'd been swimming or how far they had to go. After what seemed like hours in the dark waters, Penelope directed, *Up!* and they both rose to the surface.

There above them was the moon—big, bright, casting a yellowish silver light upon the water. They stared in wonder at it as if they were the first merfolk ever to come up to the surface.

Penelope's fin brushed against Peter's, and she was reminded just why they had come this way. "Sweetheart, it's time. I'm ready. Are you?"

The call that Peter had been feeling all day came front and center as he pulled her into his arms. "I'm more than ready, Pen."

"All right, my darling, you and I are going to move in closer to the beach. When we reach the right distance from shore, I'll swim the rest of the way on my own. If we try to go through the surf together, we'll get separated, and having to drag ourselves across the beach will really kill the mood. Once I'm ready, I'll give you the signal to come ashore."

Peter's touch on her cheek and kiss on her forehead told her all she needed to know.

"Petey, come with me. I want to mate with you."

The call became a driving force as they swam in closer. Her soft, *Wait here,* left him fuming and impatient as she swam toward the beach.

After reaching the edge of the water, Penelope curled her tail to the side, adjusted her ponytail, and the held out her arms to him. That simple gesture melted his heart. He would swim across any ocean for those arms and the sweet look on that face. She wanted him.

The driving force called him onward. He was swimming to his mate, and absolutely nothing in the world would stop him from reaching her. His tail propelled him through the foaming surf as he settled on the wet sand beside her. The feel of the water sweeping around them made him want his wife even more.

He turned his head so she could make sure his hair was secured, and then Penelope lay back on the wet sand, pulling him on top of her. Peter didn't even need to think of what to do next—it was all instinctive. His tail muscles adjusted his body until the slit to his cloaca was over hers. The lower portion of Penelope's tail slipped out from under his and then crossed over the dorsal side until she could slip her fin beneath his. She had him!

Peter felt something begin to protrude past the strong muscles that guarded his cloaca. Penelope flexed her tail, and the squeezing sensation urged him onward and inward. His body happily responded to this embrace. As he rapidly grew in length and circumference, her wall muscles grasped him, and in a series of rippling contractions, pulled him further inside.

Penelope held her mate close, and as he filled her completely, she sighed, "My husband…my mate…"

He cradled her head in his hands and could only respond to her sigh by kissing her full on the lips and invading her mouth with his tongue. No invading army had ever been more welcome.

Peter felt as though he were strolling through the surf as it lapped against the beach and was suddenly swept out to sea by a monstrous wave, his body dissolving as he was pulled to deeper water.

To Penelope, it felt as if she'd been swimming and was caught in an upwelling of warm water, lifted higher and higher, until she danced across the surface like sunlight.

For the two of them, it seemed like they were in some sort of hallway with floor to ceiling mirrors, where in either direction, you could see yourself looking back ad infinitum. Each could feel what the other was experiencing, and the boundaries of self quickly began to fade.

Penelope's body gently stroked and caressed his, pulling him deeper into her very being. Peter let go of himself, offering his heart, his soul, his very life. Penelope drank him in as if he was the only thing that could sustain her and she was the only thing that could sustain him. In that timeless moment, each understood how much they were loved by the other.

Penelope's body carried him on until he could resist no more, and he did not want to resist any more. He felt himself explode as he felt Penelope rejoice, but each wanted more of the other and continued on without pause, their intertwined tails caressing the sea foam on the sand as the moon rode higher into the sky and the water washed over them.

The stars had begun to fade and the blue-gray light that came before the dawn took over the sky. As one, they began to wake, and Peter whispered, "Penny, we should get going."

There was no cry of disappointment from her, or protestation, or complaint. She felt wonderfully alive. Penelope released Peter from their total embrace, and they both eased back into the sea.

They were in no hurry to return to the beach and put their legs on. They swam placidly together, wrapped in each other's love and the indescribable memory of their first mating. They were still in that warm and fuzzy cocoon as they crossed the channel leading to the town's harbor.

Suddenly, Peter's head snapped up. *Shark!*

Somewhere near them. He wasn't concerned with how he knew this.

Peter had begun to look around to find the threat when they were bowled over by the freight train commonly known as a bull shark. It began its turn to attack, and Peter pushed his mate away from him.

Penny, swim for it!

Penelope hesitated for a second. Peter was fresh from the merman factory and completely unarmed. Some might have thought of sharks as beautiful, but there was no way that word described this one. He was gray and aggressive—a dangerous thug with a mean and hungry look.

But, Peter…

She was knocked backwards by the force of his next communication.

NOW!

Instantly, she turned tail and swam for the beach as fast as her fin could push her, broadcasting a cry for help over every link she could think of.

The powerful, twelve-foot predator zeroed in on Penelope and began its pursuit, completely ignoring Peter. Pumping his tail hard, Peter swam in from the side, and though he was aiming for the eye, landed a punch in the gills before being blindsided by a speeding pectoral fin.

Peter tumbled over, seeing more stars than he had when he squared off against that bully in ninth grade gym class. The fine specimen of *Carcharhinus leucas* forgot about the mermaid for the moment and turned toward the merman annoying it.

At least I have its attention, now, he thought nervously.

Peter swam away as fast as he could, but he could not shake the shark, and it began to gain on him. It was time for an emergency blow. Peter began arcing upward, giving the shark a chance to shorten the distance. Peter's ascent was almost vertical, and as he neared the surface, the raging bull was only a yard and a half away.

As far as the shark was concerned, this was going to be *too* easy. But Peter rocketed up, and before his tail completely left the water, he arched his back, flipped his fin forward, and pulled his arms in. As he rotated one and a half times, Peter watched the shark broach the surface. He reentered the water cleanly, below the malicious fish.

Pumping his tail so hard he felt like his fin would break off any second, Peter held his arms straight out in front of him. *Ramming speed!*

Streaking upward, his fists landed a crippling blow behind and beneath the shark's pectoral fin, directly into its liver. The rest of his body slammed into the ventral side of the fish. Fortunately, Peter had ducked his head in the last seconds to maintain as much inertia as possible, but his back and tail took a beating. The shark rolled over, and Peter began raining blow after blow on the fish's underbelly.

You…god…damn…piece…of…cartilaginous…shit! Nobody…eats…my…mate…except…me!

Every rejection, every bit of bullying, every humiliation that had ever been laid at his feet came to the surface as Peter pummeled the shark, and his target's internal organs rapidly began to shut down. The bull desperately tried to maneuver itself into the current so it could breathe, but Peter was having none of that.

Where the hell do you think you're going?

His final blows broke the skin, and as its blood began to ooze into the water. The shark just floated there—irreparably broken.

I'd better get out of here before more of these bastards show up!

Peter took the shark's still twitching tail under his arm and began to tow it toward shore.

Bud had driven his police cruiser onto the beach and was distributing tridents and nets from the trunk as Peter's head broke the surface. Once his fin brushed against the bottom, he shifted to legs, dragging the shark into shallow water and then onto the sand.

The triumphant merman started to walk away but suddenly reversed course and delivered a swift kick to the expired animal. "Asshole!"

Peter was tired. Dead tired. He needed rest. He needed sleep, but there was one more thing he needed to do first. As fast as his aching body would allow him, he walked over to where George and Ilene were comforting a sobbing Penelope.

Peter put his bleeding hands on her shoulders and asked, "Are you okay?"

Penelope jumped, and when she realized whose hands they were, she leaned up against Peter and sobbed even louder.

Their parents caught the meaning of Peter's head nod and stepped away to speak to Grace, Raymond, and Ethyl.

After Penelope calmed down a bit, Peter tried again. "Honey, please tell me you're okay."

Between snivels, she replied, "Yes, I'm okay. I was so worried about you, sweetheart. I thought I'd lost you for good this time."

"Darling, there is absolutely no way you're going to get rid of me. I just hope you know that."

"Petey, what we shared last night...I am a mermaid, and I mated with my merman. For the second time in a week, he's shown me the lengths he'll go to in order to protect me. I'm so in love with you, and because of what we have together, my life is amazing."

She retreated into his arms, and husband and wife shared a kiss filled with warmth and solace.

"Let's go home, dear. Your injuries need some attention."

Penelope and Peter walked off the beach and up the street, followed by their parents. Neither had bothered to put on their robes, but it didn't matter. They were of the sea and Colony Island was their home.

Meanwhile, Raymond and Ethyl inspected the shark.

"Aw, it ain't *that* big," he groused.

Ethyl knocked the glasses off Raymond's nose with a slap to the back of his head. "Asshole!"

CHAPTER THIRTY-FIVE

It was the last Saturday in August—Penelope and Peter's one-year anniversary since choosing each other as mates. Given that Penelope had human friends at work, she referred to it there as the anniversary of her engagement, which, in fact, was absolutely true. A lot had transpired since she'd returned to the Harriman Company.

Peter had divided his time between Colony Island and the city, but to be honest, it was a lopsided division. The fiscal year end had occupied a lot of Penelope's time, and Peter had kept his visits to the city to two or three days at the most each week so she could have ample work time. Nonetheless, he escorted her to and from work whenever he was in town.

When he was on the Island, Peter usually stayed with their parents. He knew they'd have to give up the room eventually, but it had become home for him too, and he wanted to enjoy it while they could. It was hard to keep him out of the water these days, and the bottom of the saltwater pool was his favorite napping place. His strength and stamina had increased, and he could now do four complete legs-to-tail-to-legs cycles in twenty-four hours. This sort of thing was not totally unheard of, though Peter would readily admit he was absolutely exhausted by the end of number four.

Peter's father and uncle had been working on his training, and he'd become fairly proficient with a trident. He spent his spare time researching shark attacks and watching films of sharks in action. He wanted to thoroughly know the enemy before he had another encounter.

The incident with the bull shark had been discussed

and dissected all summer, and Peter wished he'd charged a fee every time he was asked to tell it. The common consensus was that this was the first time a mer had ever beaten up a shark, and probably the last. He'd been extremely fortunate in unfavorable circumstances, and extremely lucky—lucky he'd spent so much time back in high school watching the pretty girl in the dark green leotard on the gymnastics team.

Peter and Penelope's house was currently occupied by Raymond and Ethyl, who were on the wait list for one of the new bungalows being built. Both their daughters had gotten tired of hosting them. Lindsey had come home to Grace's house for an extended stay, and she didn't want her parents interfering. The arrangement at Peter and Penelope's place meant the house was being lived in and kept clean, though Raymond always seemed to be off swimming somewhere when Peter went over to use his office.

Setting up the home offices had taken a bit of time, but it was finally done. Peter had to negotiate with the cable company, but he was able to get a static IP address and set up a plug server in their Colony Island office. Peter created a VPN—Virtual Private Network—and the family now had its own private server accessible from anywhere.

The whole thing was hard to comprehend, but George was starting to catch on. Once he was able to retrieve a spreadsheet at the condo while visiting the city for the day, he thought it a capital idea and considered his son to be a near genius. Though there were cloud services available, Peter liked to have as much control as possible—especially where their secret was concerned.

George had finally capitulated and now sported a beard as well as a ponytail, which was a work in progress. Despite his grumping, Ilene was over the moon and wished Peter had come along sooner. As for his own locks, Peter kept them neatly trimmed and in good shape thanks to ministrations from Babs. He was waiting until after he returned to work before contacting Billy and his other friends, as growing a beard and ponytail seemingly overnight would have raised questions that he'd rather avoid having to answer.

Though Peter didn't consider himself a hunk by any standard, Penelope had an unshakable opinion of her own, and she actively encouraged him to return to Colony Island early and get some swimming in. After three months, his abs were looking good.

Partly to cope with missing Peter and partly to connect more with her human side, Penelope had developed a nonmer social life in the city. There were regular nights out with the girls, shopping expeditions, and she even taught herself to knit. Julie, her PA, was pregnant, and Aunt Penny was busily turning out booties, blankets, etc. for their inevitable trip north to meet the new grandparents. Her life had changed so much in the space of a year, and she was all the happier for it.

One day in late July, Ethyl sat at the table in the breakfast nook with her daughter. "Ilene, when do you and George plan to breed again? You're overdue at this point."

"I don't know, Mother. George and I both want to keep our focus on the children for four more years or so, just to make up for those lost years with Penny, and when they decide to breed, we'll do the same."

Ethyl wrinkled her nose at the sound of Ilene referring to Penelope and Peter as "the children." She still hadn't decided whether she liked the adoption idea or not. At the end of the day, it was her daughter's choice, and Ilene was happier than she'd ever seen her.

"Are you thinking of…"

"I'm not sure what we'll do. I've talked with Penny about it, but that's all, so far. It's still the early days for them."

"Dear, here's an idea for you. When you and George do breed, your focus is going to be on the new merbaby. Why don't you put together an album or scrapbook with pictures and things from Penelope's childhood up to the joining?"

"It was a wedding, mother."

"Whatever you say, dear. Anyway, you'll have something to hold your memories of your first child."

Ilene thought this to be one of the best ideas she'd ever gotten from her mother and immediately started going through boxes looking for old photos and memorabilia that could easily go into an album. She didn't stop there, though. She asked Peter for some childhood photos, and a week later, he handed her a stack to look through, thinking she might choose one or two. Ilene used them all.

The result was not one, but two thick volumes

chronicling Penelope's and Peter's childhoods, and Ilene even used the pictures of Peter with his parents. As far as she was concerned, his birth parents were family, so there was no reason why they shouldn't be included.

Penelope and Peter's parents treated them royally to commemorate their anniversary. Ilene accompanied the couple on the morning part of their swim, and when George met the group at the private beach with their lunch order, Ilene put her legs on and left the water while Peter and Penelope stayed with their tails. Once he was in "mermode," as he called it, Peter didn't like to put his legs back on until he absolutely had to.

After lunch, Ilene took advantage of the situation to get some photos of the two of them in all sorts of poses—looking out to sea, tails curled behind them, tails partially curled, sitting back to back, kissing, etc. By the time she was done, there was enough material to fill a third album.

With the afternoon still ahead of them, Penelope and her mother made arrangements for her to pick them up around 7:00 p.m. The couple had a late dinner reservation in Royston. Penelope and Peter slid into the surf and swam out to deeper water, where they waved before sounding hand in hand.

Ilene snapped a picture of their caudal salute, though their fins were probably too distant for a good, clear photo. *I need a camera with a telephoto lens.*

The happy couple glided through the water at an easy pace with only a small amount of fin action to keep them going. Penelope could hear the various sounds of her underwater world, but the nicest sound of all was in her head as Peter communicated with her. There were no professions of undying love. She was already well aware of what they meant to each other. Nor was it a weighty discussion of any kind. Instead, it was the ordinary talk of everyday life. She was actually living a normal life, at least for a mermaid, anyway, and it felt so good.

As they sailed over a sea grass meadow, Peter was going on about firewall appliances, and Penelope allowed her mind to wander back to earlier in the summer when the two of them had taken an afternoon nap there. They had curled up together like two quote marks, and she had felt so petite, so feminine, and so totally safe. Sure, she'd taken plenty of naps on her own down there, and would, no doubt, do so in the future, but that was the best—the best nap and the best feeling she'd ever had. It was wonderful being a mermaid.

What did you say? Penelope knew her mate had asked her a question, but she'd not yet completely returned to the present from her comfortable memory.

Peter could tell from the dreamy look in her eyes that Penelope's focus was not on security devices. He smiled at her and repeated his query. *Is it far? Where we're going, I mean.*

No, not very far at all. We might even have time for a little nap on our way back.

This was something she'd been wanting to do for almost a year. At one point, she'd even considered outfitting Peter with scuba gear so she could bring him with her, but instead, she'd decided to bide her time and wait until Peter could come with her as a merman. Their first anniversary as each other's mates seemed to be an ideal occasion.

Just a little bit further, she communicated as they began to near the reef wall.

Penelope was keeping her fins crossed and hoping against hope he would at least realize what this spot meant to her. While her darling mate was sensitive and understanding, he was still a male, and the divide that existed on land also existed in the sea.

Fifty yards or so ahead of them, there appeared to be a coral cave set into the reef wall. As they approached, the cave began to look more like a tunnel, and when Penelope prepared to enter it, Peter stopped her.

I should go in first—just in case.

Penelope shook her head. *It's perfectly safe, silly. I've been in there hundreds of times before. There's even a sort of gate barring the entrance. If the light was coming from a better angle, you'd be able to see it. Dad had Gus build it at the garage when he discovered I came here so often. Once I open it, you can follow me through, but watch your fin. Yours is a bit wider than mine, and for me, it's pretty tight. It's a short passage, so you only have to worry for two or three feet at the most.*

Peter's mate slowly entered, paused for a moment, and then proceeded. He was following George's advice about deferring to Penelope's experience, but that didn't mean he had to like it.

I'm in! See, that didn't take very long. Once you're all the way through, swim to your left so I can close the gate.

Penelope had been quite right when she'd said it was a bit close, but Peter had learned that if he used the proper tail muscles, he could curl the sides of his fin inward. That small amount was enough to easily get him through to the interior.

Penelope reached in and pulled the gate shut behind them. *Well, sweetheart, here we are.*

"Here," was in essence, a vertical coral cave. It was narrow, but there was ample room for more than one adult mer to swim up and down or side to side. The floor seemed to be mostly sand that had either been carried in by wave action, by merfolk, or both. The ceiling appeared to be almost lattice-like in spots and a thin layer of coral in others. The walls of the cave tapered inward near the top, and if they had been any further apart, the ceiling would have fallen in on itself. It still might, given time and the warming of the world's oceans.

I used to come here all the time when I was a child.

Seems a bit far for a wee lass of a mermaid to swim on her own, Peter observed.

Well, we organized swim expeditions when I was at The Academy, and we came out here a lot. Most of the other kids wanted to play tag and other games, but when we came here, I just wanted to swim in here and dream. The adults didn't mind because they knew where I was and that I was not likely to go anywhere else. In fact, it worked to my advantage, because Mrs. Herring was...how should I put this...a bit round, and couldn't come in after me.

Peter had to chuckle at that one. *Okay, then, what did you dream about in here?*

Penelope smiled, both at the memory and her mate's consideration for her childhood fantasies. *Well, when I was in here, my dreams were probably not that different from what any little mermaid dreams about—being a princess, or a bride, or both.*

Peter grinned at her. *No different than any other human girl. They dream about being brides or princesses, too. They also dream about being mermaids.*

No! Really?

So I've heard, he responded with a twinkle in his eye.

Penelope was dumbstruck. The thought that a human girl would actually dream about being a mermaid really blew her mind. She had come to love who she was and what she was, but the fact that anyone envied her was unbelievable. She began to feel sorry for humans because they were not creatures of the sea like her.

The feeling was not one of condescension or pity. It was a feeling of regret. The thought that the humans she had come to like over the past year would never see what she was able to see, or be where she was able to be, or experience the sense of exhilaration and freedom that came from having a tail and being a part of the sea, was depressing in the very least. She sank to the floor of the cave and curled her tail around her with a sad look on her face.

Peter swam down and sat beside her, laying his hand on her scales in a comforting gesture.

When I was old enough to swim here on my own, this is where I came to cry, and mourn, and contemplate the fact I was destined for a life alone. I wish it had all been different. I wish you had grown up here with me. I wish we could've swum and played together, and that I could've watched as you grew up, knowing one day we would be each other's mates.

Peter gently placed his hand on his mate's cheek, guided her face to his lips, and kissed her before asking, *Do mermaids know who will be their mate at that early an age?*

Some do, or at least think they do. There are a lot of merfolk on Colony Island, and since humans are generally out of the question, you've got a fairly good idea of the pool you'll select from, and you start laying plans to attract that special merboy to your side.

Pen, I'm sorry it took so long for me to find you.

Penelope reflected on the decade or so following her twelfth birthday. Yes, there were bright spots here and there, but things had gotten darker and darker for her each year.

It wasn't easy to escape the memory of how she'd felt and what she'd been planning to do on that Sunday afternoon in April when they'd first met. Suddenly, though, it had all changed with the sound of footsteps on the dock above her.

Don't be sorry, sweetheart. You arrived just in time.

Penelope adjusted her buoyancy and swam upwards until she was about fifteen feet above Peter. She turned and held out her arms. That gesture had become part of their mating ritual, and though Peter had expected it to be on the dessert menu for that evening, he could not ignore this call, even if all she wanted was a hug. He was only too happy to provide any and all services his mate might require of him.

Penelope watched as Peter lifted off the sand and slowly rose in the water, adjusting his course and speed with the smallest of fin flicks. It was becoming harder and harder to tell that Peter had ever been anything other than what he was now.

Penelope supposed that, in retrospect, Peter had been a merman born on land, and when his parents passed away, it became her job to find him and bring him home to where he was meant to be. In that sense, they had rescued each other, just as they had chosen each other as mates.

Peter ended his ascent directly in front of his wife, and she rested her head on his chest.

Sweetheart, I love you so much. Please don't ever leave me. It was as much a wish as a plea.

Pen, I love you so much, too. I will never, ever leave you.

Penelope drew her husband into her arms. *Then, my dearest mate, we are together forever.* She kissed Peter passionately and curled her tail around his.

EPILOGUE

"Bravo, Triton. Bravo! You've done an outstanding job. I appreciate your management of this project and putting together this highlight reel for me."

Poseidon floated in a crystalline pool set amongst the colonnades of his home. Of course, he had an undersea palace where he could take his family and hold court, but he truly enjoyed spending time here at the estate in Αἰγαὶ, Greece.

He flicked a few water droplets at the orb floating in the air before him, just above the pool's surface. "Son, I'm very proud of you. Leave the vision here in case I want to review parts of it again."

Triton nodded his head at his father and then sounded, vanishing from the pool.

The orb, or vision, was the Olympian version of Hi-Def and a DVR combined, and Poseidon was rolling it back to watch Peter's welcome to the sea when a statuesque goddess strolled in from outside the colonnades with an armful of flowers.

"Amphitrite! My sea nymph. My love. It is wonderful to have you home again. How were your travels?"

"Everything turned out rather nicely after I was done welcoming that young man, Peter, to the sea."

"I've been watching your handiwork—well done. His tail coloration, the vision in the waves, and the escort by the fish were all top-notch. Brava!"

"I cannot claim credit for the fish escort, love. It was their own idea. If you decide to do this enhanced welcome for all new converts, I suggest we get our daughters involved so we're not overloaded."

"Hmmm. Amphitrite, you may have something there. If they're going to continue to live here and sponge off of us, then the least they can do is help out with the family business," he chuckled.

"Well, I'm going to put these flowers in some water," Amphitrite said as she turned to find a vase. "And take off that silly tail!"

"Wha—what?" the god of the sea spluttered. "Amphitrite, I'll have you know, I'm on duty at the moment, and when I'm on duty, I ought to be in uniform!"

A mini tsunami leapt from the pool and rolled across the floor.

Poseidon's wife sniggered to herself. Everyone knew she had a tail of her own which she was quite fond of and enjoyed using. But even more, she enjoyed pulling her husband's tail.

Amphitrite found an appropriate sized vase, added water, and placed the flowers in it. As a goddess, she could have simply willed a vase into existence, but one thing she liked about being a goddess was that she could do things however she chose, and that meant doing things by hand most of the time. She intercepted a house servant bearing a bowl of ambrosia and carried it into the pool, deftly replacing her legs with a tail worthy of her station.

"Tell me, my dear Poseidon, what this special mission you sent me on, to welcome Peter to the sea, was all about." She settled down on his left and slipped her arm through his.

"From the beginning?"

"If you would, dear."

"Well, almost fourteen years ago, I decided to make an inspection tour of Florida and its environs. You may remember, my dearest sea nymph, that was how I came to first meet you."

"I remember that all too well, dear," she replied before giving him a tender kiss.

"Anyway, I was passing through Colony Island when I heard an anguished plea from a teenage mermaid, a cry of sorrow and despair. As you know, petitionary prayers from mermaids that age usually fall into one of three categories: they want some merboy to notice them, they want to get in with the popular crowd, or they want bigger breasts. As a rule, all such requests go directly into the bin, because I don't like to tamper with problems that will eventually resolve themselves on their own."

"But this one was different," Amphitrite offered.

"Indeed. According to the girl, there was absolutely no one for her to choose as a mate. While mermaids of that age tend to be all about drama, I decided to have a look around before moving on, and I was astounded! She was right. There was not a single match for her on the island. Not then, nor in the future—no one she could be even reasonably happy with. She so badly wanted to be able to emulate her mother—a mermaid from whom most others could take a lesson.

"It was a tragedy that could not be allowed, so I decided to find her a mate. I didn't have to go very far—just up the coast—seven hundred miles, to be exact. I found a lad about her age on holiday, sitting on the beach, with his eyes focused far out to sea as if he was searching for something. How he wound up being born so far from the sea was beyond me.

"I continued my search and found two more candidates in the Pacific Ocean and one in the Indian Ocean who were close matches, but none of them held a candle to that boy. I tell you, Amphitrite, he was absolutely perfect for Penelope. There was only one minor problem…"

"I think I can guess, my love."

"Right. He was human. I had a number of choices, none of which I particularly liked. I could have zapped him with my trident and immediately landed him on Colony Island, complete with a tail, but that would have been very traumatic and left his parents to wonder what had happened to their child. I could have zapped the boy *and* his parents, but that would have been unfair to the family. Finally, I could have done a bit of razzle-dazzle and arranged for the two of them to meet at a seaside resort every summer, but that would have been even more complicated and probably would not have worked, anyway. In the end, I decided it was best to allow them to find each other and let nature take its course. That didn't mean I couldn't stack the deck, though."

"Of course not, my dear," the goddess said with a smirk and a roll of her eyes.

"First, I used a bit…all right, a lot of divine intervention to turn him into a living, breathing, mermaid magnet. I also gave him a bit of a head start on becoming a merman."

Amphitrite raised an eyebrow at the mischievous god

sitting to her right.

Before she could chide him, he explained, "Nothing radical, dear, just a few things that would help when the time came—like a taste for merfruit juice and an early telepathic ability—you know. All of this wouldn't have been noticeable at first, but I knew he'd grow into it as time passed. However, all this brought with it a different set of problems. The last thing I wanted was for him to run into another mermaid and fall in love, so I needed to keep him out of the sea. When he went swimming late one afternoon, I arranged for him to be carried out in a rip current and nearly drown."

"You could have killed him, Poseidon!"

The god shook his head and replied, "There was never any danger. Triton was with him the entire time. The ruse worked, and he was left with a deep fear of saltwater. Of course, it was something he'd have to overcome later on, but that's what love is about, isn't it?"

Amphitrite sighed. "I suppose..."

"Finally, I had to make sure he wouldn't meet some land girl and marry her. The poor young man was right—he was indeed cursed, and I probably went overboard with that, but I knew these two simply had to meet and fall in love. There wasn't much I had to do for the mermaid. I tweaked things a bit as insurance, but that was all. Once his parents were both dead, it was time."

She gasped and sat up straight. "Poseidon! You..."

He twisted his torso to the left and took her hands in his. "Of course not! You know it doesn't work that way. I also don't *make* people fall in love. Some of my siblings might do that, but not me!"

Amphitrite visibly relaxed. "Sorry for thinking badly of you, my love."

"It is quite all right, my sea nymph. I did phrase that rather poorly." Poseidon released his grip on her hands.

"Please continue, dear," she prompted.

"Well, Peter's father was about to start a downhill slide, and there was little I could do. As for his mother, well...we were both dealing with a mess out in the Pacific, and when I finally had the opportunity to check on things, she was already gone. A pity, really. She would have made an excellent mermaid. There were even a couple of good possible matches for her on Colony Island. You know, as deities, sometimes we can do all sorts of things. Usually though, we have to work subtlety and through the system to avoid creating an even bigger problem."

Amphitrite knew this all too well. "Dear, what would you have done if they had not liked each other?"

"That was always possible, I suppose. Once his mother was gone, it was easy to arrange things so Peter would wind up in Florida, and it was just as easy to set Penelope's career path so they would wind up working for the same company. Though I did have a backup plan, just in case. Penelope's best friend, Amy, was my reserve candidate. You will notice she still has a crush on him. As it turns out, she wasn't necessary to my purposes, but don't worry. She will find her own love very soon, and it will be because of Peter that she does."

"Poseidon, I think it's wonderful what you've done, and I'm happy to have been able to play a role in all of it." Amphitrite kissed her husband on the cheek.

"Dear, it's all because I want my children to be happy. It doesn't matter to me if they spend their entire lives in the sea or live on the shore and come to visit on weekends and holidays—just as long as they're happy. They don't even need to thank me. Their simple happiness is thanks enough. If they really do feel like they have to thank me, then once a year is plenty. George Tench has the right idea about that. It's heartfelt but not fawning."

Amphitrite sought to steer Poseidon back onto the original topic. "So, what will happen next?"

"I prefer to let things run their course, and you know, dear, I intentionally do not peek into the future unless it is absolutely necessary. Still, I think more changes are coming to Colony Island and to my children as a whole. It has already started because of the wedding…"

"She was such a lovely bride," Amphitrite interrupted.

"Yes, she was, my dear. Yes, she was. Changes are in the works, and not just because of Peter, though he may well be the catalyst. I'm going to be patient and let things unfold on their own. I do know one thing, though. When it is time for this couple to bring forth children of their own…"

Poseidon whispered the rest into Amphitrite's ear.

ABOUT THE AUTHOR

Howard T. Parsons was born in Petersburg, VA during the final days of King George VI's reign. The eldest son of Lucile and Howard T. Parsons, Sr., he grew up and attended school in nearby Hopewell, VA. He attended North Carolina College in Rocky Mount, NC and graduated in 1974 with a BS in Biology. Although his interests lay in Virology and Marine Biology, the need to earn a living led him to the field of Information Technology. During his stint with the Michie Company in Charlottesville, VA, he developed the TOOL programming language, and in 2008, wrapped up a thirty-year career in legal publishing.

At present, Howard is employed as a software engineer with the Dematic Corp. and lives at The Parsonage in Charlottesville, VA with his wife and their latest two moggies in a long line of house cats. His interests include pipe collecting, Scottish Highland Games, railroads, and heraldry.

www.colonyisland.com

https://www.facebook.com/colonyisland/

https://www.goodreads.com/author/show/7315319.
Howard_Parsons